THE LONGEST EXILE

THE LONGEST EXILE

TANA REBELLIS

The Longest Exile

This book contains mature themes and subjects which may be distressing for some readers. Please visit the author's website (www.TanaRebellis.com) to view content warnings.

Cover design by Kasey Morris | Little Piggy Publishing

ISBN: 979-8-9906356-1-6
ISBN (Hardcover): 979-8-9906356-0-9

For Bubbles, Kiki, and Gabriel.

"WHOEVER LANDED HERE WAS LOST
TO THE WORLD. ISLANDS OF OBLIVION,
OF BANISHMENT…"

Norman Douglas, *Summer Islands*

(PARTIAL) JULIO-CLAUDIAN FAMILY TREE

AS RELEVANT TO WHEN *THE LONGEST EXILE* BEGINS IN 8 CE

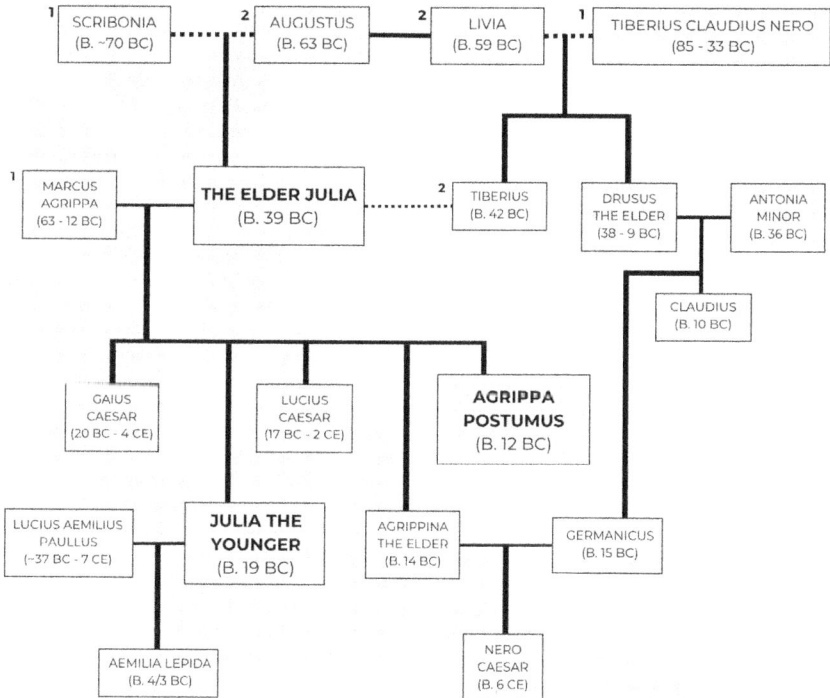

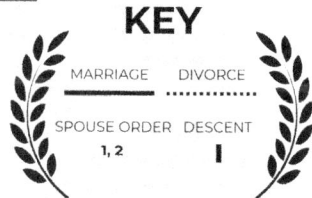

[1] SCRIBONIA (B. ~70 BC) [2] — AUGUSTUS (B. 63 BC) — [2] LIVIA (B. 59 BC) — [1] TIBERIUS CLAUDIUS NERO (85 - 33 BC)

[1] MARCUS AGRIPPA (63 - 12 BC) — THE ELDER JULIA (B. 39 BC) — [2] TIBERIUS (B. 42 BC)

DRUSUS THE ELDER (38 - 9 BC) — ANTONIA MINOR (B. 36 BC)

CLAUDIUS (B. 10 BC)

GAIUS CAESAR (20 BC - 4 CE)

LUCIUS CAESAR (17 BC - 2 CE)

AGRIPPA POSTUMUS (B. 12 BC)

LUCIUS AEMILIUS PAULLUS (~37 BC - 7 CE) — JULIA THE YOUNGER (B. 19 BC)

AGRIPPINA THE ELDER (B. 14 BC) — GERMANICUS (B. 15 BC)

AEMILIA LEPIDA (B. 4/3 BC)

NERO CAESAR (B. 6 CE)

KEY

MARRIAGE ——— DIVORCE ··············

SPOUSE ORDER 1, 2   DESCENT |

I smoothed my silky blue-green dress over my stomach with gentle, lingering fingers, although the small life within did not, at present, move. After a moment, I sighed and moved a hand to my hair, about to meddle with a particularly bothersome strand that had broken loose, but Aurelia swatted me, re-pinning a small section of the bronze curls on top of my head before she stepped away. Finished at last.

I scowled at my favorite slave, who disapprovingly pursed her lips at me in silent response before putting away the unused pins she still held in her hand. In truth, she was something like a mother to me after all our time together—and with it came more scolding than any imperial slave should be permitted to dole out.

"Stop your fidgeting, *domina*," Aurelia advised, and I knew she referenced my attentions to my pregnant belly, not to my hair.

"What are we going to do, Aurelia?" My words were quiet. I did not anticipate an answer, and none came. Aurelia could not be expected to solve all my problems, however dependable and loyal she might be. For years she had overseen much of my household and been aware of every little change in my life, every minute detail, good or bad—but even she did not have the wisdom, let alone the power, to help me now.

There was little time left to me before my pregnancy became obvious to even the most nearsighted Roman in the city. For most families, the arrival of a new, healthy child would be a joyous event; the fact that this would be a great-grandchild of the esteemed emperor Augustus himself should be cause for even greater celebration, especially if the infant were male. The only problem was that my husband, Lucius Aemilius Paullus, had been executed for treason almost a year prior, and yet my child had been conceived some four months ago at most. Even the most uneducated plebian could make sense of such simple mathematics, a fact which did not bode well for me from any perspective.

My dark thoughts were broken, if only temporarily, by the arrival of my daughter.

"*Mater*!" Aemilia cried out, trotting into the room with her nursemaid only a few steps behind, who looked, as ever, somewhat harried.

"Aemilia." I greeted my child with a warm smile, although Aurelia quickly swooped in front of me to hug her before she could muss my clean dress or carefully coiled hair. The dark-haired girl giggled happily as the slave woman fussed over her.

Aemilia was twelve now, and the only issue from my marriage to Paullus. Eighteen years my senior and much more interested in political intriguing and whoring than in a quiet family life, his marriage to me had certainly not been for love. Few women of my rank knew what such a word even meant—but perhaps they were the lucky ones.

"Your *mater* has an important event to go to, *domincella* Aemilia," Aurelia was telling my daughter. The term, 'little mistress', was one of endearment. "You mustn't touch her dress—everything must remain perfect."

Aemilia nodded solemnly, her playfulness subsiding as she turned back to me, eyes shining as they examined my dress, made of priceless imported silk, before returning to my face. "You're beautiful, *mater*." One of her small hands clasped the golden, crescent-moon shaped amulet hanging from her neck: her *lunula*.

I reached out a hand to cup her face. "And so are you, my little bird." She was becoming a young woman, and, I was told, looking more and more like me every passing day. Her dark brown eyes, set evenly if a bit widely apart, were a mirror of my own, as were her delicate features: small lips and a perfectly straight little nose. Her slightly cherubic, round face was inherited from her father, Paullus, but her perfectly pale skin, untouched by even a single freckle, as well as her wavy, bronze hair, were again a reflection of my own.

I reached out a hand to stop Aemilia from toying with her amulet. The *lunula* was a protection charm of sorts, one she would wear until she became a woman—until her wedding day.

Already she had been betrothed to one of her elder cousins, Claudius, a grandson of the infamous Marcus Antonius and Octavia, the emperor's much beloved sister. The marriage would take place within the next few years. It still seemed too soon to me, although I myself had been only two years older than her when I underwent the marital rites. An infant Aemilia arrived by the time I had seen my fifteenth summer.

I hoped my daughter's future with Claudius might bring her some measure of happiness, although that was never the point of an imperial marriage, let alone a consideration. At the very least, if she could not be happy with her husband-to-be, I hoped that she might not suffer any ills. Hoping was the most that I could do for her when it came to matchmaking.

Aurelia ushered my daughter back towards the door. "Come, *domincella*, let your mother finish getting ready. I am sure your nurse would like to have you in bed soon."

Aemilia nodded agreeably and departed with a passing glance and smile in my direction. I made a mental note to take her out into the city with me the following morning, perhaps to the market; it had been too long since I had spent a full day with her, and I worried that, as she grew from a child into a young woman, that she would soon have little time to spare for me.

My slave woman assisted me with a few simple pieces of jewelry: golden rings on several fingers, a matching, plain bracelet, and a finely beaded necklace. Nothing too sumptuous in overt appearance, but all of high quality.

Aurelia next wrapped a finely spun woolen shawl around my shoulders to fend off the still cool spring evening, and we left my residence, our feet carrying us silently across mosaicked floors that the best craftsmen of Rome had laboriously created. I did not spare any of them a glance.

A canopied litter was already waiting outside, and with Aurelia's assistance I carefully settled myself inside of it, nestling back into the pillows as I laid a hand protectively across my belly. Aurelia, after closing the sheer curtains of the vehicle, would follow on foot alongside a few other household slaves who carried as-of-yet unlit torches. We would have need of them for our return trip, as the sun was already beginning to set.

A handful of the elite soldiers from my grandfather's Praetorian Guard quickly ringed the litter and its bearers, their faces grim and voices silent as they carried out their duty. I did not expect much else from such a typically joyless lot whose sole purpose in life was unquestioning obedience to their emperor.

The slaves grunted as they lifted the wooden litter into the air, and I was jolted slightly despite their best efforts to act as a cohesive unit. Then, we were off, the litter borne across the smooth paving stones of the city which were now bathed in the golden light of the fading sun. Despite our ambling pace, the journey would be short. Our destination was, like my own home, on the Palatine Hill of Rome: my grandfather's residence.

It was a place I had been many times before, for all manner of gatherings, but this particular imperial invitation had made me uneasy. It had been delivered that very morning by messenger, transmitted not verbally, as was usual, but by a formal scroll, the summoning words written out clearly and precisely by the practiced hand of a scribe. Imprinted in the wax seal was a crisp portrait head of Augustus himself, a new design that replaced a bust of Alexander the Great.

Augustus's decision to exchange the esteemed Alexander with his own image was not an innocuous statement by any means, but I did not dare question it. My grandfather did not take kindly to being probed about his aspirations, let alone by a woman, whatever my familial relationship to him.

I felt the litter slow and moved a hand back over my belly as I prepared to be set down; we would arrive at any moment. Now that my grandfather had taken over much of the Palatine, the distance between our properties was ever shorter. My instincts were proven correct as, after another breath, the litter descended towards the ground, a gentle bump sending reverberations throughout the wood as it connected with the hard paving stones beneath. I felt more than heard a collective sigh emanate from the slaves as their burden was relieved.

Aided by Aurelia, I carefully exited the litter into one of the complex's courtyards, expectantly glancing around for other guests as I subtly straightened my dress and smoothed my shawl. The invitation had not specified, but I had assumed this was to be a family function, as most of these events inevitably were. Augustus regularly liked to gather us all together, but his efforts did not seem to stem from familial affection; instead, each visit seemed to reassure him that we were all accounted for—and behaving as he thought proper. Nothing escaped his notice.

My little sister, Agrippina, was my constant ally at such imperial gatherings, especially with our immediate family numbers being so thin at present. We that remained had to stick together for our sanity and, it seemed more and more, for our very survival.

Our father, Marcus Vipsanius Agrippa, had passed away when I was seven; Agrippina, at two years old, had been too little to remember much of him. From all that we had heard over the two decades since his death, he had been our grandfather's closest friend and most staunch supporter.

More recently, we had unexpectedly lost our eldest brother, Gaius, and a middle sibling, Lucius. Their deaths had been painfully sharp blows to Augustus, considering that he had adopted them as young boys and groomed them as his successors. The result had been an ever-shifting course of political uncertainty, although our stepfather, Tiberius, seemed to have emerged as the current favorite. Time would tell.

No one liked to talk about what remained of our family: our youngest brother, little Agrippa Postumus, nor our mother Julia, the emperor's only legitimate child by blood and whose name I bore. They still lived, if their current existences could be called that, but their futures were in doubt.

I tore my thoughts away from my family and examined my surroundings; the absence of horses or other litters concerned me. There were countless relatives and guests who could have—*should* have—been present, but as of yet, I was entirely alone. The escort of guards had remained outside the courtyard, their quiet voices drifting over the walls, punctuated by an occasional laugh. The only other noises were the trickling of a small fountain in the corner and the faint grumbling of a litter bearer's stomach.

"Are we early, Aurelia?" I asked my slave quietly. She shook her head once in response, lips set in a thin line as she performed her own examination of our surroundings.

Movement from a covered walkway drew my attention, and a tunicked slave emerged, head bowed as he approached. Aurelia stepped back from me, watching the newcomer to be sure that he showed me the proper respect. She would be the first to demand a whipping if he did not.

"*Domina*, you are to be received in the room of masks. If *domina* will follow me this way." The slave gave a small bow, his eyes still focused on the ground, and gestured to his left.

"Lead the way," I ordered, and he bowed again before guiding me away.

Aurelia remained behind; she would wait for me in the courtyard, along with the litter bearers and other household slaves. I wanted nothing more than to look back at her for whatever sense of reassurance she could give me, but I stopped myself. She was a slave; it would not be proper, especially not when there might be prying eyes in any corner. Even my own grandfather's home was not without its dangers.

My escort led me through a series of rooms, each one taking me deeper into my grandfather's sprawling imperial complex. He had slowly been expanding his residence across the Palatine Hill, buying out—or, more accurately, pushing out—various senatorial families and acquiring their properties whether they wanted to relocate or not: no one dared say no to Augustus. Some parts of the other residences were incorporated, but many had been demolished entirely in order to make way for newer, superior structures that had been designed and built by the finest architects the empire had to offer.

With every painted wall we passed, every mosaicked design we stepped over, their patterns and images showing all manner of myths and tales, heroes and monsters, my uneasiness deepened. It was too still, too quiet.

I felt eyes on me, no doubt slaves watching from the shadows of darkened rooms as my guide and I passed by, but no one emerged. The eerie gaze of a sculpture seemed to track my movement, and I fought the urge to let a shiver pass through my body. Instead, I pulled the shawl more tightly around my shoulders. This was not the setting of a happy gathering set to food and music, but that of an ominous summoning. My heartbeat quickened, and I moved a hand over my belly, as if I could protect the small life within from whatever awaited us in the room of masks.

After what felt like both an eternity and no time at all, my guide stopped beside an open door, bowing to me and gesturing inside silently: I was to proceed alone. Raising my chin and setting my face into its most bland, unreadable expression, I entered.

With no windows to the outside, the room was lit solely by flickering oil lamps. Shadows danced across the paintings on the walls, a seemingly endless assortment of theatrical masks that ranged from humorous to grotesque, all displayed within skillfully depicted architectural facades as if they had been placed upon actual, rather than painted, stands. The subtle scent of papyrus and ink, along with an odd hint of sage, reached my nose. It was a room I had never been invited to see before now, and I was not sure I would like the reason for my first viewing of it.

I was so distracted by the paintings that I barely noticed my grandfather standing in the corner of the room, heedless of the chair by his side. Now nearly seventy, he should have been taking advantage of the opportunity to rest his legs. But I was not about to suggest that to the emperor, whatever my relation to him.

"Grandfather," I spoke first, quietly. Such a right was permitted to me in private.

He held a scroll in his hands and appeared to be reading, his gaze focused downwards; it did not waver, even when I spoke. He wore not the heavy, traditional toga, but a plain, light woolen tunic that he had not bothered to belt, the garb of a relaxed man in his own home, not that of an emperor who had conquered so much of the known world.

Still my grandfather did not respond, and I nervously laid a hand across my stomach, unconsciously seeking to shield the life inside: from what, I did not yet know. The movement seemed to attract the attention of Augustus at last, and his sharp gray eyes focused on my hand, lingering for an almost unbearable length of time. I remained frozen in place.

Once a blondish man, the emperor had now been gray for years. More recently, his hair had started thinning, and he vainly tried to arrange it so that no one noticed—though no one would dare to comment on it even if they did. Wrinkles, the product of decades spent struggling for and then cementing his power, had etched his face, a tribute to his accomplishments as well as a reminder of his long-lived tenacity. What teeth remained to him did not now show themselves in a favorable greeting.

"I spared you, when your husband and your brother plotted

against me," he said, not bothering with the formality of a greeting. "I believed you, when you said that you did not know. I even defended you."

Augustus still, after all this time, refused to speak my brother's name: Agrippa Postumus, the son of his best friend and his only daughter, who had been born after his father's death and named thusly. It was young Agrippa whom my husband Paullus had drawn into his treasonous, poisonous web; it was my brother whom he had hoped to move into power as a puppet emperor, usurping Augustus. And I had been blind to it all, distracted by my own selfish desires.

My grandfather's voice was cold as he continued, efficient and deliberate, just as he was in nearly every way. "I had thought that you were different from your mother. Her betrayal…" I detected a rare note of emotion as Augustus trailed off, glancing down again at the scroll in his hands. He could not bring himself to finish his thought. "Will you give me your lover's name?" he asked, eyes still on the scroll he held. His voice was once again flat and emotionless.

I swallowed, my hands clenching at my sides in uncertainty as my mind raced. *Decimus Junius Silanus.* Thinking his name brought forth a rush of memories: his laughing green eyes; his dark, soft hair; his warm smile as he held me in his arms. He had distracted me so much that I did not see what was unfolding before my very eyes, how my scheming husband was leading my brother down a spiraling path of treason. And yet I did not regret a single moment spent with him, because, for once in my life, I had been happy.

I had known marriage with Paullus, but it was with Silanus that I had first known love for what it truly was: a most blessed gift sent from Venus herself, from whom it was claimed that my family descended. Unfortunately, given the goddess's history and my own current circumstances, it seemed that I had inherited more from my supposed ancestress than her divine blood alone. The goddess's betrayal of her husband Vulcan and her affair with Mars was infamous, an act that was rarely defended—but I would do so, now that I understood, now that I *knew* what love could be, even if it was a discovery made outside the bounds of my marriage. Perhaps it would have been better had I remained ignorant.

My grandfather was looking at me again, his cold gray eyes expectant. Calculating. Waiting. I considered naming Silanus. Even with the abundance of love for him that I held in my heart, even with his seed of life growing within me, I was a creature of my own scheming family. I was, inescapably, a product of my grandfather, who had fought tooth and nail to survive, to prevail, to conquer. Politics was no easy game, and I now wavered on the edge of the playing board. My heart hammered inside my chest as I weighed my options, and I knew that my next words would change everything. It was time to decide.

"I'm afraid I don't recall," I said at last, lifting my chin and staring past the emperor at the painted mask on the wall behind him. The light flickered across it, giving the appearance of eyes lurking beneath, a watchful presence. Judgment.

Augustus sighed, rolling the scroll back up. He held it, closing his eyes tightly for several breaths. I had disappointed him.

"Julia," he said my name, and the tone was colder than any I had ever before heard from him. "I already know who he is. I already know that you carry his child. *Silanus.*" The name was said with resignation, with disgust.

I felt as if my knees might buckle, and I bit my tongue, hoping the pain would keep me on my feet.

Augustus continued. "You have made one mistake too many,

thinking you could hide something like this from me. You are…" he trailed off, examining me like an insect under his foot, one he had tired of toying with and was ready to quash. "You are no longer a granddaughter I recognize. I cast you out. You will be relocated to one of my villas, to live there under guard, in *exilium*, away from the temptations of Rome that you cannot seem to withstand."

I tried to swallow, but instead choked, coughing. The emperor remained unmoved.

"Aemilia?" I managed to gasp out, my first thoughts racing to my daughter.

"She is already being moved to your sister's household. I trust that Agrippina will raise her well."

I wanted to scream. I wanted to beg. I wanted to die. But I could only stand there, gasping for breath, clenching my hands until my nails pierced my own flesh, drawing tiny drops of blood.

"Silanus?" I asked next, at last speaking his name: there was no longer a need to hide it, although I wavered on each syllable, drawing it out. I heard my own voice as if I were floating above, disembodied, merely an observer rather than an actor in the terror that was unfolding around me.

Augustus smiled then, his missing teeth making for a gruesome expression. "He is no longer your concern."

I remember little else after that, only being bundled back into the litter and surrounded by an even greater number of faceless guards than before. I kept clutching at Aurelia, trying to pull her into the litter with me, but she was forced away, her panicked voice fading into the distance as I was carried off at a pace faster than I thought possible. We did not return to my home but instead headed towards the external gates of Rome, bright torches lighting the way as night fell in earnest. Already my *exilium* had begun, and I had no idea where it would take me.

CHAPTER II

JULIA THE YOUNGER

After what seemed like hours, we at last came to a halt, the litter settling roughly on the ground. The thin curtains were drawn back, and a soldier gestured for me to exit.

"Please, mistress," he murmured. Half request, half order. His eyes avoided mine, and his helmet shadowed his face.

I felt numb, unable to fully comprehend what was happening, what this all meant.

"Where is Aurelia?" I asked, not yet moving from the litter. The guard shifted, uncertain. "My slave woman," I added, teeth gritted. This treatment was already proving unacceptable.

The curtains dropped, covering me inside the litter, and I heard movement outside as the soldier went to confer with someone else. Their voices were low, preventing me from making out any particular words. Once more the curtains were pulled back, and the same guard reappeared.

"Your slave will be joining us. We are to await her here. She has been permitted to return to your former home and collect a few belongings for you." Now that he had answered my question, he gestured again for me to exit the litter, eyes still downcast.

The ever-mounting tightness in my chest seemed to lessen as soon as he confirmed that Aurelia would be returned to me, and I closed my eyes in relief. All hope was not yet lost.

"Mistress," the soldier urged again, and this time I found his gaze on mine when I opened my eyes. Although his warm brown eyes seemed kind, his young face, not much older than mine, was set. He would not ask me to leave the litter again.

My expression became cold, and I made certain that my next words were in my most haughty, demanding tone. "I will await my slave in this litter. When she arrives, let me know. Until then, let me rest." My eyes dared him to argue with me, and the guard seemed slightly taken aback. He had not expected resistance.

Again the curtain dropped, and again the soldier conferred with someone else. This time, he did not return. It was a small, but important, victory. I could not let them control me entirely.

Hours must have passed, but I refused to stir. I periodically heard movement outside; quiet-voiced men and neighing, stomping horses came and went alongside flickering torches that did little to light my own surroundings, ensconced as I remained in the litter, the thin curtains drawn as if I could block out my thoughts as well as my surroundings. I pulled my shawl more tightly around my shoulders and tried not to ruminate on all that had happened, and all that was still to come.

The next time the litter's curtains were drawn aside, it was Aurelia's weathered, worried face that appeared, her blue eyes shining bright with emotion as they looked me over, her examination reassuring her that I had remained safe in her absence.

"*Domina*," she breathed, and we embraced one another, her comforting, minty scent soothing me as it filled my nose. Aurelia's arrival had set off a new burst of activity, and again I was requested by a guard to leave the litter. This time, I chose to obey.

My slave woman and I were quickly moved to an enclosed carriage drawn by two horses, who impatiently stamped their feet, and the now empty litter was borne back towards the city by my slaves, none of whom dared a glance backwards in my direction. Wooden trunks, some of them bearing what few belongings Aurelia had been permitted to pack for me, were being loaded onto a small wagon which stood in place behind the carriage. A dozen or so soldiers oversaw the entire operation, their positions strategically ringed around the vehicles in a formation that I surmised was not merely for our protection—but fleeing was the last thing on my mind.

The land journey was long and, as we moved further from the perfectly paved and well-maintained roads of Rome, increasingly bumpy. We did not halt at any inns along the way, but only paused briefly so that the soldiers could change horses and fresh beasts could be hitched to the carriage and wagon. Clearly, time was of the essence.

Food was periodically brought to us, but it was little more than fruits and bread, the former not yet quite ripe and the latter far too hard. I had little appetite, although Aurelia tried her best to coax me to eat. Eventually, after Aurelia sternly reminded me of the small, helpless life within me, I accepted some bites of the rough, grainy bread. I barely tasted it, and what I managed to consume sat in my stomach like a leaden weight.

Day ran into night, and night back into day, until I lost count of how many times the sun was carried across the sky: my best estimate was that we had been traveling for nearly a week, and the effects of the journey were increasingly visible. Trapped in the moving, stifling box that passed as a carriage, without access to a bath, I stank. Aurelia said she had not packed any of my perfumes, which I gladly would now have used to mitigate the odor of my own sweat. My face, too, was itchy and blotchy from the cosmetics a slave had applied before my fateful meeting with my grandfather, even though Aurelia tried her best to scrub me clean of the irritating kohl that now smudged around my bloodshot eyes and the red ochre that had turned my cheeks from a delightful rosy pink to an inflamed mess after remaining on my skin for too long.

Despite these hardships, as I deemed them, one morning the air seemed different. It had a tang to it, a tang that I recognized.

"We're headed towards the sea," I announced to Aurelia, and we both peered out of the carriage's tiny windows. We could not yet see the water, but I knew that it was there, perhaps just over the next ridge on the bumpy country road we followed.

My prediction was correct. By afternoon, when the sun was at its highest and hottest point in the sky above, cool blue water stretched before us. A port held a waiting ship that bobbed rhythmically in place as sailors scurried about on deck preparing for an imminent departure. The ship was small, with the look of a merchant vessel: slow, built for carrying goods rather than soldiers, and with only one mast. A handful of slaves were already in place at their oars, prepared to row the ship out of the port until the waiting sail, furled up for now, could catch the ocean wind.

Without being told, I knew that the ship was meant for me, although I still had not been informed of my ultimate destination. My grandfather had only said that I was to be sent to one of his villas; of those, he had countless, all over his empire. We could be headed anywhere.

I crudely wiped my mouth with the back of a hand as I finished vomiting again, my retching almost eerily in synch with the ship's near constant groaning as it swayed back and forth. I pushed the putrid bucket away and laid back on the cot, willing the motion to stop even as I knew that I still had a few hours more to bear.

My sea voyage was drawing to an end. Although I had remained below deck, cloistered away in a cabin for the entirety of the journey, Aurelia had reported back to me the evening before that our destination, at last revealed by the guards, drew near: Trimerus, a rocky little island in the Adriatic surrounded by only a few other equally desolate land masses. I had never heard of it, let alone known that my grandfather even possessed a villa in such a remote location.

Even though I craved relief from my seasickness, I wasn't happy about our pending arrival, as I knew it marked the true beginning of my *exilium*. Fortuna, goddess of luck and fate, had laid out a path for me that became more and more fixed with every foot I moved forward. There was no going back now.

My baby chose that moment to move, likely upset by my vomiting. I absentmindedly rubbed my belly, and he—or she—settled. The unborn infant's activity had increased at a startling rate ever since we had reached open water, as if it sensed both our lives had been upended and was making its protestations about our future known. I tried not to think about what might happen to my child, now that its existence had been discovered by the emperor: bastards were rarely received kindly.

The cabin door opened with a creak, like everything else on the damned ship, and Aurelia bustled in, frowning at me in concern. Over the week or so since my sentencing, her wrinkles had deepened, her heavy frame had thinned, and her hair seemed to have grown even whiter. Once a golden blonde, her coloring had inspired the name given to her by my mother, who had acquired the Gallic woman many years ago. In turn, Aurelia had been given to me as a wedding gift, although she had long been my nurse before that.

Thinking of my mother, the elder Julia, whose own name I bore, made me want to start retching all over again. Aurelia must have seen my face drain of blood, because she rushed over and sat on the cot next to me, rubbing my back.

"It's alright, *domina*," she murmured, her warm hands soothing me, just as they had on my wedding night before I took my husband into my bed for the first time. How scared I had been, despite my mother's assurances that I was a grown woman, and this was what grown women did.

I tried to block out thoughts of my mother and of my previous life, now gone forever, but it was hard, if not impossible, to do. Lying in my cot, torn between nightmares and the terror of my waking reality, I had little else to do but reflect. I felt hysterical laughter bubbling up inside of me as I thought of my mother again, now herself an exile, and my young brother, little Agrippa Postumus, imprisoned on an island very much like the one onto which I was about to disembark. What a family we were.

"*Domina*, we are close to the island. You should prepare yourself," Aurelia interrupted my thoughts. It was probably for the best—brooding on the past would not help me in the present.

I pushed Aurelia's hands off of me and stood, wincing as I

straightened my back and clasped my belly again. The child within was the damning cause of my exile, yet also a symbol of my final defiance, a challenge to my grandfather's authority and to the ordered life that had been laid out for me since my own birth. Whatever momentary pleasure I was able to glean from the thought faded as the ship's rocking and swaying reminded me of the imminent price I would have to pay.

The salty sea air stung my face as I slowly emerged from the stairs onto the ship's deck, and I steeled myself against the sudden chill of the breeze that rushed across the waves and battered the ship, an unnatural, bulky figure that fought its way through an endless expanse of seamless, flowing water.

I could see the island—my fate—growing closer: Trimerus. As Aurelia had reported, I now saw it was actually a small group of islands, lumped together under the same name: no one had ever bothered to differentiate between them. The largest of the land masses, to which we were destined, presented face after face of white-gray cliffs, some of them periodically broken by dark caves and grottos into which the vivid blue waves disappeared. A grassy hill rose up from the island, marking its highest point; although I could make out a scattering of dark bushes and sparsely leaved trees, vegetation was otherwise scarce.

Across a short stretch of water lay another island, smaller in size but with cliffs just as steep, and its overall manner the same as its counterpart. Beyond even that, a dark, more densely forested island formed the third of the group, perhaps the most inaccessible of them all.

Aurelia appeared with a small trunk containing some of my clothes, dragging it behind her. She moved it to the modest pile of my belongings already on deck, almost all of it my most basic, practical clothing: woolen dresses for colder weather and Egyptian linen for warmer temperatures, supplemented by a handful of shoes, underthings, and shawls. I would have no need for my fancy jewels here, nor for my collection of priceless silks; the dress I had worn to my audience with the emperor had demonstrated the fragility of the material, ruined by the sweat and dirt of our journey. Aurelia had unceremoniously disposed of it once I had changed clothing on the ship.

The slave woman approached now and wrapped a shawl around my shoulders, which I silently accepted without acknowledging that I was cold to begin with. It would have been weak to do so. I was an exile, but I still would comport myself with dignity, particularly in front of strangers.

"These soldiers are useless," Aurelia muttered in my ear, glaring at the four men in the corner of the deck who were talking and laughing amongst themselves. I imagined they were making some common, crude joke. "They didn't offer to help move any of your belongings at all, *domina*."

"I am no longer a reputable woman, Aurelia," I answered dismissively. "They are here to make certain that I remain where I have been sent. That is all. They serve my grandfather, not me. Now, I am no one." The words were true, but they still stung as I said them aloud for the first time since we had left Rome.

As rocky Trimerus grew closer with every moment, I fought down another surge of panic, another overwhelming rush of nausea. I reminded myself that my mother had only spent six years in exile on the Mediterranean island of Pandateria before she was allowed to return to the mainland—if one could even call Greek-dominated Rhegium that, considering its vast distance from true civilization, from the city of Rome.

Perhaps this was not a life sentence for me after all. Perhaps I would be allowed to return after my indiscretion proved less raw to the emperor with the passage of time. I wanted so badly to hope that this was not what the rest of my life would be.

Aurelia began to rub my back again, though she took care to be subtle. She alone could tell when I was truly upset. To most, I simply looked stern and stone-faced much of the time. My smiles had been reserved first for my family, then for Aemilia, and lastly for my lover, Silanus, whose fate even now I did not know. I was not sure I was capable of ever smiling again.

One of the soldiers chose that moment to approach, his three comrades watching warily from a distance. I ignored him, staring ahead at the nearing island. Pleasantries with common soldiers were beneath me, even now. Only a week ago he never would have dared to attempt an interaction with me.

Most of the soldiers who had accompanied me from Rome had remained on shore as the ship departed. Those that remained were clearly to be my long-term protectors—or, as I had quickly come to realize, my jailers.

The soldier reached us and cleared his throat, but it was Aurelia, not me, who acknowledged him. "Would you like to pass a message to *domina*?" she asked, as if I wasn't standing right there. Her voice was cold and forbidding as she sought to establish the appropriate order of things.

"Respectfully, given the situation, it would be easiest for everyone if your mistress and I simply spoke directly," the guard responded. I knew he was staring at me.

Holding in a sigh, I turned to face him properly. I had not had the spirit, nor the interest, to examine any of the men before now, numb and shocked as I had been since the night my grandfather sentenced me to my fate. Now, I knew that I should make note of who would be responsible for my ongoing captivity.

The guard who had spoken was probably nearing fifty, but his body remained visibly hard and muscled, its form discernable even beneath his clothing. He, like the other soldiers, wore a plain brown tunic for the time being, although all had short swords attached at their hips. Lines etched his face, acquired from countless tours across the empire, and his gray hair was cropped short in the typical military style. A single scar ran across his stubbled chin, red and angry looking as if it still wasn't properly healed, contrasting sharply with cold blue eyes that evaluated me as if I were a battle to be approached correctly.

Once his gaze caught mine, he nodded deeply in greeting. At least there was some measure of respect still left in this new life of mine. "Mistress, my name is Quintus. I was previously the *pilus prior* centurion for the Fourteenth Legion. My men are Marcus, Publius, and Titus, also from the Fourteenth Legion, now all of the Praetorian Guard." He stopped himself short of gesturing in their direction, but each man nodded respectfully at me in turn.

Marcus was tall, and would perhaps be called gangly if he were still a youth, but he looked to be in his mid-thirties. His face was cold and blank, and his eyes, far too close together, were dark and unreadable as they bored into me without reservation. Uneasy, I did not let my gaze linger on him too long, instead scrutinizing another of the men.

The next soldier, Publius, looked soft and incredibly young to me, despite his immense size; he could be no more than twenty, with a chubby, cleanshaven face and laughing blue eyes. His light brown hair looked as if it had missed its last scheduled cut, further adding to his boyish appearance. Still, I did not let his looks fool me; he was no harmless youth if he had become a Praetorian Guard.

The last guard, Titus, had a face I faintly recognized. The warm, brown eyes belonged to the same soldier who had asked me to leave the litter the night my grandfather had cast me out; without his helmet, and in the bright light out on the water, I could see he had brownish-blond hair, the shadowy traces of stubble, and fairly ordinary features that were all pleasantly tanned. He was of average height, but built strongly. Now, he gave the subtlest of nods to me, seeing that I recognized him.

I wondered what they thought of me, and I was startled to realize that this was the first time I had ever been concerned with the opinion of anyone from the lower classes. What did they see when they looked at me, the granddaughter of their esteemed emperor, the wife of an executed traitor, pregnant by her lover? Did they think I had helped my husband in his foolish attempt over a year ago to oust my grandfather and establish my young, silly brother Agrippa in his place, with Paullus and his cronies pulling the strings?

No—they probably thought that I was too stupid a woman, too busy with my lover Silanus. And the fact was, I *had* been too busy with Silanus to realize what corruption Paullus had been leading young Agrippa into, too busy to try to save my sibling. And now look where we all were.

My grandfather had accepted my innocence in my husband's treasonous plot and spared me then, trusting my word, my promises that I had not been involved. It had been the truth. But now, I was involved in an offense I could not protest. The bastard child growing in my belly, conceived well after my husband's execution, was evidence enough.

I knew the emperor had been remembering his own daughter Julia, my mother, when he cast me out. He had exiled her a decade ago, publicly claiming that the cause was her wantonness, her countless, torrid affairs with men of all classes. I knew such reports might very well circulate about me, once it became clear that I was gone from Rome.

24

Nevertheless, the gossip always remained that my mother had decided to move against Augustus and to establish a new political regime, something my grandfather could not bear to admit; he would prefer to label her a whore rather than a traitor. She never told me the truth of it, all those years ago, but I always felt it was some combination of the whispers that circulated; I knew my mother well enough to come to my own conclusions.

For Augustus, it was happening all over again. First his daughter, then his grandson, and now me. What a disappointment we were to him: traitors and whores. And all of us unsuccessful ones, in the end.

I narrowed my eyes at Quintus, returning to the present. The island was now close behind him, and the ship was slowing, sailors running about as we prepared to enter the port. The slaves were waiting to guide us closer to the island with their oars.

"You know what I have done," I said, "but also who I am. I am Vipsania Julia Agrippina, the granddaughter of Augustus, and a descendent of Julius Caesar, a god himself, with lineage tracing back to blessed Venus. I am the daughter of Marcus Vipsanius Agrippa, hero of Actium. You will all show me the respect I deserve."

There was not a particular reason why I said it, except that I wanted to remind them that I was not some common plebian, some camp whore, despite the circumstances. I did not know what the future on the island of Trimerus would bring, or how long we all were condemned to exist there together, but I did know I would do everything possible to maintain what little dignity remained to me, even if all that remained was my name.

CHAPTER III

AGRIPPA POSTUMUS

Agrippa Postumus meandered along the cliff edge, gazing aimlessly out at the ocean, which was at once both reassuring and infuriating in its endless, blue-gray sameness. Likewise, the repetitive crashing of the waves against the rocks, which almost entirely surrounded the island, both soothed and vexed him. Alas, there was nothing to be done about it. The noise haunted him, even at the very center of the land mass, when he was as far away from the water as he could get. He was no longer certain whether he was hearing with his ears or with his mind.

It had been almost a full year since Agrippa had arrived on Planasia, and now his nineteenth birthday was nearing. His last one had been spent in isolation at the villa in coastal Surrentum before his grandfather, Augustus, had ordered him to be relocated to the island. It was claimed that he would be safer there, but Agrippa knew it had nothing at all to do with *his* safety.

The year before that had been a sharp contrast, filled with the excesses of Rome, especially since his adoption by the emperor had moved him into a position of further prominence as heir-presumptive alongside Tiberius. He had had everything: women, money, privilege, power. But it had not been enough.

Agrippa's thin upper lip curled at the thought of Tiberius, once his stepfather, and he stopped his wandering. The four guards who were accompanying him on his cliffside jaunt halted at a respectful distance, and he glared in their direction, narrowing his already small, dark eyes in contempt. What did they think he would do? Where did they think he could go, trapped on this shithole of an island?

"Perhaps I should jump?" he shouted at them, a sharp laugh bubbling out of him as the guards glanced uncertainly at one another. They were a fairly fresh crop, having arrived only a month past to relieve the others, and they weren't used to him yet. He was not particularly tall or impressive in stature, but his compactly-built body emanated a sense of raw, dangerous energy that kept the new guards at bay.

Agrippa moved even closer to the cliff's edge, violently kicking off a small rock in the process, as if teasing a darker intention. "What would you tell your dear Augustus then?" He laughed again and resumed his walk, the guards jumping to move along with him, momentarily unsure of what was happening—or what might be about to happen at any given moment.

Some people thought Agrippa was entirely mad, but the exact words Augustus had used when banishing him were somewhat softer: something about an *illiberal nature*. That and the fact that he had willingly taken part in a treasonous plot with his brother-in-law Paullus to overthrow the emperor and seize power before his time were the major reasons for his *exilium*, if one were curious to know the truth of it all.

The young man had never been intended as the heir to the empire. That role had been shared jointly by his elder brothers, Gaius and Lucius, ever the favorites. Little Agrippa had never measured up, and his chance at greatness had come crashing down all too quickly, almost before it had begun. The memories brought a scowl to Agrippa's face, and he turned abruptly in the direction of the villa, the guards awkwardly shifting their own path to stay in synch with him.

The villa appeared within minutes, jutting starkly out of the ground on the island's eastern side. It was, by current standards, rather small, but it had been quite impressive when it was built some forty years ago by one private citizen or another. Since then, the island and its villa had passed into imperial hands, but it had seen little use and less renovation. It would crumble away alongside Agrippa's own youth, given enough time.

The entire complex incorporated a maritime theme throughout, from strategically placed windows looking out to the water to oceanic animals swimming and diving across wall paintings and floor mosaics; countless dolphins, whales, and mythical sea creatures danced across every surface imaginable as an abundance of brightly painted sculptures brought the theme further to life. The crowning mosaic featured a nude Neptune in his sea chariot, drawn by horses whose bodies blended with those of dolphins, the god's long hair and beard billowing in an unseen sea breeze.

The villa's original builder even had an external *exedra* constructed, essentially an outdoor theater whose main event was always the ocean itself. Beyond this, two circular fishponds were carved into the rock of the nearest cliff, uncomfortably close to the edge.

It was to the further of these ponds that Agrippa headed, stripping off his tunic in the process. Letting it drop carelessly to the ground, he approached the water and jumped in, naked, without pausing. He sank to the bottom of the cold pond and remained there, opening his eyes to stare at the fish swarming around, alarmed by the sudden disturbance in their home. Some of them would most likely be dinner later, he mused.

The four guards exchanged uncomfortable glances, and one

shifted closer to the fishpond, peering over the edge at Agrippa, who was still lurking at the bottom, a pale, murky blur.

"How long are we stuck here for?" the guard asked, to no one in particular.

One of the other men barked out a laugh. "Not nearly as long as that loony, thank Jupiter. Doesn't Neptune over there know that there are perfectly nice baths *inside* the villa?"

All four shared a rough chuckle, both at the comment and at the irreligious nickname for the youth, quieting as Agrippa finally resurfaced. White and wet, he resembled a sick little fish; goose-flesh had begun to pimple his cold skin. The youth turned to float on his back in the center of the pond, eyes closed and breathing slow, the nostrils of his wide, prominent nose barely flaring. It wasn't clear whether he was unaware or simply uncaring that his behavior was oddly disconcerting, and not a little frightening.

CHAPTER IV

JULIA THE YOUNGER

I perched on the edge of the bed in my new abode, wiping at my sweaty forehead as Aurelia set the last of my belongings in a pile in the corner. As expected, there had been no carts or litters loitering around the desolate island's modest port, and so we had all walked up the rock-strewn dirt path to the villa which was, at first glance, surprisingly well maintained for an imperial residence that had seen little if any use since my grandfather had acquired it. Still, it appeared rather small and a bit dated, probably built decades ago by some well-to-do merchant or lower ranking aristocrat who hadn't been able to afford the more posh region around Naples that had become so popular.

Three sullen slaves had greeted our party at the main door. The man, who was surprisingly fat and hairy, reminiscent of the bears I had seen in the bloody games at Rome, down to the faint stench he emitted, gave the Greek name Monimos for himself, and introduced the two women as Aphrodite and Artemis. Both mousy and brown haired with big, sad eyes that remained fixed on the ground, they looked as if they might be sisters, but certainly neither recalled the Greek goddesses for which they were named. Whoever had given them their new epithets had clearly been playing a joke.

Monimos introduced himself as the overseer at the villa and explained that Artemis was the primary preparer of meals while Aphrodite filled in as necessary, helping with cooking, cleaning, laundry, and so on. It was, compared to my residence in Rome, a skeleton crew.

My own household had consisted of a slave for every imaginable duty: I had a different girl for every hairstyle I commonly wore; a slave to bathe me, another to dry me, and a third to massage me; each cook had their own specialty; slaves whose sole job was to carry my litter; others who cared for the horses; more than a dozen tasked with cleaning. I had no idea how we were—how *I* was—to manage now with so few slaves when I had thought nothing less than a staff of a hundred could be considered respectable.

All three slaves and all four guards, along with Aurelia and myself, were to cohabitate within the villa; shockingly, there were no separate slave quarters, a circumstance I had never thought to encounter. Since the villa was modest in size, this meant that Aurelia and I would share the largest bedroom. Quintus assigned Marcus and Titus as roommates, and kept the youngest and most inexperienced, Publius, with himself. Monimos explained that he slept in the pantry, and Artemis and Aphrodite slept in the kitchen by the hearth.

The guards had been agreeable enough about moving some of my trunks up to the villa along with their own belongings, although they had perhaps been intimidated by Aurelia's ongoing, increasingly sinister glares as we first left the ship. A few of the sailors and slaves from the ship had assisted as well, quickly dumping my things in a dusty heap before they rushed back to the vessel to prepare for their next voyage. Once they were gone, there would be no escape from Trimerus.

Quintus had then quickly gone off with his men to scout the villa and its closest environs more thoroughly, leaving Aurelia and me to settle in—not that we had much with us that needed to be settled. Aphrodite had led us across the atrium to a hallway of bedrooms, including our room, meekly pointing out the direction of the bath and of the dining room, then disappeared down the corridor to help Artemis prepare a simple dinner for our motley group.

"What do you think, Aurelia?" I asked my slave, who was still fussing with the pile in the corner, the last pieces of which Aphrodite had helped to bring in from outside the villa's doors. I fought a yawn, but my mind was still racing, overwhelmed with too much newness: new villa, new slaves, new everything. I was too overloaded to fully examine my surroundings.

Aurelia muttered something indistinct about my belongings and turned around, wiping sweaty hands on her dress. "*Domina*, I think I should go sleep elsewhere. Perhaps I can sleep in the *triclinium*, and just move my things out of there for when you dine. It's improper for me to sleep right here with you!"

I almost laughed at her, but stopped myself when I saw that my slave actually looked distressed. "Aurelia, there is no need for you to sleep in the dining room. Here is fine." She looked unconvinced. "I would prefer to have you here anyway, for when my time comes."

I rested a hand on my swollen stomach, and Aurelia's gaze relaxed as she imagined the child within me. She loved Aemilia almost as much as I did, and I knew she already cared deeply for my next child, illegitimate though it might be.

"Yes, *domina*," she said. "Now, would you like to bathe before dinner? Perhaps remove the sea-stench from you, comb out your hair?"

I nodded and stood. "Let us go see if the slaves have kept the bath water hot. Bring my things." I rubbed my belly absentmindedly as Aurelia quickly sorted through the belongings she had packed for me, pulling out a drying cloth, some of my favorite oil for a post-bath massage, a comb, and clean clothing. She exited the room first, and I followed her in the direction of the bath complex.

I very shortly discovered that it wasn't quite a complex in the true sense of the word. There was just one small pool, something of a cross between a *caldarium* and a *tepidarium* in temperature, quite warm but not exactly hot, and a small adjoining sauna that also served as a changing room and the entry point to the bath itself.

It was into the sauna that Aurelia led me, closing the door behind us to keep the somewhat stale warm air trapped inside the room. I coughed as I inhaled it, and my skin quickly broke into a fresh sweat. Aurelia set down my bath supplies and then assisted me with removing my dress and underthings, unpinning my hair last of all. Once I was naked, she settled herself next to my belongings, and I stepped into the bathing room alone.

I dipped a toe into the pool, feeling water that was satisfactorily warm. I could see that a stone ledge had been built into the small pool along the walls, providing a place to sit, and I carefully stepped down onto this before further easing myself into the water in a sitting position. The warmth felt glorious, and I felt cleaner already, even though the water only rose to my distended navel.

I looked down at my body, my belly large and stretched, and my breasts almost twice their normal size. It had been so long since I had experienced a pregnancy that I had almost forgotten about the changes my body would undergo.

My first pregnancy, with Aemilia, had been both shocking and terrifying, but Aurelia had been there to soothe me, explaining that everything was as it should be. The only thing that wasn't as it should have been, at least in my husband Paullus's mind, was that I had produced a female child instead of a longed-for son.

For some time after, he had tried his very best to impregnate me once more, but it never held, my body aborting the children after two months at most. Eventually Paullus lost interest, instead entertaining himself with his whores and various political intrigues, only rarely bothering me with his attentions. I wondered, had he been alive now, if he would have believed the child inside of me was his own; perhaps he might have been suspicious that I had now safely surpassed four months of pregnancy. But such a train of thought was pointless; Paullus was long dead, and I had no one left to fool about my child's paternity.

Taking a breath, I left myself slip off the ledge into the center of the pool, my entire body now submerged. It was blessedly quiet underwater, I thought, and a part of me wished that I could simply stay there forever, if only I didn't need to breathe. The water had always been soothing to me, in any form.

Running out of air, I stood up in the pool, and even at its deepest the water only rose to just below my breasts. I massaged my scalp and ran my hands over my body, submerged myself once more, quickly, and then exited the bath. Aurelia must have heard me splashing about as I got out of the water, because she was waiting for me with the drying cloth, which she quickly wrapped around me.

"No long soak today, *domina*?" she asked, her hands rubbing me dry. "Come lie down here, on this bench, and I will rub some nice oil into you, and comb your hair. You will feel much better."

I obeyed quietly, lying on my back and letting the cloth drop around my body. Ideally, I would have been on my stomach for the massage, but the little life inside of me no longer comfortably allowed for such positioning. Aurelia got to work, uncorking the small glass bottle and pouring some oil into a cupped hand before she began to massage my body. She was extra gentle around my stomach. When prompted, I rolled onto my side, and she took care of my back.

"You have blessed hands, Aurelia," I groaned out. I had forgotten how good at bodywork Aurelia could be; she put my usual massage slave back in Rome to shame.

Aurelia chuckled quietly and continued her work, soon moving onto my hair, massaging my scalp as she teased out the tangles with a fine-toothed comb of ivory. I felt half asleep by the time she finished, pulling me to my feet and prompting me to raise my arms as she pulled a clean dress over my head. She gathered my belongings and we left the sauna, the colder air of the hallway startling me back into a more alert state. For a few minutes, I had almost forgotten that I was doomed to exile on this island, that this villa, so modest in comparison to my former home, could be my dwelling forever. The remembrance was sobering.

Monimos was lumbering down the hallway towards us, the apparent effort causing his breath to expel in sharp bursts. "*Domina*, dinner is prepared. Aphrodite and Artemis have laid it out in the *triclinium*, if you please." He kept his head bowed, avoiding eye contact, but his foul breath made my nostrils flare in distaste.

Aurelia nodded an acknowledgement on my behalf, and Monimos turned around to lead us to the dining room. My own slave quickly rushed back to our shared bedroom to drop off the bath items, but she returned before I had missed her, if slightly out of breath.

I stopped short at the entrance to the dining room, appraising the situation. The soldiers were all inside, reclining on couches, chatting amongst themselves as if they hadn't a care in the world. And the truth was, they didn't: this was simply another task to them, their next mission. It was not their perpetual fate, as it was mine.

I noticed they had at least had the courtesy to wait to begin the meal, which looked to be a modest spread of olives, grainy bread, and a variety of fish that had been lightly oiled and basted with salt sprinkled on top. There was also a small jug of what I assumed would be wine, and a container which likely held *garum*, a fermented, smelly fish sauce that had always been a favorite of mine. There was no trace of the finer dishes I had regularly consumed in Rome: soft boiled eggs in pine-nut sauce, coriander lentils, oysters, roasted peacock, stewed snails. I hoped the slaves here had simply been unprepared for the exact date of our arrival and that the quality of the meals would improve in time.

Aurelia must have been peering over my shoulder, because she let out a loud gasp at the sight of the soldiers sprawled across the room as if they owned it. Titus glanced up at Aurelia's outburst and caught my gaze; he quickly stood from his couch, coming to attention, and the rest of the soldiers followed in short order. The silence was abrupt.

Quintus, the group's commander, cleared his throat. "Mistress, apologies for our state. I should have explained beforehand that, upon a survey of the villa and its surroundings, I made the decision that it would be easiest for everyone if we dined together. Saves the slave girls some work, you see, and, given that there isn't a second dining room…" He trailed off, and for the first time I got the sense that the older soldier was slightly anxious, uncertain even. He had never been in a situation like this before. Neither had I.

I could feel Aurelia's indignant air growing behind me. In Rome, this would have been unthinkable. Just over a week ago, these men could have been executed for daring to take such liberties around me. But, now, things were different. I was too tired, too weary, to fight it. I nodded, and I could feel Aurelia bristle behind me.

"There will be no improper talk around *domina*," she spoke up harshly, and I could envision her glaring at the soldiers. They all nodded meekly, cowed by an elderly slave woman, and Aurelia and I entered the room.

Aphrodite and Artemis filled cups with watered-down wine for all of us, then retreated to the kitchen, where they presumably ate their own meal with Monimos.

There was no fancy silver or glassware here, as I was accustomed to, just basic dinnerware made of wood and simply decorated pottery, but the modest food was surprisingly fresh. Tasty, even—particularly the fish, which had been prepared with a delicate touch.

Aurelia refused to sit while I was dining, instead lurking behind me protectively, occasionally filling my plate with more food and no doubt continuously glaring at the soldiers. No one dared to speak a word the entire meal, and I suspected Aurelia played a large part in that.

The younger soldiers—Titus, Publius, and Marcus—eventually excused themselves, leaving their commander behind. He looked as if he were about to speak, but Aphrodite came in to clear the room, and again we sat in silence, his blue eyes thoughtful, if a bit wary, as he appraised me.

"So," I prompted, once the slave girl had left the *triclinium*, the pile of dishes teetering precariously in her skinny arms.

"So," Quintus mirrored me, stroking his bristled chin. "If you would like, tomorrow I will show you our immediate surroundings, which, as I mentioned, my men and I have already surveyed. There are some areas that you will, perhaps, find nice to walk. Although, I must remind you, you are not allowed to leave the villa without a guard accompanying you. Certain areas, such as the port, are off limits entirely. I will point these places out tomorrow, when you are ready." He paused ever so slightly before continuing, and his tone was slightly different than before. "And, mistress, there are four of us here. Someone will always be awake, should you require anything."

I nodded, understanding his other, more subtle meaning: that someone would always be watching. I had expected nothing less. Why else would my grandfather send guards with me? It certainly was not for my entertainment.

"Do you have any questions?" Quintus asked. I shook my head. "Goodnight then." He stood, nodded respectfully, and left the room.

Aurelia huffed. "The nerve," she muttered. I ignored her.

I remained on my dining couch for a minute longer, musing about my first day on Trimerus, about my first day dining with common soldiers. What would tomorrow bring?

"Go get some food, Aurelia," I said, waving my hand. "Take your time. I will retire to the bedroom."

"Yes, *domina*," my slave acquiesced, and I knew she was hungry; normally she would have argued against leaving me alone. Alas, she had quite a figure to maintain. No one in Rome could have said that I fed my slaves poorly, and Aurelia was no exception. It seemed that she grew outwards every year even as her age caused her height to lessen.

I stood and left the room, Aurelia following along briefly before we parted ways: she to the kitchen and me to the bedroom. I wondered if she would return with any insights from the other slaves, who had been here for longer than the rest of us. If anyone could nose out what gossip was to be found at our new home, it was Aurelia.

I paused in the atrium, which had a small central *impluvium*, a decorative pool with a pleasant dolphin mosaic across its bottom that I had not noticed earlier. Several of the depicted creatures chased one another about in play under several inches of moonlit water, the slight silver sheen catching my eye. The villa's courtyard, in the traditional style, was open to the sky; stepping out from under the walkway, I looked up. The night was clear and crisp, and I could see the stars, far better than I ever could in Rome. I found myself thinking that it wasn't altogether an unpleasant villa, even if it was rather small.

A noise made me glance to the side hallway, towards the room next to my own. Marcus, the tall and gangly looking soldier with unkind eyes, was staring at me. I tensed, his watchful gaze making me uneasy. Rather than acknowledging his presence, I walked directly past him and into my bedroom, dropping the thick door hanging behind me as a barrier, although it would not be able to stop even a mouse from entering the room.

I must have already fallen asleep by the time Aurelia returned from her meal. She gently kissed my forehead and rubbed my arm, and I realized that my cheeks were damp. I had been crying in my sleep. I wiped my face and turned over to face the wall, and I prayed for a dreamless sleep as I dozed off once more.

CHAPTER V

THE ELDER JULIA

"Really now, Mother, stop making such a fuss," Julia, the sole legitimate child of Augustus, snapped, waving a hand dismissively at the elderly woman who fought to catch her breath, fighting the tears streaming down her face. "Little Julia will be fine. So will Agrippa, just like me. They are *my* children after all, and I'll be damned if they didn't inherit some measure of tenacity."

The two women were sitting in the atrium of their villa just outside the small, bustling city of Rhegium, enjoying the spring sunshine pouring in through the open roof as two slave girls fanned them. The fountain in the *impluvium* trickled quietly, a soothing noise in sharp contrast to the wracked breathing and strangled sobs that Julia's mother, Scribonia, was trying to control. The elderly woman moaned and hugged herself, and Julia sighed, exasperated.

Sometimes it was hard to believe that Scribonia, as wretched as she now appeared, had ever been the wife of the esteemed emperor Augustus. Perhaps that was in part why she had been replaced so readily by Livia, Julia's stepmother, a conniving bitch with whom she had never gotten along. The reasons were varying, but it was mostly—although

Julia would never admit it—because they were far too similar in their ambitions.

Julia supposed her father had realized early on that Scribonia wasn't cut out for a ruthless political lifestyle—never mind the fact that she had never produced a son for him, only Julia, an ultimately disappointing specimen of the female sex. According to her father, anyway.

Despite the disappointment of her gender, her saving grace had been her appearance: she was unmistakably the child of Augustus, with the same blondish hair and cold gray eyes, as well as a nose that jutted out almost imperceptibly at its top before curving just a touch inwards. Even Julia's ears, which protruded ever so slightly more than was normal, were from her father. It was clear she had not inherited anything at all from Scribonia in a physical manifestation; the elderly woman's worrisome, sympathetic nature seemed to have eluded her daughter, too.

Julia examined a fingernail and spoke again. "Agrippa has been on Planasia for what, a year now? I'm sure he has enough slaves to care for him, and plenty of food, just as we do. Although, mind you, I am *quite* thrilled that Father finally allowed me to return to the mainland. It's not quite Rome, is it? But it's better than that dreadfully boring island, with that horrid name—*Pandateria*, please!—and certainly the quality of food has improved drastically." Julia motioned for the slave girl fanning her to increase the tempo. The sun's strength was increasing, and she felt the beginnings of a light sweat developing on her body.

"But little Julia!" Scribonia wailed, new tears pouring down her face. "And with child, no less!"

Julia frowned. Despite her current relaxed attitude, she, too, had been shocked when the news reached her that her eldest daughter had been exiled. The silly girl had carelessly gotten herself pregnant by her lover—risky enough in an affair—but, even worse, her lawful husband had long been deceased; there was no way she could pretend it was Paullus's spawn. Julia wondered if she had even *tried* to abort the child when she discovered her pregnancy.

With her older sons Gaius and Lucius dead, her only unblemished, surviving child at the moment was Agrippina—whom Julia had always thought would be the one to get into the *most* trouble, of all her children. So much for a mother's instincts.

"Now, now, Mother," Julia said, suddenly soothing.

While her mother still managed to drive her insane at times, the woman had willingly followed her into exile; her love and devotion were without question. It made Julia wonder if she had gone entirely wrong with her own children, but that was a trail of thought she didn't like to linger on for too long. She didn't like to feel guilty, for anything.

"Julia is a smart girl, a good girl," Julia continued. "I am sure Father will relent, given some time. What Agrippa did... He was—is—a silly boy, led astray, but the emperor cannot forgive treason, particularly within the family, once it has been proven definitively. Perhaps Julia will be allowed to return to Italy, as we have been, once the furor in Rome has diminished. After all, her crime was not nearly so bad as mine…"

Scribonia sniffled and wiped her face, soothed by thoughts of her granddaughter being allowed to return from exile at some point.

Julia trailed off, her eyes wandering to the slave girls, who rhythmically continued to fan the women. They both stared ahead, silent, eerily unblinking. It was hard to remember, sometimes, that they weren't deaf and mute. It was hard to remember that they were very, very capable of reporting anything they saw or heard that might earn them a pretty coin or, if the information was important enough, their eventual freedom.

"Not that any of those rumors about me were *true*, of course!"

Julia added a bit too late, with a laugh that sounded false even to her own ears. Never mind, though; the slaves were probably too stupid to pick up on any such cues.

The public reason given for her exile by her father was adultery; this, of course, was true, and Julia admitted it without reservation. But the primary reason, kept quiet and never proven entirely beyond doubt by Augustus, was treason, only she had never been as stupid as her son Agrippa Postumus to be caught out, to have let damning evidence or co-conspirators survive. Should anything change regarding provable knowledge of her involvement in any anti-Augustan plots, Julia had no doubt that she would be swiftly returned to her state of exile on Pandateria. She would *not* go back to that damned island, even at the cost of her life.

Julia ran a finger back and forth over her lower lip as she thought. "I think I should like to write a bit of poetry," she announced. "You, go fetch me some writing things. Quickly now. And not one of those wax tablets that children use, I want a proper scroll!"

The slave girl fanning Scribonia nodded, setting down the fan and scurrying out of the atrium. She returned within minutes, carefully carrying a scroll, a small bottle of ink, and a reedy pen, which she set down on the low table in front of Julia, eyes respectfully downcast. Julia waved her away, picking up the pen and unfurling the scroll as the girl returned to her fanning duties.

"Now, let's see, what silly thing shall I compose today? Perhaps a poem about love? No, that topic's been overdone, thanks to Ovid, that wretched man. Ah, I know! A musing of a mouse! One who is lost in a villa…"

Julia dipped her pen in the ink and then scratched at the papyrus, announcing aloud as she composed, aggressively crossing out sections and rewriting as she changed her mind. Soon enough, the slave girls' eyes practically glazed over with boredom; Scribonia dozed off and began to emit little snores. Nevertheless, Julia continued to talk, letting everyone know what was happening next. It was all so smoothly done that no one noticed that what Julia was writing wasn't a poem about a silly little mouse at all, but a letter.

CHAPTER VI

JULIA THE YOUNGER

Days had passed, and I refused to leave the villa. Why did it matter where this and that nice walking path was? I grew more and more convinced that I was condemned to remain on Trimerus for the remainder of my now depressingly pathetic life. I had all the time in the world to explore my prison, so I saw little point in rushing to take Quintus up on his offer to show me what he had decided were the 'acceptable' places for me to wander under supervision.

I had already explored the inside of the villa thrice over, and although it was comfortable enough, it was a far cry from what I was accustomed to, and not just due to its small size. The mosaics were well done but simple, a stark contrast to the elaborate creations my home in Rome had incorporated; I discovered that the dolphin design in the atrium was part of a larger maritime theme, with various sea creatures and oceanic scenes appearing here and there on the floors, which was common for coastal or island villas. The wall paintings were sparse, the colors faded and even chipping in places, and the furniture, while functional, was out of style by more than a decade.

There was also little in the way of sculpture to liven up the villa's interior, although I had come across a large, broken bronze statue of the god Neptune, tucked away in the back of a dusty storeroom near to the bath. Its sudden gaze had startled me: shockingly white marble had been used for its eyes, their irises a vivid blue enamel that seemed eerily lifelike, as if the god himself were watching me. I had quickly closed the door, not wanting to investigate the statue further, and even though I knew I was being ridiculous, I felt as if the eyes still followed me for some time after.

I reclined now on a couch in the atrium, dozing off as the sunshine spilled onto my body. The ever-warming rays promised that summer was approaching.

Marcus and Publius sat in the corner, playing a game of *latrunculi*, moving their little black and white pieces around as they tried to out-strategize one another. I watched them for a moment, Marcus with his cold eyes sitting still and tense, while chubby-faced Publius was a contrast, laughing every time he made a move, whether it proved to be good or bad. Funny, how different men could be from one another.

Aurelia sat in the corner behind me, stitching up a linen dress I had torn the other day. I wasn't entirely sure how I had managed it, but I didn't particularly care. No one here would be concerned about the state of my clothing or the particular fabric I was wearing that season. Gone were my precious silks, my intricately embroidered gowns that took an army of slaves countless days to complete.

Noise near the villa's main entrance carried into the atrium, and I frowned. It sounded like some sort of disagreement. I couldn't make out any words, and soon enough it was quiet again. Aurelia hadn't missed a stitch, and Marcus and Publius seemed unfazed, their swords remaining sheathed at their sides as their game continued, so I could only assume it was one of the slaves being disciplined or perhaps their comrade, Titus, being yelled at by Quintus for something or another. Nothing important.

I must have dozed off again, because I woke up to Quintus clearing his throat, standing just slightly too close to me. Marcus and Publius stood at attention nearby, and Aurelia was flanking me; I could tell she was wary. There was a newcomer in our midst, peering eagerly out from behind Quintus. I sat up quickly, blinking rapidly to clear the sleep from my eyes as I took him in.

The old man was wearing a plain tunic, but I could tell it was of high quality with just a glance, even if it was a bit faded with age. His tanned face was clean-shaven, but the abundance of hair on his head was entirely gray, a hundred different shades mixed together that seemed to jut sharply out in all directions. He smiled at me, his face becoming even more wrinkled in the process, and I saw that one front tooth was missing.

"This gentleman is Lucius Cassius Longinus…" Quintus began, but the old man fully stepped out from behind him, waving his walking cane in excitement as if he couldn't bear to remain quiet any longer.

"Allow me to introduce myself!" he interjected, and Quintus nodded after a momentary pause, his lips set into a thin, firm line of disapproval.

The newcomer cleared his throat and smiled at me again, the gap where his front tooth should have been drawing my attention once more. I tried to look away quickly, lest he think I was rude. I reminded myself that I was in disgrace, but that I was still the emperor's granddaughter, and I knew how to behave in respectable company.

"As your… friend… said, I am Lucius Cassius Longinus. Yes, quite unfortunately I am related to *that* Cassius Longinus, Gaius I mean, but *please* do be assured that I had absolutely nothing to do with Julius Caesar's assassination. Shameful family history now, that is… It's partly why I live all the way out here! Nice and quiet, nice and quiet." He smiled at me again and paused, as if waiting for me to speak.

"A pleasure to meet you," I said, but I didn't smile in return.

I wasn't entirely certain what was going on. He looked to be in his seventies, which would have made him old enough to have had a hand in Caesar's death, but in all likelihood he was telling the truth. Had he been involved in the assassination in any way, my grandfather would have had him proscribed along with the rest of those that proved a threat to his power. His very existence suggested his innocence, at least in that morbid affair. How he had wound up all the way out here in the middle of the Adriatic was a separate matter entirely.

Quintus spoke up again, his tone still disapproving. "We did not receive specific instruction regarding a situation like this," he said, and I could tell that he was uncertain how to proceed, even now. "He lives across from this island, on the smaller one, where he has a villa and some slaves. He rowed across this morning, as he had seen our arrival a few days ago–"

"Yes, I did, quite a commotion!" Lucius exclaimed, eyes dancing with enthusiasm. "Normally a ship only comes in every few months or so, whenever I need more provisions. Naturally, I had my slaves row me across, I didn't do it myself, although it isn't far, but I've added a few years since I retired out here. Anyway, what I wanted to say is *welcome*! I know who you are, your soldier here has filled me in. He was quite rude at first, wasn't going to let me come introduce myself, said he wasn't sure of the *protocol*, but I said bully that! After all, I may be old, but I *do* have some ranking still, so he has to listen to me, just a bit!"

At last I let myself smile ever so slightly at the old man, who seemed earnest in his welcome. He must have been quite lonely, although it appeared he had chosen to remain out here in the Adriatic of his own accord—retirement, he had said. What was one Roman's punishment was another's bliss, I supposed.

"Would you care to join me?" I asked, motioning at the couch closest to me. Lucius nodded happily and hobbled over, setting himself down with a sigh as he set his cane aside. A faint scent of general earthiness emanated from him, calling to mind rich soils and fresh coastal breezes.

"I'm *quite* famished," he started, but Aphrodite was already emerging with a plate of olives, which she set in front of him before retreating from the atrium.

Lucius greedily dug in, popping olive after olive in his mouth almost more quickly than I could see, spitting the pits out onto the floor and licking his fingers shamelessly. Aurelia frowned as she moved back to her sewing in the corner, and I thought I heard her mutter something about how good bloodlines don't produce good manners.

Marcus and Publius returned to their game after a nod from Quintus, who remained standing where he was, watching our new guest with an air of suspicion. I could already imagine him scribbling away at a report to be sent to the emperor when the next supply ship came to port at summer's end, asking for clarification on my visitation allowances. But, for now, his uncertainty had led to some new amusement for me, even if it might prove temporary.

"So, my dear, I would ask what brings you to Trimerus, but your man there, as I mentioned, already gave me a bit of an overview. I'm sure I'll get a letter from one of my friends soon enough, recapping the gossip from Rome. I always did hear that the emperor could be cranky, especially now that he's getting a bit older, like myself! No offense intended, of course." He popped another olive into his mouth.

I was trying to come up with some sort of politely neutral response, but it seemed that Lucius did not require, nor desire, my participation. He quickly resumed speaking, even as he finished chewing the olive in his mouth.

"It's been quite some time since I've had someone to talk to," he was saying. "Slaves don't count, of course. Their conversational skills can only go so far! My favorite was a Greek boy, but he died some time ago. Not sure why—some sort of illness. He was quite smart, even for a Greek—they're all quite intelligent, but he surpassed the others I've had. We would spend *hours* discussing all the different types of birds on these islands. I should replace him, but I figure I won't be around much longer anyway, so no matter. My family lives in Rome, and they never visit, too busy conniving, although I do have a grandson, my daughter's boy, off governing some province at the moment, some ghastly place. He's a good one, but the rest of them… They're all too involved with intriguing and trying to get into favor with you lot, by which I mean your family. The emperor's family, that is. You know. No disrespect, of course."

I simply nodded, mesmerized by Lucius. Was he senile? I couldn't tell. Perhaps. I don't think anyone had ever spoken so frankly with me before. Or so much. At least his voice had a pleasant, almost musical quality to it, one that was not entirely unpleasant to listen to.

Lucius seemed undeterred by my silence, and he continued to babble away. "My son is dead now. He was a good one too. The wife died birthing him, sadly. I was fond of her, you know, even though she only gave me the two children, that boy and his older sister. Now, when are you due to birth your own child there?" He nodded at my belly, popping another olive into his mouth at the same time.

"Soon," I said. "This summer."

"Young children are the most delightful!" Lucius exclaimed. "Too young to talk back, too young to have silly ideas. I suppose the crying can be annoying, but I wouldn't really know. When Drusilla

50

died—my wife, that is—I just had a slave take care of my son, as one does, you know. That's probably where he picked up some of his bad habits, but what can you do?"

I nodded in agreement, as he seemed to expect, then he plunged onwards. "Now, I doubt your man there, Quirius or whomever, would approve of this, but I do have quite a good cook over at my villa, imported from Gaul originally but trained in Rome from a very young age, so it would be nice for you to come visit at some point, and we could have a lovely dinner together and chat about things, literature and the like—especially birds. They're a bit of a hobby of mine, you see, an interesting study in my old age. I'm due to get some new scrolls shipped in soon as well, so perhaps I could lend them to you!"

"That would be very kind, thank you," I murmured, my words rewarded by his gap-toothed smile. My own lips curved upwards ever so slightly in response, and I was surprised to find that my smile, if small, was genuine.

Quintus, however, appeared as if his face would crack if he frowned any harder, and I almost felt badly for him. He looked as if he was straining to memorize each word Lucius and I exchanged, no doubt so that he could report every bit of it to his superiors.

"Would you like to take a walk with me, Lucius? I'm afraid I haven't gotten to see much of this island yet." My invitation was hesitant; I was not yet comfortable playing hostess in my new surroundings.

"Oh, I'm afraid I'm not much on walking these days," Lucius said, motioning towards the cane resting against his couch. A faint, sad smile ghosted across his lips. "I used to stroll these islands, watching the birds, but I'm afraid I now have to watch them from my home, although I do keep a few captive specimens."

I wanted to pinch myself for my lapse of thought. "Of course!

My apologies. I wasn't thinking."

"No worries, my dear! I exhausted myself hiking up here—took me quite a while from the port. Perhaps I should order a litter from Rome, if we become regular friends, so that my slaves can carry me about." Lucius cackled, as if imagining the scene he would create, being carted around in a fancy litter on a remote, mostly uninhabited island. Then he grabbed his cane and stood suddenly. The plate of olives was empty.

"Going so soon?" I asked, and I was shocked to realize that I felt a bit sad about his departure. What shocked me more was the realization, again, that my life had changed drastically; I couldn't recall a single time in the past that I would have enjoyed socializing with a chattering, bumbling old man who must have had little idea of the current events and fashions in Rome, and who instead busied himself with birdwatching.

"Afraid so, my dear, afraid so! Don't want to impose. That cook of mine has an early dinner being prepared for me, so I must rush back. I go to bed with the light these days, sometimes even before. You'll see one day, when you're old like me!" He laughed, and a bit of spittle flew out of his mouth, but he did not seem to notice.

Lucius hobbled the few steps over to me, took my hand, and kissed it with too-wet lips. "We'll be good friends, I think, good friends. Goodbye for now, my dear!"

"Goodbye, Lucius. Please do come visit again soon." My words were sincere.

With that, he marched to the door, Quintus following like an overly protective guard dog. After a brief pause, the soldier opened the door for the elderly man, as Lucius seemed to expect, and I caught a glimpse of two male slaves awaiting their master before the door closed again. Quintus returned, still looking perturbed.

"I'm afraid I will have to report this," he stated, his tone serious. "For now, I don't see the harm in it. But things may change, if we receive further orders."

I nodded. I had expected nothing less. In fact, I was pleasantly surprised that Quintus had even allowed the little visit to begin with, but, then again, he had spent most of his life listening to his superiors, which included those of the upper class. It would have been quite hard for him to deny Lucius entry, unless he had received specific instructions to do so.

"*Domina*, if I may speak," Aurelia piped up from the corner. Quintus nodded to me and retreated in the direction of the room he shared with Publius, quickly disappearing from my line of sight.

"Yes, Aurelia, what is it?" I stifled a yawn. My unexpected guest had tired me.

"As *domina* knows, I am saddened to see that the state of the company you now keep has been reduced to slaves, such as myself, and common soldiers. We are poor substitutes for members of your own class. Ordinarily, I would not approve of this Lucius character. His manners are quite poor, even offensive."

I turned to look at my slave, a single eyebrow raised. Aurelia was permitted to speak with me more frankly than anyone else on this earth, but even she was pushing her limits suggesting, as she was, that she could freely verbalize her opinions about my social interactions. She was *not* my nursemaid—at least, not anymore.

Aurelia blushed and looked down. She knew what I was thinking. "My apologies, *domina*. What I mean to say is that at least there is someone here closer to you in status than the rest of us. Perhaps it will bring you some comfort, some distraction, to speak with another Roman of nobility, with an education... even if it is surely not so good as your own."

I didn't bother to answer, but I mulled over what Aurelia had said once she returned to her stitching in the corner. She was right. She usually was.

Lucius reminded me, in a faint way, of my past life. Of lavish dinner parties with endless courses, all flavored with spices imported from across the empire; of heated discussions over the most recent literature, poetry, and plays that were read and performed for my pleasure; of the accepted but politely unspoken superiority of my class compared to the city's common populace. For the few minutes we had spoken, I had nearly forgotten my exile.

The remainder of my day and evening was spent quietly, but my spirits felt lighter. I went to sleep without tears, and my rest was sound for the first time since I had left Rome. When the morning light woke me, I had Aurelia dress me quickly, and I found Quintus alone in the *triclinium*, eating a simple breakfast of wheat-based porridge topped with a small amount of honey.

"Quintus, I would like to explore the island. You mentioned a few days ago when we arrived that you would show me some of the nicer places to walk. You will take me this morning. Please." The nicety had been a rare afterthought tacked onto an otherwise direct command. I hoped he hadn't noticed the slight pause before it.

The soldier swallowed his last bite of porridge and stood, nodding. "Right away, if you desire."

"I do."

Aurelia accompanied us as we left the villa, Quintus leading the way. My slave, always prepared, carried two light shawls for us, should the weather cool. I blinked rapidly as I entered the sunshine, my eyes adjusting to the sudden flood of light.

I hadn't noticed the beauty of the island when we arrived; I had been too distraught. Now, I could admire the rich blue sea, the rocky cliffs, the small hills and grassy plains immediately surrounding the villa, and a single stretch of sandy shore that was pounded by foamy waves, rushing in and then receding in an endless cycle. Birds circled overhead, calling out to one another on land, while their peers flew low over the water, seeking out their next meal.

Thinking of Lucius, I now understood why he might intentionally choose isolation in such a place. I took a deep breath, and I allowed myself to hope.

CHAPTER VII

AGRIPPA POSTUMUS

Agrippa glanced up from the scroll he was reading, scowling at the guard who had just let out a loud belch. It echoed ever so slightly in the villa's miniature theater, Agrippa's current spot of choice. He found the subtle colors of the room and its understated architecture, all meant to redirect the attention of its occupants to the stage, soothing. He had loved plays in his past life; sadly, none would be performed for him here.

Agrippa didn't bother to reprimand the soldier for his crass behavior. What was the point? He might outrank them all, but he was, when it came down to it, under their daily control, into perpetuity. Of course, they wouldn't dare to harm him in any meaningful or lasting way, but they could certainly make his existence full of little annoyances.

He focused his attention back on the scroll in his hands, the first part of Ovid's *Amores*. It had been published quite some time ago now, but Agrippa had little to select from at the villa's library, and most of the scrolls were dated. No new reading materials were ever delivered with the rare shipments of supplies that came into the port, only replacement soldiers to serve as fresh guards and foodstuffs that weren't available from the villa's small garden or fishponds. His grandfather was less than generous when it came to Agrippa's entertainment.

The offending guard had returned to chatting quietly with his fellow soldier, and Agrippa turned back to Ovid, re-reading the first line of the poem he was currently working his way through. The narrator in the piece had physically struck his lover, Corinna, but now regretted his wrongdoing. The poem was meant to show the frustrations, the struggles, of love. Agrippa thought it was all rather silly. He had never been a big fan of Ovid's, although his mother and elder sister, Julia, had been minor patrons of the poet. His grandfather hadn't approved—but he approved of little. Perhaps that was why Agrippa was currently relishing the poetry when otherwise he wouldn't have wasted his time.

A third guard suddenly entered the theater, catching both the attention of Agrippa and of the guards already in the room. He stood at attention just inside the entryway, looking more formal than was typical, decked out in his military tunic rather than the more basic, brownish ones worn by most of his guards on a daily basis. A helmet, too, was tucked under his arm—none of the guards bothered with those anymore. Agrippa briefly tried to recall his name, but rapidly gave up. They all looked the same to him anyway, with their common little noses and blank expressions. Idiots.

The two guards in the room quickly stood and approached the new arrival, and a discussion in hushed voices commenced. Agrippa lolled about, pretending to be oblivious even as his ears strained to catch their words. He couldn't be sure, but he thought he heard the name Julia. Everything else was indiscernible.

The newcomer left as abruptly as he had arrived, and the two remaining guards glanced at Agrippa as they returned to their seats. He restrained himself from asking what the unusual little discussion had been about, and instead pretended to be absorbed in his reading.

The remainder of Agrippa's day proceeded as usual. It wasn't until dinnertime, when Agrippa realized that the guard who entered the theater earlier was absent, that the oddness of the situation again piqued his interest. He performed a quick headcount: all ten of the soldiers who typically dined at the same time as he did were present. Two of the overall dozen were, as usual, missing, performing their nightly patrol, and he felt comfortable enough identifying the absent guards that he was certain the newcomer was not one of them.

"Was there a ship in port today, perchance?" he asked suddenly. The chatter in the *triclinium* quieted as the men all looked at him. No one answered. "Well?"

Agrippa placed an olive into his mouth with quick fingers, slowly chewing as his eyes moved from one man to the next. It had been months since he had bothered to speak at meals. It wasn't that he was particularly concerned or offended by the fact that he had been reduced to dining with common soldiers—he simply didn't care enough to waste his time in conversation with fools. Their class had nothing to do with it; intelligence, everything. Alas, what could one expect?

Finally, one of them, whom Agrippa believed to be the current leader of the group, spoke up. "Yes, there was."

Agrippa raised his eyebrows at the man. "Go on."

"It wasn't anything very surprising, in the end…" The soldier exchanged glances with a few of the others. One of them snickered. "Your sister Julia has been exiled. Everyone knows now that she's a whore." The rest of the soldiers broke out into laughter. "Shall I continue? She's pregnant by her lover. Not only did her traitor of a husband try to overthrow our emperor and place *you* in power—which we all see worked out so well, now that you are *imperator* of this damn rock—but he also happened to marry a common whore. Terrible luck on his part."

The group laughed again and resumed eating and drinking, ignoring Agrippa as they returned to whatever subject they had been discussing earlier. They did not see his reaction.

Agrippa felt his body go cold. He stared straight ahead, shutting out the noise in the room. Then, before any of the others could react, he managed to smash a terracotta plate over the head of the soldier who had spoken. Agrippa subsequently landed two quick punches, violently breaking his opponent's nose, before three of the guards pulled him off. Blood covered his knuckles and spattered the floor, mixing with the broken shards of pottery.

A hoarse laugh escaped him as he suffered a blow to his own stomach, and then he was dragged down the hall and thrown into his bedroom. A door, installed shortly after his arrival on the island, slammed shut behind him as he fell to the ground, and he heard it bolting. It would be days before they let him out again, but his outburst had been worth it. Agrippa made his way over to his bed and laid down with a wince, catching his breath as he recovered from the punch to his abdomen.

So: Julia had joined him and their mother in disgrace, a triad of exiles. He supposed the news had been conveyed as a security measure, so that his own guards were kept aware of any current events that might impact his imprisonment and their corresponding duties. Not that he had any way of reaching his sister, of communicating with her. She would be isolated, just like him. A prisoner.

Agrippa laughed then, the sharp, humorless sound reverberating in his room. His older sister had always tried to stay out of politics; she had had nothing at all to do with her husband's intrigues over a year ago, nothing to do with the plot that Agrippa had been a part of, that had led to his ruin. He had thought she would be safe; clearly, he had been wrong.

CHAPTER VIII

JULIA THE YOUNGER

I returned from my walk out of breath, and Aurelia practically collapsed onto the nearest chair as soon as we entered the villa, the wood groaning in protest under her weight. Neither of us were accustomed to much exertion. For my part, I had almost always traveled in carriages or litters. Using my own feet so much was a new experience, but one I had a sense I might come to enjoy.

Quintus, meanwhile, closed the villa's main doors behind us and bade us a good afternoon as he disappeared across the atrium, barely a bead of sweat on his head. I did not keep track of where he disappeared to.

The commander had shown me some of what he deemed to be the nicer places on Trimerus to walk. I noticed the entire locale of the port was excluded from the tour, but I wasn't surprised. Quintus had already made it clear that despite some of the comforts and permissions of my exile, I was still very much a prisoner. Although the port was currently devoid of ships, he clearly did not want me to become too familiar with the area.

Once we had left the vicinity of the villa, which included some small vegetable gardens and a handful of stocked fishponds, along with a pen that contained squawking chickens and a sole, skinny pig, I discovered that the island was larger than I had first thought. It also had more vegetation, and wildlife, than I expected. The number of different birds was a pleasant surprise, their varying chirps and calls blending with the rhythmic crash of waves against the island's cliffs to create a nearly constant symphony that I found soothing. Even Quintus's reminder that I had to be accompanied by a guard on any excursions didn't dampen my newly raised spirits.

The neighboring island, perhaps a third the size of Trimerus but longer and skinnier in overall shape by comparison, was where I presumed my new acquaintance Lucius lived, although I couldn't see any signs of his villa from my vantage point. I wondered if Quintus would permit me to take a small boat over to visit him, as Lucius had suggested. We would see.

Aurelia was fanning her face with a hand, still catching her breath. Her cheeks were red, and I suspected she had caught too much of the sun in addition to overly exerting herself. I forgot, sometimes, how old she was getting. I didn't like to dwell on it.

"Aurelia, why don't you go lie down?" I suggested, the hint of an order in my words. "I'll be fine amusing myself for a while."

My slave's lack of protestation was a sign of how fatigued she was. Aurelia simply nodded and heaved herself up, waddling down the hallway to our room without a word. I remained in the atrium alone, and I massaged my belly as the baby within stirred.

Craving something to drink, and not catching a glimpse of any of the slaves, which was odd considering our recent and obvious return to the villa, I decided to make my own way towards the kitchen. One of them should already have served me some refreshment.

Perhaps it was my own fault for not listening more carefully, or for pulling aside the cloth hanging without pausing to think that it may have been covering the door for a reason. I stopped in my tracks when I saw Monimos with his cock buried in Aphrodite, her long tunic pushed up around her waist. She was bent over in front of the cooking fire, a spoon still clenched in her white-knuckled hand, juices dripping from it and landing unheeded on the floor as Monimos grunted and roughly yanked on her hair. His fat, hairy belly jiggled as he drove himself into her again.

Aphrodite turned her head towards me, her big eyes blank and distant as if she barely saw me. Monimos seemed oblivious to my presence, for obvious reasons. I knew I should leave, but I felt transfixed, disgusted, even though I understood that this sort of thing happened all the time to slaves. I knew my husband had done similar things to our own slaves, both female and male, with alarming frequency.

Suddenly, I was thinking of my lover, of my Silanus, and of the last time we had made love, only a few weeks before my grandfather had passed sentence on me. My belly had been big enough that my pregnancy was already becoming hard to hide, but Silanus had kissed it softly, as if reassuring the little life within that we would find a way to protect it.

Our love had been nothing like the mindless rutting now happening in front of me, and nothing like the emotionless, joyless couplings I had shared with my husband. Silanus had been gentle and kind, passionate and fierce, in equal measure. After our final liaison he had held me for hours, whispering that he loved me, that everything would be alright. How wrong he had been.

Monimos let out a loud groan, pulling the slave girl back towards him as his body shuddered. I let the door hanging drop back into place, the fabric mercifully cutting off the sight of Aphrodite clutching the spoon as her blank eyes continued to bore into me. I fought back the bile rising in my throat.

I hastily retreated from the kitchen area back to the atrium, where I was startled by Marcus and Titus. I nearly ran into the latter, a small cry escaping me as I halted in front of him, my heart pounding as if it threatened to escape my chest.

"Are you alright?" Titus asked, a look of genuine concern flashing across his face before his more typical, impassive expression returned. His words, though, were warm and soft, an attempt to soothe. Marcus, in contrast, smirked in condescension, perhaps amused by my obvious discomfort even if he did not know the cause.

"Yes. Fine." I could feel that my cheeks were warm, and I felt confused. I was revolted by Monimos, but in a perverse way it had recalled Silanus, and now I was aroused and upset and disgusted all at once. It was too much emotion—something that I found it best to avoid.

Without further explanation, I abruptly moved past the guards and walked quickly to my room, roughly pushing aside the door hanging as I entered. I felt out of breath, panicky. Aurelia was sound asleep on her cot, snoring quietly.

I wasn't certain how long I stood there, just inside the bedroom, watching Aurelia sleep. My breathing finally slowed, and my heart stopped trying to beat its way out of my body. I wanted to get into bed with Aurelia, to have her rub my back and soothe me as she had done when I was still young and newly married, worried about being a proper Roman wife, about producing strong, noble sons to strengthen the imperial family. But I was too old for that now, and I certainly was less naïve. Having my slave comfort me would solve none of my problems, only increase my dependency on someone else. I could not afford it.

Pulling the door hanging out of the way, I slipped back out of the bedroom. Titus was in the hallway, leaning against the wall. His brown eyes looked surprised when I emerged, and he quickly stood to attention.

"Can I help you?" I asked coldly. I was embarrassed by my earlier emotional state. One of the first things I had learned as a member of the imperial family was to never allow oneself to be seen in any less than flattering capacity, especially when emotions were involved. Feelings led to weakness, and weakness in Rome could spell one's doom.

"My apologies. I…" He trailed off, looking uncertain.

"Yes?" I prompted, still cold. I narrowed my eyes on him, expectant.

Titus cleared his throat, and suddenly I realized that he was embarrassed for some reason. "I just wanted to make certain that no one bothered you." His words were quiet and hesitant.

I laughed sharply, and the soldier looked down at his feet. "That no one bothered me? Isn't that what you're doing now?"

"I'm very sorry. Please excuse me." Titus ducked his head and made to leave.

"Wait," I stopped him. "Titus, isn't it?" He nodded, still uncertain. "Tell me, have you fucked the slave girls yet? How are they?"

Titus stared at me, but he didn't answer. I wasn't sure what I was doing. Was I trying to provoke him? What did I hope to accomplish? The silence stretched.

"I have not," he finally answered, quietly. His tone was flat, with no trace of his earlier concern.

"Why? Are they not up to your standards? Although I've lately realized that most men don't have standards, so perhaps it's something else. Do you prefer boys?" I felt angry, about Monimos and his careless sex with Aphrodite, about the unknown fate of Silanus, about my exile, about everything, and even as I realized that I was misdirecting my rage at this soldier, I still couldn't stop myself.

"Perhaps we can get you one," I plunged on. "Some nice, fuckable little boy for you and your friends. No worries about getting *him* pregnant! Never any worries for you *men*." I spat the last word at him, feeling tears of anger stinging my eyes.

Titus stepped towards me, his eyes narrowed and his mouth tight. His body was coiled.

"Are you going to hit me now?" I asked him, and I laughed again, standing my ground. I found that I couldn't stop laughing, and then suddenly I was crying, sobs resounding down the hallway.

Aurelia emerged from the bedroom, her nap disturbed by my shouting, and she immediately started yelling at Titus, blaming him even though she had no idea what was going on. That was the way of it: *I* was never at fault. Not until I was exiled, anyway—I could not escape fault for that.

Leaving Aurelia and Titus to argue with one another, I wandered away, unnoticed, through the empty atrium. I mindlessly opened the villa doors and walked outside, leaving them open behind me, the spring breeze flowing in and bearing with it wisps of the outside world, the scent of grass and salt water. I wanted to be alone.

I didn't pay much attention to where I headed, but I did intentionally ignore the paths Quintus had pointed out earlier in the day. Our earlier explorations now seemed very long ago when I considered what a drastically different state of mind I had been in.

Perhaps it was juvenile, but I wanted to rebel in whatever small ways were left to me. That, and I didn't want to be found any earlier than possible, even though I knew it wouldn't take long, considering the small size of the island. There were only so many places I could hide myself away.

I reached the northern tip of Trimerus, and I stood at the edge of the cliff. A small outcropping, rocky and uninhabited, wasn't far from this vantage point; Quintus hadn't taken me in this direction, so it was something new to examine. The wind whipped at my dress, and I pulled my hair loose from its low bun, casually styled by Aurelia that morning. My curls billowed across my face and then out behind me, changing course in tune with the shifting winds rushing across the island.

In some strange way, I mused, I felt more free in my exile than I ever had in Rome, where I had been trapped in an endless cycle of imperial event attendances, parties, and social gatherings with other women, all of them concerned about the latest fashions, the most recent gossip, and who the current key political players were. They would smile and work at their looms, spinning their wool in a false semblance of humility—but they would all eagerly descend upon another of the group at the first sign of weakness, vultures circling around a wounded animal. There was always worry about whose husband would be appointed as the next governor of whichever province, boasting about whose son had begun a successful political career, snide commentary about whose daughter didn't seem able to produce any male heirs. They divorced and remarried their children as they built and decimated family alliances in an endless power struggle, quietly and carefully whispering into their husbands' ears even as they smiled into each other's faces. No, I missed none of that.

The sun was starting to set, and my skin pimpled with gooseflesh as the warm spring light slowly disappeared. It was soon completely dark, the moon absent, and still I stood at the cliff's edge, staring, now, at nothing, only listening to the waves that beat against the island, the repetitive cycle almost lulling me into a trancelike state.

I could not say that it didn't occur to me to jump. A little voice started to whisper in my mind that I should end my exile by my own hand, on my own terms, but I couldn't bring myself to do it, not yet. I rested a hand on my stomach, and eventually I turned away from the cliff's edge, shutting out the faint, dark whisper in my mind, and steeled myself to return to the villa. Aurelia, and my guards, would probably be furious with me. I must have been gone for hours.

I had moved only a few steps before a voice spoke from the darkness. "Are you ready?" I squinted at a clump of bushes, and a figure emerged, straightening up from a crouching position. Titus.

I didn't answer. Instead, I chose to keep walking, studiously ignoring the guard. Unperturbed, the soldier fell into step beside me; a pleasant aroma of leather, metal, and faint traces of honey reached my nose as the breeze carried his scent to me, and I took a deep breath. After a few minutes, curiosity got the better of me and my resolve to silence lessened.

"How long were you there for?" I asked. My tone was still icy.

"Almost as long as you were. I saw you leave, and once I escaped your slave woman—who was quite hard to evade, I might add—I told Quintus that you wanted to go on a walk and that I was accompanying you. You were within my sight the entire time." He sounded tired, although I detected a small note of pride as he spoke the last words.

"Why didn't you stop me?" The rest of his words sank in. "And why lie to Quintus?" My tone had softened.

I felt more than saw Titus shrug, the growing darkness reducing him to little more than a shadowy figure. We walked quietly for a few moments before he answered.

"I do not pretend to know what it is like to be you, to be part of the imperial family, but I do know what it is like to feel a heaviness in your soul. I understand the need to be alone." Titus paused before continuing. "And besides, where would you have gone? There are no ships in port. You couldn't have made it very far, so there was no need to worry Quintus unnecessarily."

I snorted, not caring that it was unladylike. Titus ignored the noise.

"Although," he continued, "my commander won't be pleased that we are returning in darkness."

It was my turn to shrug. "I will take the blame."

Titus's steps faltered for a moment, and I could tell he was surprised. I would not go so far as to apologize for my unkind words earlier—*that* would be beneath me—so this would have to do instead.

"My mother was a slave, before I was born," Titus announced suddenly.

I didn't answer, uncertain of the point he was no doubt preparing to make—but I was sure I would find out shortly.

"My father was of the ruling class," he said. "A senator, actually, although she never told me who, despite my constant questioning as a child. Once she became pregnant with me, he freed her. That was the only favor he ever did her, or me."

"Didn't your mother take her name from her former master?" I asked. That would have been typical for a freed slave, identifying, at least, the wider family branch of Titus's unknown father.

Titus shook his head. "No. She refused it, or at least would never use it, nor tell me what it had been. I was without a second name for a long time, only called Titus."

I frowned. There was a not insignificant chance that I had unknowingly met Titus's father at some inane social gathering or another, if he still lived. A great many senators regularly paid homage to the emperor's family.

"What did your mother do when she was freed?" I asked, choosing not to pursue my line of thought about Titus's father.

"She whored for a while. I would sit in the corner sometimes, until I was old enough to bother her clients, watchful little thing that I was. Eventually, a soldier liked her enough to marry her, but he died soon after in Gaul. I remember little of him, but I did take my *nomen* from him, Florius. Titus Florius: useless for tracing my real father. And my mother died about seven or eight years ago now, while I was on campaign."

"Oh." I couldn't think of what else to say. His life had been so drastically different from my own; it was beyond me to attempt to fully understand it, and it would be beneath both of us to pretend that I could.

"I don't need to defend myself to you, but considering that we are all here on this island for the foreseeable future, I wanted to let you know…" Titus paused, then finished his sentence in an earnest rush. "I wanted to let you know that I have never whored. I have never paid for sex, nor have I ever abused a slave in that manner. I find it distasteful."

I nodded, even though I knew he couldn't see me clearly in the dark. He had come to the point of his tale. "That is admirable. And rare." Again, not a direct apology on my part, but an acknowledgment that my assumptions about him earlier in the day had been wrong. That was as far as I was willing to go.

We walked silently the remainder of the way to the villa, Titus opening the doors to let me in when we arrived. Quintus was pacing in the atrium, and he glared at Titus after we had entered, a single vein bulging from his forehead.

"What hour do you call this?" Quintus snapped, and Titus tensed.

"It's my fault, Quintus. Calm down," I said dismissively, waving a hand at him before he had the opportunity to further berate Titus. "I got a bit confused out walking and went down the wrong path, and Titus was too polite to correct me. Then I insisted that I wanted to watch the sunset, and I was too frightened of twisting an ankle in the dark to walk back to the villa very quickly."

Quintus huffed, but he seemed satisfied enough. "Fine. Dinner has been ready for a while now." The vein bulging from his forehead seemed to have diminished in appearance.

The commander unceremoniously marched towards the *triclinium*, and I followed behind. I noticed that Titus had now moved a few steps away from me, his earlier, overt kindness diminishing as he returned to his formal duties. His faint scent lingered in my nose.

Aurelia emerged from the hallway leading to our bedroom and slipped into place behind me. I could feel her quietly seething and knew that she soon would make her unhappiness with my earlier disappearance abundantly clear. As far as she was concerned, I was to have a constant chaperone, and she was the only one up to the duty.

The rest of our awkward household was already in the dining room, and Aphrodite and Artemis appeared in short order to begin laying out the food. Aphrodite carried a large pot of barley soup, the same one that had been cooking over the kitchen fire when Monimos had had his way with her. She caught my gaze with her own, then quickly looked down.

The slave girl did not look at me again for the rest of the meal as she entered and exited the room, filling wine cups and removing empty dishes that she replaced with fresh platters of food that were, thankfully, an improvement upon our first dinner. One of the chickens who had recently stopped laying eggs had been slaughtered, and the meat was drenched in a wine and leek sauce. Again, fish played a large role in the meal, but this time they had been prepared in a type of soufflé that was a small step closer to the food I was accustomed to consuming.

If I had been less focused on Aphrodite as she moved around the *triclinium*, I may have noticed that Titus was studying me intently. Instead, I only locked eyes with him once. Neither of us so much as smiled at the other, but I sensed an understanding in his eyes, and perhaps a certain level of respect that wasn't there before, on both our parts.

Julia once again found herself in the atrium of the villa, this time with not one but two slaves fanning her. It was summer now, and it was *dreadfully* hot. She was not in the mood for much of anything, and Scribonia had quietly retreated some time ago to avoid Julia's flaring temper, a perfect match for the rising temperature.

The emperor's daughter was agitated. Not only because of the heat, but because the letter she had sent well over a month ago had not yet produced an answer, let alone any results. She was beginning to doubt that her most trusted slave was actually so trustworthy after all.

As if on cue, seemingly summoned by his mistress's thoughts, the slave in question, Felix, entered the atrium with a tray of vegetable-stuffed dormice, drizzled in honey.

"Finally! I'm starving. Come here!" Julia waved at the young man impatiently as she barked out her order, and he scurried over to her couch obediently, holding the tray aloft in front of her at the appropriate level.

She studied the slave boy as she popped an entire dormouse into her mouth, tearing into it with a vicious appetite. He had recently turned fourteen or so, and was starting to grow stubble on his chin, although his slight body remained thin and without much muscle. "You need to shave, Felix. Your chin hair offends me," she told him after she had swallowed.

Felix nodded, his eyes on the mosaicked ground. "Yes, *domina*, my apologies. Right away, *domina*."

"No, not right away, you little idiot. Right now, you are serving me the dormice I requested. Shave later, when I'm done with you." She bit into another dormouse, this time only devouring half of it.

"Yes, *domina*, of course."

Felix was one of the best things to have happened to Julia since her exile some ten years ago, hence the name she had assigned him: *lucky*. She had constantly been under guard, with most, if not all, of the slaves acting as spies for her father and stepmother, the bitch Livia. But at last, after her relocation to Rhegium, fate had intervened, Fortuna be praised.

Not long after Julia's arrival, the assistant kitchen boy at the villa had died unexpectedly—and entirely without her involvement. She had managed to convince the commanding guard, who was fresh to Rhegium and more than a little stupid, to allow her mother, Scribonia, to go into town to select a replacement slave from the options on hand. After all, Julia had sweetly suggested to the commander, who knew better how to run a household than women, and wouldn't he like to have his meals well-cooked and delivered on time?

Felix had been a boy of about ten at the time, his family recently killed or similarly enslaved by the Roman army in whatever forsaken barbarian land he had come from—she couldn't recall exactly, and she didn't care. But he had been exactly what she needed. It had taken little work on Julia's part to turn him into her own loyal lackey, answerable to her rather than to the guards: a beating here and there, intermixed with just enough affection and displays of pretended motherly love to bind him to her, to make him feel as if he could hope to be part of a family again. Julia had cleverly, and cruelly, played on his wants and needs and fears, molding him for her own purposes.

Of course, he played the part of a typical slave well, acting stupid and servile and completely ignorant of any sort of plotting. He did his daily work in the kitchen, and Julia even had him tattle on her to the guards for small transgressions, so that they would think he was just as pathetically loyal to the cause of her continued imprisonment as anyone else in the household.

But Felix's main use to her had become the transportation of letters and information to and from the villa. His regular errands into town, mostly to acquire new supplies for the kitchen, gave him more reason than anyone else to disappear for periods of time, and a valid excuse to carry a variety of goods in which a scroll was easily concealable. It was with Felix that she had sent off her letter in the spring.

"Don't you have anything else for me, Felix? I've had enough of these dormice. They're a bit overcooked." Julia placed the remaining half of the dormouse into her mouth and sucked the honeyed juices off her thumb, stretching out her body on the couch like a well-fed housecat. She blinked at the slave boy expectantly.

Felix nodded. "Yes, *domina*. Cook had me get some fresh supplies in town today. I will bring you something new now, *domina*."

As Felix scurried away, Julia pursed her lips, wondering if the slave had caught her meaning. Sometimes he was so good at pretending stupidity that she worried he truly was an idiot.

Felix returned in short order, carrying another tray which was overflowing with some sort of stuffed vegetable. Julia sniffed, uncertain about the newest food option, and daintily reached out a hand to select one. Suddenly, Felix coughed violently and shook the tray, dropping a few of the vegetables directly onto Julia's lap.

"Oh!" she screamed out, lurching away from Felix in surprise and nearly falling off the couch. The two slaves fanning Julia quickly rushed forward, doing their best to clean her up as her surprise shifted to anger. "You stupid, *stupid* boy!" she yelled, and she lashed out, slapping Felix across the face so hard that his head jerked backwards. "My dress is *ruined*!"

"S-so sorry, *domina*," Felix stammered, dropping to his knees to start cleaning up the mess on the floor. A red-tinged handprint marked his cheek.

"Get away from me!" Julia snapped at the slaves who were still trying to pick food off of her body and the couch. "And *you*," she continued, glaring down at Felix, "will get a proper beating for this clumsiness. Inexcusable!"

Julia stood up, the other slaves quickly dropping down to assist with cleaning the floor; one of them scurried away with the tray. Julia slapped Felix across the face once more as he sat on his knees, staring up at her with big, woeful eyes. She swore that she could almost see his chin quiver as he prepared for her to strike him again.

The next slap resulted in Felix curling into a ball at Julia's sandaled feet. While the other remaining slave ignored the ongoing beating, busily cleaning up the rest of the spilled food with intense focus, Felix dashed out a small hand, almost faster than Julia could see, slipping a folded-up scrap of papyrus under her right foot. Julia slapped him once more, for good measure. She was sweating from the exertion.

"Get out of my sight," she panted. Felix obeyed, fleeing the atrium without a word.

When the last slave disappeared in the direction of the kitchen with the remainder of the mess, Julia bent over, as if she had to scratch her ankle. She plucked the scrap from under her foot, tucked it into her bosom, and settled back on the couch. *I'll need to bathe now*, she thought distractedly, as sweat dripped down her body.

CHAPTER X

JULIA THE YOUNGER

I almost wanted to laugh at Aurelia, since she looked so much more miserable than I had ever seen her before, but I felt badly—she was only here because of me, and so I managed to sit quietly. We were in a rowboat, along with Marcus and Quintus, heading across the short strip of water to the island where Lucius's self-styled retirement villa was. The early summer sun was relentless even though the season had just begun, and despite the fact that it was almost evening.

I had told my slave she didn't need to accompany me, that she should rest to recover from a recent illness she had been struck with, but she hadn't listened. I wasn't surprised. The idea of me attending dinner with a man, even a quite elderly man, without an appropriate chaperone—as she didn't believe the two guards fulfilled that role—was enough to send her into a sputtering fury, never mind that she was the slave and I the *domina*. The added fact that my honor had long since been compromised didn't seem to matter to her.

Aurelia retched over the side of the rowboat again, although nothing else seemed to be coming up. Quintus politely ignored her, but Marcus scowled, his disdain and disgust evident. I don't think I had ever seen the man with anything but a scowl, frown, or leer on his face. I didn't like him.

My baby chose that moment to kick, and I winced, clutching the edge of the boat with one hand. He or she was due to arrive this summer, and while I couldn't wait to get it out of me, I was also terrified for my child's future. It was a bastard, without even the hope of passing as legitimate. I did not think my grandfather would be so cruel as to order it exposed, to let it die discarded and abandoned as some men would do if they suspected their wife's child was unlawful, but I couldn't know—and that uncertainty plagued me, although I shared my worries with no one, not even Aurelia.

I reassured myself that there was a not inconsiderable chance that the child, so far removed from the political intrigues of Rome, would be allowed to live, to remain with me in my lonely exile, surrounded only by slaves and guards for company. After all, the circle of those who knew of the unborn infant's existence was incredibly small, and if it were born female, then it would be even less of a threat to anyone. And so, I prayed daily for a daughter.

"We're almost there," Quintus announced unnecessarily, jarring me from my thoughts. He grunted as he pulled on his oar again, moving us ever closer to the rocky island.

The small port, almost more of an inlet, was up ahead, and two of Lucius's slaves were visible, patiently waiting to lead us up the hill to their master's villa. It seemed that Lucius had not yet ordered the litter he had jested about during our first meeting, and so we would have to walk. I fought a sigh, already tired at just the thought.

It had taken some convincing to get the commander of the guards to allow me to visit Lucius for dinner. Quintus had even insisted on taking two of his men over to the little island a week prior to survey the area in more detail, as well as to map the layout of the villa and to note down the number and appearances of the slaves in Lucius's service. Titus and Publius, now resting at our own villa on Trimerus, had been sent over that very morning for last minute observations. I didn't know what Quintus thought was going to happen, but the measures he had taken seemed to reassure him enough to allow me to visit my new friend, and so I was satisfied.

Lucius had only returned to Trimerus once since his initial visit, bearing his official invitation to dinner at his home. We had chatted, mostly about the scroll he was in the process of reading at the time, then gone for a slow walk as he hobbled along with his cane, pointing out some of the different birds who called the island their home, and finally we returned to the villa for a simple meal. Naturally, he had insulted Artemis's cooking and loudly criticized the manners of all the guards. It was the most fun I had had in quite a while.

I frowned. That wasn't necessarily true, upon reconsideration. Titus and I had become not quite friends, but… companions. Agreeable companions. He was my favorite guard with whom to walk, although my exercise of late had plummeted as my belly swelled near to explosion. And I wasn't always allowed to choose my own guard.

When Marcus took me out on an excursion, I felt vaguely uncomfortable, worried even. He always stared at me with his dark eyes, and I didn't like to dwell on the unknown thoughts passing through his mind. I knew that Aurelia felt the same; she always watched him, more than she did any of the others. But he never *did* anything against me, and he never even *said* anything inappropriate. I assumed Quintus knew him better than anyone else and considered him trustworthy, and so I resigned myself to my simple dislike of Marcus and left it at that.

Quintus and Publius were pleasant enough, although the former was lacking in his desire to make much conversation with me. Publius, while sometimes chatty, was always superficial. I could tell he was a genuinely nice, jovial young man, but he knew well enough to keep the barrier between us: that between commoner and aristocrat, guard and prisoner, man and woman.

Titus, though, was different. Ever since the day he had followed me to the cliff's edge, after I had insulted him and stormed off, there had been an understanding between us. He wasn't overly fond of long conversations, and I knew he tried his best not to delve into more stories of his past, but occasionally something slipped through. Perhaps that something was the real Titus. It was intriguing.

I knew Aurelia had noticed our newfound familiarity with one another, and I also knew she disapproved, although nothing that Titus and I had discussed or done was inappropriate in any way. I would not have spoken with him any differently whether she was there or not, but I could tell, in the past few weeks, while Aurelia had been too ill to accompany me on my walks, that Titus had seemed more *alive*, more free, with me. We had shared something that night when I had run off, a recognition of and respect for the other's suffering, despite our difference in station.

Our rowboat at last reached the neighboring island, and I cleared my head of thoughts of Titus and the other guards. It was ridiculous that my social life had been reduced to deciding which guard I liked the best. They were there to make certain I remained a prisoner. They were not my friends, and they certainly were not my equals. I resolved to favor Titus less, lest he think too highly of himself. Aurelia, at least, would be pleased.

Quintus exited our little boat first, extending a hand down to assist me, and I was embarrassed to see that his face scrunched in effort as he helped me onto dry land. Aurelia followed, looking pale and exhausted, with stony-faced Marcus bringing up the rear of our strange little group.

Lucius's two slaves greeted us and led the way up a steep, rocky pathway, one which I had a hard time envisioning my elderly friend navigating after finding myself struggling more than I had expected. Finally, I got a glimpse of Lucius's residence, which looked to be about the same size as our villa on Trimerus. The building style was also from a similar time period, as far as I could tell: slightly dated, but well maintained. Lucius clearly took pride in his home.

Aurelia and I were both panting and sweaty by the time we reached the main doors, the sun still beating down even though it was now early evening. I typically didn't mind the heat of summer, but I had come to realize that I absolutely despised it while pregnant, the uncomfortable labors of carrying a child heightened considerably by the hostile season. Perhaps I would have felt differently were I ensconced in one of my grandfather's cool, carefully designed villas in the countryside, where we had often retreated from the summer heat and stench of the city when I was child. Those days, I reminded myself, were long past.

One of the slaves opened the doors and we passed through into the atrium, in the center of which was a small, bubbling fountain which trickled down into the *impluvium*, lightly stirring the handful of white flower petals that had been strewn across the surface of the water. A variety of sculptures, many of them depicting the great gods and goddesses of Rome, as well as a handful of lesser-known deities, ringed the atrium; all of them were painted in bright, gaudy colors, as was the fashion. Assorted cages were placed in what few spaces remained, and they held birds of all types and sizes, the creatures within flitting about and chirping as they took in our arrival, perhaps wondering if we had food for them.

Lucius was reclining on a couch in the atrium, already indulging in some wine. The bright, glinting red of it seen through the glass suggested that it was barely, if at all, watered down. He had on a very fine tunic, and I felt my cheeks flush as I remembered the plain, pale blue dress I wore. Aurelia had done what she could with my hair, but I was a far cry from my former glory when I was in Rome, especially considering the stinky, sweaty mess I surely was at that moment.

Lucius either didn't notice my sudden embarrassment or didn't care. He jumped up as quickly as he was able and hobbled over to me without bothering to use his cane. He grinned without care for his missing front tooth.

"Hello, my dear!" he exclaimed. "So good to have you, so good! I see your grumpy old guards wouldn't let you away without them, but never mind that. You're here, at least!"

I smiled in return. "Thank you for the kind invitation, Lucius. I'm looking forward to dinner, especially having heard so much from you about your well-trained cook."

"Yes, yes, but in the meantime why don't you join me over here, and we can have a bit of wine, catch up a bit, too!"

I obediently walked over to the couch angled next to his, noticing that there were no designated spaces for Aurelia or the guards. They would all be standing, it appeared. That was the proper way of things, but I found that I had already grown accustomed to dining with them all. It felt strange that they would now be excluded.

Aurelia meekly took her place behind my couch as I settled onto it, while Quintus murmured something inaudible to Marcus. The younger guard disappeared, no doubt on another survey of the villa, while Quintus stationed himself in the corner of the atrium, ever stoic and watchful. I wondered if he missed the more exciting life on the campaign trail, following one general or another across our ever-expanding empire, striking down all manner of bloodthirsty barbarian warriors and enslaving people after people. Now he was stuck following me around an island which presented little opportunity for escape and even fewer threats of danger.

Lucius was babbling away again, and I quickly focused my attention back on my host. I reminded myself that I still had manners, despite my circumstances.

"...*all* sorts of fish, some from my own ponds out behind the villa, but even some caught down around the port, straight from the sea," he was saying, explaining a portion of the menu for the evening.

An older female slave approached from a corridor, and she served me a glass of wine as Lucius continued to chatter. I drank almost all of it at once, dehydrated from the sweaty crossing in the rowboat and the climb up to the villa.

"....and, of course, we will be having a nice little milk pudding for dessert, with some honey from the mainland, the bees having been kept solely on northern wildflowers. *Quite* a treat, I should think," Lucius added.

I smiled and nodded agreeably. "It all sounds so delicious. I can't wait."

Lucius beamed at me, then frowned. "My dear, I am so sorry, I didn't realize how hot it was in here. I'm afraid my senses must be going as I get older. You look quite fatigued. Let me have one of my slaves fan you."

The slave who had earlier served me wine reemerged from the corridor carrying a fan, as if she had been waiting to be called, and took up position at the end of my couch. Lucius reached over to refill my glass of wine himself, and I took another large swallow of the ruby liquid. The breeze created by the slave was immediately soothing.

Lucius sipped his own wine, appraising me. "Now, remind me of when that baby is coming."

"No more than a month now, I believe," I answered, stroking my belly. My child had stirred again. "Although, by the size of me, I feel as if it could be any day now."

Lucius cackled, a bit of wine dribbling unnoticed down his chin in the process, before suddenly becoming serious. "Let me know if I can be of any help."

I nodded politely, already disregarding his offer of assistance. What need did I have of an old recluse when it came to childbearing? I had Aurelia, and she was more than enough.

The rest of the meal passed without particular excitement. The food was certainly a step above what I had recently been consuming, particularly the milk-gorged snails that had been lightly fried. It was also, once again, refreshing to spend time with someone who was nearer to my own station, although the conversation was less than enrapturing, and my host would occasionally jump up to feed tidbits to his birds, all of whom worked themselves into a frenzy when their master neared their cages. I found my attention wandering more than once, particularly as another few glasses of wine had made me sleepy.

I thanked Lucius profusely for hosting me, reassuring him of the quality of the food when he worried aloud that it was a far cry from the lavish banquets I had attended in Rome, and our group departed. It was fully dark by the time we left the villa, the moon absent, but Quintus seemed unconcerned about rowing us back across the water to Trimerus. It was a short enough journey over calm water, and he had made the trip at least a few times in the lead-up to the dinner.

Feeling drowsy from the wine, I laid my head in Aurelia's lap as our little boat got underway. Hearing her stomach growl, I realized that she and the guards had yet to have their own dinner, and I sleepily hoped that Artemis would have something left for them in the kitchen when we returned to our own villa.

I must have dozed off, because the next thing I was aware of was taking a breath full of cold water as my eyes opened to an endless blackness that stung with its saltiness. I gagged and tried to scream for help, but only managed to suck in more water, choking myself. Everything was dark, and I had no sense of what was up and what was down.

My heart felt as if it was about to explode out of my chest, and my ears were roaring as my body struggled with the lack of air. I thrashed my arms and legs without clear intent, my lungs burning, and suddenly I was at the surface, coughing up seawater and gasping to catch my breath as tears streamed down my face.

After retching several more times, I managed to fight my panic and to slow my breathing, although my lungs still felt as if they burned with every shaky inhalation. I came to my senses enough to look around as I treaded water, searching for Quintus, Marcus, or Aurelia. I couldn't see anything in the darkness, and I began to shiver. My dress, soaked with water, weighed me down, and my legs began to burn with the effort of keeping myself afloat.

I had no idea in which direction to swim, no idea where the rowboat was or even where either of the islands were. I cursed myself for drinking so much wine, for falling asleep on the boat, for not knowing where I was. I cursed myself for being in this situation to begin with, on some miserable island because of my own damned actions.

I treaded water for what felt like an eternity, calling out for help a few times in a hoarse voice, and I became increasingly aware of the sense of a subtle current carrying me in a direction of Neptune's choice. I needed to decide what to do, and quickly, before it was too late.

Part of me just wanted to let myself slip back under the water, and that would be the end of it all. It was the same nagging little voice from which I had heard a mere whisper when I stood on the cliff's edge, so soon after my arrival on Trimerus. But now it was louder, more insistent: *Why continue living this pathetic existence? It would be so easy to just let go. To die.*

The ideal Roman woman should have channeled her protective motherly instincts at this point, fighting to survive for her child, if not for herself, so that Rome could see another glorious son rise to bring it further glory. I tried to summon that instinct, that desire to live, to fight, and I thought I grasped just a touch of it, but I couldn't hold on.

My legs, treading water even as they trembled with cold and exhaustion, faltered, and I slipped below the choppy surface of the water. I emerged quickly enough, coughing again, and suddenly the sinister voice was gone. My mind was now clear. I started swimming in a direction chosen at random, only knowing enough not to just go along with the faint current, since it would no doubt push me past the islands and into the open sea. If that happened, there would be little hope for my survival.

I wasn't a particularly strong swimmer, but I had learned as a child, along with my siblings. Our father had insisted that we each learn the skill, even his daughters, despite our sex. Our mother had thought it silly, but I was exceedingly grateful now, even though I had never taken to it like my brother Agrippa. He had always been a little fish, darting through the water as if it were his second home.

The passage of time as I swam was impossible to estimate. My eyes continued to try to adjust to the darkness, but there was almost no light by which to see other than a few stars. The only noise was the splashing of my own body in the water as I took stroke after stroke.

I paused, treading water once more, and looked around, silently promising the gods all sorts of honors and sacrifices if only they would guide me to land of any sort. My pregnant belly felt as if it dragged me down more and more as time passed, and I was quickly losing all hope. I felt more than heard the sinister little voice reemerging from the depths of my mind, no doubt about to remind me that I had a very easy option: to give up. To stop swimming. To let myself die. At least then I could rest.

My baby kicked suddenly, sharply, and I sucked in seawater, coughing, tears streaming from my eyes. That was enough to force me back into action, and I began to move again. I would swim until I couldn't swim anymore, and only then would I give in to that nasty little voice in my mind.

CHAPTER XI

AGRIPPA POSTUMUS

Agrippa rolled over onto his back, his naked body bobbing rhythmically with the waves. The cut on his neck from his morning shave had stung when he first entered the salt water, an all too potent reminder that he still lived, if his current existence could be called that, but he couldn't feel the tiny wound at all now. He had wanted to kill the slave who had nicked him, but, alas, the guards wouldn't allow it. They wouldn't even trust him to shave himself—not that he knew how—lest he decide to turn the blade on his own neck, or across his wrists. Only the emperor had the right to take his life, they had said.

Agrippa closed his eyes, the sun beating down on his body, listening to the gentle rush of water in his ears. A small rowboat bobbed nearby, three guards sitting in it, two of them playing a game of *latrunculi* that they had brought along to amuse themselves, while the third kept one eye on the board and the other on Agrippa's floating body.

"Still can't believe we have to appease Neptune over there, letting him swim in the ocean like a lunatic," one of the players muttered, making a move. He cursed when his opponent outmaneuvered him. "Damn you to Pluto!" he snapped, referencing the god of the

Underworld. The other man only chuckled in response.

The watchful guard shrugged. "The emperor wants him to be comfortable… Happy, even, if possible. We have our orders."

"Fuck our orders," the third guard pitched in. "How's the emperor to know if that little shit over there is happy or not? Anyway, who the fuck can be happy out here in the middle of nowhere?"

All three looked over at Agrippa, whose position hadn't changed. If the guards didn't know better, they would have thought he was a corpse floating on the waves.

"Pay attention," one of the guards said, picking up a game piece and breaking the others' focus on the emperor's grandson. The game resumed.

After a few more minutes of basking in the sunshine, Agrippa rolled over onto his stomach and started to swim lazily away from the direction of the rowboat, parallel to the shore.

"Little shit," the guard winning the game grumbled, as he had to set down his piece to pick up an oar.

The guards stroked slowly along behind Agrippa as he swam. They weren't worried about escape; the next closest landmass of significance was miles and miles away, and the summer day was clear and cloudless, allowing them to see in all directions for quite some distance, reassuring them that not a single ship was on the horizon. Suddenly, the youth disappeared under the water. The guards stopped, waiting for him to resurface. The seconds ticked by.

"What's he doing?" one asked. All three looked at one another, uncertain.

"Dunno," another guard answered, "but I hope he comes up soon."

They continued to wait in silence, but the water didn't stir.

Almost a full minute passed, and the men were all shifting their weight, glancing between the water and each other.

"Alright, someone needs to go get him," one of them finally said.

"You go fucking get him. I'm not getting wet for him. Let him drown. Then we can all go home." Silence. Still not even a ripple on the surface of the water.

"Do you really want to be one of the guards responsible for letting the emperor's grandson *drown* on our watch? We have orders to keep him on Planasia, keep him as happy and comfortable as possible, and keep him *alive*. How do you think the emperor would react when he finds out that *three* of us couldn't save his own flesh and blood when he's just out for a casual swim?"

"*You* go get the little shit, then!"

"Fine." The guard stood, removing his sandals and short sword, and then pulling his tunic over his head. In only his loincloth, he dove into the water, disappearing where they had last seen Agrippa swimming. More seconds ticked by.

Suddenly, the two guards in the boat were splashed with water from behind. Both shouted out in surprise, turning around, only to be greeted by Agrippa's laughing face as he splashed them again, then began swimming towards the shore at a rapid pace.

"You fucking madman!" yelled one of the soldiers, his comrade pulling him back from the edge of the boat by his arm.

The third guard, who had jumped into the water after Agrippa, finally resurfaced, panting and sputtering. "I can't find him!" he shouted, panicked. "I can't find him!"

"He's there," the third guard said, pointing resignedly to the pale figure swimming away. "He was just messing us around. He's fine."

They hauled their last member from the water and rowed after

Agrippa once more.

Agrippa lounged on his bed, staring at the ceiling of his bedroom. As punishment, the door had been closed and bolted by the guards who had accompanied him on his afternoon swim. He regretted nothing—after all, he had to amuse himself somehow, and his options were limited.

The door now swung open without a knock, and one of the dozen guards entered with a plate of food. It must have been time for dinner, then.

"Set it on the table," Agrippa lazily ordered, not bothering to move from the bed. The guard did as he instructed, but then stood there, watching him. Agrippa scowled. "What is it, you ignorant thug? Go away."

"Oil doesn't get made without the crushing of many olives," he said quietly, and Agrippa sat up quickly, staring at him.

Those words were something Paullus had always said to him, while he still lived, often to justify whatever misdeed he was about to commit in the name of their treasonous cause. What was this soldier playing at? Agrippa opened his mouth to speak, to interrogate the guard, but the red-haired man jerked his head in silent warning, and Agrippa closed his lips.

"Will there be anything else?" the guard asked, voice neutral.

Agrippa shook his head, lost in thought, and the guard left, closing the door behind him. Agrippa noted that he failed to bolt it. Perhaps, he mused, he was not entirely surrounded by idiots after all.

CHAPTER XII

JULIA THE YOUNGER

Silanus was kissing my forehead as I slept, his lips warm and soft against my skin. I was too sleepy to wake up, but I smiled and reached out for him with my arms, wanting to pull him closer to me, to envelop him in a hug. I couldn't survive without his love. Instead, I wrapped myself around air, and I reached for him again, panicked when I continued to find nothing. He was gone, as if he had never been. I missed him. I missed him so, so very much: his gentle voice, his soft hands, his quiet humor, his kindness.

I wanted to sleep, but it was suddenly very cold. Loose strands of my hair kept floating back and forth across my face, irritating me, and the waves crashing nearby were distracting. Waves, I thought. Why were there waves? Although I tried to shut out the annoying sounds and the disagreeable temperature in order to return to the comforts of sleep, to dreams of my lover, my body was urging me to wake up, to move. Something was wrong.

I opened my eyes, blinking rapidly as I adjusted to the bright light of the sun, and sat up, shivering. A gull had landed close to my face, its head cocked to the side as it examined me, deciding if I was some sort of large fish that it could devour. Seeing that I was now alert, it called out in alarm and, flapping its wings, took off in a hurry.

I pulled my legs up to my belly, wrapping my arms around them in an effort to warm up as I examined my surroundings. I was sitting on what amounted to little more than a pile of rocks in the sea, barely out of the water's reach. A storm of any moderate size would easily cause the rocks to slip beneath the waves, completely out of sight.

My memory of the previous night's events was hazy. I had dined with Lucius at his villa on the neighboring island, and our group had left once night had fallen. I remembered dozing off, sleepy from too much wine, my head in Aurelia's lap, and then suddenly I had been in the water, lost and alone. I knew I had kept swimming, directionless, but I didn't remember reaching this rocky outcropping. I consciously blocked out my memory of almost choosing to let go, to give up. I was not proud of how close I had come to succumbing to that dark voice inside of me that seemed to grow stronger each time it awakened.

I cradled my belly as I continued my survey of my surroundings; my baby was quiet within, not having stirred since I had awoken. I could see an island not too far away, with a steep cliff that dropped off into the sea. I realized, then, where I was. I had seen this little clump of rocks the day I had stormed off some weeks ago, when Titus had followed me despite the insults I had hurled at him. I had stood at that cliff's edge and seen the very spot where I now found myself. Breathing a sigh of relief, I realized that I wasn't far from Trimerus at all. Now I just had to hope the guards would find me sooner rather than later. Surely they were searching.

The sun was slowly climbing higher in the sky, and the temperature rose alongside it. Soon, the earlier chill I had felt was replaced with an uncomfortable heat that caused my dress to stick to my body, the salt of my sweat mixing uncomfortably with that of the sea.

Feeling my skin beginning to burn, I pulled my hair loose from its bun, hoping that it would help to cover my exposed upper arms and the back of my neck. My shoes had been lost in the sea at some point, and I tucked my bare feet under my body, away from the prying sun.

Time continued to pass, and the sun continued its journey. There was still no sign of my guards. I finally decided to stand, to move around, and I tentatively climbed across the rocks, reaching the other end of the outcropping within moments. Other than some gulls flying lazily overhead, I was entirely alone.

My bare feet began to burn, the rock scalding their sensitive pads, and I retreated to the side of the outcropping closer to Trimerus, staring at the island in vain as I waited for someone, anyone, to decide to extend their search for me in this direction. I sat again, inching closer to the water and letting my feet dangle off a ledge so that the waves touched my toes as they crashed against the rocks, the cool strokes of water a soothing salve.

I was growing impatient. How hard could it be? How could they *lose* me out here in the middle of nowhere? Surely they must have searched all of Trimerus by now, and even Lucius's island. Had my grandfather saddled me with the most incompetent of all his guards?

A new thought occurred to me, and I frowned. Perhaps they thought I was already dead. Perhaps they had already given up, and they were all sitting at the villa, drinking and eating and celebrating the end of their tour on *exilium* with the emperor's granddaughter.

My train of thought shifted. What had happened to the others in the boat, to Aurelia, Quintus, and Marcus? What if *they* had all perished? I wouldn't give a single *denarius* to save Quintus or Marcus, but my newfound worry about Aurelia made me jump up and pace uselessly on my pile of rocks, burned feet be damned. My baby remained too still within my body, but I could not yet bring myself to think of that, too.

I considered jumping back into the sea in an attempt to swim to Trimerus, even though the island was bordered by cliffs, making access difficult. I would probably have to swim into the port itself in order to return, unless I happened across the single stretch of sandy shore belonging to the island.

Suddenly, distant movement on Trimerus caught my eye, a barely visible, dark blur that was making slow progress across the grasses. Someone was by the cliff. I screamed out, not caring that the noise wouldn't be heard over the crashing of the waves, and flailed my arms above my head, jumping up and down like a fool in a desperate effort to attract the figure's attention.

I cursed the simple, pale blue dress Aurelia had laid out for me for the dinner with Lucius, wishing that she had instead packed some of the bright red and vivid scarlet gowns from my wardrobe in Rome, even though they clashed with my complexion and I had always tended to avoid wearing them. Yet if they had come to Trimerus with me, if I had worn one, perhaps then, at least, I would have been more visible; as it was, I disappeared far too easily into the water all around me.

I couldn't tell if the figure in the distance saw me. It moved away after half a minute or so, and I stood still, tears running down my sunburned face as I panted from my brief and intense flurry of activity. I was exhausted, hungry, and incredibly thirsty. None of this was what my life was supposed to be. I should have been relaxing in the finest private baths in a country estate somewhere, or snacking on a sampling of the rarest foods from across the empire, seasoned with the finest imported spices, or selecting fabrics and jewels to purchase. Anything but this. I screamed my frustration and was answered only by a single gull overhead, its call a mockery.

It was late afternoon. If I didn't start swimming, it would soon be too dark for me to try to make it back to Trimerus, and I didn't relish the idea of spending another night on the desolate outcropping. It was time. I pulled my dress off over my head, standing on the rocks in only my breastband and loincloth. I didn't want the extra weight or length of my dress to interfere with the swim I was about to undertake. Despite the heat, a shiver passed through my body: trepidation.

I felt fairly certain about where the port was—on the left side of Trimerus from where I was standing—and so I stepped into the water, pausing only momentarily to allow myself to adjust to the cooler temperature. Then, I forced myself to continue moving forward, gritting my teeth. There was rock and sand under my feet for a few steps, but then it dropped off sharply, harshly casting me into the water. Suddenly I was swimming, fighting desperately against the initial crush of waves that sought to pound me mercilessly back into the rocky outcropping from which I was trying to escape.

Once free of the rougher waters, I paced myself, pausing frequently to blink the saltwater from my eyes and to make certain that I was on track to progress towards the left side of Trimerus, where I hoped—and prayed—that the port was nestled away, as I thought it was. I could not afford to be wrong.

The outcropping slipped away behind me with each stroke I took, and I was soon in completely open water, free of any strong currents. Swim, pause, assess, swim; I found myself in a repetitive cycle, and I tried not to lose hope as I found myself tiring, while Trimerus still seemed just as far away as it had when I first started.

Abrupt movement out of the corner of my eye made me stop, sucking in water in surprise as I halted. I coughed, panicking, and floundered in the water, fighting to stay afloat. Again, a flash of gray to my right, and another to my left. I wasn't so naïve or ignorant as to believe in sea monsters, knowing them to be myths, but I also knew there were creatures that might be less than friendly in open waters.

My vision cleared as I treaded water, at last catching my breath. There it was again, another flash of gray. I exhaled, my body relaxing as I recognized the gray creatures. *Delphini.* I had seen some for the first time as a child, on a ship with my family as we went to Capri to join my grandfather at one of his villas there. They were playful, fascinating creatures, and I was in the middle of an entire group of them.

Twisting back towards Trimerus, I caught sight of a small boat. The lone figure in it was rowing frantically in my general direction. Not caring who was in the boat, hoping only that it would save me the rest of my journey, I swam towards it. The dolphins were still in a group around me, one or two coming close and then darting away as if playing a game, seeing which of them dared come closest to the awkward creature who had dropped into their midst.

The boat continued its steady progress towards me, and I could at last identify the figure inside it: Titus. It was Titus. I wanted to cry with relief. When he got close enough, he stopped rowing, leaning over the side of the boat and hauling me in as it rocked precariously with the sudden shift in weight. The dolphins remained close by, curious about the newest arrival to their territory.

I found myself hugging Titus, holding on as if I never wanted to let go. He tensed as I grabbed onto him, then slowly relaxed, one hand awkwardly rubbing my back in an attempt to soothe me as I gasped for breath, inhaling his heartening scent. My baby chose that moment to stir at last, and I started crying, overwhelmed and relieved all at once.

"How did you find me?" I asked Titus, still holding him. The dolphins, finally bored with us, begin to slip away, leaving us alone in the sea, bobbing in place as the waves lapped against the boat.

Titus kept a hand gently moving up and down my back. "I saw you from the cliff. Well, what I thought was you, anyway. I ran to get a boat to come retrieve you before I even thought of the possibility that you were a Siren luring me to my doom." After a moment of confusion, I realized he was joking, and my tears turned to a sharp burst of laughter, the unexpected sound surprising my own ears.

I was suddenly aware that I was almost naked, and I pulled away, covering myself with my hands. Titus quickly grabbed a blanket from the floor of the boat and helped me to wrap it around myself, his eyes avoiding me as his face turned red. Surely he had seen naked women before?

"People call my little brother Neptune," I said suddenly. "He loves the water, always has. I used to think it was just a silly nickname, but now I wonder if we all, my siblings and I, have a particular affinity for the god." I was only speaking partly in jest.

"Well, you certainly had more than a bit of luck, I'd say. And you even had guardians." Titus nodded his head in the direction the dolphins had swum off as he collected the oars and began rowing back to the island. "I don't think it's a stretch to say that Neptune may be looking out for you. Your father was renowned for his naval victories. It can't all be coincidence."

I didn't answer. It wasn't good to speculate on the actions of the gods. "How is Aurelia?" I asked instead.

Titus flinched as if my words had physically struck him. "Not well." He paused before continuing, taking another pull on the oars. "The boat capsized, and you were all thrown out. Quintus thinks the boat may have bumped a rock hidden beneath the water's surface."

"But everyone survived?"

Titus nodded, although the action was slightly hesitant. "Quintus was knocked unconscious—struck his head on something. Marcus managed to grab hold of him and keep him afloat on his back, but you and Aurelia were missing. Once Marcus managed to get the boat right-side up, he had quite an ordeal getting Quintus back in it, too."

"And so he didn't even look for Aurelia? Or for me?" I hissed, suddenly furious.

Titus avoided my glare. "He found Aurelia, but she was floating with her face down in the water. We aren't sure how long she went without breathing." My anger dissipated, replaced by worry. "She hasn't woken up since Marcus found her," he added quietly.

"Well, what's being done for her? We need a doctor!"

"That won't happen. If it were you, we would be permitted to call for one, but we would have to wait for the next supply ship to send out the request, and then however long for a doctor to be dispatched from the mainland. It could take months, and a doctor won't come here for a mere slave." His words were not meant to be cold, but I could not quell the rage welling up inside of me.

I wanted to blame someone, to direct my anger at the guards, or at my grandfather, upon whose order I had been exiled, but I could only circle back to myself. It was my fault that we were all here, that Aurelia wouldn't be able to be seen by a doctor. But as Titus had pointed out, even if a doctor was sent, it could take months for him to reach us. It would be too late to be of any use to her.

I switched topics, knowing that if I fixated on Aurelia and her fate at this moment then I would snap entirely. "Why did it take so long to find me?"

"Quintus is dizzy on his feet, so he's in bed, resting. Publius and Marcus searched Lucius's villa and his island this morning at first light, and are now, I believe, scouring the uninhabited island lying beyond that, on the off chance you made it that far. I've been on Trimerus, maintaining some semblance of order at the villa. I needed some air, which was why I was by the cliff, Fortuna be blessed, and caught sight of you."

"I'm happy you did," I said quietly, pulling the blanket tighter around my body.

A silence settled between us, interrupted only by the lapping of waves against the little boat and an occasional grunt from Titus as he pulled on the oars. We were nearing the island.

"Why didn't you wait for me on those rocks?" Titus asked suddenly.

I shrugged. "I wasn't sure you had seen me, and I didn't like the idea of spending another night at sea."

He laughed, and I found my spirits lifting at the carefree noise. "You make it sound like such a logical response," he said.

"It was, given the situation." I rested a hand on my belly.

Titus and I locked eyes. "You're not what I expected," he murmured, so softly that I almost didn't hear him; I wasn't sure that he had intended for me to. I didn't answer, instead shifting my gaze over his shoulder to the nearing port. The rest of the trip passed without conversation.

When we returned to the villa, Artemis and Aphrodite quickly emerged with more blankets and warm food, but I pushed them out of the way, intent on seeing Aurelia first thing. She was lying on her back on her cot in our shared room, breathing softly as if she were only asleep. A thin blanket was pulled up over her, tucked under her chin.

I sank to my knees next to Aurelia, my hands seeking out hers under the blanket. I distantly heard Titus shooing the slave girls away from the room, and then he dropped the door hanging, leaving me alone with Aurelia. I must have sat there for hours, stroking her hands as the light began to fade. Her breathing never changed, and her eyelids never so much as fluttered. Eventually, I rested my head on her cot, and I fell asleep.

Gentle hands on my shoulders woke me, pulling up the blanket that had slipped down my body. Titus was back. "You should rest," he murmured

Light from an oil lamp flickered across his face, and briefly he reminded me of Silanus, with the shadowy stubble on his cheeks and look of concern in his warm, searching eyes. I stopped myself from reaching out to stroke his cheek. "No," I said, shrugging him off instead.

Titus paused, uncertain. "Well, if you're hungry—which I'm sure you are—there's food in the *triclinium*. We've already eaten, but I told the slave girls to leave something out for you." Another pause. "I can bring you something here, if you would prefer." I nodded, and he slipped away, taking one of the oil lamps from the room. He left the other one, and by its light I could see that Aurelia's condition remained unchanged.

Suddenly the desire to bathe, to cleanse myself of my recent trials, overtook me. I quickly stood, gathered some supplies, and took off for the bath, nursing the childish hope that Aurelia would be back to normal when I returned, as if nothing had ever happened.

After setting down my belongings, I dropped the blanket from my shoulders and stripped off my breastband and loincloth, plunging into the bath without ceremony. Seeking comfort in its warm waters, I floated, dumb to the world around me.

I had brought in only the one oil lamp, and its light caused the ripples of water to move in mesmerizing shadows on the shining marble walls all around me. I found brief amusement in the thought that water, of late, had been both a source of despair as well hope for me. Favored by Neptune, indeed.

The thought called to mind the memory of the broken bronze statue of the god tucked away in one of the villa's storage closets, its blue and white eyes watching me from the darkness, and I felt a chill pass through my body, despite the warmth of the water. I quickly submerged myself and began to scrub my skin, the sudden burst of action distracting me from my thoughts.

After ridding myself of the salt encrusted onto my body, I stepped out of the pool, wrapping myself in a drying cloth. I dressed quickly in the fresh clothing I had brought, combed my hair myself, and stepped into the hallway, bumping into a body in the process.

"Oh!" I exclaimed, thinking it was Titus. I looked up, the oil lamp clutched in my hand. It was Marcus. His face had its usual unkind expression as he looked back at me, cold and unblinking. It was obvious he did not care in the least that I had safely returned to the villa.

"Are you finished with the bath?" Marcus asked, simply and directly, and I noticed he had his own bathing supplies in hand. I nodded. "Excuse me, then," he said, nodding pointedly at the door behind me.

I moved out of the way, and Marcus brushed past, bumping my pregnant belly slightly in the process. My infant stirred unhappily. Marcus did not halt, nor did he apologize for the contact. I had half a mind to stop him, to lay into him. Who was *he* to make *me*, the granddaughter of Augustus, move out of *his* way? How *dare* he? But I was too late. The door to the bath closed, and I was alone in the hallway, oil lamp in hand, all my angry words unspoken but still swirling inside of me, fighting for release.

Returning to my room, I found Aurelia in the same state as before. A platter of food, some sliced fruits drizzled in honey and bread accompanied by the fish sauce, *garum*, sat on my bed, no doubt delivered by Titus. No longer hungry, I drank only the cup of water and placed the platter on the floor, curling into a ball on my bed. I fell asleep within moments, my breathing matched to that of Aurelia.

CHAPTER XIII

THE ELDER JULIA

Julia, lost in thought, fanned herself with the letter she had pulled from her bosom once she was in the privacy of her bedroom early that evening. Although it had suffered slightly from exposure to some moisture while in its intimate hiding spot, thankfully it remained legible. Sempronius Gracchus, her admitted former lover and alleged co-conspirator from a decade ago, had finally responded to her.

When Julia had initially been exiled by her father to the island of Pandateria, the emperor had sent Gracchus to Cercina, off the eastern coast of the African province, where the accused man kept a luxurious vacation villa—only this time it hadn't been a temporary, pre-planned stay of his own choosing, but a lifetime sentence. Gracchus had admitted to his affair with the emperor's daughter—the lesser of his crimes—but the accusation of treason against him had never been definitively proven. Nevertheless, he knew better than to fight his punishment for the affair. After all, his exile had been what saved his life.

The letter contained good news. Gracchus's imprisonment was not as rigid as her own, largely because he wasn't a member of the imperial family. Guards would periodically check in on him to make certain that he remained where he had been banished, but their visits grew more and more sparse as time passed, new plots surfaced, and imperial memory faded. His freedom had grown over the years in small measures, making Gracchus, once again, a valuable asset to Julia.

Although Gracchus complained at great length of his inability to leave Cercina to take direct action, lest his absence be found out, he promised Julia that he knew of some men with whom he could make arrangements in order to enact her plans. He reported that a certain forger, known only as Audasius, was already at work creating false imperial documents. Upon their completion, the documents would be sent simultaneously to the islands of Trimerus and Planasia, each accompanied by a handful of mercenaries disguised as Roman soldiers.

If all went according to plan, Julia's children would be freed from their exile, with or without violence, and rapidly escorted to the far western provinces by the end of the year. There, an army would be mustered, Agrippa Postumus at its head. Where her son-in-law Paullus had failed, Julia would prevail.

Julia might not have bothered to include her daughter in the escape plans, except for the fact that she was carrying a great-grandchild of Augustus, one that was hopefully male. Even if illegitimate, the child could generate support for their cause. Furthermore, according to the gossip her slave boy Felix had reported to her, the public still held a surprisingly positive view of her daughter. This was perhaps enough to stimulate some measure of more tangible sympathy for the wayward family of the emperor, to include herself and Agrippa.

Naturally, in Julia's plans, her children would eventually free her from her own exile. Gracchus would call upon what allies he still had, in Rome and abroad, and join the movement. But, for the time being, Julia would orchestrate the civil war from the shadows of her confinement at Rhegium.

After re-reading the letter one final time, Julia held it above the small flame of the oil lamp in her bedroom. It quickly caught fire, and she dropped it on the floor just as it was about to singe her fingers. Gracchus's words turned to ashes, and Julia smiled, rubbing them into an even finer dust with the toe of her sandal. Now, she had only to wait.

Suddenly, the door hanging was pushed aside, and Scribonia entered her daughter's bedroom without announcing herself.

"Hello, Mother," Julia said brightly, smudging the small pile of ash on the floor with her foot to disperse what remained of Gracchus's letter. Normally she would have berated her mother for entering without permission, but she was in too good a mood. "Wonderful evening, isn't it?"

Scribonia shrugged, looking forlorn, as she often did these days. Julia wasn't about to enlighten her about the recent news. Although her mother was helpful in simple ways, Julia didn't trust her to maintain the level of secrecy needed when it came to more important matters. At least Scribonia knew better than to ask questions.

"I think I fancy a walk around the gardens. Will you join me, Mother?" Julia looped her arm through Scribonia's without waiting for an affirmative and guided the elderly woman down the hall to the villa's back door.

Two guards, who had been playing a game of dice in the gardens, quickly stood at attention as the women emerged from the villa. The light was turning dusky, but Julia had forgotten to bring a lamp.

"You, go get me a lamp. Quickly, before the mosquitos start biting," she ordered one of the guards, who obediently scurried off to fulfill her command.

The other guard remained standing at attention until his comrade returned, handing a lamp to Julia and falling in step behind the women as they began to take a turn about the small gardens. Normally she would have thrown a fit that the soldier expected her to carry her own light, but she let it go. Her temper was currently in check.

"Tell me, Mother, how did it feel when Father divorced you? On the very day I was born, no less?" Julia didn't intend meanness; she was simply curious. She had never before asked Scribonia how her mother had felt, and she was feeling particularly chatty that evening. She was nearly her old self. "And for *Livia*, no less?" Julia normally would have included some choice adjectives to describe her stepmother, but she knew the guard behind them was listening attentively and would report their entire conversation to the emperor. Better not to poke the old bear needlessly.

Scribonia, too, seemed aware that their privacy was not guaranteed and so was hesitant to answer. "Our match was not made for love. Few marriages are, as you know. But something in Livia captured your father's attention, in a way I had never before seen with him. She fascinated him, and so he wanted to obtain her." A pause. "And, when you were born female, it cemented the end of our marriage, then and there. He divorced me that very day. As all Romans do, he needed a son, and Livia had already proven, with the birth of Tiberius from her previous marriage, that she could produce one."

Julia positively cackled. "I've never understood the obsession of men with sons. *Sons*. What separates us women? Certainly not a lack of comparable intelligence or cunning." She thought for a moment. "I suppose it's simply the absence of a cock. It's all rather silly, in the end. Besides, look at Father now, still without blood sons after all these years. Livia, too, failed him in the end."

Scribonia made a noncommittal sound in response, and Julia stopped, turning around to face the guard, who immediately looked uncomfortable when he knew he was about to be addressed. Julia had that effect on nearly all her guards over the years.

"What makes *you* better than *me*?" Julia asked him, tilting her head inquisitively. Her gaze was cold and calculating as she examined him, appraising him from head to toe. The man shifted uncomfortably.

A long pause. "I don't know, mistress," the guard finally answered, avoiding eye contact. If he did know, he dared not speak it.

Julia laughed again, turning away from him and resuming her walk, her arm still linked with Scribonia's. Her brief conversation with the guard, combined with the claustrophobic garden walls that were a reminder of her imprisonment, normally would have caused Julia's temper to flare, but Gracchus's letter was fresh in the back of her mind. She would be in a good mood for weeks, waiting for her plans to come to fruition.

For the first time in a long while, she slept deeply and soundly for the duration of the night.

CHAPTER XIV

JULIA THE YOUNGER

Days had passed, although it seemed an eternity since the accident. My own ill effects from my watery adventure were short lived and barely perceptible, given my focus on Aurelia. I could think of little else while she suffered.

The slave woman's condition did not improve, her eyelids never so much as quivering, despite my soothing words and caresses of her cold, limp hands. If I were pressed to proffer a prognosis, it would not be a good one: her breathing seemed to be growing shallower, and her skin was sickly and pale, her fingers, toes, and lips all tinged with blue.

I had never before thought of Aurelia as being old, but now she looked it, as if the accident had aged her decades in such a short amount of time. I barely left her side except to occasionally find some measure of comfort in the warm bath, where I would float aimlessly, trying to ignore or at least abate my worries. Yet even when I was able to forget the condition of my nursemaid, unwelcome, distressing images of Silanus would intrude.

The worst of these imaginings showed me his bloody head on a spike with lifeless, bulging eyes, or my lover being thrown from the Tarpeian Rock to his death in the favored execution style of old. I still did not know what my grandfather had done to him, or who had betrayed us, and it haunted me.

Faced with continued uncertainty around two of the most significant people in my life, I became increasingly exhausted, and my appetite was nonexistent. I began to feel as if I were slowly fading away alongside Aurelia as my skin paled and dark smudges surfaced beneath my eyes, my fingers trembling more often than not. My unborn child, as if sensing that something was wrong, beat against my insides mercilessly, demanding that I fight on for its sake if not my own.

I wandered late one night to the bath, my thoughts racing between Aurelia and Silanus, even as I hoped that the warm waters might make me forget them both, at least for a time. The door to the preliminary room was not bolted, and I pushed it open. Transfixed by my miserable thoughts, I had not noticed the light flickering at the small gap between the door and mosaicked floor.

I walked in on Marcus sodomizing one of the slave girls: Aphrodite. She was lying face-down on the bench, her hands clutching its sides, as Marcus straddled her, forcing himself into her over and over again, one hand wrapped around her neck from behind in a painfully tight grip.

I dropped the oil lamp I was carrying when I saw them, my lips parted in a silent gasp of surprise, and Marcus turned his head to look at me as the crash of pottery seemed to resound throughout the villa. Despite my presence, he kept going, squeezing Aphrodite's neck harder as he locked gazes with me, as if daring me to speak out, to stop him. Then he raised a hand and harshly slapped the slave girl across the buttocks, still without breaking eye contact with me.

Disgusted and slightly frightened, I turned and fled the room, my feet slipping precariously in the hot oil that now seeped across the floor.

Marcus's gaze, his sneer, had felt like an unspoken but clear threat: that he could do the same thing to me, and what would I do about it? What *could* I do about it? Monimos's sexual conduct with Aphrodite some time ago in the kitchen had been distasteful but, ultimately, normal, whatever my personal opinion might be on the use of slaves. Marcus's behavior was something else entirely: intentional cruelty, revelry in his power. It was that which excited him, not the sexual act itself—that much was clear.

My heart was still racing as I moved down the hallway, reaching the atrium, which, bathed in soft moonlight, was a peacefully stark contrast to the scene I had witnessed only moments before. Wanting to calm myself, I perched on the edge of a couch, my nails digging into the wood until I forced splinters to prick my fingertips. I couldn't yet bear to go back to my room and see Aurelia still just lying there.

I felt helpless, trapped. The feelings were not entirely new to me. After all, I had been constantly surrounded in Rome by ever-present slaves, watchful guards, and opportunistic aristocrats; my entire life had been laid out for me by my grandfather from the very moment of my birth, if not even before. But at least there I had had Silanus as an escape, a heady breath of freedom I hadn't known I needed until I had tasted it. Now I had no one.

"Are you alright?" a voice asked from the corner, and I jumped up, startled again. A shadow moved forward, and I could make out Titus's features.

"Yes. Fine." I stopped. I wasn't fine. But how could he understand?

"What happened?" the guard asked, examining me. "You have something on the hem of your dress. And you smell," he sniffed, "like oil."

Looking down, I realized the oil from the lamp I had dropped had splattered on my dress. In hindsight, I was lucky I hadn't caught on fire.

"Marcus," I began, "is sodomizing Aphrodite in the changing room by the bath. He forgot to bolt the door." My toneless voice surprised me.

Titus exhaled sharply, his warm brown eyes concerned as his eyebrows grew closer together in a grimace. "Quintus has already had a word with him before about his… treatment of Aphrodite. The slaves are not to be irreparably harmed. He knows that."

I frowned. The fact that Quintus had had to reprimand Marcus about such matters suggested Aphrodite had already been injured in one way or another before this. I had never noticed anything.

"You know that slaves are often treated this way, and worse," Titus said gently, taking a step towards me.

My pride flaring, I glared at him. He stopped, the moonlight making his eyes shine. "Don't lecture me, Titus." I did know that many slaves were worse off than Aphrodite, but knowing about their treatment and seeing it with my own eyes were two entirely different things. I had never been responsible for punishing my own slaves, and while I had heard of the arduous labors undertaken by slaves in the fields and mines, I had never witnessed their treatment directly.

Titus shrugged and retreated to his chair in the shadows, letting the silence between us stretch. The lengthening quiet irked me; as much as I did not want to admit it, speaking with Titus, a common soldier, was one of the only things to quell my racing mind and heart of late.

"How is Quintus?" I asked, my voice tight as I sought to reestablish our conversation. I had only seen the commander of the guards a few times since the accident in the rowboat. We had not exchanged many words.

"Improving. Almost back to normal, in fact. The knock on his head was pretty hard, but there wasn't any lasting damage." His tone did not betray any lasting irritation with me, and I drew my next breath more easily.

"That's good," I supplied, half-heartedly. A thought occurred to me then. "Who would have been next in command, if Quintus had died?"

Titus answered readily enough. "Marcus. Why?" I didn't respond. "Oh," Titus said then, picking up on my thoughts. "He wouldn't hurt you, you know. Marcus isn't the nicest or most cultured man, I know, but he understands his duty. He wouldn't have been selected as one of your guards if he wasn't trustworthy and reliable. You have nothing to fear from him."

I wasn't convinced. "The way he looked at me…" I trailed off. "I don't think a man would understand. Or *could* understand."

The following silence grew so long that I thought Titus had decided not to answer me. Then, quietly, he said, "I wouldn't let him hurt you. You have my word."

I left the atrium without replying.

The next morning, when I awoke from a tangled mess of nightmares, I found that Aurelia had passed away sometime during the night. Rather than running out of my room to tell anyone, I sat with her body for an hour or more, holding one of her icy, lifeless hands in my own as I kneeled next to her cot.

I had thought I would be inconsolable, that I would cry aloud with wracking, violent sobs that tore my body and spirit apart. But instead I was silent. Eventually I kissed her gently on the mouth, as was the custom, then fixed the blanket tightly around her body. Her eyes had never opened, and now they would remain forever closed in death.

Wrapping a shawl around my shoulders, I left the room, padding barefoot down the hall. I found all the soldiers gathered in the *triclinium* for breakfast. All four of them ceased chattering when they caught sight of me in the doorway, quite clearly still in my night clothes despite the shawl I had had the presence of mind to pick up. My hair hung loose and tangled down my back, a scraggly bronze mess that I did not currently have the pride to try to tame.

Titus stood and moved as if to approach me, but he stopped when I looked at him sharply. He had not even made it a full step.

"Aurelia has died," I announced, simply. "I will care for her body. You will all build a pyre for her, on the highest point of this island. When it is ready, we shall cremate her." I didn't ask—I ordered, and my expression dared any of them to defy me.

Quintus nodded, and I turned around to leave, making mental notes of what I had to do next. None of them had spoken.

Aurelia's body needed to be placed on the ground, washed, and then dressed in something appropriate. I also needed to find a coin in my belongings to place on her mouth, lest the ferryman not let her progress on her final journey. Whether or not that particular story was true, I didn't care: I didn't want Aurelia to pass into the Underworld unprepared, just in case.

After stopping by the kitchen to get a basin of water and a cloth, I returned to my room, where I gently pulled Aurelia onto the floor, trying not to jar her too much. I removed the simple, loose clothing in which she had been dressed after the accident, and I began to wash her body, gently rubbing away what faint traces of her minty scent still lingered.

It occurred to me that I didn't know the Gallic death rites—I didn't even know if Aurelia would have preferred those over the Roman death I was giving her. But I could do only what I knew, and so I continued, telling myself that Aurelia would understand that I only meant to honor her. Perhaps her Gallic gods would still find her, would welcome her to their own afterlife.

Aurelia had rarely spoken of her life in Gaul before coming to Rome as a slave. I did not know if she had brothers or sisters; I did not know any stories of her childhood. In fact, I realized, it seemed that I had barely known Aurelia at all, and yet she had been my most constant companion for nearly all my life. I had thought of her as more of a mother than the woman who had birthed me, and still I had not bothered to ever truly speak to her on a level beyond my own needs and wants.

Aurelia had known about my affair with Silanus. As an older, wiser woman, she had warned me against it, but, as my slave, she had been complicit, through no desire or choice of her own. She had passed messages and letters between us; helped to coordinate our trysts; counseled and soothed when some silly lovers' spat proved briefly disruptive. Without Aurelia, Silanus and I could never have succeeded in our affair.

She had been, at the time, a blessing seemingly sent by Fortuna herself; in hindsight, her aid had been a curse. If our relationship had failed before it had truly begun, there would be no bastard child now, no endless exile. All of this would have been prevented.

I forced my thoughts away from such a treacherous path, reminding myself that I did not regret my affair with Silanus, nor my refusal to give his name to the emperor. I loved him, then and now, wherever he might be.

I smoothed the cloth down Aurelia's limp arm, wiping it clean. The repetitive, tactile process was soothing to my grief, something I found surprising. It occurred to me that funerary rites were perhaps just as much for the comfort of the living as they were to ensure the safe passage of the deceased's spirit. I had never before been the person so involved with the details of death, nor had I been so affected by another's passing, even that of my elder brothers or my father. It was not something I hoped to ever repeat.

When I finished washing Aurelia's body, I found one of her nicer dresses, which I thought I remembered gifting to her on a past Saturnalia, despite her protestations that it was far too fine for a lowly slave. I wasn't sure if she had ever worn it; now, she would.

Sweat dripped down my face when I was done clothing her, and I slipped one of my golden rings onto her finger, a final token. I certainly no longer had need of it.

It was now time for her body to lie in state in the atrium, her feet pointed towards the door in symbolic readiness to depart the realm, and home, of the living. She would remain there until the pyre was prepared.

I left the room once more, in search of the men; I couldn't move her body by myself. I didn't care that Aurelia had been a slave, and that the guards, all of them free citizens, might resist taking part in her funerary rites, seeing it as beneath them, as unnecessary for a person of her status. They *would* assist me.

I found Monimos sweeping the floor in the atrium, unaware of my arrival. "Monimos," I greeted him, quietly. Now was not the time for cheeriness.

He paused his sweeping, bowing his head respectfully. A sheen of sweat glistened on his forehead. "*Domina*, how may I assist you?"

"Where are the guards? I have need of them, now."

"Outside, *domina*, on the large rise nearby. They are constructing the pyre for your slave woman, as you instructed them."

I nodded, considering asking Monimos, too, for his help, but the thought of that sweaty, crude bear of a man touching Aurelia made me pause. Titus. I wanted Titus to help.

I permitted Monimos to return to his work and left the villa. The midday sun made me squint my eyes as I opened the atrium doors and stepped outside. I quickly bumped into someone and jumped back in surprise, losing my balance.

"Easy," a familiar voice said, and, as my eyes adjusted, I looked up at Titus. His hand was gripping my elbow, a gentle, stabilizing force. I recovered after another moment, and he let go of me, stepping away to a respectful distance.

"Why aren't you helping the others?" I asked, a hint of accusation in my tone.

"Quintus has us alternating shifts in the villa. You, as always, are our priority. I was just on the way back to take my turn." I saw, then, that Titus was sweaty, with dirt smudged across his hands and left cheekbone. I felt ashamed that I had thought he was evading the work I had requested to honor Aurelia.

"Oh."

"And where were you headed?" Titus asked. I tensed, ready to snap, insulted that he was about to interrogate me, before I realized that his eyes were crinkled in humor. He was trying to jest; we both knew very well that there were few places I could go. "Back into the sea, Siren that you are?"

I didn't quite smile, but I relaxed—which seemed to have been his goal. "To find you," I said, simply. "Aurelia needs to be moved into the atrium, to await the pyre. I need assistance moving her."

Titus nodded, motioning for me to re-enter the villa ahead of him. He closed the door behind us, sighing in relief as the cooler air of the atrium embraced his sweaty body, the tang of his odor causing my nostrils to flare.

I frowned as I looked at him, a thought crossing my mind. "Would you mind bathing first?"

Titus raised an eyebrow. "Excuse me?"

"It's just that I've already washed and prepared Aurelia's body and you're…" I trailed off as I examined him, noting the sweat marks and dirt on him for a second time.

Titus looked down at himself, and then nodded. "Of course. I'll be just a few minutes." A pause. "Strictly speaking, I'm not supposed to leave you unattended. My orders are to stand guard in the atrium."

I wanted to roll my eyes, but I remained enough of a lady to stop myself. "We've discussed this, Titus. There's nowhere for me to go. I will wait in my room with Aurelia until you are ready." Titus seemed slightly hesitant. "You have my word."

Titus nodded then, and we headed down the hall, he to his room to collect his bathing supplies and me to mine, to await his return.

Aurelia remained on the floor, and I sat on my bed, looking down at her. Without the spark of life, her body seemed so very empty, so unlike her—a mere shell. It was difficult to envision that the lifeless flesh in front of me had once been such an animated woman, one who had been through so much of my life with me, every sadness one that she had shared, and every triumph one that she had rejoiced in, too. My future, without her in it, now seemed unbearably long and lonely.

I finally started crying then, silent tears rushing down my face in a hot stream. I was barely aware of Titus entering the room, clean and freshly dressed, and even though I saw him crouching in front me, saw his mouth moving as he spoke to me, I couldn't hear him; a sudden rushing in my ears rendered me deaf to the world. One of his hands reached towards my face, but, just before he touched me, it dropped away.

Without thinking, I reached my arms out and hugged him. His body immediately tensed. He was rigid. Uncomfortable. But I didn't let go. At this moment I didn't care that what I was doing was inappropriate, unbecoming of a Roman lady. I only knew that I needed some measure of comfort, and that Titus was able to provide it. I had no one else.

After a few more moments, his arms wrapped around me, returning my embrace, and I felt his body soften as he let out a gentle exhale. We stayed like that for some time, and eventually I felt my tears dry up, my breathing return to normal. The rushing in my ears disappeared, and I felt my senses fully return. I pulled back from Titus's enveloping warmth, and he immediately let me go, standing and taking a step back. He avoided my eyes, instead looking down at my feet.

"I'm sorry," I whispered. It was the first time I had apologized, to anyone, since I had been a child and broken one of my mother's perfume bottles. The words felt foreign as they passed my lips, some strange vocabulary that I had almost forgotten.

Titus didn't acknowledge my apology. Instead, he cleared his throat. "May I take her now?" His impassive gaze was still on my feet, and his tone was suddenly formal, cold and removed.

I nodded. "Yes."

Titus bent and gently scooped Aurelia into his arms. I knew it must have been some measure of strain to carry her large body, but he didn't so much as grunt as he began to walk with her down the hall to the atrium. I trailed behind, feeling lost.

Monimos had returned, and Titus instructed him to move one of the couches so that its foot faced the villa doors. There, Titus gently laid down Aurelia, respectfully placing her arms so that they didn't dangle off the sides before he moved away. I moved forward to place a single coin on her mouth: the ferryman's price for her entry to the Underworld.

Titus and I remained together in the atrium for the next few hours, neither of us speaking. Eventually, Quintus and the other two guards returned, all equally sweaty and dirty after a long day's work. None of them commented on Titus's comparably pristine state.

"We should light the pyre tonight," Quintus suggested to me as he glanced down at Aurelia's body. "It's not good to let the dead linger for too long. Let her finish crossing over, so we all might find some peace."

I nodded in agreement, and the four guards each moved to pick up the couch from a different corner. It would go on the pyre with Aurelia.

Our procession was small and quiet, without the dramatic wailing and hair pulling of the professional mourners that I was accustomed to witnessing at the funerals of the wealthy in Rome. Only Monimos and the slave girls, Artemis and Aphrodite, followed behind me as we moved up the rise to the highest point of Trimerus, the overseer carrying a large torch that would serve to light the pyre.

When we reached the windy rise, the guards placed Aurelia on the constructed pyre without too much difficulty, moving back once they were certain the couch was secure. Quintus, at my nod, took the torch from Monimos and set everything alight. The grasses around the pyre's base caught fire quickly, the flames slowly spreading upwards as the salty wind coaxed them to further action, a spiraling inferno. We all stood quietly, watching as Aurelia was enveloped, plumes of purple smoke rising into the sky as the sun began to set.

Soon it was dark. The pyre was still burning, doing its duty to help Aurelia's spirit wholly pass on. The orange brightness was a glaring contrast to the surrounding darkness, the flames' tongues lipping mercilessly at the night as if in battle. It was one that we all knew the night would win, in the end. Fire never lasted forever.

Monimos and the slave girls had departed some time ago to prepare the evening meal. Even though I knew Aurelia's ashes wouldn't be ready to collect until at least the following morning, I wasn't ready to leave yet. My eyes burned from staring endlessly at the flames, the smoke from the fire occasionally drifting into my face as the sea winds changed the course of the ashy plume. Still, I remained.

Sometime later I found myself nearly asleep on my feet; Quintus awoke me with a polite clearing of his throat. He was close by my side, although he had not been so presumptuous as to lay a hand on me.

"Mistress, I will have Titus remain on watch with the pyre throughout the night. We should return to the villa for the evening." The commander looked insistent, but not unsympathetic. I thought about arguing with him, but my eyelids were so heavy, fighting against me even as I willed them to remain open. "Her spirit is already gone," Quintus said quietly, as if guessing my thoughts.

I nodded in sad agreement. I knew he was right.

Quintus led the way back to the villa, where the slaves had prepared a simple meal. I had no appetite, and so I left the guards to dine alone, retreating to my bed. The absence of Aurelia's quiet, rhythmic breathing was shockingly disruptive as I laid awake, waiting for sleep to claim me.

CHAPTER XV

AGRIPPA POSTUMUS

It was just past dawn, and Agrippa was lounging in the villa's atrium as the light strengthened, soon rendering the bright oil lamp by his side useless. He did not bother to extinguish it.

He was working his way through the villa's limited selections of scrolls for the umpteenth time, ignoring the gentle snoring of the guard in the corner who had fallen asleep by midnight the evening before. Agrippa no longer bothered to stay on a typical schedule, instead choosing to sleep only when he felt the need to do so. It perplexed the guards, who seemed to enjoy routine and order above all else.

He had recently finished his most recent re-reading of the *Amores* and had moved onto the *Ars Amatoria*, which was nearing a decade old now. Nevertheless, when Agrippa had been in Rome, it had still proven to be one of Ovid's most popular works, even overshadowing some of the poet's newer pieces. This was due, without a doubt, to the collection's erotic nature—always a popular topic amongst Romans— and the fact that it was common knowledge the emperor himself had taken a disliking to the poems, as they conflicted with his program to restore family values and traditional morals amongst the people. Agrippa scoffed just thinking about it. Morals, indeed.

Augustus encouraged stable marriages and rewarded abundant childbearing in an effort to strengthen the Roman populace. In contrast, Ovid spun tales of seductive, passionate love, even going so far as to condone extramarital affairs. Everyone, from the basest commoners to the most refined of the ruling class, couldn't get enough of it. Naturally, that infuriated the emperor.

A few other guards stumbled into the atrium, waking the sleeping soldier, who unceremoniously retreated to his room to finish his rest before he had to return to duty. One of the men, seemingly still drunk from the night before, let out a loud belch as he passed Agrippa.

"What're you reading there now?" the soldier asked.

Agrippa wrinkled his nose at the guard, who smelled as if he hadn't washed in days. "Ovid," he answered, not looking up from the scroll. "*Ars Amatoria*, to be precise."

"He speaks!" the guard exclaimed, letting out a laugh. The others had paused, watching the interaction.

Agrippa shrugged. "I'm feeling rather chatty this morning. Besides, I thought you could benefit from some culture." The guard's grinning face slowly darkened. "Can you even read?" Agrippa asked, his eyes still skimming across the scroll. "Allow me to share a selection with you. Perhaps you can use some of these lovers' skills on one of your fellow guards." Agrippa paused, looking up at the burly man for the first time. "Or, perhaps, they should use some of these techniques on *you*…"

One of the other guards had approached and placed a hand on his fellow's shoulder, ready to restrain the man as he glared down at Agrippa, who simply raised an eyebrow and smiled faintly in return. The man shook off his comrade.

The newcomer spoke up. "Maybe Ovid used some of his own

teachings on your sister," he said.

Agrippa had resumed reading. "Whatever do you mean?" he asked, nonchalantly. The insults against his sister had already become old fodder for jokes, so he was surprised that the guard was recycling material.

"Ovid was exiled, shortly after your whore of a sister was sent away from Rome. He's gone off to that shithole Tomis, all the way over in Moesia. Can't be a coincidence, can it? He must have been fucking her too, like every other man in Rome."

The burly guard who first had spoken to Agrippa perked back up, laughing. His breath smelled of stale wine. Agrippa silently digested the new information but, when it became clear that he wasn't going to come up with a clever retort, the guards all moved off, except for one who remained with him in the atrium as he stared down at his scroll. Agrippa wasn't reading, but thinking.

He had met Ovid before in Rome, several times, and he knew that Julia had been acquainted with the vain yet talented poet as well. Many aristocrats were, so there was nothing odd about that in itself. However, he seriously doubted that Julia would have been involved sexually with the poet, who was nearly twice her age. The affair resulting in her exile had proven shocking enough, given his sister's normally reserved manner. There was simply no way she would have had yet another lover, too.

Furthermore, although Ovid wasn't popular with the emperor, Agrippa also doubted his grandfather would have exiled him for a collection of poems that was, by now, rather old. Something must have happened that he didn't know about, and Agrippa Postumus didn't like not knowing.

Agrippa had not yet had a chance to reconnect with the guard who had repeated his former brother-in-law's oft-used phrase to him some time ago: *Oil doesn't get made without the crushing of many olives.* The soldier had turned and left, and Agrippa did not follow: he needed more time to think, to consider the potential implications of what was happening and to decide how he might proceed.

It was possible that the guard was a direct agent of the emperor, tasked with nosing out the names of any conspirators who had been left undiscovered from Paullus's ill-fated plot years before. Perhaps he might even try to set a trap for Agrippa, to coax him into some new treachery, so that more proof could be acquired, justifying his execution, should his grandfather change his mind and wish him dead.

Further reflection, however, led Agrippa to believe that the soldier was sincere. Too much time had passed for an investigation into Paullus's intrigues to still be ongoing. And if Augustus wanted him dead, he needed no proof to carry out an execution, which could be covered up easily enough. He was, after all, the emperor. What need of due process did he have?

Agrippa decided to join the guards for dinner, and he sought out the red-haired soldier in question with his boring gaze, waiting for the man to look up at him. When he finally did, he gave no inclination that anything strange had transpired between them, instead returning his attention to his comrades, laughing and joking.

It was hours later that Agrippa was jolted out of his sleep, a hand roughly clasped over his mouth to prevent the predicted cry of surprise from escaping his lips as he sat up in bed. When his eyes adjusted to the darkness, he made out the features of the mysterious guard, and the hand was removed.

"Tell me now," Agrippa hissed, "who you are."

Dark eyes considered him, and the man's voice was low when he finally spoke. "You may call me Rufus, as the other guards do. I would have returned to you before this, but…" he trailed off briefly as he glanced towards the closed door. "There is little freedom of movement for me here."

"Well, *Rufus*," Agrippa repeated the alias with condescension, "you would do best to explain to me what your purpose here is, before I expose you to the others."

Rufus sighed. "There are still those in Rome who harbor similar goals to Paullus, devoted to the cause of bringing you to power."

"Who?" Agrippa demanded to know.

The guard frowned, setting his lips in a tight line. "You will know all, in time."

Agrippa began to argue. "Do not test me, or I will gut you myself." The threat was anything but empty.

Rufus quickly stood and moved away, ignoring Agrippa, who remained in his bed like a petulant child. The soldier pressed his ear close to the door as he listened for the other guards assigned to patrol at night. Before Agrippa could speak again, Rufus disappeared into the dark hallway, and the youth dared not follow.

CHAPTER XVI

JULIA THE YOUNGER

I gazed out at the pile of rocks where I had found myself just over a week ago, after the accident. Aurelia's ashes lay buried some distance behind me, having been collected and placed inside an old culinary amphora. It was the best I had been able to manage for her, considering no one had thought to bring a funerary urn amongst the other countless supplies. No one had been expected to die.

The grassy perch near the cliff's edge had become my favorite place to sit, and I spent most of my days there now, basking in the summer sun for hours on end. Had I still been in Rome, I would have gone outside in sunny weather only under a parasol, or within a covered litter, to keep my skin pale and unblemished, the perfect upper-class woman. Now, I had finally progressed from a reddish burn to a golden-brown tan that kissed every inch of my exposed skin. My mother would have been horrified, but I felt reborn, the newest acolyte of the sun god Sol.

Aphrodite hovered behind me some ten paces or so away, looking bored and hot as she picked at her dress. Not long after Aurelia's death, Quintus had come up with the idea to assign the slave girl to me in order to assist with bathing, dressing, hair styling, and so on. It wasn't at all necessary, but Quintus had decided that it was proper, even if Aphrodite didn't know the first thing about her supposed duties.

Although I acquiesced to the commander's wishes, in part because I hoped to shield the girl from some of the attentions forced on her by Monimos and Marcus, I had drawn the line at her sleeping in Aurelia's cot. Instead, I chose to keep the room to myself.

Publius was the third member of our small group that day, sitting on a rock to my left. Unlike Aphrodite, the young guard didn't seem to mind lounging around outside all day. He was singing quietly and weaving together some long grasses into a design or figure, but I couldn't quite make out what it was meant to be. The faint sound of his song drifted towards me over the wind, and I wished I could mimic Publius's carefree attitude.

I dreaded birthing my child without Aurelia to help me, and my anxiety grew with each passing day. The time was coming. I still remembered my pain and fear from when Aemilia had entered the world after a long and difficult process. But Aurelia had been there through it all and had been a primary figure in my daughter's life, as was typical amongst women of my standing. The details of my child's life—feeding, clothing, bathing—had never been my concern.

I hadn't thought I would ever again go through another pregnancy, given my repeated failure to bring any other of Paullus's children to term after Aemilia's birth. But then I had met Silanus.

If all had gone according to our plan, I would have withdrawn from Rome on the pretext of illness and the need for fresh country air, birthing our child in secret. While the infant might never mature into a public statesman or the wife of a senator, given its illegitimacy, we still could have provided it with a comfortable life. But we had been betrayed. Someone had named Silanus as the offending adulterer, outing him to my grandfather. Had we truly been so careless that our affair had become obvious? Who had known?

I wondered if our child would ever know its father; I wondered if I would ever see my lover again. Yet each sunset on this island further drained away my hopes, a subtle but consistent lessening of my drive for restoration, and I began to wonder less and less. My unborn child and I might be fated to become Trimerus's permanent residents—if she was allowed to remain with me. I did not dwell on what might happen if I produced a son instead.

I laid back on the grasses, closing my eyes to the summer sun, although its golden glow warmed my lids. Publius's song mixed with the repetitive crash of waves below us, and I began to doze off, too tired to keep worrying. But suddenly something was different; the guard's quiet song had ceased, replaced by the cheery trilling of birds as they cast around on their constant quest for food.

I sat up, opening my eyes and blinking rapidly until they had adjusted once more to the sun's full force. Titus had arrived, and he was speaking quietly with Publius. Aphrodite was picking her way through the grasses towards me, her hands awkwardly grasping at folds of her clothing to keep them from catching on the foliage.

"What is it?" I asked as she approached.

"*Domina*, your friend, *dominus* Lucius, has arrived at the villa. He would like to see you, *domina*." The slave girl avoided eye contact with me, as she always did—as was proper for a slave. I felt a sharp pang as it made me realize, once more, how close I had been with Aurelia, who had been astoundingly bold in private.

I stood up, brushing myself off, and headed back towards the villa, Aphrodite falling into step behind me at an appropriate distance. I didn't bother to wait for the guards.

This would be the first time I had seen Lucius since the dinner… since the accident that had led to Aurelia's death. I knew he was aware of what had happened, or at least my initial disappearance, given the fact that some of the guards had gone to search his island while I was missing. They would have informed him why they were there. But he wouldn't know of Aurelia's passing, and I wasn't sure if he would care. After all, she had been merely a slave, when all was said and done; no one else had known her as I did.

Titus trotted up to my side, slightly out of breath as he slowed his pace to match mine. I didn't acknowledge him. The guard and I had barely spoken in the week since Aurelia's death, since I had broken down and clutched him to me, sobbing, desperate for any sort of soothing salve to calm my broken heart. He had been there, and I had used him as I needed. It was weak. Embarrassing.

"Are you alright?" he asked quietly, words that seemed to have become his too-frequent question to me.

I was acutely aware of Aphrodite's presence at our rear. "Fine," I answered. I was sharp, unwilling to engage in further conversation. Titus seemed to grasp the hint in my tone, and he increased the distance between us, soon dropping back to walk with Publius the rest of the way to the villa.

I decided it was for the best if we did not maintain the tenuous friendship we seemed to have established. After all, when it came down to it, he was just another one of my jailers. To think that he saw me as anything except a task he had been ordered to undertake would be a mistake, and I could afford to make no more.

Lucius was seated in the atrium when I arrived, but he jumped to his feet as I entered the room, using his cane to brace himself. A small cage sat on the ground next to him, a little brown and gray bird hopping

131

around inside of it, pecking about with a tiny black beak in search of seeds.

"My dear!" Lucius exclaimed. "I am *so* relieved to see you well! I was positively devastated with worry when the guards came over to search for you on my little island. Your man, Quintus I think it is, let me know that you had been found, but I didn't want to intrude—I am sure that you have been recuperating, getting your strength back after *such* a fright. Terrible business!"

I offered up a small smile, gesturing for the old man to return to his seat. Aphrodite scurried off, presumably to prepare some refreshments, while Titus and Publius took up watchful positions in separate corners of the atrium. Marcus and Quintus must have been elsewhere.

Lucius resettled himself on a couch, plucking a small glass of wine from the tray that Aphrodite had returned with in short order. I sat across from him, taking a sip of my own drink as the slave girl retreated, but she stayed within earshot, should we require anything else. The caged bird emitted a series of chirps, but Lucius still did not comment on it.

"So, do tell me, *how* did such a thing happen? If I recall, the night was fairly calm when you left, no storms or the like. So odd!" Lucius was leaning forward expectantly, reminding me of the shameless gossips in my old social circle in Rome. A bit of wine ran down his chin, and he dabbed at it, still watching me intently.

"I'm afraid I don't know," I answered truthfully. "I had dozed off, from too much wine, I suppose. Quintus was knocked unconscious at some point during the accident and doesn't have any memory of what happened. He barely remembers being at your villa. His man who was with us thinks we struck a rock, perhaps some outcropping between the islands, hidden just under the water. Aurelia, my slave woman, died as a result." I forced myself to keep my tone neutral, removed. It was as if I were reporting an accident that had happened to someone else entirely, some story that I had heard and was merely repeating.

Lucius was nodding, looking sympathetic, but he didn't have a particularly strong reaction to my announcement of Aurelia's death. I wasn't surprised. To him, she was like any other nameless, unimportant slave: an equivalent replacement could be found in almost any market across the empire. He had not known her. I clenched my teeth together.

The old man took another sip of his wine, thinking. "I've been out here now for quite some time, quite a while. I've made more than a few trips back and forth, over the years, between your island and mine, but I've never had such a thing happen." A long pause, as if he were processing something, then his gap-toothed smile emerged. "Just bad fortune I suppose! As I said, I am *so* relieved that you're here, unscathed!"

Unlike Aurelia, I thought, but I just returned Lucius's smile, although mine was devoid of any feeling. He did not seem to notice.

"Oh, yes, I nearly forgot!" he exclaimed, seeing that my eyes had drifted back to the cage by his couch. "I brought you a little gift, one of my sparrows! She's a chatty little thing, the great-great-granddaughter of the very first pair of sparrows I brought out to the island with me. I thought that you might like a friend." The old man beamed, smile earnest as he waited for my response.

"Thank you," I said quietly, examining the bird as she chirped again, her shiny black eyes examining her new surroundings. I motioned for Aphrodite to carry the cage to my bedroom, and she disappeared with the sparrow. I had never felt the need for a pet when I had lived in Rome—and Aurelia had always felt that they were too dirty—but it seemed that I would now have one. It would have been rude to refuse, especially since it was clear the old man cared greatly for his birds.

Lucius and I chit-chatted for a while longer, and then he made his excuses and departed. "I wanted to see that you were well, and as I have, I shall bid you farewell!" he had said, adding that he wanted to beat the sunset lest he find himself in an accident like my own.

I chose to skip dinner with the guards, which was becoming a new habit of mine, and instead bathed for an extended period of time. I would take my meal later in my bedroom, alone with my dark thoughts.

As usual, the warm water of the bath was a welcome presence, a comforting friend that made me feel weightless and free as I floated. My ears were submerged just under the surface to create a soothing hush, a world removed from my present reality. It was a sharp contrast to the night of the accident, when the water, cold and harsh, had been my enemy.

I so wished that I hadn't fallen asleep in the boat. Something about the accident bothered me, but I couldn't clearly remember what had happened, and it haunted me. I hadn't been awake, hadn't been aware.

Why had it taken so long to find me? I had called for help, more than once, as I treaded water. There was a current, but surely I hadn't been pushed so far, so quickly from the boat. I sighed, letting my head slip under the water as I thought. It must have been chaotic, confusing in the dark, and Marcus had only managed to save Aurelia and Quintus, by the grace of Fortuna. I was being paranoid, pointlessly replaying my memory of the events over and over again. I could recall nothing out of the ordinary, but something still didn't feel right.

A sudden, sharp pain in my belly made me cry out, forgetting that I was under the water. I stood up in the bath, coughing and spluttering, clutching my stomach. Again, another pang, and I groaned, realizing with a mixture of excitement and fear what was happening. I was going into labor. My child was finally coming.

"Aphrodite!" I called out, moving to the edge of the pool and grasping the ledge with a white knuckled hand. "Aphrodite!"

The slave girl, who had been waiting for me in the changing room, entered the bath, looking confused. "Help me," I hissed at her as she stood at the edge of the pool, staring at me blankly. "My child is coming."

Understanding finally flooded her face, and she rushed towards me, helping me out of the water. She disappeared briefly back into the changing room, reemerging with a large drying cloth which she wrapped around my dripping body.

"What do I do, *domina*?" she asked, and for the first time I realized how young she really was, how removed from the world she must be, out here on some island in the Adriatic. I had no idea where she had come from or how long she had been here—but now was not the time to ask.

Another pang, and I gritted my teeth. "Help me to my bedroom. I need to lie down." The slave girl nodded and hurried me out of the bath and through the changing room, although we stopped every few steps so I could gather myself. When we emerged, Titus was in the hallway. He looked shocked to see me, half naked and hunched over, dripping water.

"*Domina*'s child is coming!" Aphrodite barked out, surprisingly forceful in her address as we pushed by him.

Titus stood there helplessly, and soon enough we were past him, entering my bedroom. Once the slave girl had helped me onto the bed, she dropped the door hanging behind us. The sparrow flitted about in her cage in the corner of the room, chirping in excitement as she witnessed the flurry of activity.

I groaned as I laid there. I dreaded what has happening, wishing that I could delay it, even as I recognized the inevitable, hoping that the process would occur as quickly and smoothly as possible. I didn't bother to pray for a painless birth. There was no such thing.

"What do you need, *domina*? How long will it take? Is it coming?" Aphrodite hovered by the doorway, uncertain and anxious. She looked pale, her eyes wide.

"I will be here for quite some time, if I recall," I grumbled between gritted teeth. "When the child is almost here, I want you to—" I broke off as more pain hit me and caught my breath before speaking again. "For now, just bring me some warm compresses. Sponges, cloth, anything will do. It will help with the pain."

Aphrodite nodded and hurried off, and I let my head fall back onto the bed. The drying cloth had fallen open around me, but I did not bother to fix it. There was little need for modesty now.

Already this was so very different from my experience with Aemilia's birth, at which a skilled and well-practiced midwife had been present, ordering about numerous slaves, having me sip soothing concoctions, reassuring me even as Aurelia held my hand and assisted in her own way before I was moved to the birthing stool for the final push. Now, I was surrounded by male guards and had only a clueless slave girl to help me bring my bastard child into the world.

Aphrodite returned with a basin of steaming water and a number of cloths draped over her arm. In the brief moment that the door hanging was pushed aside, I saw Titus hovering just outside the room, his face lined with worry. Our eyes met for only a second, and then the hanging dropped back into place, coinciding with another burst of pain that caused me to groan aloud.

The slave girl followed my directions, placing damp, warm cloths on my belly in an attempt to mitigate some of the discomfort. She replaced them regularly as the hours passed, exiting and reentering the room as needed for more hot water, and eventually she lit several oil lamps as full darkness swallowed the island. Their flickering light cast ominous shadows throughout the bedroom, and the sparrow's silhouette danced across the walls as she restlessly hopped back and forth in her cage, unsettled by all the activity.

Aphrodite stayed by my side throughout the night, and I was grateful for her presence, despite her inexperience. She was by no means a replacement for Aurelia, but her companionship was certainly far better than going through the ordeal entirely alone. As the actual birth approached, I found myself grasping at her, seeking what comfort I could through human touch. She agreeably held my hand, squeezing back as if she could impart additional strength to me.

I was aware of daybreak's light filtering into the bedroom as I began to push in earnest, but the combination of pain and exhaustion made me feel as if I were in a daze. It was almost as if the entire process was happening to someone else; although I could recognize that it was my voice that was screaming out, that the moisture running down my face was my own salty tears, I felt removed from it all, distant.

Aphrodite hovered over me, murmuring something in a language I didn't know and didn't have the energy to analyze. Just as I felt that I could no longer go on, that I could no longer push, it was over. Aphrodite helped pull the child clear of my body, awash in wetness and sticky blood that filled the air with its coppery scent. After a brief moment of silence, the baby opened its lungs and screamed, announcing its arrival to the world. The sparrow, too, cried aloud, whether in alarm or mimicry, I couldn't tell.

The slave girl quickly cleaned the infant with a warm cloth, then cut its cord as I instructed, as I had seen the midwife do when my little Aemilia had been born. She wrapped the baby in a clean cloth and handed it to me to hold. I brought the child to my chest, its ongoing screams reassuring me of its vitality, of its strength, and I wept. I had a son.

CHAPTER XVII

OVID

Ovid perched precariously on a wobbly-legged stool he had dragged up to the ship's deck, furiously scribbling away at the stack of papyrus sheets in his lap. The wordsmith, just past fifty and with a visibly receding hairline that he could currently muster neither the vanity nor the energy to disguise, was hard at work crafting his next collection of poetry—even as the ship sped him mercilessly away from Rome, across the Ionian Sea, and onwards to his exile in Tomis.

The very thought of his future residence caused Ovid's lined, worried face to blanch before he frantically dipped his pen into the small, chipped inkpot by his side and scratched out another stream of words, as if he could rewrite Tomis into something better, not the good-for-nothing outpost in far-flung Moesia that it was, part of a sadly underdeveloped province that he had absolutely no desire to see with his own eyes. Yet there was little Ovid could do; Emperor Augustus had decreed his punishment so, and, with barely enough time to pack his belongings and kiss his much younger wife—the sweet, innocent Fabia—farewell, Ovid had been cast out from his beloved Rome, forced to leave behind everything he knew and cherished.

The poet scowled in silent warning as a sailor moved past him, eyes carefully averted. Only a day ago Ovid had thrown an inkpot at one of the men who had dared ask him to move from his chosen perch on the deck—never mind that his position proved a continuing hinderance to their duties. Now, they knew well enough to leave the brooding man alone, particularly when he had out his writing utensils.

Once the sailor passed by, Ovid resettled himself, staring down at the words he had written as he considered how to continue. The sailing had been fairly smooth thus far, as if the gods themselves wished for the poet to reach his wretched destination with speed and safety, but a tranquil voyage did not fit well with Ovid's plans. After all, who would pity him for having an easy journey? Who would pity him for a comfortable exile? No, it wouldn't do, not at all; his readers needed to understand the horrors of his new reality.

These works he was now composing were to be sent back to Rome, to Fabia—dear and loyal thing that she was—who would see that they were published, that they reached the attention of the emperor, who, gods willing, would have mercy and recall him from forsaken Tomis, practically at the world's end. Ovid had never been to the town, but he didn't need to in order to know that it would be like living in the darkest recesses of the Underworld. He clenched the reedy pen in his hand, then proceeded to scratch out a few more words.

In his newest creative work, Ovid was writing of frequent and threatening storms, cold winds that nearly cast the ship over. According to his draft, all aboard the ship were constantly mere moments from a watery death; terror was a frequent guest, threatening to stifle his creativity—he went so far as to name the great Homer himself as incapable of working under such brutal conditions.

The poet paused, resting his hand, the pen still as a single drop of ink hung quivering from its tip. He re-read his own work with a muted sigh; it was, he thought, just enough to rile up some public pity for his hardships, already begun, but not too over the top. Ovid was pleased, too, that he had managed to include a little comparison to Homer, a subtle suggestion that he, when all was said and done, was the superior artist, capable of producing great work even under extreme duress. No one had ever claimed that Ovid was a humble man, and he was not about to convince anyone otherwise.

Still, in his wildest and most optimistic dreams, Ovid's newest work would never *have* to be published in Rome; he would be recalled long before that, negating the need for his woeful accounts of his already-begun exile. But Ovid was old enough, and wise enough, to know that he would likely have to endure some considerable length of banishment before the emperor would extend forgiveness to him, especially after what he had done.

The poet stilled, genuine sadness overcoming him as he recalled his final night in Rome. His wife had clutched him with desperate, trembling hands, weeping uncontrollably and promising the gods all manner of offerings if only they would change her husband's fate. He bade Fabia farewell two, three, four or more times, but still he hadn't been able to tear himself away, even as time slipped dangerously by and the sun began to rise, its pale pink glow signifying the beginning of his *exilium*. To have remained any longer would have been to invite not only his own death, but to threaten Fabia's future—and for all his shortcomings, acknowledged or ignored, Ovid could not bear to think of any misfortune befalling his wife.

When Ovid had finally made to leave his home, the doors mere steps away, Fabia had thrown herself at him, pledging that she would follow him into exile, but he forbade her. He needed someone in Rome, a true and trustworthy ally, to manage his properties and to keep things in order for his eventual return, if things went well. Most importantly, he was entrusting her with the publication of his work created in exile: his restoration depended upon it.

Ovid silently cursed the imperial family, the whole lot of them: Augustus and Livia, for their iron-fisted control of Rome, from which none could escape; the elder Julia, for her constant machinations, from which he had barely escaped just a decade ago; and the emperor's grandchildren, particularly Agrippa Postumus and the younger Julia—not to mention the latter's treasonous husband. It had all begun with a poem, a simple poem… and now he was on his way to exile in Tomis, having committed only what he would admit was an error—but it was an error that the emperor would not easily forgive. Ovid could not bear to think of it.

The light was beginning to fade, and the ship's crew wouldn't allow him to use oil lamps in his cabin to write. They didn't trust him not to set fire to the vessel, whether by accident or with intention. It was like being a prisoner or, worse, a barbarian, a man without the right of Roman citizenship, without the corresponding treatment that accompanied such a rank. Ovid bristled at the offense, every sunset reminding him of his new, and much lowered, status.

There were not any guards accompanying him, but he was scheduled to meet with the governor of Moesia upon his arrival, who would no doubt send a dispatch to Rome to confirm the poet had made it to Tomis. The report of his arrival, obedient and well-behaved despite his unwilling state of disgrace, would in turn help to safeguard Fabia, and so he would bear it—for as long as he could.

It wasn't that Ovid wouldn't have a chance to escape whilst on his journey—it was that he had no desire to. After all, he would be killed on sight upon his return to Rome, and his wife would be stripped of their properties, their income, their slaves, herself turned into a miserable wretch without a future. No—he needed to secure a formal recall from *exilium*, a clean and clear restoration to his former life.

Ovid knew his best chances for setting himself on this path laid in expressing regret at his involvement in the numerous errors of judgment the emperor had accused him of, some of them rightly. He also needed to conjure up enough pity amongst the populace and powers-that-be of the city that his exile would be reconsidered.

At this point, his future, his life, literally depended upon his work. Ovid clenched the pen in his hand, scribbling a last few lines with the fading light, a new desperation tinging the words he wrote.

CHAPTER XVIII

JULIA THE YOUNGER

I stared down at my baby, my little boy, as he continued to scream at me, his cheeks flushed a rosy pink and what little hair he had sticking up in all directions. It made all the pain, all the suffering, worth it. Already the hardships of my pregnancy and the delivery were distant memories.

After countless minutes of simply admiring my child, I at last thought to move him to my breast, which very quickly appeased his cries. I had never fed my daughter, Aemilia, myself; that had been up to her wet nurse. Alas, there was no wet nurse for me here, and so I resorted to old-fashioned motherhood. I soon found that it felt startlingly right.

Aphrodite came over to pull a blanket up over me as I nursed, and I leaned back onto the bed's pillows, suddenly realizing how very tired I was. In no time at all, I was dozing off, my son contentedly suckling away.

My dreams were strange, vivid. Silanus appeared to me, but he was far away, and with every step I took towards him, the distance increased. I found myself running, then sprinting, and still he moved further and further away. He stared back at me, but he did not beckon, nor did he try to close the distance between us. Just as I began to lose sight of him, I heard his laughter, as if he were mocking me, and I felt confused, distressed.

And then, my lover disappeared. Instead Titus was there, close enough to touch, but he was on his knees, holding Aurelia's dead body, his face stricken as he stared up at me.

"I'm so sorry," he said, and his words were endlessly repeating, until they ran together, increasing in volume. I pressed my hands over my ears and begged him to stop, closing my eyes as tears streamed down my face. When I thought I couldn't take it anymore, at last there was silence.

Opening my eyes, I saw only darkness. I heard water dripping somewhere close by at a constant interval, but I couldn't make out what was up and what was down, what was in front or what was behind. I felt weightless, senseless save for my hearing, which I soon found made me even more disoriented.

"They'll take him, you know," a man's quiet voice announced from the darkness. It was the most beautiful sound I had ever heard, recalling the gentle crash of waves, the soft crush of sand under my bare feet, the deep mystery of the ocean. It came both from everywhere, and from nowhere.

I wanted to ask who he was. I wanted to see him, to put a face with that magnificent voice. But instead I found myself asking, "Who? Take who?"

A sigh, exquisite even in its clear frustration. "Your son." I finally saw the face of the speaker, a bearded man with long, rich hair, whose skin had an almost ethereal glow to it. He seemed familiar, his eyes a startling, glowing white with vivid blue irises that seemed to swirl, drawing me further in. "An illegitimate great-grandson of Augustus won't be allowed to be reared. You must know that."

"No," I said. "No, no, no, no, no…" I found myself screaming, my words running into each other as I reiterated my denial again and again.

I woke up screaming. Aphrodite hovered anxiously near me, holding my son as her big eyes watched me, uncertain.

"Give him to me! Give him to me!" I cried out, sobbing, and Aphrodite quickly handed him back.

"I am sorry, *domina*. You were so upset in your dreams, speaking aloud… I worried that you might drop him, *domina*." The slave girl looked abashed.

I didn't answer, instead clutching my son to me, his quiet breathing soothing me as I regained my sense of calm. It was a dream. Nothing more, nothing less. Everything was fine. My sleeping baby was safe in my arms, where he would remain. He was a threat to no one, least of all my grandfather. If there had been orders for him to be taken from me, it already would have happened. We were safe—*he* was safe.

It wasn't long before I fell back asleep, and this time, thankfully, it was dreamless. I woke only periodically as my son stirred, feeding him as needed, both of us then drifting back to our sleep together. We needed the rest.

Aphrodite brought me a small breakfast the following morning, which I found myself devouring with little heed of manners once she lifted my sleeping son from my arms so that I could eat. Her counterpart, Artemis, had prepared several wheat pancakes, drenched in honey and dates, which I washed down with water. I made a mental note to praise the slave for her cooking, wondering if it had truly improved with time and practice or if I had simply grown used to it.

When I finished, Aphrodite cleared up, passed my child back to me, and took the empty plate to the kitchen. I quickly found myself dozing off again in the sunshine: I had not stirred from my bed, and I had no plans to do so any time soon. My baby was nestled in my arms, content to share my nap. Each minute that ticked by reassured me that he would remain with me, safe and sound, far removed from the perils of Roman politics.

I slipped in and out of dreams again, but the morning sun brought happier images than the night before: dolphins playing out at sea as two children, a small, dark-haired boy and an older girl, ran across a sandy strip of beach, laughing as they played. I tried to see their faces more clearly, and suddenly I realized I was seeing myself and my little brother, Agrippa.

The sound of movement at the door hanging made me flutter my eyelids back open, expecting to see the slave girl returning. Instead, it was Quintus.

"Good morning, Quintus," I said politely, although a wave of alarm rushed through my body. I pulled my blanket further up around my body with one hand as I adjusted my hold on the baby, who stirred only slightly.

The guard didn't answer, and upon closer examination I saw that his face looked tired and drawn. Quintus had never struck me as old or worn out before that morning, but now it seemed as if he had aged decades in the two days or so since I had last seen him.

"What's wrong?" I asked. My grip tightened on my son, my turbulent dreams from the night before flooding back into my mind. *They'll take him, you know… An illegitimate great-grandson of Augustus won't be allowed to be reared…* They had been dreams, just silly dreams.

That was all.

Quintus finally made eye contact with me, and I saw tears in his eyes. He still didn't speak, but he moved towards me, resolute firmness evident in every inch of his body.

"No," I said. The guard didn't stop. "No." Another step closer. "No!" I screamed at him. Quintus was at my bedside.

"Give him to me," he said, quietly. "I don't want to tear him from you."

I shook my head, pressing my son closer to my chest. He was beginning to stir, awakened by my scream. The sparrow had awoken in her corner of the room, and she, too, cried out, disturbed by the panic in my voice. Quintus reached out with both hands, placing them on my baby.

"Stop it," I whispered. "Don't do this. Don't do this. Don't take him from me."

"I have to."

"No, you don't. Please don't. I'll do anything. Anything you want." I had never before begged in my life, but suddenly I had lost all of my former pride. I didn't even care. Nothing was too much to ask, if only he would let me keep my baby.

"I have to," he repeated, and his grip tightened on my son. The baby woke up, his sleepy eyes opening to an unfamiliar face.

"No one has to know he's here," I said, trying to reason with the guard. My voice became more hysterical with every syllable I uttered. "We live in exile. He can live his entire life here, with me, far away from Rome. He's not a threat. He's just a baby."

Quintus stopped answering me, and new resolve hardened his face. Gone were the tears that had earlier pricked his eyes; there was no going back, not now. He began to pull my son from me, and my baby started to wail, cries of fear, of pain. The sparrow beat her wings against her cage.

"Stop it!" I screamed, pulling my son back to me. "What harm can he cause? He's only a day old! He doesn't even have a name!"

Marcus suddenly entered the room, and he was holding me back, pushing me down on the bed, much the same way he had abused Aphrodite. The assistance of the newly arrived second guard finally allowed Quintus to rip my crying son away from me, and within seconds he was carrying him out of the room, out of my sight.

I screamed like a dying animal, writhing as Marcus held me down. My baby's cries were growing fainter as he disappeared into the distance. Soon I would lose track of him, lose him entirely. Soon it would be too late.

My struggle against Marcus seemed hopeless. He was too strong. My sobs were making it hard to breathe, while my panic was making it difficult to focus, to plan, to try to think of some way that I could free myself and save my child. I forced myself to inhale and exhale, and I tried to clear my eyes of tears. When I succeeded, what I saw infuriated me: Marcus was leering down at me, utterly without empathy. But what I *felt* frightened me: his arousal was pressing against me. The sick bastard was enjoying this, enjoying all of it.

I let my body go limp, and in response I felt the guard relax, ever so slightly. It was all I needed. Lurching up, like a wild, rabid dog I once had seen in the streets of Rome, I seized the guard's nose in my mouth, biting down with as much force as I could muster. Marcus let out a pathetic scream as his blood rushed into my mouth, choking me, and as his hands flew to his wounded face, I found myself free of his grip. I knew my opportunity would not last long.

Still naked, but now with Marcus's dark blood running unheeded down my chin and breasts, I staggered towards the door, appearing like one of the barbarian warrior women I had seen in the gladiatorial games of Rome, wild and savage. Flinging the door hanging out of the way, I tried to run down the hallway to the atrium, assuming that Quintus had already taken my baby out of the villa. I could not afford to be wrong, to head in an erroneous direction: there was no time.

I hadn't planned for the other two guards, Titus and Publius, to pose any hindrance, but they were on their feet in the atrium, as if waiting for my arrival. Their twin expressions were ones of pity, but there was an underlying resolve as their attention fixed on me. They had received their orders, and they meant to obey.

I came to a halt, some of Marcus's blood dripping from my body onto the floor in a series of small, crimson splashes. "Let me go." I tried to make it sound like a command, but in reality I knew that it was no more than a final plea. My voice broke on the final word.

Neither guard answered. Marcus had apparently regained some degree of composure and was now approaching from behind, one hand clutching his shredded nose as blood continued to drip onto the mosaicked floor. The other hovered dangerously over the handle of his short sword. I was surrounded.

The last thing I remember was screaming, a cross between an Amazonian war cry and the enraged wail of a wounded animal, as I lurched towards the two guards blocking my path, keeping me from my child.

I don't know how much later it was that I awoke in the changing room of the villa's bath. A blanket had been draped around me, and I was lying on a bench. My body and my head ached, and, for the briefest of moments, I struggled to recall what had transpired, why I was here. Sticky blood made my skin itch, and suddenly I remembered everything.

I sat up, the blanket falling away, and groaned, clutching my head. My son. I needed to find my son. I managed to stumble to the door, but I found that it wouldn't open, no matter how hard I pushed against it. I realized I had been locked inside, kept away from my child, and a rush of words thundered through my mind, each syllable a painful blow: *they were killing him.*

Beating on the door senselessly, I screamed until my voice was hoarse. I scratched at the wood, splinters digging themselves under my nails until my fingers bled, and still I continued. Worst of all, I knew that it was too late. That *I* was too late. My son was already dead. I had pushed down my worst fears, consoling myself with prayers for a daughter who might be allowed to live and willfully ignoring the dark fate that had always awaited a bastard son. In the end, my dreams had been right: the illegitimate great-grandson of Augustus would not be allowed to be reared, lest he challenge the emperor's dynastic plans. My grandfather never did like surprises. I should have known better; I should *done* something. But how could I?

Sinking to my knees, I ceased my scratching and beating on the door and quieted my screams. My son had been doomed from his conception, and I had been too stubbornly blind, too foolish, to foresee it. Better had I aborted him, better had I never even met Silanus. It had all been for nothing. What love was worth all this suffering?

I retreated from the door, crawling across the floor to the bath like a wounded creature, unable to stand on my feet. My bleeding fingers left dark smudges on the floor, a grotesque trail. Perhaps I would drown in the pool, a watery death to reunite me with my child. The dark little voice in my mind uncurled itself, awakened and intrigued by the idea, and it gently urged me forward. It would be for the best.

Rolling my tired body into the bath's water that day, I had every intention to die. I thought it would be so simple, to just stop breathing as I lay on the bottom of the pool. Unfortunately, it wasn't so easy. My body's most base instinct to survive forced me to return to the surface again and again before I lost consciousness, every time. Had I had a knife, I would have taken the more honorable, and efficient, method of suicide by blade, but even that route was, for now, blocked. I was trapped, my own continued breath a prison from which I could not free myself.

Eventually, I gave up. I floated in the bath, catching my breath for the hundredth time, and tried to think of absolutely nothing at all. Naturally, my attempts were in vain. How could I so quickly forget what had just transpired? My belly was still distended, my body sore and sensitive from my son's birth. My breasts were aching, more than ready to spill milk that was no longer needed.

I couldn't cry anymore; I couldn't scream. I felt numb, empty, except for a small grain of self-hatred that I knew would fester for the rest of my life. I had failed my child. I might as well have killed him myself.

A sudden shadow from the door to the changing room briefly distracted me from my thoughts, but I ignored it. I made no effort to cover my naked body, nor to see who had entered the bath. Perhaps it was Marcus, come to seek his revenge for his shredded nose. Let him— I no longer cared.

Minutes passed, and the shadow was so still that I began to believe I had imagined it all. But, just as I started to close my eyes, to at last doze off in the water, it moved, and a figure emerged. Titus.

We locked eyes with one another, wordless, as I continued to float in the water. The guard looked shaken, exhausted. I could only imagine that I must have looked the same, if not worse. My eyes continued to examine him, and I noted a small amount of blood on his tunic. I wondered, somewhat distantly, if any of it was from my son.

Titus suddenly stooped, removing his sandals. Then, standing, he pulled his tunic off over his head. Left only in his loincloth, he stepped towards the bath and quickly entered the water, submerging himself. I still had not moved, save for my gaze, which tracked his movements. The old me, the more proper, imperial Julia, would have been horrified at what was happening—alone in the bath with a semi-naked man who was certainly *not* my husband. My current self no longer had the energy to care, let alone react.

Titus reappeared above the pool's surface, throwing his head back to clear his face of water as he took a gasping breath. He caught my gaze again, and we simply stared at one another as time passed, two sets of brown eyes locked together. Eventually, I stood up, looking down at the man before me, who remained crouched in the water. He looked abnormally small as I, for once, towered over him. It would have been almost laughable, if it had been any other time. But right now, the last thing I felt like doing was laughing.

"Did you help to kill my son?" I asked. My cold, emotionless tone surprised me, but I felt my hands clench under the water. I knew that, depending on his answer, I might try to murder him myself.

Titus shook his head in denial. "I didn't know," he answered, his voice barely more than a whisper. "I didn't know those were the orders Quintus had received." His warm brown eyes begged me to believe him, to find the truth inside of him, and I found that I did.

I nodded in recognition of his words, but I needed to ask one more question. I needed to be certain. "The blood on your tunic, then?"

A brief flash of confusion crossed his face, then remembrance. "Marcus. From the nose job you did on him."

Again, I nodded. I didn't bother to ask him why he hadn't helped me, why he didn't fight for my child, but instead stood in my way. Titus was, after all, a Roman soldier, a member of the elite Praetorian Guard, sworn to obey the emperor even if it led to his own death. His dutiful obedience was so ingrained in him that expecting him to have acted differently than he had would have been unfair—impossible, even.

And, I realized, he owed me nothing. Titus had no allegiance to me, let alone my bastard child, whose innocence was cancelled out by virtue of his very bloodline. At best, the guard and I had exchanged a few conversations, a kind word here and there. I had no right to presume anything about him or to expect anything from him.

"Why are you here?" I asked next, focusing on the present. His decision to join me in the bath was anything but an ordinary course of action.

Again, a flash of confusion changed his features, and his eyes darkened. "I don't know." A pause, and then sudden resolve in his next words. "That's not true. I do know."

I did not speak, instead waiting for him to continue.

"I wanted to be with you," Titus finally said, as if it were the simplest thing in the world. The earnest expression on his face left me feeling confused this time. I was somewhere between angry that he dared to approach me at such a time and grateful that another human being sought to provide some form of comfort to me when I felt so very alone.

I didn't respond to his words. It might not have been fair of me to expect him to have tried to save my child, but I did not have the strength to care about fairness when my baby lay dead somewhere. Our conversation changed nothing.

I climbed out of the bath, walked slowly through the changing room, and found the door unlocked, thanks to Titus's earlier unannounced entrance. Without bothering to find a drying cloth to wrap around my naked body, I moved down the hallway to my room and laid down on my bed. The blessed numbness of sleep rushed to me, blacking out the terrors of my waking world. I could only hope that my dreams would leave me in peace.

CHAPTER XIX

THE ELDER JULIA

Julia had sweet-talked some of the guards into accompanying her into town for a brief excursion. She had a particular craving for some of the street foods Rhegium had to offer, an ill-bred habit she had developed once her more refined palate began to see less and less use, entirely against her will. Gone were her days of imperial banqueting, but, although Julia would never admit it aloud, she no longer particularly minded. The partridge stew and pork sausages from one of her favorite shops were a far cry from flamingo tongue or sea urchin, but they were absolutely *divine*.

Of course, her father didn't technically permit such *excesses* as shopping or street dining in her new, curtailed life. He had even restricted her diet for the first few years of her exile, going so far as to forbid her consumption of wine. That was when she knew for certain that he was a cold, heartless bastard, both as a father and as an emperor.

Nevertheless, Julia knew enough about the nature of men that she occasionally was able to convince her minders that a small deviation from the rigid rules of her confinement was not the end of the world, so long as nobody important, such as the emperor, found out. It was her blessed combination of womanly wiles and dagger-sharp threats that had always gotten Julia her way, in the end.

Smirking, she fanned herself as the litter slowly moved down the hill from the villa, gazing out at Rhegium's late summer landscape; the once green grasses now had a brownish tinge, worn down after months of endless sun. One of the slaves bearing the litter suddenly stumbled, jarring her, and her smirk quickly turned into a scowl. Normally, she would have had that particular slave whipped upon their return to the villa, but, as her little adventure wasn't allowed, she would instead play nice, lest someone decide to make a scene and her father found out she had been bending the rules.

Scribonia sat across from her daughter, sweat dripping down her face. It was both a combination of the heat and her anxiety about their visit to town. While Scribonia was at Rhegium of her own free will, keeping her exiled child company by choice, she didn't want to draw any more of her ex-husband's attention to herself. It was only by Augustus's grace that she was allowed to be here now, and her circumstances could change in the blink of an eye.

"Really now, Mother, relax. We've done this before and everything was *fine*." Julia twirled a loose strand of hair around her finger as she noted that her words did nothing to reassure Scribonia. At least she had tried, she thought, as her mother resumed staring anxiously out of the litter.

Julia was growing tired of waiting for her plans to come to fruition. Sempronius Gracchus hadn't sent word since his last letter, which, combined with the unchanged behavior of her guards and their current lax attitude about her little excursion, suggested that the rescue attempt on behalf of Agrippa Postumus and her daughter Julia had yet to occur. Surely it would happen soon, she thought, as summer's end was approaching.

An autumn timeline was workable, but winter seas were practically impossible to navigate safely, which would make any rescue attempt, already a high stakes gamble, significantly riskier. Even once the mercenaries safely reached the islands and successfully retrieved their quarry, they then still had to escort the imperials to the western provinces, a journey which would include further sailing for both ships.

It would also be preferable if Julia's daughter was retrieved before she birthed the bastard descendant of Augustus she was carrying, so that there would be no doubts about the child's identity—and so that it could be protected. It would be a target for countless scheming good-for-nothings, all of whom wanted to use it to their own advantage. Naturally, Julia did not consider herself among them.

She couldn't precisely recall when her new grandchild was due to arrive, largely due to her uncertain knowledge about exactly *when* her daughter had been exiled; she hoped her plans would not come to fruition too late. News always reached Julia slowly and unreliably, which was a near constant source of irritation. When she had been in Rome, she had known things before the people involved even knew it themselves. Now she relied on what the guards deigned to tell her and what gossip her slave boy, Felix, reported.

Another jolt of the litter brought Julia back to the present, and she had to bite her lip to keep from loudly cursing the offending slave. Thankfully, they were entering the outskirts of the town of Rhegium. With Fortuna's blessing, the guards would allow her to do a bit of her own shopping, even if it meant having to walk around under a parasol.

The streets soon became more crowded, and Julia's guards moved in closer, tightly ringing the litter. While they permitted this small excursion against the guidelines of their emperor, they would die a thousand deaths before they allowed Julia to be harmed… or abducted, willingly on her part or otherwise.

The people of Rhegium, many of them Greek-speaking, knew the emperor's daughter resided in the imperial villa on the hill outside their settlement, but they also knew enough to stay away. No one wanted the negative attention of the guards and, by extension, of Augustus himself. It could easily spell doom for them all. And so, the litter continued its journey through the streets unimpeded, the assortment of merchants, slaves, transient sailors, and common people all making way.

Another jolt of the litter caused Julia to finally lose her patience. "Get it together, you idiot!" she snapped, moving to poke her head out of the litter to glare at the clumsy slave in question.

Just as Julia's head emerged, she realized it hadn't been a slave losing his grip again. People were rapidly clearing the streets, panicked, and her guards were yelling at the litter-bearers to turn around and go back to the villa. Another jolt, and then a second, followed by a third, all in quick succession, and suddenly it was as if the earth was alive underneath them. They had gotten themselves trapped in an earthquake.

Scribonia was whimpering as she cowered in the litter, and Julia screamed as a building collapsed to her left, a large stone smashing one of the slaves on his head. He fell to the ground, unconscious or dead, and the litter collapsed before a guard was able to take the slave's place. Julia was aware of tumbling out of the litter amidst screams and widespread panic, and then her vision faded to black as she hit her head on the road.

Over a month had passed since my newborn son had been ripped away from me. Just over a month since my baby had been *disposed of* on my grandfather's orders, lest he grow up and challenge one of the emperor's future successors for power. Never before had I despised my cursed bloodline with quite so much vehemence. The same lineage that could guarantee power, money, and prestige could also seal one's doomed fate.

I barely ate for an entire month, although Aphrodite tried her best to coax me, bringing me a variety of concoctions that her fellow slave, Artemis, thought I might enjoy: the last of our available dormice, stuffed with meat and vegetables before being dipped in honey; a mixture of dried fruits from our reserves; even *moretum*, an herbed cheese spread she remembered Aurelia once mentioning I liked. None of it appealed to me; what little I did manage to eat all tasted bland, sitting heavy in my mouth before I forced myself to swallow it down.

Most of my time was spent in bed, caught somewhere between the terrors of my dreams and the horrors of my waking reality. My baby's screams haunted me without respite. The sparrow's chirping, too, had begun to recall my son's wailing, and I had Aphrodite move the bird into the atrium, safely out of earshot—but I found the silence in my room proved just as deafening.

All of the guards except for Titus avoided me. Even Lucius had not made an appearance after he was turned away a handful of days following the incident, when he had arrived unannounced. For obvious reasons, I had not been inclined towards receiving visitors.

I still had not seen Quintus since he had taken my child away. I thought he was ashamed, as he should have been. While the rational, coldly political part of me could understand *why* it had happened, *why* Quintus had been duty-bound to carry out such a sentence on my child, the mother in me could never forgive it. I would gladly have given anything for my son's life, even my own.

I had caught sight of Marcus just once, lurking down the hallway as I headed to the bath, and his glare had sent shivers down my spine. His nose was missing a small chunk, and it was incredibly red and swollen, possibly even infected from my bite. Publius had been there too, and he placed a hand on his comrade's arm, as if ready to restrain him, should the need arise.

I realized that although Marcus may not have been particularly kind or friendly to me before, at least he had not been overtly threatening. Now I had a much bigger problem in the form of an armed, and angry, enemy; I had no doubt that he would seek some form of vengeance, if the opportunity arose. Certainly Marcus wouldn't dare cause me any permanent damage, but he could make my life deeply unpleasant. The memory of his arousal as he held me down on the bed, as he prevented me from trying to stop Quintus from carrying away my child, still made me queasy.

Titus seemed to sense my unease, and he became my constant shadow. He was the only guard whom I tolerated in my presence, and so he was the one who accompanied me to my bath, waiting outside until I was finished; he was the one who set up a cot outside my room, allowing me enough peace of mind to even try to sleep at night; he was the one who escorted me the first time I left the villa since my son's death.

We were walking on the sandy strip of beach close to the port, Titus a few steps behind me at a respectful distance. We still had not spoken about how he had come to me in the bath that day a little over a month ago. In fact, we hadn't spoken about that day at all. It was better, I thought, if the memory of my child died as quickly as he himself had. I didn't know if I could go on otherwise. Perhaps it was a somewhat callous way of thinking, but it was survival.

"Funny, isn't it, how a new death makes us so quickly move on from another?" I asked Titus suddenly, musing on how I hadn't spared Aurelia a single thought recently. "When my slave woman died, I felt as if my world had changed drastically. I couldn't even imagine what was still to come."

I could hear Titus plodding along behind me through the sand at his consistent pace, but he didn't respond. In truth, I didn't really expect him to. How could someone answer a question like that?

Suddenly, I found that I wanted to keep talking, wanted to share something of my pain, even if no one could lessen it. "I didn't much notice when my father died, nor my brothers, if I am honest. I saw them all rarely enough. It was like I barely knew them, in the end."

Titus did not answer, but I plunged onwards, words suddenly tumbling out of me as if they were water let loose from a dam. "How long did it take for you, after your mother died, to feel..." I trailed off, uncertain of the words for which I was searching.

"Whole again?" Titus supplied.

Stopping, I finally turned to look at the guard, shading my eyes as he came to a halt in front of me. Although it was now autumn, the afternoons were still hot, and sweat trickled down the sides of his face and lightly stained the front of his tunic. I nodded.

Titus shrugged, looking down at me with an unreadable expression. Pity? Concern? I couldn't tell.

"I know I mentioned my mother to you before... She was a whore. A common whore, when all is said and done, even if she managed to catch the attention of a senator." Titus's words were even and measured. "She didn't abandon me, the inconvenient child who resulted from their brief liaison, which says something good about her. But she was never truly prepared to be a mother. She didn't know how to show real love. I don't blame her, though. Her life was hard."

I said nothing, waiting for him to continue. I didn't think I'd ever heard Titus say so many words at once; then again, I don't think I had ever spoken so much before, either.

"I don't think we ever are whole again, after the death of someone important to us," the soldier said. "Or, perhaps we are, but we're different. We change. Maybe some part of us dies with them, but then there's a newness that comes after, as we move on and continue to live without them." He cut himself off, and I saw that he was blushing, embarrassed by his rambling. It brought a very small smile to my face.

"At least I made you smile," Titus said gruffly. "You haven't smiled in a very long time."

"I haven't spoken with a philosopher in a very long time," I countered jokingly. Titus merely grunted in response.

Suddenly, I felt guilty and ashamed that I was able to smile, to joke, while my murdered baby's remains rested Jupiter knew where. I turned sharply away from Titus and marched off, not seeing his surprised, and saddened, expression. A short time later, I felt more than heard his presence behind me, and we continued on in silence until we reached the end of the beach, further passage blocked by the rocky face of a cliff.

After a month spent inside the villa mourning, I couldn't bring myself to return there again so soon. I hadn't realized how much I had missed the sunshine on my skin, the sea breeze toying with my hair, the sound of gulls crying and waves crashing as sand crunched softly under my bare feet. The villa had become a prison that stank of death and fear, but here—I could finally hear myself think.

"Is my lover dead?" The question surprised me as the words fell from my lips. It was something I long had wondered, but I had lacked the courage to ask, just as I had avoided asking directly about what orders the guards might have received about my bastard child. I no longer wanted to live in willful ignorance. "Did my grandfather have him executed?"

Titus looked me over, his face again sad. He seemed to weigh his words carefully before he finally spoke, and his voice was soft. "He lives."

I felt my heart drop to my stomach, and my body quivered. Silanus was alive. "Where is he?" I barely remembered how to speak, and my words came out in a rush.

Titus examined me for what felt like an eternity, his eyes searching; what they were trying to find, I didn't know. At last he responded. "He is in exile. I'm not sure where."

A thousand more questions were bubbling to the surface, fighting for a chance to be asked. For the first time in months, I felt a true sense of hope. "How long have you known?" I wondered if I had somehow missed a ship in port, perhaps bearing a messenger with news from Rome.

The soldier briefly looked down, avoiding my gaze. "Since the night your grandfather sent you away."

"Why didn't you tell me?"

Titus's voice was cold as he answered, and his eyes once again met mine. "I didn't want to break your heart."

I was confused. "What do you mean?"

The guard sighed then and turned his back to me, his head raised to the sky and his eyes closed as if in prayer. He remained facing away from me when he finally spoke again. "He saved his own skin."

My confusion did not lift. "I don't understand."

Titus whirled back to face me, an intense, fiery heat in his eyes, and I stepped backwards, suddenly afraid of his coiled energy as he spewed out his next words. "He betrayed you. He betrayed you, to save his own neck."

I shook my head. "No. Silanus would never do that. You're wrong."

He briefly closed his eyes again, but when he opened them he seemed calmer. "Your grandfather already had his suspicions. But when he called Silanus for an audience—not long before your own meeting with the emperor—your lover did not hesitate to admit to everything. He did not even try to shield you, or your child, from the fate he surely must have known awaited." His words were factual, without malice.

A rush of emotions overwhelmed me. I wanted to defend Silanus, to argue for him. But why would Titus lie? I felt confused, betrayed. Lost. I had lied to my grandfather to protect my lover; I had withheld his name, willing to suffer whatever lay in store, for the sake of what I thought had been love. Evidently Silanus had not done the same, not even for his own flesh and blood that had taken hold of my womb.

"How do you know?" I whispered.

Titus sighed, resigned. "Everyone does."

"Except me."

He did not answer my self-pitying words, which only cemented their truth. I started crying then, the tears rushing hot and wet down my face, and within a single breath Titus was there, holding me, his strong arms hugging me to his body so tightly that I almost couldn't breathe.

I cried again for Aurelia, realizing that I would never fully recover from her death; I cried for my baby, whom I hadn't even named; I cried for Silanus, whose survival I now cursed knowing that it came at the cost of a cowardly betrayal; and I cried for myself, for the very different person I had been before any of this had happened. Titus held me through it all.

Titus and I did not mention Silanus ever again, but I could tell from the way he watched me that he was waiting for another breakdown. Another fit. Perhaps he thought he had been right for withholding what he knew about my former lover for so long, but he remained quiet on the topic—and I was grateful for his silence.

My days became routine, each one a ritual of pointless habits that I told myself over and over again would ease not only the passage of time, but also the raw wounds of my soul. I doubted my own prescription, but still I persisted. Every day I forced myself to walk the same sandy strip of beach where Titus had revealed what he knew of Silanus and his role in my exile. For me, it was a daily damnation of his memory, each step an attempt to cut him from my heart.

Titus was once again my loyal shadow on a particularly overcast afternoon. Dark clouds were rolling in across the water, evidence of a brewing storm, but, to his credit, the guard did not complain or suggest we cut my walk short. He knew I would not heed him anyway. Still, Titus watched the approaching storm with apprehension.

"Dolphins," I announced, movement on the horizon catching my attention. A group of them were speeding along parallel to the island, occasionally surfacing on the crests of the growing waves.

"What?" Titus asked distractedly, his focus still on the impending poor weather.

I gestured out into the water. "Dolphins. There—look." I wasn't sure what possessed me—perhaps a touch of the madness that was said to afflict my poor brother—but I turned to the water then, pulling my dress off and dropping it to the ground as I moved towards the waves. I hadn't bothered with a breastband or loincloth that day; it had all seemed like too much effort at the time.

"What are you doing?" Titus asked, slightly panicked. He had finally torn his watchful gaze from the storm and caught sight of me, but now he seemed too dazed to move.

"Going swimming," I answered simply, bracing my feet as a wave crashed and rushed in, the salt water briefly coming up to my ankles before it receded. I took a further step into the sea, and then another. Finally Titus cursed, seeming to break his immobile spell, and he rushed towards me. The water had reached my thighs, a wave threatening to knock me over and drag me away.

Titus's body suddenly collided with mine, arms wrapping around me as if he could singlehandedly fight Neptune from calling me into the sea. "Are you mad?" he snapped as a wave crashed into us both.

I laughed. "Perhaps I am. What does it matter?"

Titus still held me, and his expression softened. I became increasingly aware of his body, firmly muscled and warm, pressed against my own naked figure as gulls circled overhead, their mocking cries sounding aloud. I felt his hands move up from my back, ever so slowly, to either side of my neck, gently caressing my skin, then up to my hair, which was tied back in a simple bun. He pulled it loose, and my hair spilled down, tendrils of it waving in the wind as Titus moved his hands to my face.

He stroked a thumb over my lower lip, so lightly that I barely felt his touch, before tracing his fingers up and over my cheeks, my nose, my brows. I closed my eyes, at once anxious and terribly excited, and I felt the briefest brush of his lips against each lid. Exhaling, I opened my eyes and saw that Titus had pulled back just a few inches, although he still cupped my face with his hands. He was watching me, a mix of hesitation and want clear on his face.

"It matters," he murmured. "Please know that it does matter."

I didn't answer. Instead, taking his face in my hands, I closed the distance between us, and I softly pressed my lips to his. It was like setting a pyre alight on a dry, windy day.

Waves continued to crash and rush in, water swirling around our legs, the laughing gulls our only witnesses as began something that neither of us would ever forget. A thousand thoughts rushed through my mind, a thousand feelings coursed through my body, from excitement to fear, from worry to arousal, but still I could not tear myself away as we stood entwined.

At last we did part, and both of us stared at one another in a combination of awe and shock. Titus was the first to recover, and he pulled both of us out of the increasingly dangerous waters and further onto shore as the storm loomed ever closer. The strengthening winds quickly chilled my body, and I redressed, shaking the sand from my dress. Titus, still clothed in a tunic that was now soaking wet, watched, seemingly immune to the cold.

"You're not what I expected," he announced, appraising me.

I studied him in return, admiring the traces of stubble on his cheeks, the way the wind caught his hair and how the receding sun seemed to make some strands glint gold. But most of all, I admired the way he looked at me. His expression was not calculated, wondering if and how he could use me to his own advantage, nor was it judgmental, weighing my worth as a potential broodmare or as another pretty, voiceless decoration for his villa. Both were looks I was more than familiar with in Rome.

No—I realized that to Titus, I was not a prisoner, not an imperial, but an individual in my own right, despite my sex, my family, and my current circumstances. It was refreshing. Even Silanus, at the end, had looked at me as a tool, a way to avoid a harsher punishment even if it cost the life of his own child. Perhaps Titus was different.

"Neither are you," I replied, stepping closer to him, and we embraced again. This time I could feel a faint trace of his arousal, but he made no move to progress beyond our current entwinement.

Titus broke away, and he looked troubled as we both caught our breath. "What are we doing?" he asked. "What do we expect to come of this?"

I didn't know how to answer, at first. I thought about it, reflecting on the man who was in front of me, on what possible future we could have together. I knew there was none. "We can't expect anything," I finally told him. "There is no future, not like this. We must always keep this secret. Do you think Quintus and your fellow guards would allow this, if they knew?" I did not bother to mention a scenario in which I were recalled to Rome; the reasons preventing us from being together there were obvious enough.

Titus's face was stony. "I will not just use you. You deserve better."

I threw back my head and laughed, the noise blending with that of the gulls above us as their mocking cries swiftly turned to panic. Jupiter's thunder boomed in threat. "Do you think I would be here with you now if I thought you just wanted to use me? Do you think I'm so weak as to let myself be used against my wishes?"

Titus's cheeks reddened, and he looked slightly abashed. I realized that he must have forgotten with whom he was dealing. While I certainly was not the same cold, aristocratic woman he had first met the night my grandfather cast me out, I still had a strong sense of pride, instilled in me since birth, and it wasn't disappearing any time soon. Silanus had fooled me; it would not happen again, whatever path Titus and I were now headed down. I would make sure of it.

"One thing that I have learned, far too well since my *exilium* began, is not to plan for the future or to expect anything from it." My words, while grim, were earnest.

I wasn't angry. It was just that I had come to realize there was little, if any, place for optimism in my new life. To open the door to hope for a happy future would inevitably lead down a path of disappointment and regret. I could deal with no more of either.

Thunder crashed again, and then the rain began, pouring relentlessly from the sky. At least it would wash the salt of the ocean from our bodies.

Titus did not respond to my ominous words. Instead, he pushed me against the rocky wall of the looming cliff, kissing me roughly and deeply, as if he were saying goodbye. In a way, he was—for a time, anyway. We were headed back to the villa, where there would be no opportunity for lovers' play. If discovered, it would lead to a harsher imprisonment for me and to a death sentence for Titus. I was certain of it.

CHAPTER XXI

AGRIPPA POSTUMUS

Agrippa stared off at the sunset as he stood near the cliff's edge, a small group of guards huddling together at a reasonable distance as they waited for him to finish whatever it was that he was doing. They often found it easier to play along than to challenge the emperor's grandson, although their patience was very tried at times.

The nights were becoming increasingly chilly as autumn arrived in full force, and the seas were growing rougher. It hadn't stopped the youth from taking his regular swims, although it did mean the last supply ship of the year would be arriving soon, before the journey became too treacherous with the change of seasons. Winter on Planasia, in Agrippa's past experience, was uneventful, save for the fantastic storms that regularly battered the island and would easily smash a ship to pieces. Such a storm looked as if it was brewing even now.

Turning away from the sea at last, Agrippa began to walk back towards the villa, the soldiers quickly moving into step behind him as they continued some inane conversation. It was interesting, Agrippa mused, how the guards changed their interactions with him: sometimes accommodating, sometimes cruel. At times, Agrippa was the clear master; at others, he felt his imprisonment deeply, in every sense.

Each fresh crop of men that arrived to guard him appeared, at first, to be slightly different: variations in coloring and in build, with a range of accents from across the whole of Italy. But in the end, they really were all the same to him: stupid, uncultured brutes.

It was what Agrippa most despised about his *exilium*: the lack of any sort of adequate companionship. There were no whimsical poets, talented actors, or barbaric gladiators to entertain him, no learned senators or wise philosophers to debate. He should have been at the head of a vast empire, but instead he was on an insignificant island, wasting his youth and his talent, all because his grandfather didn't trust him, didn't value him. He had been *driven* to rebellion by the old man. And it had all been for nothing.

The group reached the villa just as thunder boomed and the skies opened, pounding rain flooding down onto the island as the wind picked up. The storm matched Agrippa's mood perfectly, an observation that did not escape the guards. It would not be a good time to antagonize the youth.

Agrippa paused in the atrium, coldly noting the influx of rain through the open roof as the oil lamps flickered precariously. The handful of slaves in residence at the villa had pushed back the room's furniture to a safe distance, keeping everything out of the weather. Some of the guards had already dispersed to whatever leisure they might find, their duty done for the day, while two remained with the youth, as they always did. They were his constant, unwanted shadows.

Suddenly, Agrippa grabbed one of the oil lamps and headed down the hallway. The guards, taken aback by his unexpected movement, hurried to follow, the bobbing light of the lamp leading them behind their charge to the small library, where the villa's collection of old scrolls was housed. Agrippa had read and then re-read all of them, some of them multiple times. He stood there now, in the center of the room, the lamp held aloft, his back to the guards. They exchanged a glance but remained unperturbed; it was more likely than not that Agrippa simply wanted to select more reading material.

The guards were not prepared for what happened next. Agrippa, as if in a frenzy, began to tear scrolls from the shelves, throwing them all on the floor, violently ripping some in the process, while furniture was tipped over in every direction. The sound of splintering wood melded with the cracks of thunder that seemed to shake the villa.

The two soldiers remained outside the library, unwilling to intervene. Considering the young imperial's current mood, they thought it prudent to avoid a direct conflict—especially since Agrippa did not seem particularly interested in attacking them directly, but instead was focused on the destruction of the scrolls, which were of little interest to them.

Their indifference dissipated when Agrippa threw the lamp against the wall, the crash of pottery resounding throughout the villa. Hot oil splattered across the scrolls, strewn throughout the entire library, and the fire, small and innocuous before, suddenly spread, violently engulfing everything in its path.

The guards, panicked, began to shout for help, yelling for the others to bring water, lest the entire villa go up in flames. Agrippa's tunic caught a small lick of fire then, and, as it grew, the youth only laughed, surrounded by the chaotic destruction of his own creation.

Agrippa awoke to searing pain on his back and the stench of charred flesh. He yelled out and tried to move, but his body remained in place: he had been tied belly-down to his bed, his limbs all immobile. Gritting his teeth, Agrippa tested the restraints. They were firm.

"It's for your own good," a voice told him.

Agrippa whipped his head around as far as he was able, and Rufus stepped into sight. He held a small jar in his hands.

"A salve, for your burns," the guard explained.

Agrippa closed his eyes, teeth still gritted. "Get on with it, then," he snapped at Rufus.

The guard was gentle as he dabbed the salve onto Agrippa's back and spread it over the burns, but the pressure of Rufus's fingers on his wounded skin still made the youth curse.

"Why did you do it?" Rufus asked quietly, his fingers dipping into the jar to scoop up more of the salve.

Agrippa did not answer, and Rufus continued to silently apply the salve. The youth himself did not know why he had been in such a fury. Boredom? Resentment? Both, he supposed. But a darker voice fluttered at the corners of his mind: the curse of his insanity.

"They say I'm mad," Agrippa told the guard at last, and for once his voice reflected some level of uncertainty—and of fear.

In response, Rufus pressed a finger harshly into one of the youth's burns, and Agrippa howled. "You must stay sane enough, for now," he murmured gently, even as his finger pushed violently against another wound, threatening. "We need you."

Agrippa fought back tears of pain as he glared at Rufus. "I'll kill you."

"No," Rufus said with a smile, finally removing his hands from Agrippa and standing. "Right now, you need me. You need *us*."

"Who is *us*?" Agrippa asked, still seething.

Rufus ignored his question. "Paullus failed. He was too arrogant, too careless. He rushed. And it is his fault that you are here now. My master will not make the same mistake. We will protect you, and we will give you Rome."

"How?"

Rufus smiled at him again. "Have patience. In the spring, I will depart with the other guards, once the new squad arrives. Amongst them will be another like me."

"Tell me!" Agrippa shouted, straining at the ropes that bound him to his bed. But Rufus was already leaving the room.

Agrippa was so furious at Rufus's treatment that he considered turning him in to his fellow soldiers at the soonest opportunity, revealing him as the traitor he so clearly was. Once he began to regain his temper, though, his line of thought changed. After all, they believed Rufus was their loyal brother in arms, while he was the mad, traitorous grandson of their emperor. It was not very hard to imagine whose word they would trust.

Even as Agrippa mused on his dislike for Rufus as an individual, it became increasingly clear to him that the man was his only ally on the cursed island of Planasia. If, as Rufus promised, his master could accomplish what Paullus had not, and establish Agrippa as emperor, then no price was too much to pay.

CHAPTER XXII

JULIA THE YOUNGER

I lost track of how long it had been since Quintus dared show his face to me, but he finally reappeared. Our reunion was not a happy one. The man could hardly bear to look at me when we encountered one another for the first time since *the incident*, as I had come to think of it.

Calling it *the incident* made it easier to protect myself from collapsing further into the misery of deep despair and self-destruction, a bottomless pit to which I sometimes found myself precariously close if I thought too long and hard about my baby's death. The dark little voice in my mind had strengthened over time, and it would seize any opportunity to push me over the edge. Titus was the only thing that kept me halfway sane, and even he was sometimes not enough.

I was leaving the bath in the evening, Titus, my loyal shadow, flanking me, when I came face-to-face with his superior.

"Mistress," Quintus murmured, so quietly that I could barely hear him, even though he stood barely a foot away from me. His eyes quickly scanned my face before he stared past me, his body tense.

I wanted to strike him, to scratch his eyes out; I wanted to scream at him, to curse him to an eternity of torment at the hands of the most creatively vengeful gods. Instead, I stood there, frozen and blank.

Seconds passed, but it felt like minutes, hours even. Neither Quintus nor Titus pressured me to move or to speak, and we all three stood there as I tried to work through my rush of emotions, the hundreds if not thousands of things I wanted to yell out at the world in my rage.

At last, I managed to open my mouth to speak, but only a quiet croak emerged from my throat. I wet my lips and tried again. "I understand why," I managed to whisper. "I understand why, but I can never forgive. Never." I could hardly hear my own words, but I saw in Quintus's eyes that he had understood me. Before he mustered any sort of response, I quickly brushed past him, practically running to my bedroom as Titus hurried to keep up.

Barely making it inside, I dropped to the floor as if my muscles had ceased to work. I couldn't breathe, I couldn't see, and panic was surging up inside me even as the sinister little voice emerged, whispering at me that it would be so easy to take all the pain away, to never feel anything again. Suddenly, Titus was there, sitting behind me as he wrapped his arms and legs around my body, holding me. As my senses returned, I realized that he was rocking me back and forth, whispering gentle, soothing words quietly into my ear.

"How can I do this?" I finally managed to ask him. "How can I see my child's murderer every day and manage to live with it? How is it that I can rationalize it, that I can understand *why* Quintus isn't really to blame? What type of mother does that make me?"

Titus said nothing, just continued to hold me, his earthy scent wrapping around me like a calming balm. He had no answers, and I didn't expect him to. It was enough, for now, that he was simply there.

I didn't remember falling asleep, nor did I recall Titus carrying me to my bed. I awoke with a start from an unsettling dream, in which the familiar bearded man smelling of sand and salt was chasing me through a city under the sea, closing in no matter how fast I swam. He had appeared to me before, foretelling the impending murder of my child. Perhaps I would do well to heed my dreams in the future, where he appeared.

As I fought to catch my breath, I realized that the villa was silent and still, blanketed in darkness: it was the middle of the night. Rising from my bed, I tiptoed to the door, pulling back the hanging halfway as I peered out into the hallway. Titus was sound asleep on his cot, his breathing deep and even, save for an occasional disruptive snore.

Without thinking, I softly padded past the guard, headed towards the atrium, and, beyond that, to the villa's main door. I felt stifled, trapped. I needed air. No one appeared out of the darkness to stop me; only the sparrow emitted a quiet chirp, a single, shining black eye cracking open from her sleep to peer at me as I passed by. In less than a minute I reached the door, easing open the simple latch that kept the villa closed to outsiders.

The stars shone bright, and a cool breeze rippled the grasses and caused the trees' branches to wave at me in a beckoning gesture. I took off at a slow run towards my favorite cliff, leaving the villa wide open behind me. I realized belatedly that I was barefoot, wearing only a thin white dress, but I didn't mind. The grass was soft underfoot, and I was free, entirely alone for the first time in recent memory.

I reached the cliff's edge, breathless and excited as I came to a halt. The moon cast an eerie silver light over the rise and fall of the sea's waves, calling to me, and I inched closer to the rocky ledge, hearing the crash of water far below. The dark little voice unfurled itself from the recesses of my mind, intrigued by my sudden, and unexpected, situation.

Standing there, I raised my arms out from my sides, closing my eyes as I tipped my head back and breathed in the salt, the wind, and the crisp night air.

"Gods," I murmured, "if it be your desire, take me now."

The seconds ticked by, and the cyclical crash of the waves mesmerized me. I was so close to the edge, so very close. It would be so easy to be free.

Suddenly, I felt a firm grip on my wrist, pulling me harshly away from the cliff's edge and breaking my spell. I opened my eyes and, turning, saw Titus. He was pale, breathless, and had an expression somewhere between fury and relief.

"Stop this madness," he spat out at me, the anger clear in his voice. Something else was there, too, underlying his words: fear.

I didn't respond, instead choosing to close the distance between us, my lips finding his. At first, he seemed resistant, confused, but within seconds he melted into me, his body betraying his attempted resolve. New life seemed to flood into me, and I began to pull at Titus's tunic, trying to remove it as our passion intensified. His hands found mine and pulled them away, holding them at my sides even as I struggled. I didn't just want him, I *needed* him, my sudden raw desire consuming every fiber of my being.

Frustrated, I pulled away from him, although he still clasped my hands in his, holding them tightly, as if he feared that I would return to the edge of the cliff to tempt fate once again. His eyes betrayed his worry, even as a trace of lust colored them.

"Please," I beseeched him.

At first I thought he might refuse, but then his expression softened, and he pulled me back towards him. This time, he did not stop my hands as they escaped his grasp, and I tugged his tunic off even as his own hands softly pulled my dress from my shoulders, the garment dropping to the ground.

I shivered under his touch, his calloused hands lightly exploring my body. A soft brush across my shoulders, a stroke down each arm and then back up, a gentle caress of my breasts. A finger teased my navel, and then both his hands grasped my hips, pulling me forcefully into him as I gasped. Our bodies pressed against one another, and his touch moved to my back, his fingers tracing down my spine. Groaning, Titus brought his mouth to mine again, his tongue pushing against my own as he tried to pull me still closer to his body.

Abruptly, he spun me around, and we stood, back to front, the endless ocean stretching out before us. One of his hands teased a breast, toying with the nipple, while the other lazily drifted downwards, so slowly that I wanted to scream with anticipation. Just as I thought I could bear it no longer, Titus's hand reached his target at the same time that he gently bit my neck, the pressure almost painful before he kissed the spot better.

I moaned from the overload of sensations in my body, my knees shaking. Sensing that I wouldn't be able to stand much longer, Titus broke contact, silently leading me by the hand to a soft patch of grasses. In a daze, I followed, allowing him to help me to the ground. Lying on my back, I was distantly aware of the beauty of the night, admiring the stars overhead even as I anticipated what was about to happen. Titus situated himself between my legs, and he cupped my face in his hands as he gazed down at me.

"Are you sure?" he asked.

I nodded, stroking his stubbled cheek. Turning his face to kiss my hand, he began to press himself into me, and I closed my eyes, a hundred emotions suddenly rushing through me. Titus, as if realizing that I was processing things, paused. When I opened my eyes again, it was to stare up into his, and I smiled. I was ready.

He finished pushing into me, and I could tell that he was holding himself back; his arms were shaking. In encouragement, I shifted my body underneath him, urging him on. Titus needed no more signs, and we at last fully consummated our affair under the open sky in the nighttime air of Trimerus: the emperor's granddaughter and one of the guards tasked with ensuring her imprisonment.

We lay together afterwards, our bodies still partially entwined as we watched the stars, listening to the waves crashing all around. I wondered what it would be like to be away from the ocean, to have silence again, and found that I couldn't even imagine it. My past life in Rome seemed a distant memory, a vague dream of endless intrigues and maneuverings. It occurred to me that perhaps it was for the best that I never returned.

Titus interrupted my thoughts. "We should go back to the villa before we're missed."

I wanted to protest; lying there with him was the most at peace I had felt in many months. But I knew that he was right. We already had risked too much.

"Titus," I started. He turned his head to look at me, and the reflection of the moon in his eyes made me pause. I realized how pure he was, how uncorrupted by Roman politics he appeared to be, whatever else he may have done in his life as a soldier. It made me want him even more.

I shook my head, and Titus didn't press for more, instead helping me to stand up. We both retrieved our clothes, dressed quickly, and set off for the villa. We still had hours before daybreak.

The villa's entrance remained wide open, as it had been left. Nobody had stirred, not even the sparrow this time. Within minutes, I was back in my bed, Titus in his cot outside my room. As I drifted off to sleep, I found myself thinking that the wool blanket I had pulled up around myself was a poor substitute for the warmth of his skin. At least the lingering trace of his comforting scent still clung to my skin, and I breathed it in.

Aphrodite's arrival with a small breakfast woke me in the morning, and I surprised her by finally eating everything she had brought me. I had entirely forgotten what it was like to have an appetite, but I found I couldn't resist the small amount of fruits, honey, and bread she had laid out.

"*Domina*, would you like me to bring you more?" Aphrodite hovered uncertainly as I devoured the last piece of bread, watching me with ever-anxious eyes.

Swallowing, I nodded, and the slave girl disappeared back to the kitchen. I dressed myself in the few minutes that she was gone, and, rather than waiting for her return, I decided to head to the atrium, through which she would have to pass anyway. Titus met me as I left my room, and our eyes lingered on one another, each of us recalling the night before. The guard's gaze broke away first, and the faintest hint of a blush bloomed across his cheeks. I hid a small smile.

Titus perched himself on a chair in the corner of the atrium while I stretched out on a couch, enjoying one of the last warm mornings of the autumn season. It was the first time in quite a while that I had placed myself in such a public location of the villa, and Aphrodite seemed surprised to see me there when she emerged from the kitchen area.

"*Domina*, if you please," the slave murmured, placing a tray before me. Assorted fruits, covered in honey, tempted me, but just as I was about to reach for an especially plump date, the villa doors swung open. Publius entered, followed by Lucius.

The old man's gap-toothed smile appeared as soon as he caught sight of me, and he pushed Publius out of the way with his cane as he hobbled towards my couch. The young guard shook his head as if resigned and closed the doors as he resumed his duties outside.

"My dear! So long since I've seen you!" Lucius exclaimed, spittle spraying from his mouth.

I returned his smile but remained on my couch. "Hello, Lucius. Would you like some fruit?" I gestured to the tray in front of me, but he shook his head.

"I've been awake for hours," he explained. "I'd much rather have my noonday meal, if you don't mind obliging…"

Inwardly, I was laughing at Lucius's gall to make such a request at a home not his own, but I simply gestured for Aphrodite to remove the tray, and she obeyed. Similar behavior in Rome would lead to one being socially ostracized, but, alas, we both were now two nobodies in the Adriatic. There was no society from which to be cast out.

"Bring something suitable for Lucius," I called to the slave's retreating figure.

My guest settled himself on the couch next to mine, and as he was about to speak I caught sight of Marcus, scowling as he entered the atrium from the direction of the kitchen. I frowned, wondering if he had been abusing the slaves again, but there was little I could do about it at the moment, considering Lucius was present: it would be improper to complain about household matters in front of a guest. But even if I had not had company, I was not sure anyone would listen to my grievances.

Marcus, whose nose was still red but slightly less inflamed, leveled a very direct and distinctly unfriendly glare in my direction. The small, missing chunk of flesh had seriously hampered what little appeal his unkind face might hold for anyone.

"Didn't finish your breakfast?" he murmured as he passed behind me, so quietly that I barely heard him. I didn't understand his point, unless he was simply stressing that he had been in the kitchen after all: he knew that I was bothered by his mistreatment of the slaves, particularly Aphrodite.

Titus looked uneasy, and he was half-rising from his chair until his fellow guard disappeared down the hallway leading to the bedrooms and bath. He resettled himself, but his attention remained elsewhere, as if he were waiting for Marcus to pop up again behind me.

I realized that Lucius was still speaking, and I hadn't heard a word that he had said, so distracted was I by Marcus's unexpected presence.

"I'm sorry, what did you say, Lucius?" I asked, refocusing my attention on the old man with a small, polite smile. I realized my heart was beating too quickly, and I felt a shiver run down my spine knowing that Marcus was somewhere behind me, no matter how far away he was inside the villa.

"I was commenting on how well you look, my dear, now that you are no longer with child," he repeated.

I froze, staring at him. Did he have no idea what had transpired a little over a month ago, when my newborn son had been taken from me?

He continued, "Women just look *so* unhappy when they're pregnant, so shapeless and so… so… heavy! Alas, I suppose it is a sacrifice we all must make to produce the future sons of Rome. How is your child, anyway? You have a boy, I hope?"

I realized, then, that no one had told him anything. He had tried to visit before and had been turned away, seemingly without explanation. I could not be angry with him, since he did not know, but the wound of my unjustly lost child was still raw, and I felt my eyes begin to well with tears.

"Oh, my dear, I'm sorry." Lucius realized that he had upset me, although he did not yet know why. "Did you lose the child? It happens quite often, as I am sure you know. We must be robust about it, as life does go on."

I shook my head at him, finally finding my voice. "My son was healthy, alive and well. He was taken from me on the orders of my grandfather, the emperor, and killed, lest he become a threat to the succession." I spat out the final words. Better that I had never been born into such a wretched family.

Even Lucius recognized then that he had been incredibly out of order, although unknowingly, and his face paled. He didn't stay much longer, only uttering a few words about how he hoped I was enjoying the little sparrow he had brought me, then rushing back to his own villa on the neighboring island as quickly as he could make an excuse to leave. He did not stay for lunch.

Drained, I retreated to my bedroom, with Titus, my shadow, following behind to stand guard. He was the only one who heard my anguished cries, but he dared not comfort me when the others might see.

CHAPTER XXIII

OVID

Ovid had established his residence in coastal Tomis, on the edge of the Black Sea, shortly after his arrival. A modest *domus* in town had graciously been granted to him by Aulus Caecina Severus, the governor of Moesia, under whose watchful eye Ovid was to spend his banishment. The governor had even gifted the exile a small household to serve him so that the poet would not have to manage entirely on his own, which was just as well; back in Rome, Fabia had overseen their household slaves, always making certain that her husband was comfortable, fed, and happy. He had little idea how to cook or launder his own clothing.

Despite this small stroke of fortune, it still made Ovid's blood boil that, of all the places he could have been sent, the emperor had specifically selected this location. Nearly two months in Tomis had done little for his adjustment, and Ovid resented the settlement just as much as he had the very day he arrived, sweaty, tired, and feverish from a mysterious illness that in truth, due to his distress, he may have half imagined.

Barbarian Thracians and Dacians stomped about the city in their silly, slouching hats, the stench of meat and animal skins emanating from them in an alarmingly wide radius that suggested they had little idea of the benefits of bathing. What Greeks remained in the city so long after its foundation were now cowed by the presence of the barbarians, threatened by their proximity even though the Roman soldiers on hand reassured everyone that the settlement, its wider region, and all those contained therein were now allies or subjects of Rome.

In his writing, Ovid freely lamented the mistake that had led to his exile, but, he maintained, it was one that had stemmed from naivety, not from malicious intent. *Certainly* he never would have been involved in open, violent rebellion against Augustus, as the emperor's own family members had been plotting; he had simply neglected to speedily report a few tidbits of information that had innocently made their way to him. What Ovid would not admit was that he had been hoarding such knowledge until he felt it was an opportune time to promote his own interests; it was a pesky habit that even dear Fabia had been unable to break him of.

When Ovid wasn't pitying himself, he spent his time writing, composing and editing all manner of poems and letters to be dispatched to his wife. He would refuse to divulge it, if there had been anyone around who cared to ask him, but the scenery was not quite so bad as he was leading his future readers to believe: the small residence in which he was situated had a nice view of the sea—once one was able to look past the barbarians—and the autumn breeze was a refreshing contrast to the city-stink of Rome. But, Ovid was a creature of the *urbs*, and so he set his sights on securing a recall from exile at any cost.

He was in the middle of his most recent poem, praising the emperor Augustus, when the sudden wailing of a baby interrupted him. Sighing, he rested his pen, waiting for the aggravating noise to cease; he wouldn't be able to focus until silence was restored.

The source of the cries was one of his house slave's children. The woman had produced twins not long before his arrival, whom he jokingly thought of as Romulus and Remus. Irreverent, perhaps, but amusing to him nonetheless.

The second infant had now been set off by its brother, and both of them were screaming in tandem. It was as if they wanted to drive him insane.

"Shut those brats up!" he yelled, hoping that the house slave, Galla, would hear him and do something about her cursed babies.

Their native-born Dacian father, Didas, was now a *libertus*, or freedman, who still worked for the household, saving to buy his children and his lover out of bondage so that they could be a proper, legal family. He was now out in the city, purchasing some needed supplies. Otherwise, Didas would have made certain Galla kept a better eye on their offspring, to avoid upsetting Ovid. The poet would be perfectly within his rights to cast the infants out.

More time passed, and still the little brats were screaming. Ovid pushed away from his desk, striding swiftly out of the room as he headed towards the source of the noise. The house was modest enough that it took him only seconds to reach the small room shared by Galla and Didas, where the swaddled babies had been left, alone.

Although Ovid was a father and grandfather himself, by way of his ex-wife—Fabia's predecessor—he had never dealt with childcare. His only regular, paternal involvement in his young daughter's life had been some adjustments to her education and, when the time came, the organization of an appropriate marriage for her. Ovid suspected the infants had soiled themselves or were hungry, complaints that he was both unable and unwilling to address, even if he did sympathize with their relatively helpless state—he himself felt much the same in his exile.

"Galla!" he called out again.

A few moments later, a heavyset slave woman appeared, slightly out of breath.

"Where were you?" Ovid asked accusingly. "These brats of yours have been screaming for quite some time now, and I am attempting to work on some *very* important materials. See to them immediately, or I will have them thrown out onto the city's trash heap." The threat was cold but half-hearted; Ovid was already redirecting his attention to his work.

"Yes, *dominus*," came Galla's meek response. She knew that no excuse, however valid, would be acceptable to the poet.

The poet turned on his heel and retreated to his workspace, sighing in relief as the upset infants finally quieted with their mother's presence. Picking up his pen, he resumed where he had left off, praising the emperor:

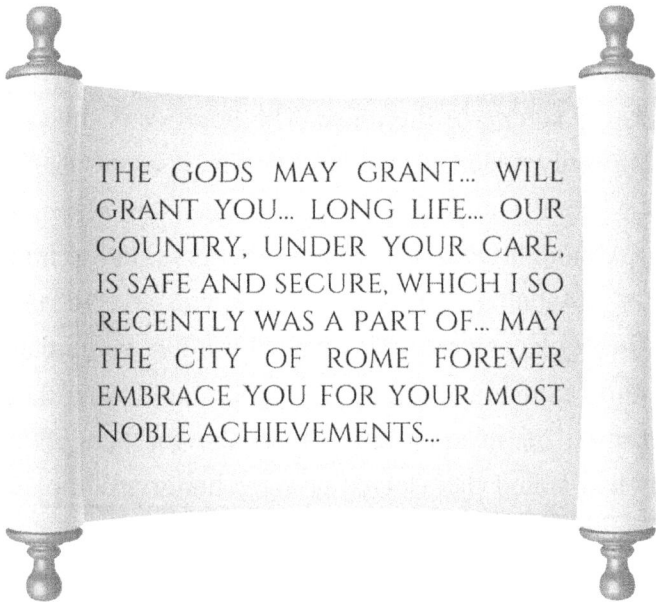

THE GODS MAY GRANT... WILL GRANT YOU... LONG LIFE... OUR COUNTRY, UNDER YOUR CARE, IS SAFE AND SECURE, WHICH I SO RECENTLY WAS A PART OF... MAY THE CITY OF ROME FOREVER EMBRACE YOU FOR YOUR MOST NOBLE ACHIEVEMENTS...

They were a few lines amongst many, all in a similar vein, praising the emperor as if he were a living god. Ovid could only hope his words might have some effect on the emperor when they reached him; it was his only chance to return to the life he knew.

Tucked underneath Ovid's ode to Augustus lay a poem dedicated to his wife, both a reassurance to her of his love and a silent promise that he would do whatever was necessary to return to her. The words were written out more clearly than those about the emperor, as if they had been composed with a greater degree of certainty, a greater degree of devotion. Faintly, it made Ovid recall why he had been so drawn to poetry in the first place, against the wishes of his father: it had been for love, and there was no greater calling.

CHAPTER XXIV

JULIA THE YOUNGER

I returned from my morning walk, flanked by Aphrodite and Publius as I entered the atrium. Titus and I had decided that I should spend more time with the slave girl, as well as with the only other guard whose presence I could currently bear, lest Quintus, or anyone else, become suspicious of our frequent contact with one another.

Considering the commander's role in the death of my son and his subsequent, understandable desire to maintain a sense of calm civility in our little island community, I doubted Quintus would dare to broach such a subject with me, even if he did question the extent of my relationship with one of his guards. Nevertheless, Titus and I needed to err on the side of caution. I did not think I could survive the inevitable heartbreak if we were found out.

"*Domina?*" Aphrodite prompted me, her eyes downcast and hands held out in front. She was requesting the shawl I had draped over my shoulders. I removed the garment and wordlessly passed it to the slave girl. She disappeared down the hall to return the clothing to its proper place in my bedroom.

The days were growing increasingly chilly, and, for the first time in recent memory, I had wanted an extra layer for my excursion. Soon I would switch to my warmer, winter clothing made of thick wool, of which Aurelia had packed too much when she prepared for my *exilium*. The slave woman had acted as if I were being sent away to the furthest edge of the empire, some mysterious locale with an unknown climate, not to an Adriatic island with mildly cold weather. I doubted we would even see snow, come wintertime.

Still, I had taken pity on the little sparrow, whom I had long since banished to the atrium, and had Aphrodite move her cage back into my bedroom, where it was considerably warmer. The bird's chirping no longer reminded me of my poor baby's wailing, and her beady black eyes, always watching me, had looked increasingly lonely.

Once I seated myself on a couch, Publius settled himself in the corner of the atrium, preparing for a game of *latrunculi*. The question as to who his partner would be was answered when Titus entered the room, no doubt alerted to our return by Aphrodite's movement down the hallway.

"Mistress," Titus greeted me, accompanied by a quick bow of his head.

I could feel my eyes light up as the guard entered the room. My heartbeat quickened and my breath caught. Just as rapidly, I pushed these feelings down, admonishing myself, and I managed to keep my face bland and unimpressed. I reminded myself that I was no virginal girl to be excited by the mere sight of a soldier; I could not let my emotions betray me, not when others might see.

Just as I wondered what was taking Aphrodite so long, the slave girl returned to the atrium, looking slightly flushed.

"I am sorry, *domina*. I dropped some of your clothing when putting the shawl away." The poor girl looked genuinely horrified, and once again I was reminded that she was far out of her depth when it came to serving a Roman lady. It wouldn't surprise me if I had to organize my own clothing for the change of seasons, carefully boxing up my linen and cotton fabrics until they were needed again.

I waved my hand at her with a sigh. "No matter, Aphrodite. Bring me something to nibble on. Olives, perhaps, and some wine."

Aphrodite bobbed her head and scurried off to fulfill my command. In the meantime, I turned my attention to the game played by the two guards in the corner. They both appeared to be evenly matched, for the moment. Publius captured one of Titus's pieces, the latter guard laughing good-naturedly as his younger opponent grinned at his small, if temporary, victory. Within a few turns, Titus had evened the odds and then overtaken his comrade, whose smile had now slipped as he sought to recoup his losses.

After a few minutes, Aphrodite returned, bearing a small bowl of pitted olives and a cup of wine. She set both on the low table in front of me before retreating to stand behind the couch, remaining nearby should I need anything else.

I ate a few olives as I continued to watch the guards at their game of *latrunculi*, taking a sip of wine just as Titus captured another of Publius's pieces. Thinking it tasted a bit odd, I took a second, larger sip, rolling the liquid across my tongue before I swallowed. The wine still didn't taste right.

"Aphrodite, this wine tastes off. Was it only recently opened?" I sniffed the wine, but it smelled as it always did: fruity and faintly sour.

The slave girl spoke up. "Yes, *domina*. Monimos sampled it himself this morning and said that it was fine."

I snorted. Of course Monimos had *sampled* the wine, no doubt under the guise of quality control. I took one more sip of the wine, and it confirmed my two earlier tastings of it. I was not willing to finish the remainder.

"Remove it. And tell Monimos to throw out the rest of this batch. Something is wrong with it." I set my cup down and placed another olive on my tongue, hoping to rid myself of the wine's unpleasant aftertaste.

Aphrodite disappeared towards the kitchen with the offending drink, and I suddenly found myself feeling somewhat queasy and incredibly tired. I moved to put back the olive I had just picked up, my fingers shaking, but instead it dropped onto the floor, rolling away. My eyes struggled to track it as it disappeared amongst a scramble of geometric mosaic designs.

Titus and Publius seemed unaware that anything was wrong. They continued to play their game, and I could hear their laughter, but only as if it were far, far away from me, not in the corner of the same room. Thinking I just needed to rest, I went to fully recline on the couch, practically falling back onto the pillows instead of slowly and gracefully stretching my body out.

My stomach ached, a dull throbbing that was periodically broken by sharp bursts of pain, and my body felt as if it were slowly being engulfed in flames. A cold sweat broke out across my forehead, and the shaking that had started in my fingers spread throughout my arms and reached into my chest. I opened my mouth to call out for Titus, but I found that I couldn't speak. I could barely even emit a dry croak, a pathetic cry that would reach no one's ears. My throat was closing up, and very soon I wouldn't be able to breathe.

Managing to lift my head, fighting the dizziness that was consuming me, I saw Aphrodite peering at me from the hallway leading to the kitchen. The slave girl made no move towards me even as she took in my distress. Anxious tears ran down her face, and suddenly I understood what was happening. She had tried to poison me. I was dying.

Gasping for breath, I managed to fling my shaking hand out, knocking the bowl of olives to the ground. The resulting crash at last drew the attention of the guards, and suddenly there was a commotion of shouting and action. As I began to convulse in earnest, Titus dragged me from the couch to the floor, holding me tightly as I lost control over my body.

"What happened?" he was shouting at me over and over, but I could barely hear him. Publius stood nearby, watching with an expression of combined shock and horror as I felt my eyes roll back into my head, losing sight of my surroundings. Aphrodite had disappeared entirely.

I suddenly felt my body being turned to the side and then fingers were in my mouth, pressing themselves insistently down my throat. I retched and began to vomit, spewing out the morning meal I had ingested before my walk, as well as the more recent handful of olives and the few sips of wine. The wet mess splattered across the floor, a putrid mixture that resembled blood. Perhaps some of it was. The fingers pressed again and again, until my stomach was entirely empty, and I could only produce dry heaves that felt as if they tore apart my throat. Then I at last slipped into the welcoming darkness of unconsciousness.

Titus informed me later that I slept for three full days, and no one thought I would survive. My dreams, although I could not recall them once I woke, caused me to moan and speak aloud even as I remained unconscious, as if I were possessed. Names poured from my lips:

Paullus, my dead, treasonous husband; Aemilia, my daughter in Rome; Silanus, my betrayer; and Titus, my redemption.

Quintus was in an anxious frenzy, believing the emperor would blame him directly for what had happened; I had been exiled, not sentenced to death, and allowing me to be killed on his watch would be much the same as if he had murdered me himself. He made twice-daily sacrifices to all manner of gods for my quick and full recovery.

Publius had been the one to find Aphrodite's body. The slave girl had fled through one of the villa's windows with a kitchen knife, with which she must have planned either to defend or to kill herself before she could be captured, tortured, and executed. That would have been the only available course of action, given the situation. She had served the tainted wine, and then she had attempted to flee; her guilt was obvious, and her fate was sealed.

However, there had been nowhere for Aphrodite to escape, trapped as we all were on the island. It turned out that she did not ultimately have the courage to end her own life with her stolen weapon, slicing her wrists or plunging the knife into her heart as any respectable Roman would have done. Instead, Aphrodite had chosen to throw herself off the cliff's edge, from the very same place where I so often liked to sit.

Her body, mangled and bent, lay on the rocks below, her head violently smashed in by the fall. The blood, Publius had reported, was still fresh when he found her, although the crashing waves made quick work of cleaning up the scene. No effort was made to retrieve her corpse: a poisoner deserved no funerary rites. Better that her body become food for the more deserving creatures that dwelled on the sea's floor.

The main concern that ran through my mind was why Aphrodite had done it. I posed this question to Titus when he visited my bedside, but he was similarly clueless.

"Perhaps she was mad," he said with a shrug, but I could tell that he didn't believe his own suggestion. "Some slaves lose their minds. They can never forget their homes, their families, their lives before slavery. Eventually, they act rashly, in some ill-conceived plan for freedom."

"Why me, then? I've no control over these slaves' freedom. They aren't even mine. I am as trapped here as they are."

"Maybe she wanted to make a statement. I don't know." Titus shrugged again. I was getting tired of that gesture.

"Well, she certainly can't think she would have escaped. There isn't a single ship in port. There should be one arriving soon with our winter supplies, but she didn't even wait for that." I frowned. "She sealed her own fate, one way or another, without any clear reason." The entire thing was beyond perplexing, now that I had recovered enough to think about it all.

I had never done Aphrodite any harm. No one could accuse me of having been a cruel or harsh *domina*, who might have driven her to such an extreme and desperate act. In fact, I had been worried about her treatment, particularly at the hands of Monimos and Marcus. I even felt that I had, to some extent, tried to protect her once Aurelia had passed away and the girl had become my personal slave. The more time she had spent with me, the less time there was for her to be abused by others.

"Do you know what it is that she put in the wine?" I asked Titus.

He shook his head. "Whatever it was, we should thank the gods that she either misjudged the dose or didn't pick something deadly enough."

"Hmm." Something was tickling my mind, some vague memory that seemed related to all this, but I couldn't quite grasp onto it. My head was starting to ache and so, with a sigh, I let it go, at least for the time being. The danger was past; my would-be murderess was dead and gone.

"Quintus has already suggested that Artemis try to help you, in place of Aphrodite," Titus said, gauging my reaction. He looked unconvinced by the idea.

I shook my head, confirming his guess about my feelings on the topic. "I can manage well enough on my own. Aphrodite wasn't much help to me anyway. Although I assume Quintus will have to send a report back to Rome when the next ship arrives. Perhaps he will put in a request for another slave or two."

"Do you want another personal slave?" he asked. "Quintus could ask. I am sure your grandfather would want you to be comfortable, even here."

"No," I answered quickly. "No. I'm fine."

"Fair enough," Titus responded. "I wouldn't be surprised if one was sent anyway, once the emperor learns of what's happened."

A figure appeared in the doorway then, peering inside at us past the hanging that had been pulled over to one side. Publius.

"May I enter, mistress?" His voice was subdued, and the young man looked more somber than I had ever seen him.

I nodded, and Publius stepped into the room, briefly exciting the sparrow, who always looked to new visitors for a tidbit. Unamused by the energetic little bird, he wrung his hands for a moment, looking at the floor, and then back up at me.

"Speak if you have come to do so, Publius," Titus admonished the younger guard. "Otherwise, we should leave our mistress to her rest." He stood and moved away from me, taking a place beside his fellow soldier.

Publius swallowed. "I wanted to apologize, mistress. I should have been paying more attention. Perhaps I would have noticed something. We failed you." He hung his head; his shame was obvious.

I cleared my still-tender throat, preparing to speak. "Publius, don't blame yourself. No one could have known." My words seemed to reassure him, and he nodded at me, a hint of his usual smile playing across his lips.

Titus clapped Publius on the back and gestured the younger guard out the door. He remained a moment longer. "Do you need anything?" he asked me, eyes warm with concern.

I didn't answer. My headache was worsening, and my throat still felt raw and swollen from whatever it was Aphrodite had put in my wine; I hadn't been able to eat anything since I had awoken. Titus sensed that I needed to rest, and he left me in peace, dropping the door hanging into place. I slipped back into sleep even as he exited my bedroom.

When my eyes opened again, it was dark, and the villa was quiet. I saw that a pitcher of water and a cup had been left in my room close to the bed, and I rose to quench my thirst, my dry throat itching. My legs trembled as I took the few small steps necessary to reach the water; my hands trembled just as much as I poured the cool liquid into the waiting cup.

Just as I was about to take a sip, I hesitated. Ripples crossed the surface of the water as my hand continued to shake. I knew I was being ridiculous. Aphrodite was gone. No one was trying to kill me. Still, I set the cup down without drinking. I couldn't recall if it had been in the room when Titus had visited me earlier, and paranoia or not, I could not bring myself to drink it without knowing who had brought it and when.

I stepped quietly across my room. Pushing the door hanging back, I saw that the cot in the hallway was gone, and Titus was nowhere to be seen. I wasn't particularly surprised by this development, but

Titus's absence still wrenched my heart ever so slightly. I had grown used to him as my constant shadow, and knowing that he slept just outside my room had brought me a great sense of comfort ever since my son's abduction and murder at Quintus's hands. I would never forget how the commander had entered the room unannounced, his face set hard as a rock as he coldly carried out his orders.

No doubt it was Quintus who had ordered Titus to return to his normal sleeping arrangements, sharing a room with Marcus. I was certain the commander had only allowed Titus to shadow me for as long as he did in some sort of attempt to appease his own sense of guilt: at what he had done to me, and to my innocent child. Clearly, he had recovered from his shame and decided that Titus serving as my personal guard was no longer in line with protocol.

Grabbing a clean dress, I padded softly down the hall to the bath, craving the comfort of its warm water. After three days of unconsciousness, and then restless, fitful sleep, I wanted to bathe. I smelled vague traces of vomit on my dress and realized nobody had changed my clothes since Titus had forced his fingers down my throat, likely saving my life. Had he been a moment longer in his reaction, I might have died.

I went to push open the door to the bath's changing room but found it locked. On impulse, I knocked. A few moments passed, and then the door opened, a small amount of light from an oil lamp reaching my feet and illuminating the room enough for me to recognize its occupant. My impulse was rewarded: Titus was inside, a drying cloth wrapped low around his hips. For only a brief moment, he looked surprised to see me, and then the low heat of desire flooded his eyes.

Silently, I entered the changing room, Titus closing and locking the door again behind me. I was about to turn and interrogate him about the change in sleeping arrangements when he wrapped his arms around me from behind, and the desire to talk fled my body entirely.

CHAPTER
XXV

THE ELDER JULIA

No one had died in Rhegium's earthquake towards the end of the summer. Well, no one who mattered, anyway. The litter bearer who had been struck on the head by a falling stone did pass away, but in Julia's mind he didn't really count as *someone*; she hadn't even been certain of the slave's name. Naturally, the common people in the city below didn't count either, in Julia's estimation.

What concerned Julia more was that her little trip into town had unfortunately been relayed to her father. The emperor had dispatched a small group of trusted men to check on her wellbeing after news of the earthquake had reached him in Rome. Her own guards had done little to defend her, or themselves, when confronted with a barrage of questions regarding the incident.

As a result of her unapproved excursion, Julia's guards had all promptly been replaced, and the small pleasures that she had managed to stash away in the villa over time—namely a collection of fine wines and numerous dietary delicacies— were removed.

It was like reliving her initial, harsher exile to the island of Pandateria all over again. The emperor had been so furious with her then, laying out a list of simple foods she was allowed to consume, entirely banning her consumption of wine, and ordering her guards to remove what she considered to be all the interesting scrolls from the library. She had been a prisoner in every sense of the word, the accompanying soldiers harsh and strict in the enforcement of their orders.

Her father's anger had lessened after a handful of years, and eventually she had been allowed to return to the mainland, to Rhegium. Although she remained an exile, the conditions of her captivity were significantly improved. Now it appeared she had lost the small freedoms that she so recently had managed to regain.

Two of the fresh Praetorian Guards leered at Julia as she strolled the garden with Scribonia, and she scowled at them.

"Go suck my father's cock!" she hissed as she passed by. Their expressions did not change in the least.

Scribonia squeezed her daughter's arm in warning. "Don't make it worse, Julia. You know they'll report back to the emperor everything you say."

"I don't care." Julia was seething.

"You should. I'm still here. He could have forced me to leave you, kept me away from you. But he didn't."

Julia didn't answer, but not for lack of a clever retort. Instead, her attention had been drawn to the slave boy Felix, who had taken up some gardening tasks outside.

Although Felix primarily worked in the kitchen and ran errands for the cook, it wasn't odd in itself that he was gardening; the boy was used to picking up assorted jobs that sometimes fell through the cracks with the villa's limited household. What *was* odd were his subtle, repeated glances at Julia. He had something for her.

The guards still had their gazes fixed on Julia as she strolled the garden, and she knew she wouldn't be able to retrieve a note from the slave boy, if that was what he had brought. Luckily, in Julia's experience, Felix wasn't as stupid as most slaves—or most people, for that matter.

The two women paused by the slave boy, standing over him as he continued his work. Aware of the guards nearby, Julia spoke loudly enough for them to hear her. Better to make her interaction noticeable; quiet words and furtive glances would raise suspicions.

"Felix, isn't it?" she asked, her voice carrying. A glance to the side assured her that the guards had not changed their position.

"Yes, *domina*," Felix answered, pausing his work but keeping his eyes on the ground.

"Whatever are you bothering for with these plants over here? Winter is coming. They'll die soon enough anyway." It was true. The few remaining flowers in the garden were hanging limp, their petals already tinged brown at the edges.

Felix raised his glance ever so slightly to make eye contact with Julia. "It is their last chance to bloom, *domina*. In a week or two, *domina* will see the results and know if it has been successful. Change is coming, and with change can come good things, as *domina* knows." The slave boy, finished speaking, returned to his work.

"One would think you were a poet, Felix, you speak so eloquently. Carry on. I expect these results you have promised. Don't disappoint me." Julia continued her stroll, her mother following. The guards hadn't shifted a single step.

To them, Julia, bored with her captivity and lack of appropriate, patrician company, had just had a simple exchange with one of her slaves about the garden. But to Julia, a new wealth of information had just been communicated.

Felix had confirmed that the plans to rescue her children, Agrippa Postumus and Julia the Younger, were finally about to be enacted within the next week or two, before winter roughened the seas and prevented travel for the remainder of the year. In a very short amount of time, she would know at last if her plotting would result in a new, brighter future for them all. Julia was counting on success.

CHAPTER XXVI

JULIA THE YOUNGER

I hadn't yet returned to the cliff's edge where Aphrodite had thrown herself to her death. It was now another site of violence on the cursed island, which thus far had claimed three lives: Aurelia, my son, and the slave girl. I had very nearly joined that list.

The guards were alternating watch for the expected supply ship, which was due to arrive at any time. The sea was already growing rougher as each passing day brought winter nearer, and soon approach to the island would be much more difficult. Once the supplies arrived, we would not see a ship again until the spring, which would mark the completion of my first year in *exilium*.

It was hard to believe that so much time had passed, that so much had happened. Pregnant, I had been cast out from Rome by my grandfather, torn away from my family, my lover, and the only life I had ever known; all this, too, coming after my husband's execution for treason. I had survived an accident at sea and a poisoning attempt, but I had lost Aurelia, whom I had known for almost as long as I had been alive, and had my son torn from my arms so soon after his birth. So much of my life seemed to have vanished, including, I realized, a large part of my own identity.

Publius, unaware of my musings, lounged in the grasses at the highest point of the island, taking his turn to watch for the arrival of the supply ship. He hummed quietly. I had opted to join him, with Titus, as usual, accompanying me to make for a group of three.

Quintus, understanding that I wanted little to do with him or Marcus as a result of their involvement in my son's execution—for that's what it was—did not press the issue of either of them ever having more direct interaction with me. Besides, as always, there was nowhere to escape; the presence of the guards was, in many ways, nominal at best.

"Do you have any family, Publius?" I asked suddenly. It occurred to me that despite the amount of time we had all spent together on Trimerus, I still knew little about the young, chubby-faced guard.

He grinned at my question. "Indeed I do, mistress. My older sister, Publia, is married with a few little children, although they're probably much bigger than I remember. It's been a few years since I've seen them all."

"They're in Rome?"

The young guard shook his head. "Herculaneum, near to Pompeii. They run a small shop. Merchants."

"You'd be a terrible merchant," Titus chimed in, briefly stopping work on the chunk of wood he was carving up with a small dagger. "You're far too nice. Everyone would talk you into giving away your goods for free."

Publius laughed. "As usual, you're probably right."

"Why did you become a soldier?" I asked, waving off the men's joking. I found myself genuinely curious. In my past life in Rome, I had had little interest in the common people of the empire and, as a result, little knowledge of them.

"The women," Titus answered for his fellow guard, causing both of them to laugh again.

"No, no," Publius finally said, once their laughter had subsided. "In part, I was inspired by the stories of Julius Caesar. My father taught me to read, using Caesar's tales from the Gallic War. I grew up on them."

"That's it?" I was disappointed, having expected something more insightful, perhaps more romantic even.

Publius shrugged. "In truth, mistress, being a military man means guaranteed work and, for the most part, reliable pay. It's a tough life at times, but it offers security. When my service is done, I'll have the chance to settle somewhere, maybe have a small farmstead. Or maybe I'll join my sister and her husband in Herculaneum and become a merchant. Only the gods know."

Titus had resumed work on his chunk of wood, cutting away small pieces of it, and our short conversation ended as Publius refocused his attention on the horizon and resumed his humming. I was content to soak up the remainder of the afternoon sun, gracing us with its presence before winter would soon suck away its lingering warmth.

After an hour or so of companionable silence, Publius stood up, his gaze fixed in the distance. "Titus, do you see that?"

Titus paused in his work, leaving the small wooden figure on the ground as he got to his feet. The chunk of wood was starting to resemble something, but I couldn't with any certainty tell what, half-covered as it was by grasses.

Shading his eyes, Titus looked in the direction indicated by Publius. "What? I don't see anything."

"Right there." Publius pointed again.

There was a long pause before Titus finally answered. "I see it now."

"What is it?" I asked, unable to see anything at all.

"*That* is our supply ship," Publius responded cheerfully. "Hopefully laden with plenty of wine to get us through winter in this shithole."

I blinked at Publius's foul language, more surprised than offended, and, as Titus sharply smacked his fellow guard on the arm, he realized his mistake.

"Apologies, mistress." Publius looked meek, his face red. "I don't know how to behave in civilized company."

I laughed, and Publius rewarded me with a smile, although his cheeks were still flushed. Titus just shook his head, resigned.

"They won't make it here before nightfall," Titus mused, eyeing the distant ship once more. "They'll anchor out in the sea and approach in the morning, when there's enough light. No sense in rushing the final stretch and hitting the rocks. They've already taken long enough, and we won't run out of wine in one more night."

Publius trotted ahead of us to the villa in order to alert Quintus to the supply ship's arrival, leaving Titus and me to meander back at a slower pace together.

"What are you making?" I gestured to the wooden figure clutched in his fist.

Titus lifted his hand, his fingers uncurling to reveal the wooden object resting in his palm. It was a dolphin.

"Oh," I breathed, reaching out to touch it. Instead, Titus pressed it into my hand, and I gently stroked the rough wood.

"It still needs some smoothing out," he said.

"It's beautiful. Why a dolphin?"

Titus appeared to be blushing. "They appeared around you that day, when you were trying to swim back to the island after the accident in the boat. And then again, the first time we…" he trailed off, and I knew he was remembering the first time we had kissed.

"I'm not a very religious man, but I do recognize the power of the gods, and it seems clear to me that Neptune favors you. Think of this as a small charm, a token of good luck, in his name."

I closed my fingers around the wooden figure. "Thank you."

While I didn't believe that Neptune, or any of the other gods, favored me, I still appreciated the gesture, especially because it came from Titus. I had very few belongings of personal value or sentiment, but the little wooden dolphin immediately became one of them.

When we reached the villa, the three other guards were gathered together in the atrium, and a general feeling of anticipation hung in the air. Although the arrival of a supply ship carrying wine, food stuffs, and perhaps some other odds and ends from the mainland, including letters, would not ordinarily have been cause for celebration in my previous life, even I felt a twinge of excitement at the prospect of a change of pace from our daily habits on the island.

Artemis and Monimos were both scurrying back and forth from the kitchen to the atrium, bringing out seemingly endless jugs of wine and platters of food that were a level above our typical fare. With the pending arrival of new goods, they could afford to be less than frugal. Despite the small number of vegetables and fruits that were grown in the villa's gardens, and its handful of stocked fishponds, a not insignificant portion of our better meals still depended upon the supplies sent from Rome.

Two chickens, kept for eggs until now, had been freshly slaughtered and presented in the Parthian style, seasoned with caraway and mixed with dates; fish of several types had also been prepared, roasted and basted with an added touch of olive oil and a light sprinkling of salt. Artemis placed out a bowl of my favorite *moretum*, a cheesy spread with herbs, which the guards, between all four of them, promptly devoured; I only managed to get a few mouthfuls. Monimos next delivered an oil-drenched salad and soft-boiled eggs in a pine nut sauce, just as Artemis returned with a large bowl of lentils, flavored with some of the valuable spices we had brought with us from Rome in the spring.

The more proper setting for our decadent little feast would have been the *triclinium*, but I think all of us wanted to enjoy the last vestiges of warmth in the atrium before winter forced us into thicker clothing and into the more easily heated, closed-off rooms of the villa. When they were done serving, even Monimos and Artemis were invited to join us and excused from refilling empty wine goblets; it was as if Saturnalia, the winter festival associated with general merrymaking and revelry amongst all classes, had come early.

As night fell in earnest, the moon and stars shone brightly into the atrium, illuminating the scene so that the few flickering oil lamps spaced throughout were hardly needed. The sense of celebration, of joyousness, had never before been before in the villa; laughter and jokes abounded, and even stony-faced Quintus appeared relaxed for the first time in memory.

Even after all that I had been through in recent months, I surprised myself that I could take pleasure in the celebration; I was actually enjoying the evening. I reveled in a sense of freedom that was both new to me and ironic, considering my state of imprisonment, of exile. I never would have guessed, only a year ago, that I would find any level of companionship with slaves and Praetorian Guards on a remote island.

Everyone had had far too much to drink. Monimos and Artemis had disappeared, presumably back to the kitchen, while Publius and Marcus had become embroiled in a loud and argumentative game of *latrunculi* in the corner. Quintus, his large frame awkwardly draped over a couch, had fallen asleep and was snoring rather loudly.

Titus stood from his own couch and made a show of stretching and yawning, glancing at his drunken peers in the corner before subtly gesturing to me with a nod of his head. He disappeared down the hallway leading towards the bedrooms, and after a few minutes I followed, Titus's wooden dolphin figurine still clutched in my hand. Marcus and Publius were too drunk and too distracted to notice our absence.

The noise from the guards' game followed me faintly as I moved away from the light of the atrium. I stepped farther down the hallway into darkness, my eyes attempting to adjust as I searched for Titus. Suddenly, I found myself pushed against a wall, lips pushing insistently against mine as familiar stubble brushed across my cheek.

"Took you long enough," Titus's voice was rough and impatient as he broke our kiss to speak.

I didn't answer, instead choosing to close the distance between us once again, my tongue teasing his. I was rewarded with a low groan, and Titus's body pushed mine back against the wall with more force, his knee forcing itself between my legs.

Thinking I heard a noise from the atrium, I broke away from him. "What was that?" I asked, breathless.

Titus stilled, trying to calm his own breathing as he listened. "Nothing. Just Publius and Marcus at their game."

I wasn't so certain, but his mouth was back on me, teasing my neck with small, gentle bites followed by soft, soothing kisses. I moaned, feeling my legs weaken beneath me.

"Let's go somewhere else," I managed to say, even as Titus's focus shifted downwards on my body and he sank to his knees. "Titus!" I hissed at him insistently, and he looked up at me with a cheeky grin.

"Fine. This way." He stood and, leading me by the hand, started off down the hallway, with a brief stop for me to put the wooden dolphin in my bedroom so that I wouldn't lose it.

We reached the end of the hallway, where a large window was cut into the wall above our heads, its shutters tightly closed for the night. Titus, instructing me to stay where I was, disappeared, returning in a few brief moments with a chair, which he positioned in front of the window. He set about standing on it, swaying slightly as he opened the shutters. Moonlight suddenly flooded into the hall, bathing Titus in its silver glow.

After some awkward maneuvering and a fit of laughter, Titus boosted me through the window; in short order, he followed, landing in the grass with a soft thump.

"How are we going to get back in?" I asked, suddenly worried.

"Don't worry. Marcus and Publius are so drunk that they'll pass out soon and be none the wiser. I unlatched the villa's main doors earlier this evening, and I doubt they'll notice." Titus looked pleased with himself.

I raised an eyebrow at him. "You're cleverer than I give you credit for."

Titus smiled again, more relaxed than I had ever seen him. The god Bacchus had worked his magic on all of us through his wine. "I know."

Warmed by drink, we took off for the sandy beach we had walked together some time ago, where we had first acted on our passionate impulses and shared more kisses than I could recall. Laughing and stumbling, we found ourselves leaving a trail of clothing as we headed across the sand.

Tripping again, I found myself caught by Titus, who gently laid me down on the sand. Under the moonlight, the sound of crashing waves mingled with the noise of our lovemaking.

CHAPTER XXVII

AGRIPPA POSTUMUS

Agrippa lay in bed, studying the ceiling. He had been untied at last and, sick of being on his stomach night and day, had decided to switch positions. The shift caused him to wince as his burned back made contact with the bed, but the recently applied bandages provided some cushioned relief.

Although the bedroom had originally housed a handful of guards, he had forced them to switch spaces with him once he caught sight of the beautifully painted scenes of Neptune that decorated its walls and ceiling. The commander of the guards had been accommodating at the time, recognizing Agrippa's superior station and ordering his men to clear out. Now, the youth doubted that the commander would so much as offer him the choicest piece of fish. Time had worn away their sense of protocol, eroded what little respect they still held for him.

In one of the ceiling's painted scenes, Neptune was pulled in a chariot by unruly seahorses; in another, the longhaired, bearded god conquered a monster with his trident; and in a third, he was accompanied by his *paredrae*, Salacia and Venilia, themselves minor deities of the sea.

Movement by the door drew Agrippa's attention. It was one of the guards who had been made responsible for changing Agrippa's bandages—but Agrippa was not in the mood.

"Later," he said, his gaze already shifting back to the ceiling.

The guard retreated wordlessly. He knew better than to antagonize the youth.

Structurally, the villa had suffered little damage in the fire started by Agrippa. The blaze, once it had eaten the entirety of the library's scrolls, had mostly fizzled out on its own, helped along by the buckets of water brought by the small army of guards, as well as the incessant downpour from the sky above.

Apparently, one of the guards had even taken it upon himself to tackle the emperor's grandson to the floor, beating out the fire on his body; Agrippa remembered none of it. The guard had probably saved Agrippa's life, but there would be no thanks given to the commoner.

Movement at the door again distracted him. He sighed angrily, prepared to lose his temper. "I said *later*, you stupid fool."

A body crashed to the ground in his room, dark blood pouring onto the mosaicked floor from an open wound in its chest. The guard who had been there only moments earlier was dead.

The sudden noise of shouting and fighting reached Agrippa's ears. Something was happening. He sat up, swinging his legs over the edge of the bed just as a new figure entered the room. The man was armored, but his gear was distinctly un-Roman; Agrippa couldn't place it exactly, but it was, perhaps, Gallic. The man's sword, free of its scabbard, shone with blood, and the figure peered at Agrippa.

"You are Agrippa Postumus?" he asked. "Grandson of Augustus?" He spoke in Latin, but it was heavily accented.

Agrippa nodded, for once in his life struggling to find words. "Are you here to kill me?"

The man, who Agrippa noted was incredibly tall, threw back his head and roared his laughter, an eerie sound that rose above the screams and yells of bloodshed in the villa behind him. "No, we are here to rescue you. Come with me, boy."

Agrippa didn't pause to ask questions or to think twice. He stood from the bed, wincing as his burns stung his body again, and pulled on a tunic before he followed the giant into the hallway.

They headed towards the atrium, passing a handful of dead and dying men. Some of them were Agrippa's guards, others were members of his rescuer's party, whoever they were. The youth stooped to grab a sword from one his fallen guard's hands; the man, still barely alive, resisted, blood spewing from his mouth, but Agrippa simply kicked him in the stomach, wrenching the sword free.

"Who sent you?" he asked his new ally, having to shout over the sounds of conflict as he followed along. "I demand to know." Perhaps this was connected to Rufus and his mysterious master.

The man laughed at him, and Agrippa frowned. He did not abide laughter at his expense. "I command you now, tell me on whose orders you are here." Agrippa's hand tightened on the sword he held, but his rescuer did not seem concerned. The underestimation was another strike against the warrior.

The giant man made quick work of cutting down one of Agrippa's guards, but another surged forward from the side, slicing him across the back. He groaned in pain, turning to engage the newcomer, while Agrippa stood by, ignored by everyone.

The youth looked around as the men fought, noting the casualties on both sides, as well as the few ongoing skirmishes. It seemed that his guards were winning, beating back the attackers. He caught sight of Rufus stabbing an intruder through the stomach, and the red-haired guard shouted at Agrippa to hide somewhere before he turned to engage another enemy.

Clearly, whatever was happening was *not* part of Rufus's plan.

Agrippa hefted the sword in his hand, eyeing his large, would-be rescuer and the guard who fought him. Making a decision, he swung out, cutting the large man across his neck from behind, instantly felling him. For good measure, he stood over his body, stabbing into it several more times, hot blood spraying up into his face. He laughed.

When he was done, he saw the rest of his guards had claimed victory over their own opponents, and they were catching their breath, watching him with expressions ranging from bewilderment to horror. Rufus was the only one whose face remained unreadable.

Agrippa dropped his sword and headed towards the villa doors, a few guards trailing wordlessly behind while others checked the bodies of the attackers for any signs of life. Many of those who still breathed were dispatched without hesitation. One or two of them would likely be kept alive for torture, to see if any more information could be found out.

Standing outside, the wind whipping his hair and clothing, Agrippa could see the distant port. From it, a ship was sailing away in a hurry, a few figures rushing about on its deck.

As if unperturbed, he turned and headed back inside the villa, fighting a wince as the pain of his burns, masked earlier by the rush of adrenaline, returned to him.

The current commander of the guards greeted him in the atrium, where the bodies of the deceased were being sorted into two piles: the honorable fallen and the enemy. The former would be given funerary rites, while the latter would most likely be tossed into the sea without ceremony.

"Why didn't you try to run?" the commander asked him. The remaining guards all paused in their work, wanting to hear his answer.

Rufus looked particularly intent.

"He disrespected me," Agrippa answered, gesturing towards the corpse of the giant man who had found him in his room. The commander only blinked at him. "And, upon examination, it seemed that your men by far had the upper hand. Had you been losing, I gladly would have joined in with the attackers to kill you." He shrugged. "It's a matter of odds, isn't it?"

With another laugh, Agrippa, still blood-spattered, headed back towards his room. Lying down on the bed, he resumed his study of the ceiling as if nothing at all had happened.

CHAPTER XXVIII

JULIA THE YOUNGER

Drip. Drip. Drip. I turned my face to the side, trying to evade the annoying, constant trickling, but suddenly it was harder and faster; soon, my entire face was streaked with water. I shivered, my body alarmingly cold.

Opening my eyes sleepily, I blinked up at the weak morning sun. A gull was flying overhead, calling out as it retreated to its nest. The rain was falling harder, and it looked as if a storm was brewing. Titus was still sound asleep next to me, lying naked on his stomach in the sand. I grabbed his arm.

"Titus, wake up." He didn't stir, so I shook him. "Titus," I said, louder.

The guard started, looking confused as he awakened. When he realized where we were, and what time it was, alarm flooded his eyes, and he cursed.

"We need to hurry," he said, already standing and in the process of redressing himself. He tossed bits and pieces of my clothing to me. "It's very early. Considering how drunk everyone was, they may all still be asleep."

I pulled my dress over my head without responding, then quickly slipped on my shoes. If they weren't asleep, if we were found out…. Titus, sensing my worry, paused. He cupped my face in his hands as he looked down at me.

"It will be alright." He sounded so sincere, so certain. I believed him.

I nodded, and we set off, rushing across the beach back towards the villa even as the rain began to fall harder, soaking us to our skin. Just as lightning struck and thunder boomed, we reached the villa's doors, and we were relieved to find they had remained unlatched throughout the night and into the morning. Perhaps we would escape detection after all.

The atrium was still messy; Monimos and Artemis had not yet cleaned up. The game of *latrunculi* lay half-finished in the corner, its black and white pieces still stationed across the board, but Publius and Marcus, its most frequent players, were absent. The couch on which Quintus had fallen asleep was empty, the pillows left askew. We were alone.

"Go to your room and rest," Titus whispered. "The supply ship will be arriving today, but we should have some time before we need to be presentable." The ship wouldn't just be delivering supplies; it would serve as a check on my existence, on my continued *exilium* on Trimerus. In addition to whatever reports Quintus might send to the emperor, our visitors would also make note of their own impressions.

Nodding, I set off towards the hallway of bedrooms, but I stopped in my tracks when Marcus emerged from the shadows. He looked exhausted and still half-drunk, but his eyes shone with animosity. His disfigured nose remained red and swollen.

"Hello, you two," he greeted us with a taunting tone. "Had a nice night, did we?"

In barely a second, Titus had surged forward, standing

protectively in front of me.

"She wanted to go for a walk this morning, before it rained," Titus lied.

Marcus laughed. "Liar. I've suspected for some time now that things weren't quite… *right*… between you and the whore of Rome here." Titus tensed as if prepared to strike his fellow guard, but Marcus seemed either oblivious or uncaring.

"I saw you two disappear down the hallway. I saw the chair by the window. And, all night, I saw your empty beds. I considered latching the door, locking you outside, so that Quintus could find you in the morning himself, but…" Marcus trailed off, shrugging.

"Where are the others?" Titus asked, wondering about Quintus and Publius. Feeling sick to my stomach, I leaned against the wall, using it to hold myself up. Did they all know?

"They've gone down to the port to await the supply ship. It's funny, really. Neither of them even noticed your absence, not yet. I was instructed to stay here with you and the whore. Such an outstanding, observant commander we have." Titus and I were silent, but a small measure of hope surged within me: only Marcus had found us out. Perhaps Quintus wouldn't believe him. "Aren't you going to ask me why I didn't tell Quintus about your little love affair?"

Titus practically growled. "Why?"

Marcus laughed. "Because I wanted you both to be here when I humiliated you."

Titus moved as if to punch the other guard, but he caught himself at the last second, which only caused Marcus to laugh again. Titus reached back and grabbed my hand, pulling me down the hallway with him. Marcus's mocking laughter followed us, but the guard did not move.

When we were alone, I realized that I had been crying. Tears ran down my face.

"Quintus won't believe Marcus," I suggested hopefully. "He knows that Marcus dislikes me, especially after I ruined his nose. We can convince him it's all a lie."

Titus was shaking his head. "No." I was about to speak again, but Titus cut me off. "No. Marcus is not a good person, but he has always been a good soldier. Quintus has no reason *not* to believe him. He trusts him."

"What are we going to do, then?" I asked, my panic growing. "We can't just… just…" I was fumbling for words. "We can't just *admit* to it! You'll be executed!"

Titus was smiling sadly, and he reached out a hand to my face, a single finger wiping away a fresh tear that rolled down my cheek. "Quintus isn't as harsh as you think he is. He's done some bad things, yes, but he isn't a bad man. At worst, I will be discharged from service without my retirement. At best, I will be reassigned to some backwater province. I don't think he would rat me out to your grandfather."

"But you don't *know* that," I seethed. "He *killed* my son! My newborn infant, without even a name." I was crying fresh tears. "You can't leave me. You can't leave me."

His arms were around me then, holding me tightly. "Shh," he breathed into my hair, stroking my back.

Eventually, I managed to pull myself together. "What do we do?" I asked. This time I was ready to listen. There wasn't much time.

"Go clean up. I'll do the same. And then we will oversee the arrival of the supplies, and we will face Quintus. Because it's what must be done. We don't have a choice."

Feeling numb, I nodded, stumbling away from Titus to my

bedroom. I found a clean, appropriate dress and pinned my hair up in place. I could do little to counteract my splotchy face and red eyes.

We reconvened in the atrium not long after. The room was freshly tidied by Monimos and Artemis, all traces of the previous night's celebration now gone. The growing storm was sending rivets of rain through the open part of the roof, and the heightening winds caused stray droplets to strike the mosaicked floor that ringed the central pool. Thunder boomed again.

Marcus was sprawled lazily on a couch, his face the most cheerful I had ever seen it. Pettily, I was pleased to see his injured nose in better light, and I hoped that it would remain painful and ugly for the remainder of his wretched life.

The villa doors were suddenly pushed open, and Quintus and Publius led a group of seven dripping wet men inside out of the growing storm. All wore sensible brown tunics with short swords attached at their hips, just as my own guards did, and had their hair cut in typical, short military fashion. There was no sign of the supplies.

Quintus, I noticed, looked uneasy, although it didn't help that he was clearly suffering from the previous night's festivities. Perhaps he was simply hungover, and I was misreading his expression.

"Are the supplies following?" Titus asked, having noticed the same things I did.

Quintus shook his head, the trace of a frown tugging at his lips. "It's not a supply ship. These men have orders from the emperor to release his granddaughter into their care. It appears that her *exilium* has ended. She has been recalled to Rome."

I felt faint. "What did you say?" My voice trembled, but I wanted to hear it said again.

Quintus lifted up a crisp document. "The orders are here. The emperor has placed his seal upon the document himself. You are to return to Rome immediately."

I marched over to the commander and snatched the leaf of papyrus from him, wanting to examine it for myself up close. I couldn't believe that this was happening, that my grandfather had relented.

All thoughts of Marcus exposing my affair with Titus flew from my mind. Instead, I imagined seeing my daughter Aemilia again, and my sister, Agrippina. I would be there to watch my daughter become a bride and, perhaps, a mother herself. I would have all my clothes, my jewelry, restored to me. I could go to the games and the theater, to the circus and the market. I would have the newest literature at my fingertips, the best and most exotic foods. My life could return to normal, despite everything that had happened.

As I raised the papyrus up to look at it, to read the fortunate words myself, I noticed that the newcomers were watching my own guards warily. All seven of them had their hands resting on their swords, as if they expected trouble. Why? They were Roman soldiers amongst their comrades. They had nothing to fear here.

Returning to the document, I noted that it had been written by a scribe; I would have recognized my grandfather's personal handwriting. Still, that was typical enough; Augustus often had someone else write down his thoughts, his commands. It stated that I was immediately restored to my position and recalled to Rome by the emperor. I was to join the squadron of Praetorian Guards he had sent with the orders, who would escort me on my journey. The words were a godsend.

But the document's seal was wrong. It showed the head of Alexander the Great, a design that the emperor had replaced shortly before I had been exiled in the spring. The seal should have been a portrait of my grandfather himself. I had seen it with my own eyes on the fateful letter that had called me to Augustus's presence, so that he could cast me out by his own hand, with his own searing words.

I let the hand holding the papyrus fall to my side as I looked again at the seven strangers. Their posture had not relaxed at all. Something was wrong.

Deciding to announce that the seal was incorrect and to demand an explanation before I placed myself in the care of these outsiders, I made eye contact with one of the new men. As if he sensed that I was about to raise the alarm, he pulled his sword from its scabbard in one smooth motion and attacked the guard closest to him: Publius.

I felt as if it all happened in slow motion. Publius, who had been standing there, relaxed, was cut down before I could even blink. I could see the shock in his bright, blue eyes as he saw his own blood spill onto the floor, his hands clutching the gaping wound in his belly as he fell to his knees.

Pandemonium ensued. The newcomers, prepared for a fight, rushed my guards, who were taken completely by surprise. I felt the document drop from my hands, a distant part of my mind realizing that it had been a forgery. I was not being recalled from my *exilium*; my grandfather had not sent those orders. Without knowing who had, I did not intend to place my fate in the hands of strangers. I would not be a pawn in yet another political game, no matter whose it was.

The papyrus floated to the floor, softly landing in Publius's blood, which had seeped across the atrium. As if it were an unstoppable crimson tide, it soaked the papyrus through, next reaching my sandaled feet. Publius was lying on the ground, his eyes wide open in the fixed stare of death as his fellow guards strained to expel the enemy from the villa.

Someone grabbed me, and I screamed, slipping in Publius's

227

blood. In another second, the hand that had been clutching my dress was cut off from its body, joining the mess on the atrium floor. The man to whom it had belonged fell, screaming, before Titus stabbed him in the throat, his life ending with one last gurgled cry.

Titus stooped to grab the fallen man's sword, which he then forced into my hand, wrapping my cold fingers around its hilt. I stared down at it uncomprehendingly. He was shouting at me, but I was too stunned, too shocked, to hear him. Titus shook me, and some sense finally returned to my body and to my mind.

"Run!" he was screaming. Crimson drops had splattered across his face, and his kind brown eyes were now wild. "Go through the window in the hallway!"

A blade caught Titus on the side, and he winced, turning to engage the new enemy even as wet blood blossomed across his tunic. I couldn't tell how badly he had been wounded.

Terrified, holding a sword that I did not know how to use, I took off, running away from the chaos of the atrium. My sandaled feet slipped in a puddle of blood, and I left a trail of smudged red footprints in my wake as I fled.

The chair which Titus had pushed under the window only the night before was still there. At first, I was shaking so much that I fell off of it, but the sounds of conflict carrying down the hallway pushed me to try again, and quickly. Needing both of my hands, I tossed the sword through the open window, my fingers grasping the ledge as I stood on the tips of my toes. Last night I had had Titus to help me. Now I was alone.

Groaning, I finally managed to half jump, half pull myself up and through the window, spilling out onto the wet grasses below with a violent thud. I landed uncomfortably close to the sword, which I picked up again with a shaking hand before I stood. The pounding rain quickly soaked through my clothing, and I couldn't tell if I trembled from the chill or from fear.

Without thinking twice, I started running towards the cliff's edge, to the same place where Titus and I had first made love, the same place where Aphrodite had thrown herself to her death after she had tried to poison me. I would hide there until this was all over and my guards had repelled the invaders. I refused to think that there might be another outcome.

I found a suitable niche of rocks and grasses and tried to hide, pulling my knees to my chest, trying to make myself small, invisible. I clutched the sword like a child, uncertain if I was capable of using it for its intended deadly purpose. Hopefully, I wouldn't have to.

The storm surged to its height, lightning striking all around and thunder booming. The island shook. This was the type of weather that convinced people of the power, and the fury, of the gods. I hoped that, if they were present now, they would favor my own guards.

I didn't know how much time had passed, but I thought I heard someone calling my name. I listened, but I didn't hear it again, and I convinced myself the storm was playing tricks on my mind.

Without warning, sandaled feet appeared before my hiding spot, and I yelped in surprise and fear. Just as I was about to lash out with the sword, I recognized Marcus. For the first time, I found myself relieved to see him, whatever our past history. As Titus had said, he might not be a good man, but he had always been a good soldier. His presence surely meant the skirmish at the villa had subsided, one way or another.

"What happened?" I asked him, standing up and brushing myself off. The hand with the sword dropped to my side. I realized that I was still shaking, and it wasn't only from the cold rain.

"Is Publius…" I trailed off, unable to finish my question when I already knew the answer. There was no way that Publius was still alive; I had seen his death stare with my own eyes. "Quintus? Titus?" I asked instead.

Marcus didn't answer, instead studying me with a surprisingly cold gaze.

"Marcus?" I said his name again, questioning.

I had no time to react. Marcus's fist surged forward, punching me in the face. I felt my nose crunch, and blood rushed forth. Yelling in pain, I bent over, dropping the sword to clutch my face with both hands. Marcus kicked me sharply in the side, and I fell to the ground. The impact knocked the wind from my body.

"Stupid, stupid bitch," he snarled at me. "You should have stayed where Titus could help you."

Fighting to breathe, I tried to roll away from him, but he kicked me again in the stomach. His foot sent me flying and dispelled what little air I had managed to suck into my lungs since he had first knocked me to the ground. Blinking through blood, I saw that Marcus held his sword in his hand, and he was moving towards me with deadly intent.

CHAPTER XXIX

OVID

Aulus Caecina Severus, the Roman governor of Moesia, wearily stepped into the small house, his motley retinue trailing behind him as the slave woman Galla ushered them all inside, her lips pursed in disapproval as she took in the dark, sticky mud they were bringing inside on their boots.

"Aulus Caecina!" Ovid called warmly, beaming as he reached out with widespread arms to greet his guest and benefactor. In Rome, his Fabia would have been present to play the pristine and welcoming hostess by his side; now, he was on his own. Ovid's smile became strained for the briefest of moments as his wife's face flashed through his mind, but he forced himself to return to the present, to the man before him whose single word could influence his future.

Aulus had connections in Rome, and he was more than capable of putting in a positive mention of the poet to the emperor, potentially helping to secure Ovid's recall from exile. There also remained the fact that Ovid's arrival in Tomis might have been very different, and much less comfortable, without the aid of the governor, and for that alone the poet owed him a significant debt. It was Aulus, after all, who had gifted to him the very house in which he now lived, as well as the slaves who looked after him.

Ovid's welcoming smile faltered only slightly when he took in Aulus's attire. The governor, who looked worn and exhausted, the skin around his green-brown eyes creased in fatigue, wore leathers and wolf-furs. He stank of sweat, campfires, and wet wool; a faint, underlying coppery scent caused Ovid's nostrils to flare: blood. The poet swallowed, examining his own clothing: ever urbane, he had opted for one of his very best togas, crisp and clean—but it was never good to outshine one's benefactor.

"Busy week?" Ovid asked, his smile now stretching on for too long. Perhaps, he thought, he should go change his clothing to better match his guest's.

The governor, who either didn't notice Ovid's formal toga or didn't care, allowed Galla to take his furs before responding. "The natives have been causing some problems over in Illyricum." He gave an unconcerned shrug as he ran a hand through too-long hair that hadn't seen a proper wash in weeks. "The usual… concerns."

"Ah, yes, well, typical barbarians!" Ovid's smile was still firmly in place. He was determined to remain upbeat and cheery; Fabia would have insisted upon it, if she were there. "This way, please, Aulus Caecina. Galla has prepared something edible for us, although I can't say it's as good as the food in Rome, as I'm sure you know."

Aulus shrugged again, following the poet. To him, food was food. It was sustenance, required fuel; he cared little what was served, so long as it was edible. "Do away with my second name, if you will. I've never much liked the sound of Caecina."

"As you wish, Aulus." Ovid smiled again, ushering the governor into the house's tiny dining area. It wasn't fit to be called a *triclinium*, but it would have to do.

The governor's retinue remained outside the room, as there weren't enough provisions to feed them all, while the two men settled themselves on couches. Galla served wine and scurried off to the kitchen so that she could bring in the first dishes.

Ovid debated spilling his cup of wine on himself intentionally, so that he could make his excuses to go change into something less showy, but he decided against it. It was his best toga, a gift to him from his wife, and he doubted the laundering services in Tomis were up to par: better not to ruin it. Anyway, he supposed, it was preferable to be overdressed than to appear as a sloppy fool who couldn't handle his wine. He needed to remain on Aulus's good side, whatever it took.

Galla returned with two platters. On one were seasoned balls of venison meat, hunted by the slave woman's man, Didas. The other had strips of cooked fish, lightly oiled and salted shortly after they were plucked from the sea. Aulus hungrily dug in, pausing only to drink a sip or two of wine before he would spear another piece of meat and bring it to his mouth. He seemed less than chatty.

Ovid delicately sampled some of the fish, watching his guest. He was preparing himself to inquire about Aulus's next correspondence with the emperor, thinking that he could perhaps convince the governor to include in it a favorable mention of him, when one of the slave woman's babies started screaming.

Galla's face fell as she heard her child's wail, preparing herself for Ovid's rebuke, which was, without fail, sharp and immediate.

"How many times—" Ovid started shrilly, but he was cut off by the governor.

"How are your children?" Aulus asked Galla, surprising the poet. Who was he to care about the whelps of a slave? The governor had stopped eating and now watched Galla intently as he waited for a response.

"Well, *dominus*," she answered quietly, her eyes avoiding both men.

The governor wasn't satisfied by the simple answer. "Which one is it crying, then, if they are well?" There was a tinge of annoyance to his words, though Ovid could not tell if it was due to the disturbance or because he was concerned with the infants' welfare.

Galla shifted her feet, looking uncomfortable. The crying infant had set off its brother, the wails now doubled.

"The first to cry is always Duras, *dominus*," she explained. "He is a demanding child, always wanting immediate action. His brother, Scorilo, is led by him."

Aulus looked thoughtful, but he did not immediately speak again. After a short pause, he waved Galla away.

"Go see to them, then. I want to enjoy my dinner in peace." Aulus shoveled another piece of fish into his mouth as he finished speaking, already turning his attention away from the slave woman.

Galla hurried away, and her absence was shortly followed by blessed quiet. No doubt the babies were nursing, appeased at last.

Ovid dared to ask the new question on his mind. "Why concern yourself with the wellbeing of slave children? There are two of them. Should one die, there's always its brother." He did not mean his words to be cruel, but a mere statement of fact.

Aulus stared at the poet coldly and sipped his wine before answering.

"May I remind you, Ovid," he began, "that these slaves only serve you because I made it so. They were my household before yours, and they can be mine again in a heartbeat." Another long, slow sip of wine. "The freedman, Didas, need not even be here, but he wishes to keep his family together. I expect that you, too, will wish to keep them together. The children are of particular value to me, personally."

Ovid sipped his own wine, wisely choosing not to ask any more questions—not that his first one had been answered in any clear manner at all.

The only reason Ovid could think of to explain the governor's concern with the wellbeing of Galla's noisy brats was that they were, perhaps, the governor's own. While Ovid couldn't see the appeal of the heavyset slave woman, he supposed that one could get rather desperate when stuck in Moesia for long periods of time. Liaisons between masters and slaves were not unheard of, and Aulus wasn't too different from any of his contemporaries, in Rome or elsewhere—although Ovid silently promised himself that he would be true to Fabia, never mind the dalliances of his youth and the erotic nature of his earlier work, which had been inspired by far more than his mere imagination.

The remainder of the governor's visit passed uneventfully, but Ovid's mind continued to churn at such a rate that he entirely forgot to ask Aulus about his upcoming reports to the emperor. Something was out of place in Tomis, the poet mused. He would find out what it was, sooner or later, and, more importantly, he would find a way to use it to his advantage.

CHAPTER XXX

JULIA THE YOUNGER

My vision was hazy, but Marcus's motion towards me with his drawn sword was unmistakable, as was his intent. I was trapped between a murderous soldier and a cliff, below which a pile of rocks jutted threateningly out of the water. Either way, my death was assured.

Fumbling for the sword I had dropped, I barely brushed its hilt with my fingers. Unfortunately, Marcus's earlier kick had sent me flying slightly too far away from the weapon. I needed just a bit more time to get my hand around it. It was my only chance.

"Why are you doing this?" I managed to gasp out, loudly enough that Marcus could hear me above the rain. My voice sounded nasal and strange, confirming that the guard had indeed broken my nose with his first, unexpected punch.

Marcus now stood over me, one leg on either side of my chest. Rather than dispatching me immediately, he teased his sword back and forth over my neck, the sharp tip threatening my exposed skin. The cold glint in his eyes reminded me of his arousal when he had held me down as Quintus took away my baby, and it chilled me to my bones.

"I really can't believe that you never connected anything," he said, as if he were on the verge of laughter. The sword's point pressed down into my neck ever so slightly, the tip drawing a small drop of blood that was quickly washed away by the rain.

"Did you really think that stupid slut of a slave decided to poison you on her own? *I* gave her the poison. *I* forced her to do it. At least the bitch saved me the trouble of killing her, although I think I would have enjoyed splitting her soft skin open."

Marcus bared his teeth at me and pressed his sword down further, and I felt my flesh give way, the blood trickling out faster. I wanted to whimper, to roll away, but I feared that any movement would result in my immediate death. I realized that I had even stopped breathing, lest the rise and fall of my chest cause the sword to cut just a measure too deep.

My fingers continued to stretch out, teasing the hilt of the dropped sword towards me. I couldn't tell if I was making much progress or not.

"Of course, I had hoped to kill you *and* your unborn brat the night of that insipid little dinner party with the old man, but you just wouldn't die. Instead, I had to settle for the death of your pathetic old slave woman, who was always hovering around you, and hope that Quintus wouldn't remember anything after I bashed him over the head and threw you into the water."

There had been no accident in the boat that night. Marcus had attacked us all, wounding his commander and causing Aurelia's death in an effort to murder me. Aphrodite's attempt to poison me had been the result of Marcus's threatening instructions, her suicide the only way she knew how to save herself from murder by a madman or torture and execution by the rest of my guards.

I hated myself for not having realized it before. I hated myself for not remembering what had truly transpired the night of the accident after visiting Lucius, which would have stopped Marcus then and there. I hated myself for not protecting Aphrodite from him, for not really asking *why* when she had poisoned me. Most of all, I hated myself for not trusting my instincts about Marcus. Deep down, I had always known what he was. His revelry in my suffering, even now, confirmed his sickness.

The soldier's eyes were finally drawn to the movement of my fingers, which were desperately trying to grasp onto the hilt of the sword still lying just out of my reach. He stepped a foot forward, crushing my wrist beneath his sandal, and continued to stare down at me.

A small blessing from Fortuna meant that Marcus's brief movement had resulted in the slightest upwards shift of his sword, allowing me to take a gasping breath without fear of cutting my own throat. Still, the blood from my small wound continued to flow out at an alarming rate, one that even the rain was not able to wash away fast enough.

"What do you have to gain?" I wanted to understand not the sequence of events leading up to this moment, but why he wanted to kill me at all. Once the other guards found out what he had done, he would be executed. Surely there was no happy ending in store for him.

Marcus decided to move his sword to my trapped arm, poking it sharply and unexpectedly into my forearm. I screamed, and my cry was rewarded by his cruel smile.

"Riches from Rome, an estate in Campania. The satisfaction of cleansing the world of another worthless, privileged bitch." Another poke with his sword, another scream from me as my flesh tore open again in a new spot. "I have a benefactor who will reward me handsomely for your demise. Quintus did me the favor of killing your illegitimate spawn, so now it's just you."

"The other guards will kill you," I hissed at him through clenched teeth. "I'll be dead, but so will you."

Marcus laughed. "They may be alive still. They're good soldiers, good fighters, although the odds weren't in their favor when I left. Naturally, I couldn't pass up the opportunity when I realized you were out here alone, without your shadow." The thought of Titus, possibly lying dead inside the villa, made my stomach churn.

"It will be easy enough to convince them that your would-be rescuers accidentally killed you, especially when I report back that, hard as I tried, I couldn't find your body. You'll wind up in the sea, just like the slave girl. Perhaps I could even say you fell, in your haste to get away from the conflict in the villa."

Marcus's words were harsh and confident, but for the first time he appeared somewhat uneasy. A quick glance over his shoulder in the direction of the villa revealed that he thought his fellow guards were, perhaps, faring better than he had earlier implied.

Remembering something, I eased my free hand up to my head, finding the end of one of the long, sharp pins entwined in my hair. Marcus's gaze returned to me, and I could tell by its heightened intensity that this was it: he would kill me.

"That's enough talking, now," he said, and he raised the sword up and away from my bleeding arm, aligning it with my heart for one final, swift blow that would be the imminent cause of my death.

I knew I had to act. I roughly wrenched the hairpin free, the rapid motion distracting Marcus just long enough to delay his sword from its downward trajectory. With as much force as I could muster, I stabbed the pin into his exposed skin, forcing it into the side of his knee until I felt the grating touch of bone. Marcus grunted in pain, but still his sword descended towards me at an alarming speed. I managed to roll slightly to the side, but the sword sank into my shoulder. It missed its fatal mark, but I still let loose an agonized scream as my flesh tore open.

"Fucking bitch!" Marcus yelled at me, and already he was pulling the sword free of my shoulder, preparing to strike again. This time, I did not think he would miss, even with my hairpin sticking gruesomely out of his leg.

The searing pain in my shoulder was close to overwhelming me entirely, and I fought the urge to lose myself to unconsciousness. My eyes, struggling to remain open, landed on the sword that I had dropped earlier. It was now within reach.

My fingers closed around its hilt, and Marcus was too full of rage, too focused on finally killing me, to notice. Sweat and rain dripped down his angry face, and our eyes met. I whipped the sword up and drove it into his thigh, the feeling of slicing through skin and muscle simultaneously sickening and fascinating me. I was not prepared for the copious amounts of blood that suddenly spurted out, nor for Marcus's sudden fall forward as he cried out in fury.

The soldier dropped his sword, but he landed on top of me, knocking the wind from my body. Even as I felt the hot blood from his leg pour out onto me, I realized that he was still alive, and he was beyond furious.

I felt his hands clawing at my neck, his nails scratching my skin, and then he was strangling me, crushing my throat in his relentless grasp. I had no fight left, no strength. I was so, so tired.

Blind hatred filled his eyes as he slowly killed me, spittle frothing around his mouth as if he were a rabid dog. My arms flailed, pathetically beating at his hard body, and my vision blackened more and more. Eventually, my arms fell to my sides, and I finally lost consciousness. My last thought was one of relief. It would all be over soon.

It was still raining when I awoke an immeasurable time later, pinpricks of water hurting my eyes when I finally opened them, blinking. Marcus, cold and heavy, lay on top of me, the grasses around us stained with blood, both his and mine. I was alive.

The soldier's hands were resting on the ground at either side of my head, lying open and limp as if they hadn't been around my neck, squeezing the life out of me, only a short time before. I realized then that he had bled to death just before he managed to kill me. Only a few moments more and I might not have awoken.

I was so tired… too tired to push Marcus's corpse off of me, too tired to crawl back to the villa only to see if my heart would be broken into a thousand pieces by finding Titus's mangled and bloody body lying on the villa's floor. I didn't want to know anymore. If he still lived, he would find me. Until then, I would simply wait.

And so I lay outside in the cold rain under Marcus's lifeless body, my wounds still slowly oozing blood. Thankfully, my mind, barely present, wandered. If I thought too much about what had happened, what might still come, I knew that I would break.

I wondered, had I died, if I would have seen my infant son again in the Underworld, awaiting me with my elder brothers and father. Would our ancestors be there, too? How would I recognize them, whom I had never met? It occurred to me that I had never given the afterlife much thought until then—but if my blood did not stop flowing soon, then perhaps I might discover the answers to such mysteries earlier than anticipated.

My philosophical musings were interrupted when Marcus's body was pulled off me with a loud grunt of effort, and I smiled deliriously up into Titus's panicked face.

"Titus!" I breathed, my raspy voice barely audible after Marcus's final assault on my neck. "You're hurt."

An open and still bleeding gash ran from his forehead to his ear, crossing his brow but narrowly missing his left eye. His right was bruised and swelling rapidly shut. I couldn't see the rest of him, but the fact that he was here meant that he was alive and well enough.

Titus fell to his knees and embraced me, and I was distantly aware of the sound of him sobbing as he progressed from holding me to checking my body for wounds. He found plenty.

"Why did he do this?" he asked. "Why did he do this to you?"

Titus's gaze travelled from my broken nose to my bruised and bloody neck and down to my arm, scattered with bloody holes of varying size. The deep wound in my shoulder still bled sluggishly, and Titus pressed his hands against it.

I was too dizzy and faint from blood loss to answer, but I managed to smile at him again. I wanted to tell him that I loved him, but instead I slipped into the welcoming blackness of unconsciousness.

My next awakening was far more pleasant than the last. Instead of opening my eyes to stinging rain, I opened them to the soft, flickering light of an oil lamp. Instead of the cold, heavy corpse of a guard who had tried to murder me multiple times, I was under a warm wool blanket. My dress was clean and soft, and my skin felt washed, my hair dry.

Peering around, I found Artemis sitting quietly in a chair in the corner of my bedroom, half asleep. Once she saw that I was awake, she rushed over to my bedside to pour me a cup of water, which she gently helped me to drink. My swollen throat caused me to choke and sputter as I sipped.

Very shortly, I realized that I ached and stung all over, and I wanted nothing more than to return to sleep. With no one to stop me, I gladly closed my eyes.

The bearded man who smelled of salt and sand was in my dreams again for the third time, his long hair now pulled back with small, glowing white seashells braided into it here and there, setting off his eerie eyes. We were in a boat, bobbing in place as waves passed underneath us. There was no sign of shore.

"Who are you?" I asked, my dream voice clear and strong, but he didn't seem to hear me. Or perhaps he chose to ignore me.

I wanted to move towards him, to grab him in an effort to elicit some reaction, but my body refused to respond. As if sensing my intentions, the man turned to look at me, and I stopped struggling, inexplicably calmed by his unnatural, swirling blue irises. He did not speak, but the memory of the broken statue of Neptune, tucked carelessly away in one of the villa's storage rooms, crashed into me with such force that, had I been standing, I would have been knocked over.

"Neptune," I breathed in recognition. He—a god or a hallucination, whatever reality or manifestation of madness I was seeing before me—did not speak again, and I was in no state to determine if I was having a prophetic vision or had simply lost my mind, as my little brother was reputed to have.

Time passed, but I couldn't tell if it was an eternity or merely a second. Dreams are odd like that. Without seeing any movement, I was suddenly aware of Neptune pointing into the distance. Squinting, I followed the line of his finger. Nothing.

"What is it?" I snapped at him, oddly bold despite not being certain whether I was insane or in the presence of a god. Once again, there was no answer, and I wished that I would wake up and end my own frustration.

Preparing myself to ask again, I stopped short, suddenly catching sight of a small, floating object in the distance. It was moving at a strangely unnatural angle to the waves, but it was gradually coming closer to our boat.

Eventually, I was able to make out a swaddled baby, rosy pink in the cheeks and sleeping contentedly as a dolphin nudged his miniature boat along with its snout. They were coming nearer.

Standing, I felt as if my heart had stopped beating. I knew in my bones that it was my son out there, my stolen baby, whom Quintus had killed on my grandfather's orders.

"Why?" I cried, warring with my dream self between conflicting feelings of fresh hope and renewed misery.

As the baby neared, I reached my hand out, and then I was falling an endless distance that seemed to stretch on and on. I never hit the water. I awoke with a hoarse, strangled moan and felt the wet traces of tears on my swollen cheeks. It was only a cruel dream, I told myself, a madness that had taken hold of me. My son was dead, and there was nothing that would change that, not even a dreamed-up vision of a god claiming otherwise.

The wind whipped at my hair as I stood on the hillside above the port, clutching a thick wool shawl around my chest and shoulders. Below, I watched the long-awaited supply ship finally get underway for its departure.

Autumn seemed to have faded away with alarming rapidity after the attack on the villa only two weeks before, winter making itself known with increasingly cold nights and ever harsher winds. The sea was more gray than blue these days, choppy and changeable, matching the sky above. The sailors, still weary from their initial trip, would be lucky to reach the mainland without further incident. Storm after storm had delayed the supply ship's initial departure and then its progress. The decisive change of seasons would only make their return journey to the mainland even more uncertain.

Titus rested a hand on my good shoulder, and I couldn't help myself: I flinched. The events of the fortnight before were fresh on my mind, and the marks still raw on my body, the brutally painful sting of the vinegar used to flush out my wounds a vivid memory. My right arm remained in a sling, but, thankfully, the wound in my shoulder would heal, given time.

Rather than letting go after I flinched, Titus tightened his fingers, and, after a moment, I relaxed into the guard's hold. His presence, his touch, reminded me that I was safe now.

"I was starting to think they had been lost at sea, they took so long to arrive," Titus announced, nodding down at the ship as it pulled out of the port, bobbing rapidly on the uneasy waters as it began its voyage. "There won't be another until the spring, now."

I nodded halfheartedly in acknowledgement of his words. The springtime supply ship wouldn't just bring more food and wine, but also new, fresh guards to replace those who remained. I had been informed by Titus that he and the other men had been assigned to me, and thus to Trimerus, for only a year. For me, this island was now my entire life; for them, it was simply a brief tour of duty. And, for Marcus and Publius, it had been a fatal one.

I had always known, on some level, that Titus wouldn't be permitted to remain with me for the full duration of my exile, however long it might prove to be. For now, I tried not to dwell on his departure, which, although inevitable, was still months away.

"What was in the letter that Quintus sent with the sailors?" I asked, breaking the silence that had begun to stretch between us.

Titus continued to watch the ship below, his hand still lightly grasping my shoulder.

"Other than the basics," he began, "a report on your attempted abduction via poorly forged documents and the subsequent attack when we didn't hand you over. Notification of the deaths of Marcus and Publius in the line of duty, with a request for additional guards in the spring." He glanced at me and then away, so quickly that I barely noticed it. "Confirmation that your child was... removed." He chose a kinder word than I would have to describe what had happened to my baby.

I tensed. Despite everything else that had happened to me, the murder of my child remained the rawest of all my wounds, and I knew it always would be. But instead of seizing on the tentative mention of my son, as Titus perhaps feared that I would, I fixed my attention on his nonchalant mention of Marcus.

"You said notification of the death of Marcus, in the line of duty," I said. "Does that include how he tried to kill me? How he caused the deaths of Aurelia and the slave girl, Aphrodite? Or how he attacked Quintus?"

Titus turned towards me, his normally warm brown gaze intense as he placed his free hand gently on my other shoulder, careful to avoid aggravating my wound as he held me firmly in front of him.

He said only a single word. "No."

I blinked at him, not comprehending. "Why not?"

"Quintus and I discussed it, and, given the circumstances, we think it better that we let it go."

"Let it *go*?" My voice was quiet, but I knew Titus could sense the swelling rage beneath those three small words.

"Yes." He rubbed my shoulders, looking at me intently, almost beseechingly. "Think about it, Julia. We have no proof, just our word."

"You mean my word," I hissed, trying to pull back from him. He held on, forcing me to stay in place. "*I am the* granddaughter of Augustus! My word is *everything*."

Titus briefly closed his eyes, as if fighting for patience.

"Yes, *your* word. The word of an exile," he said. I continued to glare at him, but his stream of words didn't stop. "The word of a disgraced woman who was pregnant with her lover's child and whose husband was executed for treason. The word of a prisoner who probably

247

would like, very much, to escape this forsaken island. The word of someone who has a vested interest in getting rid of her guards."

"Get off of me," I said coldly, and I shoved him. He barely moved. There was no way that I could overpower him, and we both knew it. At the very least, I could retain some of my dignity, and so I decided not to struggle.

"How *dare* you insinuate that I fabricated some sort of lie about Marcus, or that I was involved in this… this… *plot*." I spat the last word at him. I was furious.

Titus's hands still held me, and I felt as if he were trying to avoid shaking sense into me.

"Julia, I *know*." His words were pleading. "But without proof— and we may never know who bribed Marcus to try to kill you, or who sent your would-be abductors—you will always be thought guilty. You are dangerous simply because of who you are. It's why you're here in the first place."

I tried to muster another glare, but my heart was no longer in it.

"And there's another thing you didn't think of." Titus finally let go of me as he spoke, turning back towards the sea. The supply ship was growing increasingly small as it sailed from the island.

I wanted to stomp away, to dwell in my childish tantrum even as Titus's words continued to sink in, worming their logical way into my brain despite my unwillingness to listen. But I stayed.

"And that is?" I asked.

"Quintus and I could be implicated in this, unless more information turns up indicating who was behind the abduction attempt."

I frowned, surprised. "What do you mean?"

"Some of the attackers managed to flee, taking their ship with them. The others were all killed. There is no one to torture, no one to question. To some, it wouldn't be inconceivable that those closest to you—us—had some involvement, working from the inside. If we hurled accusations against one of our own, who also died in the attack and now can neither defend nor incriminate himself, it may look suspicious."

"That's ridiculous," I scoffed. "You're members of the Praetorian Guard, some of the most trusted soldiers of Rome. Surely no one would think that you and Quintus had anything to do with an attempt to abduct me, or that you killed Marcus to keep him quiet."

Titus once again caught my eyes, his gaze serious.

"Sometimes you are surprisingly naïve, Julia. In reality, it doesn't matter if we had anything to do with it." He sighed, hanging his head. "Someone will have to pay the price for this, and Quintus and I are the easy targets here. If there is the slightest doubt about our loyalty, or if the true offender isn't discovered…. That's how it works. Surely you can understand that."

His words weren't meant to be harsh, but they struck me as if they were a physical blow. I'd had enough insults for the day, and so I didn't answer. Instead, I began to retreat to the villa. Titus, my ever-present shadow, trailed behind at a short distance, allowing me room to seethe. He didn't speak again, but he had said enough already. I knew he was right; my prideful self just wasn't ready to admit it yet.

The villa had been meticulously cleaned by Artemis and Monimos, the latter of whom had survived the attack by hiding himself under a pile of flour bags in the storeroom. Quintus had almost stabbed him to death as he did a final sweep of the villa, scaring them both as he tripped over Monimos's quivering body. Artemis had been hiding behind a barrel in the same room.

Other than the noticeable absence of much of the villa's furniture—many pieces had been damaged beyond repair in the conflict—and some deep cracks and chips in the mosaicked floor of the atrium, little had changed. Artemis, aided in part by a slave sent over from Lucius—who had appeared only long after the threat of danger was gone, despite having admitted to seeing the false supply ship's arrival—had dutifully spent many of her daylight hours scrubbing the reddish-brown blood stains from between the thousands of tiny tiles until the floors gleamed as if new. The villa was now cleaner than I ever remembered it being.

The bodies of the attackers, after being searched by Quintus and Titus, had been thrown unceremoniously into the sea, which was also where Titus had dumped Marcus's corpse once he found me half dead on the cliffside. None of the attackers carried anything that might provide further clues as to who sent them. The only thing we had to go on was the forgery that ordered my immediate release into their care, but even that was almost entirely ruined, having been nearly soaked through with blood during the attack.

Publius had been given a proper funeral pyre, as he deserved. His ashes were collected and placed into a discarded amphora, then buried by Aurelia, morbid mementos of two of the lives that Trimerus had claimed. There were no mementos for the slave girl, Aphrodite, nor for my unnamed son. They had lived and died as if they had never existed.

I blew through the atrium when we reached the villa, my mood matching the worsening weather. Titus still followed behind, lurking outside my room as I stopped only briefly to collect a drying cloth and clean clothing. Storming down the hallway, I let my shawl drop unheeded to the floor as I pushed open the bath's door.

I moved to slam and latch the door behind me, but it connected sharply with the palm of Titus's hand, which forcefully halted its motion. Sighing in exasperation, I turned my back on the guard. I began undressing, removing the sling from my arm and trying to avoid wrenching my shoulder as I carelessly threw my clothes to the ground with more force than was necessary.

A quiet thump confirmed that Titus had entered the room and latched the door behind us, but I ignored him, instead stepping towards the warm bath. I was not in the frame of mind to continue our earlier discussion. Just as I was about to enter the bathing pool, Titus's arms wrapped around me from behind, and he pulled me back against him. His breath was warm and quick against my ear, and I shivered.

"Julia," he breathed. His voice was soothing.

My body remained tense despite his efforts.

"Let go," I whispered. I was still angry.

I felt Titus shake his head as he continued to hold me, and it only took another moment before I broke, my naked body melting backwards into him as my resolve softened and faded away entirely. His hands were moving then, tenderly avoiding my cuts and bruises as they traced my skin, firmly grasping me where they could. Gentle kisses and soft bites teased my ear and covered my neck, and then moved downwards to my uninjured shoulder. I moaned, my hands seeking out the guard's tunic behind me and pulling at it.

Titus released me only to remove his own clothing, and then, with him guiding me from behind, we stepped into the warm water, our bodies already beginning to tangle together. My earlier strong emotions resurfaced, and I spun around, pushing the guard down onto the pool's ledge as I straddled him. Sensing that I needed this, Titus let me have my way, his head falling back as I spent my anger, my frustration, and my fear.

Minutes later, I remained on top of Titus, our arms wrapped around one another as we both caught our breath.

"I'm sorry," I whispered. The words felt strange on my tongue; apologizing still wasn't something I was used to.

Titus merely grunted and rubbed my back. I was happy he didn't make an ordeal out of my apology.

"Do you really think that you—and Quintus—will somehow be blamed for what happened?" I asked. This time, I was willing to listen.

The guard didn't answer right away, instead continuing to move his hands over my back, fingers lightly tracing my spine, which had become far too prominent since we had left Rome.

"Maybe," he said at last, "but probably not. It's a possibility, but only if the actual source of the plot isn't discovered. Somehow, knowing your grandfather's reputation, I expect that he may already have an idea who was behind it all."

A sense of relief washed over me. "That's good, then."

"Yes. I'm sure Quintus and I will still have to answer some questions when we return to the mainland in the spring, but perhaps it will all be resolved by then."

Titus's words reassured me, but I couldn't tell how confident he was in his own suppositions. For his sake, and for mine, I hoped that he was right.

Lying in bed that night, I once again found my thoughts drifting back in time. Who was the mysterious person who had been able to bribe Marcus so handsomely, to promise him so much, that he would risk unspeakable punishment in order to kill me? He had been a Praetorian Guard. He should have been above such corruption.

And who had the men been sent by, with their forged document? Had they succeeded, where would I be now? I hesitated to think it, but a small part of me wondered if I should have gone with them willingly. I could have escaped my exile; perhaps I could even have been reunited with Aemilia one day. But I knew that my rescue would have come at a cost, one that I might have been unable or unwilling to pay.

Despite my racing thoughts, there were no forthcoming answers. I found myself tossing and turning for hours as an early winter storm raged outside the villa, battering the island. Marcus was dead and gone, taking his secrets to his ocean grave. Perhaps for the latter questions, at least, we might have an answer come spring. I had no doubt that my grandfather's network of spies and informants would turn up some information about who was behind the abduction attempt.

At long last, I was lulled to sleep by the constant, pounding rain and the sparrow's intermittent chirps. I dreamed of stolen babies and crooked guards, spies and treachery. The longhaired man who smelled of salt water and sand—Neptune—did not appear.

CHAPTER XXXII

THE ELDER JULIA

The shutters on one of the villa's windows were cracked open, allowing some cold air in to freshen the room, and a lone bird just outside chirped pitifully, no doubt looking for a stray crumb of which it could make a modest meal. Autumn had come and gone, and Proserpina, whose presence or absence was said to dictate the seasons, had once again disappeared to join her husband Pluto in the Underworld, taking the last vestiges of warmth along with her.

Julia, her obvious, icy mood a perfect complement to the chilly season, was sprawled on a couch in her winter receiving quarters, heavy furs draped across her lap. A scowl remained fixed on her face as she stared downwards at an unfurled, yellowed scroll clutched tightly in her hands.

It had been over a month since the plans to free her children from exile had failed, but even now Julia couldn't stop herself from rereading the scathing letter the emperor had sent after both the incidents had been reported to him. In the end, it hadn't taken much to piece together the trail that led back to her. Handsome bribes and merciless torture led to loose lips, unfortunately.

I AM DEEPLY SADDENED, ONCE AGAIN... TREASON AGAINST ROME AND YOUR OWN FATHER... I WILL SEND AWAY SCRIBONIA IF THERE IS EVEN ONE MORE INCIDENT... IT WOULD NOT BE BEYOND QUESTION TO SEND YOU BACK TO THE ISLAND OF PANDATERIA... YOU SHOULD BE GRATEFUL...

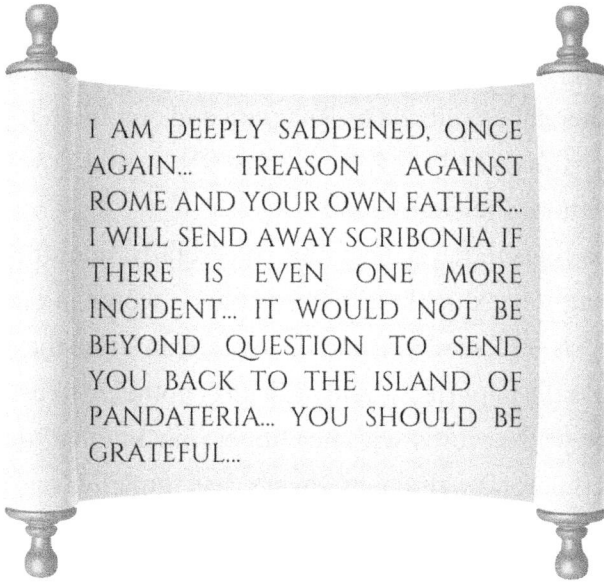

It was the first direct contact she had had with her father in years, and it was every bit as disappointing as she had expected. Julia clenched her fist, partially crushing the scroll. Better had he sent his usual messengers, who merely droned out a verbal relay of Augustus's words.

She knew her father did not make empty threats, and so she remained on her best behavior despite her fury. Although being the only blood child of the emperor lent itself to a level of favoritism, even in her state of disgraced exile, this was not without limit, and Julia knew when to cease pushing. That time had come.

It was obvious that Julia could not have accomplished her scheme singlehandedly, from within the lonely confines of the villa at Rhegium. Naturally, someone had had to pay the steep price for enabling her plotting.

The slave boy Felix had been found out, with some unprovoked assistance from Julia herself. He had been a sacrifice she had to make in order to protect her own future. Under torture, he had confessed to his role in delivering letters to and from the villa. When all was confirmed, Felix was then taken outside of Rhegium and crucified. It took him three days to die. Julia's only regret was that she would now have to find a new slave whom she could trust.

Julia relaxed her hand and then carefully smoothed the letter out before rolling it back up, holding her father's words in one hand. After a long pause, she reconsidered and once more unfurled the scroll, her eyes raking across the papyrus. Augustus hadn't bothered to use a scribe. Julia traced some of the words with her finger, musing that, despite his clear anger, the emperor's writing, as always, had remained constant and rigid, just as he was. He had never been a joyful father, in any capacity.

Starting by ripping the scroll in half, Julia methodically tore the letter into tiny pieces, letting them drop one by one to the floor. A breeze flowed in through the window, swirling and scattering the shreds across the room.

Some of the pieces fluttered to the feet of one of her new guards, who steadfastly ignored them, a large hand resting on the hilt of his sheathed sword. Julia now had many new soldiers after her most recent misbehavior; she lost count after a dozen. She wasn't quite certain what had happened to the others, who had only so recently been stationed in Rhegium after the earthquake.

A ghost of a smile fluttered across her lips as she mused that she went through guards like she once had gone through lovers, in her youth. Times had certainly changed. It would be a while before she could identify those new guards who might be sympathetic to her desires, whether that was leaving the villa to go shopping or turning a blind eye to the comings and goings of the villa's slaves, one or more of whom, ideally, would be working to secure Julia's interests.

Julia had found that all men, even those amongst the elite Praetorian Guard, were corruptible. It was simply a matter of finding out what they most craved. For many, it was money and sex. Others aimed at something slightly higher: power and influence. But all of them had a price.

She would certainly be in need of new accomplices. Sempronius Gracchus, her onetime lover and most recent ally, would be lying low, if he still lived. If he had been linked to the escape attempts, his execution would not be out of the question. His role in organizing the forged letters meant to secure the release of Julia's children was pivotal, and thus gravely punishable. Regardless, he would clearly be of little use to her in the future. Even if Gracchus were still alive, the forgeries had proven abysmal failures, leaving a bitter taste in Julia's mouth. She would have to explore new options, new alliances. She could not tolerate incompetence, whatever relationship she once may have had with the man.

While Augustus remained, for now, furious and watchful, it was only a matter of time until the emperor's attention wandered and his anger lessened. The old man had too much else on his plate to keep a constant eye on his wayward daughter and troublesome grandchildren. Julia would find a way, as she always did. After all, she was her father's daughter.

CHAPTER XXXIII

JULIA THE YOUNGER

Although the winter days were bleak and seemingly endless, I realized that I was, in some inexplicable way, happy. My shoulder had, for the most part, healed, as had my other wounds. I would bear permanent scars on my body, and my nose would always have a new tilt to it, spoiling its once-perfect straightness, but there was no other lasting damage. Fortuna had been looking out for me.

The immediate threat to my safety, Marcus, had been eliminated, and any approach to the island by other would-be abductors would be suicidal given the harsh and unpredictable winter seas. As a result, Titus and I were making the most of our last few months together, often ensconced within the villa as Monimos and Artemis looked the other way. Our most recent brush with death had made us both heedless of the consequences.

Quintus, too, largely turned a blind eye to us. Ever since the attack, he had kept mostly to himself. He disappeared for long stretches of time for solitary walks on the island, even in the most questionable of weather, or simply shut himself away in his room. None of us knew what he did in there for hours on end.

I thought, to some extent, that he felt defeated. The death of young Publius, whom he seemed to have favored amongst all his men, weighed heavily on him. Once I had fully recounted Marcus's scheming since our arrival on Trimerus, including the guard's cliffside confession as he made his final attempt to kill me, Quintus's demeanor had changed even further. He had repeatedly overlooked an assassin lurking within his own ranks, one who had even attacked him directly—although, through no fault of his own, he couldn't remember it.

As if it weren't enough that he appeared to blame himself for some of the more unfortunate events on the island, his future career, and life, remained questionable. Only springtime might bring an answer, as warmer, calmer waters would signal the impending arrival of the next supply ship.

On that ship would be news regarding the imperial investigation into the abduction plot, as well fresh soldiers. These newcomers would do one of two things. They might take my surviving guards into custody, implicating them in what had transpired, if only to have public scapegoats for an embarrassing attack. Or, they would reassure them that their service was unquestioned and admirable before they were sent onwards to their next assignment.

The nasty, vindictive voice in my mind told me that I shouldn't be overly concerned with Quintus's fate, responsible as he was for carrying out my child's murder, but I knew that his future was very much connected with Titus's. If Quintus became a scapegoat, so too would Titus.

Besides, I had recently managed to come to a peace of sorts with the commander's role in my son's death; it was with great effort that I constantly reminded myself to channel blame to my grandfather instead, upon whose orders the sentence had been carried out. In the end, it was perhaps better that I saw Quintus even less now than I had before. It made it easier to maintain my ongoing attempts at forgiveness.

It was a quiet day when Lucius chose to come for an unannounced visit, his most reliable slaves rowing him across the calmer than usual stretch of water that separated our two islands.

Titus and I were moving towards the kitchen for our noontime meal, laughing unreservedly at an outdated joke, when we caught sight of the old man in the atrium, bossing Artemis about in his usual way as she tried to help him with his cloak. His own two men stood nearby, their faces chapped and cold from the salty winter wind.

"Lucius!" I called out, my voice warm. Titus subtly increased the distance between us as I spoke, returning to his official and public role as my guard. Lucius, at least, had no idea of our relationship. It would be better to keep it that way.

"Ah, my dear, my dear!" Lucius greeted me in return. "Hurry up now with that cloak, you silly girl," he muttered as Artemis finally untangled him from his own garment. She quickly disappeared.

"Will you join us? I'm afraid Artemis probably has made only a light soup, but there is plenty."

"Us?" Lucius asked, raising a grayed eyebrow as he at last registered Titus's presence behind me.

I recovered quickly. "Yes. You know by now that I take meals with my guards. There is no sense in maintaining decorum when there's no one here to see." I made sure to roll my eyes, as if I were perplexed by the new status quo.

"Is Quintus joining us? I was hoping to have a word with him."

"I'm afraid I'm not sure. He's kept to himself since… Well, since everything happened, as you know." There was no need to bring up the bloody details once more.

Lucius nodded, looking apologetic. "Terrible business. Just

dreadful. Don't suppose they were pirates, do you? I remember hearing all about how Julius Caesar, when he was just a young man, was taken off by some of them, and had to live amongst them for quite some time. Ghastly. I can't even imagine." He shook his head, looking put out at the very thought.

"We aren't certain what it was all about, but I'm positive my grandfather will have some idea. Come spring, we may know more. I'm just relieved that they left you alone, Lucius. I would never have forgiven myself if I had brought trouble upon you as well." My words were the truth. Despite his oddities and shortcomings, Lucius had become a friend of sorts.

The old man flashed his gap-toothed smile at me, stepping closer to take my hand, which he patted in a manner he meant to be reassuring. "You've been through quite a lot, dear, you really have," he said soothingly.

I simply smiled and, linking my arm with Lucius's, escorted him to the *triclinium*, where we would wait to be served our meal. Quintus did not appear before Artemis brought the soup, which left the cozy threesome of Lucius, Titus, and myself sprawled on our respective couches.

Since Titus was firmly back in his proper role as my guard, much of the conversation was led by our elderly guest, who took great pleasure in recounting various stories, most of which I had already heard at some point or another. Nevertheless, I played my own role of the well-bred hostess, smiling politely and encouraging a pleasant atmosphere.

"My daughter's son, the one who's a governor, now he's a good man," Lucius was saying, waving his hand so that wine sloshed out of the cup he was holding, leaving a spatter of the ruby liquid on the floor. It was too early for me to want much to drink, but my guest seemed to have no such reservations.

"Indeed he is," a new voice spoke up, and I started, looking to the door. Quintus had joined us.

"Ah, Quintus, another good man!" Lucius raised his wine cup in a toast to the commander before taking another sip. If he wasn't already drunk, he was close to it.

Quintus looked tired, his large frame now surprisingly small in appearance as he hunched in the doorway. He looked as if it cost him every ounce of effort he had to even remain standing. I knew Quintus wasn't a young man, but his age was ever more apparent as winter progressed. His face was drawn, a graying beard was growing out in uneven tufts, and purple marks under his eyes were evidence of his many sleepless nights.

"You know Lucius's grandson?" Titus asked, sharply. I had been so surprised by Quintus's appearance that I had failed to make the connection. Clearly, it hadn't escaped my guard.

It was Lucius, not Quintus, who answered Titus's query. "Yes, I helped to…" The old man seemed to choke on his wine as Quintus whipped his head towards him, his gaze intense.

"What I meant to say," the old man corrected himself, now choosing his words carefully, "is that I helped my grandson, when he was merely a child, to learn some basic fighting with a proper soldier, just by sponsoring a few lessons, you know, that sort of thing... A gift from his dear old grandfather. And it turns out that Quintus had actually taught him the sword, by chance…" Lucius trailed off, taking a large sip of wine as he gazed downwards. Everyone was silent.

Titus was still watching Quintus intently, and his examination of his commander did not cease throughout the remainder of the meal, even when Lucius regained his energy and began to babble about other topics.

Notably, he did not mention his grandson again.

By the time a rather drunk Lucius departed with his slaves, I had almost forgotten the entire incident, as brief and insignificant as it had appeared to be. Titus, however, had not. As soon as Quintus retreated to his bedroom, Titus was at my side, bursting with coiled energy.

"What's wrong?" I frowned at him, fighting a yawn brought on by the small amount of wine I had had with my soup. I was ready to take a nap.

"I've known Quintus for a long time now. If he knew Lucius, directly or indirectly, through his grandson, he would have said something long before this, to all of his men."

I scoffed. "Titus, I am sure that he had no idea whose grandson he was training, or however it was they met one another. No doubt it just came up in some conversation they had, and they realized their connection many years later. It's not unheard of—such things happen all the time."

"No." Titus seemed certain. "The story Lucius told us never happened."

"Why not? What reason would either of them have to lie about something so silly?" I was on the verge of laughter, although it was somewhat endearing that Titus was so proactive with his information-gathering. "And why not just go *ask* Quintus about it if you know him so well?"

"Julia." The way he said my name wiped away any lingering trace of amusement, and I focused my attention on him. "What if Marcus wasn't acting alone?"

I didn't know what to say. The idea that Quintus was somehow working with Marcus to ensure my demise was absurd, but Titus seemed so certain. His hands were holding my arms now, forcing me to look at him, and the earnestness in his eyes showed that he truly did suspect Quintus of being another assassin.

"Marcus attacked him on the boat that night, coming back from dinner with Lucius. If they were working together, wouldn't Quintus have *helped* Marcus?" It was a logical counterargument, and so I proposed it.

"Accidents happen. He may have fallen out in the struggle. Perhaps Aurelia tried to protect you. We can't know for sure. But we can't trust that Quintus doesn't remember."

I sighed. "Even if that were the case, how does the fact that he somehow knows Lucius's grandson tie into all of this and mean that he was—or still is—in league with Marcus and whoever his master was?"

"What if Marcus's unknown benefactor is Lucius's grandson?" I was unconvinced, but Titus continued. "He's some governor, no doubt involved in all sorts of scheming and intriguing to try to advance his position in Rome. It isn't insane to think he might believe that killing you would bring him some sort of power or influence."

I frowned, still uncertain.

"Why else would Quintus lie about it?" Titus pressed. "As long as I have known him, I have never heard him lie. Something is very wrong. Maybe I'm missing something. I'm sure that I am. But the only thing I can think of is that, somehow, Quintus is involved in all of this. And so, it seems, is Lucius." Titus stared at me, willing me to believe him. To trust him.

"Is that what you really think?" Both of us spun around to see Quintus standing once more in the doorway.

Titus surged forward reflexively, his hand already moving to draw his sword. I screamed as Quintus landed a heavy blow to my lover's nose before he could raise his weapon, blood rapidly welling up as he fell to his knees with a grunt.

"Stop it!" Quintus boomed, holding his hands out front in an appeasing gesture even as Titus prepared to surge forward once more, despite his injured nose. "You bloody fool! Let me explain!"

"Titus!" I snapped, my heart racing. I wasn't sure what was going on, but, in my bones, I still didn't feel that Quintus was a true threat. Nevertheless, I backed a few more steps away from the commander. Titus joined me, holding his now-drawn sword aloft even as his other hand tried to quell the blood streaming from his nose.

Composing myself, I focused my attention on Quintus. "Explain." The single word was a cold order.

The large man sighed and moved to sit on a couch, resting his head in his hands. Titus shifted his own position, prepared to strike down his own commander if he made any questionable move. Just as I was about to prompt Quintus again, he spoke.

"I was hoping neither of you would have noticed that I commented on Lucius's grandson. I wasn't thinking… I haven't been able to think much, lately. But I trained you too well, Titus, and you weren't going to let my slip-up go, especially after that ridiculous story the old badger came up with about me training his grandson to use a sword." He sighed again and took a long pause, rubbing his face. "I do have an… acquaintance of sorts with Lucius's grandson, but only since a few months ago, towards the end of summer."

I felt lightheaded, but I forced myself to remain standing. "This summer?" I asked, my voice barely a whisper. But Quintus heard. He nodded.

"Yes, this summer," he confirmed.

This past summer. Around the time my baby had been born. Around the time my infant son had been stolen from me and murdered.

Titus seemed to sense that I couldn't think of how to continue, and so he took over the questioning. "How are you *acquainted*, then?" he asked, his voice strangely nasal as a result of his newest injury. The flow of his blood had already slowed.

Quintus finally lifted his head from his hands, and he directed his answer not to Titus, but to me. "He's in the province of Moesia. It's where he's been assigned as governor. There's a small city called Tomis, right on the sea, where he spends much of his time. His name is Aulus Caecina Severus."

"Go on." Again, it was Titus who spoke, but I barely heard him. I was transfixed, my gaze locked with that of Quintus. I held my breath as he spoke his next words, once more addressing me in his response.

"I couldn't bring myself to kill an innocent babe. I couldn't kill him. Gods know I tried. I stood at the cliff's edge for hours, willing myself to throw him away, telling myself that he would pass quickly, almost painlessly, even. But he just stared up at me. He didn't even cry." Quintus's voice was forlorn as he recalled the memory.

I fought the rushing in my ears, sitting down heavily on a couch as I felt the breath leave my body.

Quintus continued speaking. "Eventually I went to Lucius, praying to the gods that he wouldn't turn me in for my wretched inability to obey my most important order—for treason, because that's what it was. He seemed positive his grandson would help, and so he wrote a letter and sent his most trusted slave with your child on the next supply ship that came to his island. Aulus Caecina Severus, Lucius's grandson, has your child."

Quintus placed his head back in his hands, hiding his face as if he could take back all his words, perhaps even his actions. No one spoke for a very long time.

My son was alive.

CHAPTER XXXIV

AGRIPPA POSTUMUS

Agrippa carefully scratched away at a scroll, the wet words left by his pen glinting in the light of a nearby oil lamp. Sighing, he stopped, balling the letter up and throwing it to the ground, where it joined several other discarded attempts. Once again, he began anew, absentmindedly smoothing a fresh piece of papyrus with his hand as he thought about what to write. At last, he started with an address, writing out the words '*Esteemed Grandfather*,' just as he had on each previous letter.

Agrippa was in a rare period of heightened clarity of mind, and he was not sure how long it would last.

After the attack in the fall, when first he had willingly gone with and then turned on one of his would-be rescuers, he had simply returned to his bed, waking the next day covered in dried blood that flaked off his skin and clothing as he rose and surveyed the damage. The events of only hours before were foggy and confused in his mind.

He knew that he was not right. For all that his family referred to his 'illiberal' nature, Agrippa knew it was more. He was not so silly as to think he was a good man; after all, what member of the imperial family was? They all were ready to throw their closest friends and family members to the barbarian hordes if it meant a rise in status, an increase in power. He, too, would do no less. But it was more than that.

He had tried to control himself in the past, and he had failed, again and again. And every time, the disappointment shone more and more greatly in his grandfather's eyes, his grandfather who so desperately wanted a blood heir for his empire. The final break had come when Agrippa moved against Augustus in the ultimate act of treason, a grasp for power Agrippa had blamed on those around him, blatantly protesting his own willful involvement even though, for much of it, he had been sound of mind.

Agrippa suspected, although he did not yet know for certain, that it was his mother who had engineered the rescue attempt. He knew she would never cease her quest for power, for control, as long as she lived, and Agrippa remained her best chance for this: through her son, the elder Julia sought to establish her own reign. While they both lived, there would be no peace.

Despite knowing that the emperor had likely already discovered who was behind the most recent plot, Agrippa put his suspicions into words. A normal man may have shied away from betraying his own mother, but Agrippa was not normal. It was a coldly calculated act formulated to bring him into a more favorable light, an act that he may not have been able to fully think through while trapped in his increasingly frequent bouts of *illiberal* behavior. It was strictly the business of survival—even his mother would understand.

At last, Agrippa finished his letter and set it aside to dry. It would not be sent until the next supply ship had come and gone in the spring, but he was pleased that he had been able to utilize this particular period of clarity in a way beneficial to his future. Perhaps there was yet a chance for his recall to Rome.

He was not sure how much longer this sharp frame of mind would last; already in the past week he had insisted on taking a winter swim outside in the fishpond, nearly freezing to death before his guards forcibly removed him from the water and carried him inside the villa. It was only a matter of time until it happened again.

The young man laid out another piece of papyrus, writing across the top 'MY DEAREST SISTER JULIA.' He did not know whether the letter would reach her; certainly it would be opened and read, possibly even sent to the emperor for approval before it would be passed along to his elder sibling, who, presumably, was still sequestered in her own miserable exile. It was just as likely the letter would be burned by his own guards as soon as they took hold of it.

Nevertheless, Agrippa began to write, unreservedly honest in his stream of words. She had always been his favorite, because she had always been the one least interested in politics and power. Her care for her little brother was genuine, something he still understood even as his mind slipped more and more away from him. Whatever she was going through, Agrippa knew that she, of everyone in their family, deserved it least of all.

***

The guard Rufus skimmed the letters with a calculating eye. Agrippa had foolishly entrusted them to him, but it wouldn't do to send them onwards to their intended recipients. He rolled both scrolls up and placed them under his bed, not quite ready to destroy them; they might prove useful in some manner he couldn't yet anticipate. Rufus was certain his master would have more insight, come spring.

Agrippa's suspicions that it was his mother behind autumn's attack were not particularly interesting, as Rufus had already suspected as much. No, it was his willingness to betray the woman who had birthed him that was revealing. There was hope yet for the youth to be fully bent to their will, if he would stoop so low. The fact that Agrippa would discard his own mother, one of his last allies, meant he would be even more isolated, more vulnerable. It would make his mission all the easier.

Agrippa's letter to his sister was another matter, and it brought to light something Rufus had not yet considered. It was abundantly clear that Agrippa maintained a surprisingly strong affection for his disgraced sibling. Perhaps, Rufus mused, Julia could be used to further their cause, even if she only served the purpose of controlling her brother.

I paced my bedroom, just as I had done every morning without fail since Quintus's revelation that my son was alive and well in the care of Lucius's grandson, Aulus Caecina Severus, the governor of Moesia.

I awoke each day with an unstoppable stream of thoughts and anxieties, an ever-building sense of excitement, and fear, as I pondered my child's daily existence and the various futures that might await him. There were a thousand questions to be answered, a thousand scenarios to be thought through and planned for.

Lucius had avoided the villa since Quintus's verbal slippage revealing his connection to the old man's grandson, and so the commander, Titus, and I had rowed across to visit him, unannounced, on a calm winter afternoon a week since his last appearance. Although taken aback by our unexpected arrival, Lucius had seemed relieved when Quintus informed him that their secret was now known openly amongst us all.

"My dear, I am so very sorry for the deception," he had gushed, holding my hands as tears sparkled in his eyes. "I am also most sorry for baiting you about the child, when you had just had him taken from you and thought that he was no longer of this world."

I thought back to Lucius's first visit after the birth, when he had appeared and asked after the baby, callously commenting on my figure and inquiring if the infant had been stillborn, as if he had no idea what had transpired. Although my anger briefly surged at the memory, at how coldly I had been manipulated, I pushed it down. Quintus, in an effort to protect us all, had instructed the old man to play the role of unknowing dolt, and Lucius had played it exceptionally well. I could bear no ill will against him when he had orchestrated the survival of my baby.

Unfortunately, since the delivery of my child to Lucius's grandson at summer's end, there had been no word of his wellbeing. This was intentional, for the safety of all parties involved, but proved to be exceptionally frustrating.

Now, with Proserpina's return bringing warmer temperatures and fresh, green growth to the island, we expected a supply ship any day, the arrival of which would also signal the imminent departure of Quintus and Titus.

Taking a breath, I forced myself to stop pacing, pushing back the door hanging as I stepped into the corridor. I nearly collided with Quintus, who averted his eyes with a mumbled apology as he gestured for me to proceed in front of him. Although words could not express how grateful I was to the soldier for sparing my child at the final moment, a lingering part of me resented how both he and Lucius had intended to keep their silence on the matter forever. Only Titus's vocal suspicions had prompted the commander to speak out, finally confessing that my son still lived.

How to proceed next was a contentious topic. Quintus and Lucius had both refused to contact Moesia's governor regarding my child's welfare, and they also made it clear that they strongly believed I should merely take comfort in the knowledge that my son was alive; to take any further action, they claimed, would lead to the downfall of us all.

Titus remained mute on the topic, at least in group settings; as it stood, he was still under Quintus's command. In private, he reassured me that we would think of something, but no formal plans had materialized as of yet, and time was running out. Every blooming flower and fresh green blade of grass reminded me that the spring supply ship neared and Titus's departure was imminent. And, so, I spent my days pacing, worrying and imagining.

The glimpse of a ship on the horizon one bright morning brought about a brief frenzy of activity, which only subsided when it finally passed away into the distance. It was not bound for us. A full week passed before another ship was sighted, and its gradual increase in size confirmed that we were, at last, the intended destination.

I refused to remain in the villa as Titus packed up what few belongings he had with him, instead choosing to stand alone by the cliffside as the supply ship drew ever closer. Neither remaining guard insisted on accompanying me. What threat was left?

When he was finished, Titus joined me, wordlessly attaching himself to my side.

"Promise me you will find my son," I said, not bothering with a greeting. "Find a way, whatever it takes."

There wasn't even a pause before his answer came. "I will."

"I know I may never see him again. I know that. But if you can care for him, teach him and protect him, then I will be happy. Love him for me, as you love me."

Titus nodded, repeating his words. "I will."

I turned to him then, and we embraced, hugging each another fiercely. Our tight hold on one another quickly became sensual, a sense of desperation tinging our kisses as we knew that these were our last few hours alone together. I could not know my future, nor could I plan for it, and so I prepared to say my final farewells to my friend, my protector, my lover.

I cried as we made love in the same spot where we had first consummated our forbidden bond—the same place where I had considered throwing myself to my death; where Aphrodite had killed herself; where Quintus had thought to cast away my son; where Marcus had tried to strangle the life out of me. It was a place of life-altering decisions, a place that had come to mark the most significant events of my exile, all within a mere year—a stretch of time that had seemed to pass in a way that was at once painfully sluggish and brutally rapid, bearing with it grief and hardship alongside redemption and deliverance.

We lay together afterwards as a warm spring breeze flowed over us, gulls calling out as they observed the island, searching for an easy meal. The supply shipped inched closer and closer.

"What should I call him?" Titus asked suddenly, stirring me only slightly from my sleepiness.

"Hm?" I traced a finger across his haired chest, my eyes still closed, warm under the spring sun. It was nice, if only for a few moments, not to think too much about all the things I had no power to change.

"Your son. What should I tell him his name is, when I find him?"

I blinked, uncertain. In all this time, I had never decided on a name. To name that which was dead was to hold onto the past, to hold onto hope.

I realized now that I had reason to hope; if not for myself, then for my child, now removed from the intrigues and plotting of Rome and, for all intents and purposes, dead to the powers that be. He could live a life unencumbered by the politics of my family, free to pursue a path of his own choosing. He could be safe.

Custom was to name a child after his father. In my son's case, that would be after my last lover, Silanus, who had willingly and knowingly betrayed me and our unborn child in an attempt to save his own skin. It all seemed so very long ago now, a different life entirely. There was no going back, to any of it.

"Call him Titus," I said after a few moments. My words were decisively firm.

I felt the soldier's body tense beside me in surprise, and then he softened. "Titus," he breathed his own name, and we gazed at each other silently.

Eventually, we began to dress, preparing to return to the villa to await the supply ship. We would soon find out the official fate of Quintus and Titus, the new arrivals bearing news of the investigation into last autumn's abduction attempt. Soon, too, I would be surrounded by a mass of fresh, unknown faces. We walked slowly, each step taking us closer to our questionable futures.

"I don't know when I will be able to reach Tomis," Titus informed me. "The ship is bound to return to Rome, and Quintus and I both must report in… unless we are to take the fault for the attack."

I began to protest, but Titus quieted me. We had been through this many times before; although it was unlikely that he and his commander would be punished for last autumn's attack, it was nevertheless a possibility.

Titus continued. "I will likely be entitled to some period of leave, and it is then that I will travel to Moesia. Quintus has made it clear that he will not pursue this, nor help in any way. As far as he is concerned, your son… Titus," the name quivered on his lips ever so slightly, "is to be forgotten about. He is to be on his own."

I dragged my feet as the villa rose into sight, and Titus looped his arm through mine, helping me to walk forward.

"I will find him, Julia," he said. "I will find him. I promise you."

"I know you will." I blinked back tears, and Titus fiercely embraced me once more.

"Come now," he murmured, and we entered the villa together, Titus slowly slipping back into his role as a soldier. I did not know if I would ever get to see him again in any other capacity, and he was not so cruel as to pretend that he knew otherwise, either. There would be no promises of a lovers' reunion, because we both knew that such promises could all too easily become unwitting lies.

Monimos and Artemis were busy cleaning up the villa and preparing a meal to receive the new guards. Quintus had dressed himself in proper soldier's garb, fit to officially hand over command to whomever was to be next in charge of my exile, and he nodded at us in solemn greeting.

"Best prepare yourselves," he suggested. "Receive them now as you mean to treat them for the duration of their term here." The latter order was addressed specifically to me.

I nodded, taking his meaning. A year ago I would have bristled at his tone, but now I could appreciate his warning.

These were fresh guards, unknown to us all. To be anything less than what I was—the granddaughter of their esteemed emperor—was to show weakness. I was an exile, but I remained an imperial; I was a prisoner, but I had my dignity. It didn't seem so long ago that I had promised myself I would carry that prideful sense of superiority with me even as the ship bore me to my island prison, and I now renewed that vow.

Following Quintus's advice to prepare myself, I headed to the bath to get cleaned up. I lingered in the warm water, my mind racing. What if the entity who had bribed Marcus to kill me had already turned one of my newest guards?

Although Quintus and Titus had discussed the situation and agreed that it was better not to report what Marcus had done, since there was no tangible proof, I still feared another attempt on my life. Both soldiers had reassured me that the newest arrivals would have undergone the most extreme vetting possible considering the attack in the autumn, and even Titus seemed to dismiss my worries as out of hand. I remained unconvinced, but neither of them could help me now. I was on my own once more.

Finally leaving the bath, I dressed myself in my finest clothing and called for Artemis to help me fashion my hair. I had no doubt that I was well out of style with the current trends in Rome, but it was all that I could do. Perhaps some new clothing would arrive with the other supplies.

We all gathered in the atrium, an indeterminable amount of time passing at an unbearably slow pace as we waited for the new arrivals. No one spoke, and the repetitive clearing of Quintus's throat was the only noise. All of us started when the knock on the door came at last, and Titus and I exchanged a lingering, loving look as Quintus went to grant the newcomers' entrance.

Everything from that point on was a blur. I counted some dozen soldiers, a sharp increase from the original four who had first accompanied me into my *exilium*. There was a small handful of slaves, male and female, to handle the additional work created by the increased number of guards, and an immeasurable load of supplies streamed in. I caught sight of food stuffs, including grain and preserves, as well as trunks that might contain clothing or bedding. Assorted pieces of furniture, fresh from the craftsmen of Rome, were set down in a half-organized heap, pending their later placement in the appropriate rooms of the villa.

The new commander approached, and he and Quintus saluted one another respectfully. Formalities over, the new man removed his helmet, revealing a closely cropped head of blond hair and alarmingly bright blue eyes. He and Quintus embraced, both men laughing as they clapped each other on the back. Clearly, there was to be no arrest of my soldiers, and I let out a breath I hadn't even known I was holding. Titus would be safe.

"Never thought I'd see you again, Gaius!" Quintus was saying.

The newcomer, Gaius, chuckled. "Last I saw *you*, you had a Gallic dagger sticking out of your back!"

I raised a brow. "Excuse me," I interrupted, somewhat more harshly than intended.

Quintus's smile faded, but I could see in his eyes that he approved of my tone as he turned to face me. I had treated him the same when we had first met on the ship, establishing my authority despite my unfortunate position as an exile. I needed to do the same now.

"Mistress, please excuse us. Gaius and I go back a long way. I had no idea he would be replacing my command here." Quintus's tone was formal.

I sized up the new commander, standing straight and tall as I did so. At last, I sniffed. "He will be satisfactory," I announced.

Quintus hid a small smile, and I felt Titus, standing on my other side, relax. There was already a level of trust amongst these soldiers, and I had to believe that was a good sign.

I soon excused myself and dined separately, the raucous noise of the soldiers drinking and talking reaching me even in my bedroom. There would be only one night of overlap between the two groups of guards, and then the ship would be underway in the morning.

I did not see Titus again until sunrise, when the sound of movement in the hallway stirred me from my half sleep. I felt exhausted. Even when the noise from the men had died down, I had not been able to quiet my mind enough to find any rest. When I had managed to drift off for brief periods, my dreams had been fitful and strange. Neptune, with his familiar long hair and salty ocean smell, appeared throughout, but he was never able to speak to me. His mouth was moving, but no words came forth that I could hear, leaving me with a strong sense of foreboding.

I dressed quickly, the sparrow's insistent chirps reminding me that she had not yet had her breakfast, and I raced to the atrium to find Quintus and Titus preparing to depart. They were joined by Gaius, who, despite his obvious hangover, looked alert enough. The sailors were already preparing the ship for departure from the port below.

"I simply came to wish you farewell. May your journey be safe and quick." There was little else I could say in front of Gaius; those few words would have to do. Titus and I had said our real goodbyes the afternoon before, but I wanted—needed—to lay my eyes on him once more, to fix the memory of him in my mind.

Quintus spoke for both himself and Titus. "Thank you, mistress." It was formal and slightly cold. It was the way it was meant to be—the way it *had* to be, for all our sakes.

Titus sent me a look into which I read love and reassurance, and then they were leaving. Gaius was chatting away with Quintus as they turned their backs to me, pushing open the atrium doors and stepping out of the villa. There was no backwards glance from any of them, and then the door slammed shut in my face. I felt nauseated; my heart pummeled my chest. Titus was leaving. He was leaving me here.

I simply stood there, staring at the closed door, a war of emotions battling violently within me, a small voice urging me to run after them, to get on the ship, to hug Titus once more, a final embrace. The more logical voice within me proffered a reminder that to expose Titus as my lover was as good as to sign his death warrant with my own hand. Better to let him go, to remember that, soon enough, he would find my son, the boy I had named after him. That would have to be enough.

It wasn't until some of the new guards began to stir, their snores turning into morning grumbling, that I at last left the atrium, lest they find me standing there, gaping at the closed doors. I wasn't ready to deal with any of them yet.

I hurried along the corridor until I reached a window that oversaw the area around the port, and I stared down at the water. I saw Titus standing on the deck beside Quintus as sailors scurried back and forth. I could make out little else, although my eyes tried their best, sucking up every last visible detail.

At last, the ship got underway. It somehow took both an eternity and no time at all for it to sail from Trimerus, bearing my lover away from me without ceremony. When I could no longer see the ship, I turned from my vantage point, only to find two guards watching me with perplexed expressions. Rather than addressing them, I raised my head and marched past to the atrium doors. It was time for my morning walk.

CHAPTER XXXVI

OVID

Ovid, despite his worst fears and endless complaints regarding his purported cruel and ongoing confinement, had survived the bleak and frigid winter in Tomis, emerging from his residence only when absolutely necessary, and even then ensconced within layers of wool. The poet had had his slave woman, Galla, keep the fires of the small house burning without fail while he passed the winter months composing his various works and preparing to dispatch them all in the spring to Rome, into the safe care of his wife. Fabia was waiting for word from him, and he would not disappoint her.

Spring had come at last, and Ovid's small collection of poems and letters was now in the care of exceedingly well-paid handlers. For the first time in quite a while, the poet allowed himself a respite, and with it came the opportunity to reflect upon matters other than his own wellbeing and future.

The governor, Aulus Caecina Severus, had paid him a handful of visits throughout the winter, and each time it had become increasingly obvious that the man's interest in Galla's twins exceeded what could be considered normal. All the while, Ovid had been quietly observing his household with a much keener eye than before, and he now felt as if he had reached a conclusion about what was going on beneath his nose.

Although Aulus always took care to inquire after the health and care of both infants, favoring neither above the other, it did not escape Ovid's notice that the twins were growing more and more dissimilar with the passage of time. The one called Scorilo now bore a striking resemblance to his mother, with tanned skin, dark hair, and almost-black eyes, along with thick, blunted features. In contrast, the other boy, Duras, had finer features, lighter skin, bronze curls, and dark brown eyes. He exhibited no likeness to his mother or his brother—nor to his supposed father, Didas. It was Duras whom Ovid suspected of being the governor's bastard, pawned off on a slave woman who, with a babe of her own, could serve as a wet nurse. But he had to be certain.

"Galla, come here for a moment," Ovid called out, knowing that she would hear him in the small *domus*: it seemed that one could never be out of earshot when there were so few rooms in the house.

The poet frowned as he recalled his much more luxurious accommodations back in Rome, a delightful residence that Fabia took such pleasure redecorating frequently, concerned about keeping up with all the current fashions, however ridiculous or expensive they might be. Nevertheless, Ovid had always indulged her without fail; after all, what did a handful of coins matter when his Fabia's smile was beyond any measure?

Ovid sighed wistfully and gazed out the window as people bustled about on the street below. It was an interesting combination of humanity here, he mused: Romans, Greeks, Dacians, and Thracians all living alongside one another, often easily enough. Although he would never admit it to anyone but himself, part of him had grown accustomed to the way of life in Tomis; he had even picked up a few words and phrases used by the local Dacian people, thanks to the assistance of the freedman Didas. But with any luck, he would soon return to Rome—and to Fabia—where he would have no need of his new vocabulary.

Galla appeared then, and the heavyset slave woman bobbed humbly to the poet as she stood in the doorway. "I am here, *dominus*. How may I help?"

"Bring your children in here, Galla. I'd like to have a look at them."

A brief flash of concern crossed her face, but she did as he bade without protest. "Right away, *dominus*."

Galla disappeared for only a minute or two, returning with a rosy-cheeked boy on each hip.

"Bring them closer," Ovid ordered. Galla hesitated only briefly, but she obeyed once Ovid glared at her in warning.

Ovid studied Duras, who smiled at him with the joyful innocence of an ignorant child, as if he were immune to the world's evils. The poet tried to find the features of the governor in the infant boy, but he still could not be certain.

"Tell me, Galla, these boys are twins, are they not?" Ovid fixed the slave woman with his gaze.

She bit her lip as she appeared to briefly consider her answer, but she ultimately responded in the affirmative, though her tone betrayed a hint of uncertainty. "Yes, *dominus*."

"Why is it that they look nothing alike?" Ovid asked. "Why is it that little Duras here looks nothing like his brother, nothing like your husband, and nothing like you? It's quite curious, isn't it? Strange, even. In fact, they aren't even the same size, what with Scorilo always being just a bit smaller than his brother."

Galla began to look worried. "I do not know, *dominus*. The gods decide."

"Indeed they do." Ovid paused. "Hand me Scorilo," he ordered.

Again, a slight hesitation, but Galla complied quickly enough, passing the darker boy to her master. Ovid suddenly stood and held the boy outside the open window, hanging him above the street below by his little, chubby legs, and Galla cried out in shock.

"Don't worry, Galla, I won't drop him. Just tell me about the other child, Duras. I know he isn't yours."

Galla began to cry, tightly clutching the child in question to herself even as she stared in horror at Scorilo dangling out the window.

"Come now, Galla. I don't have all day." Ovid sighed impatiently, though the arm holding the infant trembled—not from weariness, but from uncertainty. He didn't enjoy what he was doing, but he saw no other way; he needed to know the truth of it all, for his own sake.

"I am sorry, *dominus*, but the governor made me promise not to say," she wailed.

"I am your master now, and I order you to tell me. I don't like having secrets in this household, and this has gone on long enough."

Galla broke quickly, her teary gaze fixed on the child in Ovid's grip. "Duras is not mine, *dominus*."

"I know that, you silly woman," Ovid snapped. "It's obvious enough. But is he the governor's brat?"

Galla sniffed, her nose running. "Didas and I always thought so, but the governor never told us. He just appeared one day, knowing that I was to have my own child soon, and brought the infant with him."

"Go on," Ovid urged, his tone now soothing. He brought Scorilo back close to his body, safely away from the open window. The infant warbled at him and waved its arms happily, completely unaware of its uncertain fate only moments before. Ovid breathed a nearly silent sigh of relief, for the infant's sake as well as his own.

"He didn't say who he belonged to, only that we were to treat him as our own son, if not even better, and that he would check in on us, make sure the child was provided for. He threatened us with lashings if we told anyone, or if we did not treat the child well." Galla looked at her master beseechingly. "I don't know anything more, I promise. But I have come to care for Duras as if he is my own. Please don't take him from us, *dominus*."

Ovid sighed, frowning as he handed back the child. "You may go," he muttered. "Say nothing to the governor about this... conversation." The slave woman retreated faster than he had ever seen her move before, the happy gurgling of one of the infants drifting back to him.

Ovid briefly closed his eyes and took a deep breath as he pushed down the queasiness that had arisen in his stomach, telling himself that his threat on the baby's life had been necessary. After all, he had promised Fabia he would do whatever was needed to return to her—and now he knew for certain that the infant Duras was not Galla's whelp, but was no doubt the governor's bastard brat from some other woman. Ovid could press the issue with Aulus and use it to his advantage.

It was clear that the governor cared for the boy; Aulus hadn't bothered to expose the child, but instead intended to have it raised, checking in on it with a reliable regularity that betrayed a sense of ongoing duty and concern that would surely extend beyond its infancy. But certainly the governor's wife, left behind in Rome, wouldn't take kindly to the tangible evidence of her husband's infidelity abroad, if Duras's existence were to come to light...

Although affairs and bastard children were certainly not uncommon amongst Rome's elite, ruling men, their wives often looked the other way—so long as everything was conducted quietly and any resultant issue was pushed to the shadows and wholly ignored. No woman wanted to be made a mockery of amongst her peers because it was *her* spouse who seemed to favor his whore more than his wife, or who valued his bastards above his own, legitimate children.

But already Aulus had proven that he cared for his bastard more than was ordinary or respectable. If word got out in Rome that the governor was making a fool of his wife—who, if Ovid recalled correctly, had brought her husband almost the entirety of his wealth when their marriage was arranged—the humiliation would not soon be forgotten, creating a series of potential consequences that Aulus might prefer to avoid: divorce, bankruptcy, the loss of his position in a regime that so proudly yet so hypocritically proclaimed its devotion to morality...

Ovid hurriedly scratched out a note to Fabia, instructing her to become friendly with Aulus's wife; the woman would have to trust the source of the news, when it came time to be delivered, or else she might not lend it credence. Fabia would also be entrusted with quietly planting the seeds of gossip amongst Rome's leading ladies, if the need arose, to ensure that anyone and everyone who mattered would hear of Aulus's behavior, and thus guarantee his wife's thorough humiliation. Rumors could be such a reliable tool.

Now, if Aulus would prove agreeable to Ovid's demands—sending a few letters that sang the poet's praises, importing some better foods for him while he awaited his recall, and so on—then no one in Rome—including his wife—would be the wiser to the governor's doings in Tomis. Still, Ovid knew he had to proceed cautiously, lest he push the governor too far; Aulus did not strike him as a stupid man, nor a cowardly one.

CHAPTER XXXVII

JULIA THE YOUNGER

Amongst the newly arrived slaves on the supply ship was a plump and well-shaped woman about my age named Claudia, dark haired and eyed with surprisingly fine, pale features. She, I was told, was to be my new companion.

Claudia was more than up-to-date on the current fashions in Rome, from clothing to hair to cosmetics, and she seemed to take some measure of delight in filling me in on all that I had missed, chatty, overly indulged thing that she was. One of her favorite topics was the games, particularly the most handsome—and winsome—gladiators, whom her former mistress, a young woman from a self-made family named Flavia, loved to watch, and flirt with, regularly.

Claudia was a shockingly stark contrast to the matronly Aurelia, as well as to the quiet, submissive Aphrodite, and recalled the simpering, backstabbing women I thought I had long ago left behind in the city. I didn't trust her in the least.

We were passing through the atrium one day, returning from a walk around the island, when I noticed that she was not so subtly preening under the leering gaze of a few of the guards who were at leisure.

"Stop that," I snapped at her in front of everyone. "No slave of mine is to have relations with any of the guards. I'll whip you myself if I have to. Now come along." I set off down the hallway.

Claudia looked ashamed, her face flushing red, and she meekly followed me back to my room without a word—or a backwards glance to her admirers.

I didn't bother to apologize, nor to explain myself; I required no reason to chastise her, although the guards were another story. While they owed me a high level of respect due to my imperial status, they remained, ultimately, my jailers. I would have to tread carefully with them.

Still, the gazes of those men had reminded me far too much of Marcus, sadistic creature that he had been. I would not let another man abuse and manipulate my personal slave again, although I had to admit my concern was only partly for *her* wellbeing. I was more worried about my own safety, should another assassin be lurking amongst us. Claudia could prove to be another weak link, in the same vein as Aphrodite.

In addition to guards, slaves, and supplies, the ship had also borne a letter from my sister Agrippina, who had been entrusted with the care of my daughter, Aemilia, for the past year. It was to this that I turned my attention, rereading it for the umpteenth time.

I felt guilty that I had spared little time to think about my daughter. In my absence, she had reached her thirteenth birthday, another milestone on the road to womanhood, but she had also had her betrothal to her cousin Claudius dissolved by the emperor—a blow that further reflected my family's fall from favor, between my late husband's treachery and my own disgrace. Aemilia's future was to suffer not because of any fault she had committed, but because of her parentage.

Agrippina wrote that a new betrothal was, without question,

forthcoming, but that she was not sure of all the candidates currently under consideration by our grandfather. Certainly it would be no one as high profile as young Claudius, but I hoped it would at least be someone kind. Kindness, I had come to realize, went a long way for a woman, whatever else her lot in life.

Otherwise, my sister reported, Aemilia was happy enough, although her patience was sometimes tried by Agrippina's own very young children. My sister's eldest boy, Nero Caesar, had seen three years now, but was still prone to noisy tantrums at odd hours. He was also increasingly set off by the wailing of his new little brother, Drusus, who had been born shortly before Agrippina had written her letter to me.

I had had to pause after reading that line. I hadn't even known my sister was carrying her second child. She must have fallen pregnant not long after I had, before my *exilium*. I wondered how much she knew about my own bastard child, her illegitimate nephew; it had been one secret I had not dared share with even her, and I doubted our grandfather would discuss it now. If Agrippina knew, she would be wise not to pursue the topic.

After that inclusion, my sister went on to write that Aemilia asked after me often, and Agrippina assured me she told my daughter only that we were well and that I sent my love. Better that Aemilia not know the full truth of everything that had happened, not yet—not the cause of my exile, nor everything that had transpired since.

It was here that my sister's letter then became strange, a particular section to which I returned time and time again since I first had read it:

OUR MOST DEAR GRANDMOTHER, LIVIA, SENDS HER BEST WISHES FOR YOU, GIVEN YOUR CURRENT STATE. I SAW HER JUST THE OTHER DAY, AND WE DISCUSSED A BIT OF HISTORY, ONLY TO PASS THE TIME AS WE WAITED FOR OUR NOONTIME MEAL.

I RECENTLY HAD THOUGHT TO RENAME TWO OF MY SLAVES CORNELIA AND AFRICANA, AFTER THE MOST ESTEEMED MOTHER OF THE GRACCHI— SO VIRTUOUS A ROMAN WOMAN THAT SHE WAS—AND I MENTIONED THIS TO OUR GRANDMOTHER IN PASSING, THINKING THAT SHE MAY FIND THE IDEA HUMOROUS.

QUITE RIGHTLY, SHE REMINDED ME THAT CORNELIA AFRICANA HAD NOT BEEN A WOMAN TO TRIFLE WITH, WHETHER IN LIFE OR EVEN IN DEATH, DEPARTED SPIRIT THAT SHE NOW IS; DID I NOT RECALL THE LENGTHS TO WHICH SHE WENT IN ORDER TO ADVANCE HER SONS' CAREERS? BETTER NOT TO USE HER NAME IN JEST, LEST A FURY IS CALLED FORTH.

I became convinced that it was some sort of hidden message, but I could not yet decipher it in full. My letter had clearly been opened before I had received it, which was to be expected; had there been anything obviously amiss in it, it never would have been delivered to me at all. Whatever Agrippina was trying to tell me thus *had* to be conveyed in disguise, cloaked within seemingly normal words that would raise no alarm. Even then, she still would be endangering herself and her own family to tell me something. The question remained: to tell me *what*?

The first odd words were those lovingly describing Livia, our grandfather's wife, who in truth was no blood relation to us at all. She had never been a kindly figure, and there was no warmth between her and Augustus's descendants by way of his only daughter, my own mother. Perhaps Agrippina had only said as much since she knew her letter would be opened and read. After all, it would not do to fan the fire by airing our familial unrest.

The considered renaming of her slaves also confused me, as Agrippina had always favored exotic names for her household. Not a one of them had ever carried a truly Roman-style name, although there had been countless versions of Apis, Zmaragdus, and Viticula, amongst others that now escaped my recall. Why the change?

Finally, Agrippina's apparent heeding of Livia's warning about trifling with spirits did not ring true to my ears. As much as my sister and I had always shown the appropriate level of piety, as was expected of imperial women, neither of us had ever been particularly fearful of the gods, nor wary of magics and omens.

Why the inclusion of such a silly little story? Agrippina was not one to mince words, and yet she had used valuable space in her letter to recount a strange interaction with Livia that was so out of the ordinary that I was not even certain it had occurred at all.

"*Domina?*" Claudia spoke up meekly, stirring me from my musing. She still appeared contrite after being disciplined for her earlier flirtations. "Will you be bathing soon?"

I made a noncommittal sound, waving a hand at the slave woman in an effort to silence her as I tried to recapture my thoughts, but it was too late. Whatever idea had been forming in my mind was now lost.

I sensed that my new, too-talkative companion was about to address me again, and I scowled at her just as she began to purse her lips to speak. "No, Claudia, not yet. I will let you know. Now be silent, unless I wish for you to speak."

Claudia sighed and resettled herself, looking bored. No matter to me.

Although I spent a few more minutes trying to evaluate my sister's letter, I was not able to generate any particular revelations, and I ultimately set the papyrus aside.

I dined alone that evening, with only Claudia for company. I did not bother to engage in conversation with her, and so she sulked over her bowl of cabbage and honey-vinegar as the sound of laughing guards reached us from the *triclinium* down the hall. Eventually, all was quiet, and we went to bed, Claudia's soft snores lulling me to sleep.

It was perhaps some hours later that I awoke with a start, gasping into the darkness as I flailed with my arms, confused about where I was. It took only another breath to remember it all, and I sank back into my bed, my heart already slowing its beating. Claudia's snores were consistent; she did not stir.

Although I waited for sleep to reclaim me, it would not oblige. It was slightly too warm in the villa, Claudia's presence was a distraction, and thoughts of my son, and of Titus, kept my mind racing. I did not think I could bear to wait for news, knowing that it would be months at least before he reached my child.

At last, worried that I would go mad if I continued to lie there motionless, trapped in my own thoughts, I quietly stood from the bed. I selected a shawl to wrap around my shoulders and moved into the hallway and towards the atrium. My companion's breathing remained constant, her sleep undisturbed by my movement as I left the bedroom.

The assorted snores and grunts of sleeping men emanated from the guards' various resting places, yet I encountered no one as soft moonlight guided my bare feet to the villa's doors. Just as I raised a hand to open them, movement caught my eye, and I turned sharply towards the corner of the atrium.

Gaius, the new commander, sat there, barely a shadow. I would have missed him entirely if he hadn't shifted in his seat, and I realized that had been his intent: he had wanted me to see him.

"Good evening," he said quietly, sitting back.

I responded in kind, and we simply stared at one another for a few breaths. I was the first to break the silence. "Will you escort me on a walk? I can't sleep."

"Neither can I." He didn't address my request.

Instead of waiting, I raised my hand to the door again in an attempt to open it. It did not budge. I tried again, and then I caught sight of the padlock affixed to the door, keeping it closed against my efforts.

Gaius spoke, observing me from his shadowy corner. "Recently added."

"I noticed," I answered dryly, turning back towards him. I wanted to be furious, but I couldn't find the energy.

The new commander's tone of voice sounded surprisingly apologetic as he spoke again. "Orders, from above, because of what happened before," he explained, referencing last autumn's attack on the villa. "Nothing much to be done, I'm afraid. The doors will always be locked from sundown to sunrise now."

I mentally scoffed at the presumption that a little padlock on a set of wooden doors would stop a small army of violent men bent on breaking through, but I kept my opinion to myself. It would be unheeded regardless of its validity, and I suspected anyway that the padlock was in truth partly for me, to make sure I did not wander.

"No one ever told me who was behind the attack, the attempt to abduct me," I said instead of commenting on the new lock. "Who was it?"

I sensed Gaius's hesitation as he considered what, and how much, to tell me—and that is how I knew with certainty that the mastermind of the plot had indeed been found out.

I never had had much time to ponder the attack itself. I had been far too busy fighting for my life as Marcus tried his damnedest to kill me. After his death, instead of feeling secure, I had been left with even more questions and anxieties, wondering who had sent him, why they had done it, and if another assassin would find his way to me after Marcus's failure.

Although the attack had been frightening, it had always been clear that I was a living target, not to be harmed beyond reasonable repair; I was meant to be abducted, not murdered. That knowledge lent itself to a certain reassurance that I still was not able to find when it came to Marcus's attempt on my life. Nevertheless, now that the opportunity for answers presented itself in the form of Gaius, I was willing to pursue it.

Finally, the man spoke, his words coming slowly, as if he measured each one before letting it leave his mouth. "It was your mother, for the most part. There were some accomplices, naturally, but she engineered it from her own place of exile."

I kept my expression carefully blank as I considered the guard's revelation, trying to weigh my own emotions. Truthfully, I was not particularly surprised. "Is it beyond doubt, that it was her doing?"

"Yes." A quick, confident answer.

Had my family been ordinary, perhaps I would have been pleased that my mother had apparently tried to save me from my fate. But I knew better. She had not engineered a rescue on behalf of my wellbeing, but for the sake of my usefulness, my potential role in whatever games she was plotting. I was a tool to her, nothing more.

"Thank you," I simply said, filing the knowledge away. Ultimately, it changed nothing. I was still an exile, as was my mother, and, presumably, my brother, Agrippa. We all remained cursed. Perhaps we all deserved it. Still, the sudden thought of my similarly disgraced sibling prompted another question from me. "Is my brother, Agrippa, well?"

A long pause. Hesitation. "I'm afraid I can't speak to that, mistress."

Liar. He knew something. I considered pushing him but thought better of it. Perhaps another day.

We remained in the atrium in silence for another moment or so, and then I turned and headed back towards my bedroom, leaving the moonlight, and the commander, behind.

"Goodnight, mistress," Gaius called softly from the corner's shadows. I did not answer.

Claudia's snores continued just as before, the slave entirely unaware of both my earlier, extended absence from the room and, now, my presence. Sleep, I mused, was a strange thing, rendering one dangerously susceptible to the threats of the living world even as it allowed for a blissful escape into the fantastical realm of dreams.

Julia returned to the villa, pushing through the doors and giggling like a young girl as she twirled her new, beaded necklace around a similarly decorated finger. Her mother lingered behind, along with the stony-faced guard who had discreetly accompanied them into the market that chilly autumn morning.

As Julia had known would happen, the passage of time had once again eased the terms of her confinement. Over the summer, memories faded, precautions lessened, and her freedom increased—so long as there was something in it for her jailers. Scribonia slipped a small money pouch to the guard, who, after a single grunt of acknowledgement, then sidled away, as if nothing at all had transpired.

"We really should be more careful," Scribonia belatedly urged her daughter, her lined face looking tired and anxious as she glanced around the empty atrium, seemingly expecting another guard to jump out at them and to betray their most recent infraction to the emperor.

Julia only laughed, the sound shrill and surprisingly cold. "Mother, *you* are not an exile. Father lets you remain with me knowing full well that you have your own resources. I am quite certain he knows that you couldn't bear to see me go without a new bauble every so often." Her mood swiftly soured as a new thought occurred to her. "Although no one of importance will ever be able to admire my good taste, so long as I remain here."

The matching necklace and ring suddenly felt infuriatingly heavy on her body, and Julia took them off, carelessly tossing them onto a small table before sinking down onto a couch with a heavy, woeful sigh.

Julia's sour mood remained steady for several days, so much so that her interest was barely roused even when a disheveled messenger appeared at the residence, loudly demanding to speak with the commander of her guards. A slave summoned the commander, who quickly admitted the messenger after a few quiet words, and both men rapidly disappeared down the hall, passing by Julia in the atrium as if she were merely a statue.

Julia truly did try to remain on her couch, but curiosity shortly got the better of her, as it often did. No guard was present in the atrium at that time, and Scribonia was taking her afternoon rest, so she stood and swiftly moved in pursuit of the commander and the mysterious messenger, her feet silently padding across the mosaicked floors. She soon heard voices behind a door hanging, somewhat muffled and hushed, but filled with strong emotion that intensified as she approached. Surprise, shock, confusion—what in Jupiter's name was happening? It must be something big to warrant a messenger in the flesh.

The first voice Julia was able to make out belonged to the messenger, she presumed, since she didn't recognize it. "Terrible defeat… three entire legions, completely destroyed… yes, right there in the forest, in Germania… barbarian scum…"

The commander spoke next, and Julia managed to catch most of his words. "Varus should have lost his command before this… possible end of occupation in Magna Germania… emperor is not handling the news well…"

The messenger then said something unfavorable about Tiberius, Julia's most recent ex-husband and the emperor's current heir, to which the commander responded with a stymied laugh.

Julia's mind began to race as her thoughts led her down various paths. Would Augustus really end his occupation of the region? If what the messenger reported was true, and three full legions truly had been lost, then it was perhaps the worst defeat in Roman history. Her father would be livid.

Julia's elder sons, Gaius and Lucius Caesar, would not have permitted such a blow to go unanswered, if only they still lived. The emperor would have dispatched them to reconquer the territory and slaughter the Germanic peoples into utter, bloody submission, once again proving their worth as heirs to their grandfather's empire. Yet fate had not been kind, and her most treasured sons were no longer of this realm. Now it would all be left to Tiberius, Livia's wretched spawn.

Julia started as she heard movement in the room behind the door hanging, and she rapidly retreated to the atrium, once more taking her place on the couch, although her heart still beat too quickly. The commander and the messenger passed by, once more without acknowledgment of Julia's presence, and the latter departed without ceremony.

Julia felt the commander's eyes on her, but she did not meet his gaze, and, after a few moments, he left without a word. She wondered if anyone would bother to tell her the news directly.

Her heart finally returning to its normal rhythm, Julia turned her focus towards the situation at hand. She would find some way to use this most recent tragedy to her advantage; it was only a matter of time.

CHAPTER XXXIX

JULIA THE YOUNGER

I felt as if I were the only inhabitant of Trimerus to remain unexcited by the anticipated arrival of the autumnal supply ship, meant to replenish the resources used up over the summer. It would be the last one until the spring, at which point the next ship would, presumably, bear a change of guards alongside foodstuffs and anything else that the villa and its inhabitants might need by then.

I spoke little to any of the guards. In fact, I could see little difference between them, large and faceless brutes that they all were. I always dined alone, with only Claudia for company, although the commander, Gaius, would periodically force his polite attentions on me. I was not so naïve as to think he cared for my welfare beyond my most basic survival; without a doubt, his meetings with me were merely for inclusion in the reports I knew he was preparing for his superiors, to be dispatched with the departure of the next ship.

My conversations with the commander consisted of forgettable, generic exchanges about the weather and his endless war stories, tales of bloodshed that he only sometimes remembered to water down for my well-bred female ears. My contributions were minimal, but Gaius didn't appear to mind, so long as he had an audience.

Sometimes, I would find myself spending hours fantasizing about the path my life might have taken if the attempted abduction a year ago had gone to plan. What if I had gone with them, willingly even? Now that it was confirmed that the entire thing had been my mother's doing, I had the hindsight to know my life had not been in danger. Had I been agreeable, joining them on their ship without resistance, might they even have spared my guards? Spared Titus?

A pang shocked my body as I thought of him. I had become quite skilled at avoiding any memories of my lover, of the man now tasked with finding my lost son. I took a shaky breath, refocusing myself. It had been a silly thought to begin with. My guards would never have let me leave without violence, so the question of their fate was pointless. I let the image of Titus's face fade from my mind, and I felt my heart return to its normal rhythm.

What, though, would have been my mother's next steps, once I was free of Trimerus? If anyone knew, they wouldn't have bothered to tell me, and any contact with my mother was out of the question. It wasn't as if I could write her a letter and simply *ask*. And so, I resigned myself to never knowing, unless my grandfather might relent and recall me to Rome, where gossip, truth, and lies all flowed plentifully. Perhaps I would find answers there, eventually.

Still, I no longer felt hope surge up within me when I thought of my former home. My daughter Acmilia was a distant thought, as were the parties, the dinners, the politics. Everything was a lifetime ago. I did not know how to return, or even if I truly wanted to. That lattermost thought disturbed me on some level, but I had little desire to address it. Who was I, if I was not a woman of Rome? Who was I, if I was without a city, without a home? What did it say about me if I no longer wanted to be those things, to be that person?

A sudden cry rose up from a guard outside my room, and then there was an outbreak of noise. Cheerful shouts, claps on backs. The supply ship must have been sighted. Claudia rushed in, breathless and rosy cheeked, her dress slightly askew.

"*Domina*, there is a ship on the horizon! The men think it's headed our way." She smiled at me expectantly, perhaps hoping for me to be happy, to praise her for being the bearer of what everyone else felt was good news. But I felt nothing.

I nodded, lest she stand there and gape at me all day, and she ran back out of the room, not even waiting for a proper dismissal. I didn't bother to recall her for a scolding.

The supply ship sailed into Trimerus's port the following day, and Claudia sulked for most of the afternoon, since I preferred to take my daily walk rather than be present at the villa as the goods were carried in. As usual, I paid her no mind. What did catch my attention, however, was the arrival of a rowboat from the small island across from us: Lucius.

My spirits rose at the old man's arrival, as I hoped that he bore news of my son, and of Titus. The guard should have arrived in Tomis by then, if all had gone to plan. I knew that he would not waste any time in completing his mission. I hastened back to the villa, Claudia following along behind, no doubt confused by what she thought was my sudden interest in the supply ship.

"*Domina*—" she started to ask once we were inside the villa, but I cut her off.

"You may go. Stay out of trouble."

The slave girl did not question her sudden change of luck. She happily disappeared in search of treats and new, if temporary, companions, leaving me alone in the atrium except for one half-asleep guard who looked as if he already may have helped himself to the fresh wine stores.

It felt as if an eternity passed before there was a knock, and I threw open the doors, quickly admitting Lucius and his accompanying slave. The sleepy guard started, shaking his head to wake himself as he eyed the new arrivals with suspicion before he recognized them. Bored, he once again appeared to doze off.

Gaius had been told of Lucius and his occasional visits by his predecessor, Quintus, and he had been agreeable enough, even if only as a favor to his old comrade. I hoped the next commander, come spring, would be as willing to accommodate the only friend I had left.

Lucius graced me with his familiar gap-toothed smile. "My dear, you look a bit tired. All the excitement of the new supplies, is it?" He reached out to grasp my hand, and I clasped his in return, the comforting warmth of human touch a reassurance I had missed. It had been too long since his last visit.

I shook my head. "I could care less about the supplies. I—"

Lucius squeezed my hand tightly and fixed me with his eyes as he interrupted me. "You may go. Make yourself comfortable and quiet somewhere," he addressed his slave, although he did not spare the man a glance. The slave nodded and obediently disappeared towards the kitchen, where Artemis might give him a tidbit or two from her cooking.

I bit my lip, realizing that Lucius had stopped me from inquiring, in front of too many untrustworthy eyes and ears, about what I really wanted to know.

Lucius let go of my hand, gesturing towards the couches in the atrium. We each took up position on one before he spoke again. "Now, my dear, what I came here to ask about was actually the status of your supplies and if, perhaps, you think there may be enough to keep an old man and his small household fed for the winter, if the need arises."

At first, I thought Lucius was simply trying to distract the guard in the atrium from my earlier near-misstep, but his expression and tone were sincere.

"What has happened?" I asked.

Lucius sighed. Normally chatty and cheerful, he now seemed tired, exhausted even, and frightfully old. I had never considered him *old* in the most basic sense of the word; while he was gray, had more than a handful of missing teeth, and usually moved about with a cane, it had never truly occurred to me that his health might fail in a debilitating way, or that his heart might one day simply cease its beating while he slept. This belated realization alarmed me more than I liked to admit.

"We had an early summer supply ship—a small one as we always do—but I expected another, larger one a month ago, and it still has yet to arrive. Perhaps it was lost at sea… That's not unheard of, and in fact it's happened to me before, since I've taken up residence out here in the Adriatic. But I'm afraid that my household hasn't been rationing supplies as it should, and, well…" he trailed off, for once at a loss for words. His gaze was downcast, looking at his folded, wrinkled hands, speckled with age spots.

"Please don't worry yourself, dear Lucius," I tried to soothe him. "I will speak with Gaius to make any adjustments to the guards' and slaves' diets, and my own, rather than let you go hungry. It will be fine."

Lucius's eyes met mine, and they were sad. The skin sagged around them, making them droopy, and his scraggly, emerging beard looked in desperate need of shaving. I silently chastised myself for being so focused on my son, and on Titus, that I did not even notice his state when I first saw him at the villa's doors. I owed Lucius more than I could ever repay after what he had done for my child.

"Thank you, my dear. I am in your debt. Although," he smiled, seeming more like his usual self, "with Fortuna's blessing, the ship will arrive any day now, and I'll have embarrassed myself here for nothing at all!"

I smiled in return, and we shortly turned to other topics, covering everything except for that which I most desperately wanted to know: whether he had had word of Titus's arrival in Tomis, and whether my son had been located.

Finding that I could bear it no longer, I took control of our conversation. "How is your grandson?" I asked. The question, if overheard, was harmless enough. I knew Lucius would understand that I specifically asked after Aulus Caecina Severus, and all that a mere mention of the man implied.

The sadness returned to his face, and Lucius's voice was somber as he answered. "The summer ship bore me no letters, I'm afraid. Perhaps the missing supply ship might bring news." There was a pause. "I miss all my grandchildren quite dearly. It saddens me not to hear more from them all." The last part was clearly an addition made solely for the benefit of the nearby guard's ears, although, upon my last glance, he seemed asleep on his feet once more.

I tried to quash down the surge of disappointment, of anxiety, that flooded me. What if Titus, or Lucius's grandson, had sent word via the missing ship? What if something had gone wrong? My heart was racing, and I placed a hand across it, willing it to slow even as it pounded against my chest. Lucius only looked on sadly.

"Ah, Lucius, what a pleasant surprise!" Gaius entered the atrium, a half-empty wine cup grasped loosely in his fingers. Neither of us responded to the commander, but he plopped himself onto a third couch regardless. "I was just getting the—" An unexpected hiccup interrupted the man, but he recovered quickly. "The *news* from the sailors." He looked at each of us in turn, as if expecting us to ask him what this news was, but neither Lucius nor myself were particularly concerned. The affairs of Rome no longer had much effect on us.

Gaius shrugged to himself and continued. "We've lost three entire legions in Germania, believe it or not. Your grandfather," Gaius shifted his focus to me, hiccupping again, "is *beyond* furious. Bloody stupid Varus... never much liked him, but Jupiter's *balls*, what a bad way to go!" Another hiccup, followed by a slurp of wine. "His family will never recover from this. To be in command when a massacre like that happens..." He sighed, as if envisioning it.

I examined the floor, processing the news. My grandfather would be feverish with fury, no doubt. His empire, his grand plans, taking one hit after another. First his inability to produce a male son, then the deaths of my elder brothers and the exile of my younger, all of them at one point meant to succeed Augustus. Now the conquered peoples of the empire were fighting back anew, with, it appeared, some measure of respectable success. Oh, yes, my grandfather would certainly be angry.

Would such a turn of events lead to my recall, or to that of my younger brother? Would our grandfather relent and consider our restoration, valuing the blood of his family in light of sudden uncertainty in the empire?

Gaius belched, recalling my attention to the present, and then he wandered off in search of more wine and gossip. Lucius and I exchanged glances, and I could tell that his thoughts were similar to my own. He was no fool. Still, only time would tell, for all our questions. Lucius's next supply ship would hopefully bear news of Titus and my son, perhaps any day now. Spring might deliver further news of my grandfather's plans for his empire, and what roles my family and I might have to play.

The supply ship and its crew departed the following morning, and the days turned into weeks, each one progressively colder and drearier than the last as winter continued its slow but relentless approach.

Lucius's missing ship never appeared, and although Gaius was generous enough in agreeing to evaluate our own rations so that we might aid the old man and his household, I remained forlorn, convinced that the lost ship had taken with it some information about the fate of my son.

I saw less and less of Lucius as some illness took hold of him, wracking his body with violent coughing fits and, apparently, leaving him bedridden much of the time. As much as he was a friend, and thus I worried about him in such a capacity, I became increasingly concerned about how news of Titus and my son might be conveyed to me, should Lucius be lost to Pluto's deathly realm.

Claudia seemed to feel that I had lost my mind, as I had secured permission from Gaius for her to take specially prepared draughts to Lucius, meant to ease his discomfort. She was regularly ferried across the small strip of sea separating our villas in a rowboat with two guards, and upon her return I would interrogate her about Lucius's health. To her credit, the slave girl obeyed my every instruction and answered my every question, although I could tell she did not understand my obsession. So long as she obeyed, I did not care what she thought. Lucius had to live.

There had been several times before that I felt I had reached the lowest point of my life, but that autumn began to reveal new depths of quiet despair. I realized how truly powerless I was, unable to act on my own, and limited to what information the guards deigned to share with me, once they received it. But, worst of all, my only connection to Titus and to my lost child was Lucius, an old and increasingly frail man. Without him, they might be lost to me forever.

CHAPTER XL

OVID

Ovid heard the main doors of his residence open, then muffled voices. He sighed, irritated. He was in the middle of a new poem, and he could not afford for his concentration to be broken.

Shuffling steps outside the room, shortly followed by heavy, labored breathing, signaled the arrival of Graecus, the somewhat elderly—and incredibly ornery—man whom the governor of Moesia had begrudgingly supplied to Ovid after the loss of the slave woman Galla and her family. It had been an unfortunate happening, but, Ovid had protested to the governor, completely unforeseeable.

The governor had been in *such* a rage when he had paid a visit to the poet and learned of the slave woman's escape, along with the two infant boys, Scorilo and Duras, all aided by her freedman husband, Didas. Ovid had simply awoken one morning and the family was gone, without a trace. What the poet did not relate to Aulus was that it had taken him some hours to even realize they were missing, once his breakfast had failed to be delivered in a prompt manner. It had taken him even longer to find someone who could carry a message to the governor.

Ovid knew that Aulus was not particularly concerned about

Didas, Galla, or Scorilo. In the end, as far as Ovid knew, they were like any other slaves or freedmen, easily replaceable. But Duras—ah, yes, Duras. No wonder the governor was in such a frenzy if his favored bastard son had been stolen away from him.

Of course, Aulus would never freely admit as much to the poet, and Ovid had not yet found the ideal opening to use these suspicions to his advantage. Now, with his leverage disappeared into the wilds of Dacia, Ovid worried that the chance had entirely slipped away from him. After all, what point was there in extortion when the only evidence had vanished? Aulus would never confess the truth of it, not now.

Graecus cleared his throat, a harsh, grating noise that irritated Ovid to his wit's end.

"What is it, Graecus?" the poet snapped, still tightly clutching his pen. Nothing was going as he had planned, and Fabia's disapproving face flashed through his mind. The pen snapped, and Ovid cursed, already seeking out a replacement.

The slave cleared his throat again before speaking, his voice raspy. "There's a man here, *dominus*." He paused to breathe, and Ovid fought to keep his eyes from rolling in exasperation. "He is asking after the missing slaves."

"Send him away," Ovid snapped. "I've already recounted everything to Aulus. I'm assuming it's another one of his men, come to ask more questions, but I have nothing else to say. I have work to do. Important work."

"Yes, *dominus*," Graecus said, bowing as he shuffled away.

It was another few minutes before the elderly slave returned, his breathing once again labored after the effort of two trips back and forth. A trace of sweat ran down his cheeks, a sheen highlighting every age line on his face.

"What is it now?" Ovid snapped, throwing his pen down. Ink splatted the table. He would never finish his new poem at this rate.

Graecus took a gasping breath, wiping at the perspiration that moistened his face. "He will… not… go, *dominus*."

The poet cursed and stood, marching past the slave and to the doors, throwing them open violently. Outside, a well-built man waited expectantly, one hand resting casually on the hilt of a short military sword, although he wore a plain tunic rather than an issued uniform. Brown eyes, one of them narrowly missed by the faint scar that ran above it, met Ovid's squarely as the man spoke.

"You must be Ovid. I'm here about the slave family that was here with you. I need to find them." No introduction, no nonsense, straight to the point. Definitely an army man, at least at some point in his life. Perhaps he was a tracker Aulus had hired.

Ovid glared at him. "I already told the governor everything I know. I have work to do, and I would *appreciate* some quiet."

The brown eyes narrowed for a moment in consideration. "Have you any idea where they may have gone?" There was a sense of urgency underlying the words.

The poet sighed in frustration. "As I already said to Aulus, I have no doubt that they scurried off into inner Dacia, back to whatever little barbarian tribe they came from." Ovid narrowed his eyes at the man. "Give me your name, soldier. I would like to register a complaint with the governor for all these interruptions when I next see him. I am not impressed at all with the lack of organization in his efforts to locate these escaped slaves."

The visitor hesitated for a moment, his shoulders tensing as if he were considering a lie, for reasons unknown to Ovid. "My name doesn't matter. I'm here on behalf of the governor." His words were dismissive.

310

The more Ovid examined the man on his doorstep, the more curious—and suspicious—he became. "Tell me, where is the governor now? You look like you've come from quite a way." The soldier's tunic and cloak were mud splattered and worn, and his hair and beard were too long for standard military style. Ovid caught sight of a travel pack thrown over the man's shoulder, although he shifted subtly under the poet's gaze, as if to hide it from view.

"I'm afraid I'm not at liberty to say," the soldier responded curtly.

Ovid could smell a lie; he was well acquainted with them. He was about to interrogate the man further, now doubting his connection to the governor at all, when a crash in the residence behind him briefly drew his attention away from the door. Graecus had no doubt knocked something over in the kitchen, clumsy oaf that he was.

When Ovid turned back around, the soldier was already moving away, a limp from some unseen injury hindering his speed only slightly as he dodged the handful of other people on the street. The man did not spare a backwards glance as he turned a corner and disappeared.

Ovid scowled, his sixth sense for intrigue tingling, but another crash from the kitchen led him to close the door and redirect his attention, for the time being. He would be sure to follow up with the governor about the mysterious man on his doorstep, but he was already certain Aulus would have no idea of whom he spoke. Who, then, was this man working for? And to what end?

CHAPTER XLI

JULIA THE YOUNGER

For the first time since the supply ship's departure, Gaius had firmly insisted that I dine with him. I was certain he simply wanted to produce further reports on my wellbeing, since his most recent ones had been dispatched with the ship, and so I resigned myself to a long evening of war stories and drunken boasts, with minimal participation on my part.

We were alone in the *triclinium* except for Artemis's occasional interruptions to bring in platters of food. She had some additional assistance in the kitchen now, but she remained the primary cook, especially when it came to preparing meals for me or for the commander. The slave had developed quite a knack for seasonings and sauces in particular.

That evening, Artemis had prepared seasoned pork, the pig freshly slaughtered that morning. There were only a few others that had been delivered with the ship, and they would be eaten sparingly. The sailors had also delivered live dormice, more chickens, a handful of doves, and a sole goat, whose life I surmised would be short, as he was already aggravating the guards who were charged with retrieving him every time he escaped his pen.

Artemis also brought out some lightly oiled and salted fish, a sampling of boiled vegetables with sauce, and a platter of dried figs, drizzled with honey. Gaius dug in without hesitation, while I picked at the offerings more daintily. All of them were delicious, but more often than not I found myself with little appetite. My clothes had all hung too loose for quite some time.

Between swallows of food, Gaius gestured at the platters. "Eat something, mistress," he said, taking a gulp of wine.

"I am," I responded with a sniff. I nibbled on a piece of fish to prove my point.

The commander shrugged and tore into a piece of pork. "I'd rather not have to report back that you're wasting away for lack of appetite, what with all these good meals."

It was my turn to shrug. "Report what you will. I don't think it will matter much, in the end."

Gaius's blue eyes fixed on me. "It matters more than you know."

My attention sharpened. "What do you mean?"

The commander chewed thoughtfully, pondering his answer. "There are those in Rome concerned with your... wellbeing."

I took a sip of wine, mulling over my next question. I sensed I was on the precipice of something important, but I didn't yet know what. "Who would be concerned?"

Gaius smiled at me tightly, and I detected regret in his blue eyes. He hadn't meant to say as much as he had. Still, he did not answer my question, and he pointedly changed the topic of discussion.

In short order, the commander had drunk enough wine that he shifted towards his typical tales of slaughtering barbarians, his voice rising as he recounted the various battles he had been involved in. I thought I had heard some of the stories before, but, in the end, they all ran together, their themes overlapping regardless of their smaller details.

I tried one more time to return to our earlier topic, to tease some more information out of him, but he only laughed at me and launched into another story, as if I had never spoken.

Eventually, Gaius stumbled off to his bedroom, in which he was the sole occupant; he had refused to share it with any of his men, instead forcing them to triple or even quadruple up in other spaces. I relocated to the atrium, where two guards noted my appearance and then resumed their quiet conversation in the corner. They had the night shift, and although little of note ever occurred on the island now, the atrium doors continued to bear their heavy padlock from dusk until dawn.

I spent a few quiet minutes observing the stars through the open roof, exceedingly bright on that clear, cold autumn night, before I caught myself in a yawn. Claudia was probably already asleep in our room; unlike Aurelia, she didn't bother herself with waiting up for me. I had begun to suspect the slave girl had been sent off to Trimerus because of her clear lack of suitability to her role.

The guards' eyes briefly followed me as I set off down the hallway, and then the quiet murmur of their voices resumed. I heard snoring from behind Gaius's door hanging and, without stopping to think, lest I lose my grasp on my sudden burst of courage, I brushed through into his room, swiftly dropping the hanging into place behind me.

Gaius was sprawled on his back with one hand and one foot hanging limply off the bed; he still wore the clothes he had dined in, although he appeared to have kicked off his shoes. A sole oil lamp still burned in the corner of the room, casting an eerie shadow of his body against the wall, making him seem immensely larger than he truly was.

My heart was racing, but I forced my breath to remain even and quiet as my eyes searched the room. In moments, they landed on their target: Gaius's letter box. Stepping as softly as I could, I moved to where he kept his writing supplies and, hopefully, his reports. The commander's snoring continued.

After what felt like an eternity but what could only have been seconds, I reached the box and opened it, a small creak startling me as the wood shifted and groaned in protest. Thankfully, Gaius did not wake. Inside I found only one scroll, and I gingerly picked it up. It had not yet been sealed with wax, so perhaps it was a draft. Glancing behind me, I saw that Gaius remained in exactly the same position, and so I focused my attention on the letter, unfurling the scroll carefully.

It was hard to read in the dim lighting of the room, but what I found was dry and ordinary: a recounting of what supplies and slaves had arrived, notes on which guards took which shifts, and so on. There was nothing abnormal at all, and no mention of me in any direct capacity. I carefully rolled the scroll up and placed it back inside the box, closing the lid and gritting my teeth as it creaked once more, the sound shockingly loud in the quiet of the night.

Turning, I took one more look at the sleeping soldier, who had not stirred at all. Disappointed with my lack of findings, I was about to make my retreat into the hallway when something caught my eye. The edge of a small wooden box peeked out from under Gaius's bed, beckoning.

I had no particular reason to think that the box contained anything special. From what I could see of it, it was ordinary in every way. It could have contained clothing, military gear, or any other number of things: bath and shaving supplies, personal tokens, a sewing kit for clothing repairs. I couldn't explain it, but I felt that it held something else, something important.

Clenching my teeth, I moved slowly towards the box. I came so close to Gaius that his occasional snores caused wisps of my hair to shift, and I found that I was holding my own breath as I crouched down, my hands seeking the edges of the box. My skin touched the soft grain of well-used wood, and I lifted and pulled the box from under the bed, careful not to bump it.

Gaius snorted and rolled towards me, and I froze, my heart in my throat as I wondered if he would wake and discover me. After a moment that stretched an eternity, he gave another snore and seemed to settle back into whatever dreams he was traveling through that night.

I considered escaping the room with the box in hand, but I had enough sense to know it would be difficult to return it without its absence having been noticed, should Gaius awaken—and I would have to avoid the night guards a second time. This could be my only chance. I took one step and then another away from the bed before gently setting the box on the ground. Kneeling, I at last lifted the box's lid. It opened silently.

Inside were various small clothing items, which I quickly set aside: wool socks and linen loincloths, mostly. They were of no interest to me. Underneath these, however, was a small, folded piece of papyrus, its edges slightly frayed. It bore no wax seal.

I lifted it with trembling fingers and carefully opened it, my eyes already seeking to make sense of the string of letters I saw scrawled across the yellowed surface. My eyes skimmed the writing, and although I did not see my name spelled out, I knew that it referenced me.

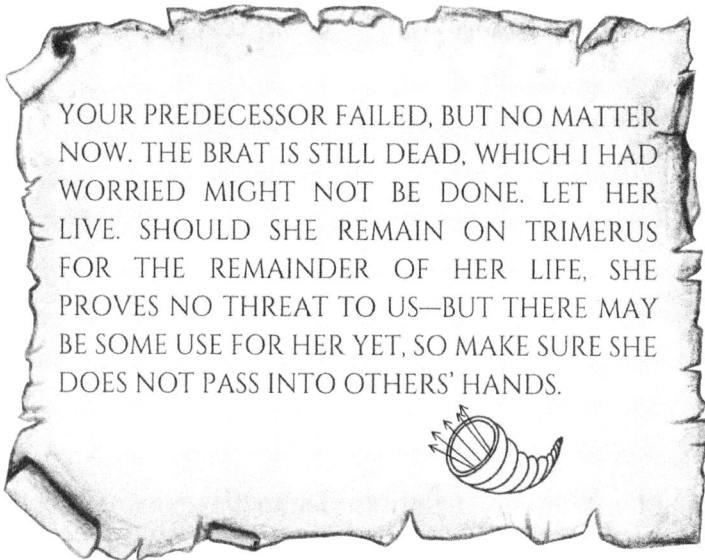

YOUR PREDECESSOR FAILED, BUT NO MATTER NOW. THE BRAT IS STILL DEAD, WHICH I HAD WORRIED MIGHT NOT BE DONE. LET HER LIVE. SHOULD SHE REMAIN ON TRIMERUS FOR THE REMAINDER OF HER LIFE, SHE PROVES NO THREAT TO US—BUT THERE MAY BE SOME USE FOR HER YET, SO MAKE SURE SHE DOES NOT PASS INTO OTHERS' HANDS.

Predecessor. That must be Marcus, though he was not named. The brat was my son, believed to have been eliminated. The remainder of my life—there would be no recall, if this person had their way. I didn't know what to make of the notion that I would be useful to them in some capacity, but the anonymous writer's orders now seemed to suggest that Gaius, rather than killing me, was instead to protect me.

I skimmed further down the page, and in place of a signature there was a design drawn, one that seemed strangely familiar even though I could not place it. A small cornucopia held, in place of fruits and vegetables, five sharp-tipped arrows. I felt as if I were on the verge of remembering where I had seen it when a voice spoke up from behind me.

"I thought you had better manners than to enter a man's room uninvited."

I froze. Gaius was awake.

He laughed, and I could tell he was still drunk. "No matter. Run along now." He did not move from his bed, crossing his arms lazy behind his head.

I seized my chance and fled, dropping the piece of papyrus behind me on the floor as Gaius laughed again at my retreating back, the sound seeming to follow me even long after I had reached my own bedroom.

Gaius did not mention my nighttime visit to his room, nor my discovery of the letter he had in his possession. I would have thought that perhaps he had been too drunk to remember the incident, but I knew better. I could tell he remembered everything by the way his blue eyes tracked me across the room whenever he saw me.

His silence on the matter unnerved me more than I liked to admit. Why did he not speak? Why did he not seek to punish me for rifling through his belongings in the dead of night? Perhaps, I realized, his silence was punishment enough, as was the knowledge that, at any given moment, he could have killed me, had his orders been different. I had thought Gaius could be trusted, since he was an old and trusted comrade of Quintus. My relief at their familiarity had been a potentially deadly mistake.

Winter continued its ceaseless approach, but I took advantage of a warmer than usual afternoon to perch at the cliff's edge. I gazed numbly out at the gray water as Claudia shivered and shifted her weight from foot to foot behind me in an attempt to keep warm, pulling her wool shawl tightly around her body. Two guards, accompanying me for my excursion, muttered and sent glares my way, missing the warm fires of the villa.

My mind was blank, and I didn't notice that Claudia had wordlessly retreated from me. In her place now stood Gaius, and he stepped forward, situating himself directly next to me.

"Aren't you cold?" he asked, rubbing his hands against one another. He wore a thick cloak with furs around his neck, and his face was pale.

I froze, my back stiffening in surprise.

Gaius didn't wait for answer. "I suppose you're rather frightened of me now, aren't you?" Again, he seemed neither to want nor to expect an answer. He sighed. "You shouldn't have been sneaking around. But you know that."

"Who is it?" I asked.

Gaius smiled sadly, but he ignored my question. "I should have burned the letter as soon as I read it. Silly mistake. Amateur, really."

"Very." My voice was cold, and my body remained tense.

The commander shrugged, rubbing his hands together again. "You needn't worry now," he said quietly. "You read the letter. You are to be protected, not harmed. Marcus failed, but it all worked out, in the end. Your son is dead, and you will remain here, safely imprisoned, for the rest of your life, unless there's a need for you. You won't cause any trouble."

I wanted to vomit. I wanted to scream. I wanted to shove Gaius off the cliff. But I remained silent, still. The only thought that kept me sane was the knowledge that my son was alive, and that Titus would find him, protect him. They, at least, were safe.

"Quintus mentioned Marcus's betrayal to me, as he was leaving. He thought I might provide an extra layer of protection for you, should someone else come calling." Gaius smiled, shaking his head slowly. "I think his wits are slipping. Too many blows to the head over the years. Makes a man too trusting."

"Whose orders are you following?" I asked again, my mind picturing the symbol of the cornucopia filled with arrows. I found myself remembering the image in mosaic form, but I could not remember where I had seen it or when.

Gaius continued to ignore me, following his own train of thought. "There will be others like me, with every change of guards. I don't know them, but I know they will be here. It's best to just go along with it, you know. Don't cause too much trouble for anyone, and you'll be treated well enough."

I realized the man thought he was providing kindly advice. He actually thought he was helping me, his blue gaze intense and earnest as he spoke.

I closed my eyes, trying to pull the eyes of my memory up from the mosaicked floor with the arrow-filled cornucopia to those in the room around me. I was young, sitting at a loom. We were spinning wool. My mother was there, sulking and irritated as she cursed her work and muttered about having better things to do. There was someone else there, too, but I could not see her face. I could not remember.

Gaius continued speaking. "There will always be someone watching you, passively waiting for a change of orders. For your sake, I hope those orders never come. But we can never know what Fortuna has in store for us, can we?"

The commander turned to leave, retreating to the warmth of the villa. It was then that I recalled the face of the other woman in the room with the mosaicked floor, the cornucopia filled with arrows. I had asked her once what it meant, and she had smiled at me and answered that a bountiful life could only be achieved through strength, and even violence when necessary. I didn't understand, then. She told me that one day I would.

"Livia," I said, and Gaius stopped in his tracks. "Livia." It was louder this time.

Gaius did not turn around, but his voice was rigid when he spoke. "It would be better for you to forget Rome. Forget your life there. There is no going back."

"Why?" I asked him, wanting to know more, to *understand*. But he ignored me, his strides taking him further and further away from me until he was out of sight. "Why?" I whispered again, my voice caught by the autumn wind and carried away.

I already knew the answer to my own question. I had been pregnant with an illegitimate child, but one who was still related to the emperor, to Livia's husband. Worse, it had been male, a greater threat. My mother's failed rescue attempt had cemented the need to eliminate my child before he could be used against the reigning powers of Rome—but by that point, he was already far gone, believed dead. Livia thought she had succeeded, one way or another.

Livia had never borne Augustus a living heir, and she had never accepted my mother's offspring—Augustus's grandchildren—as her own family. No—she had only ever sought Tiberius's rise in station, and now she had it. My older brothers were dead, and Agrippa Postumus had been cast off, condemned to an island much like my own. I knew then that he would never leave his prison alive, so long as Livia and Tiberius still breathed.

My nephews, Agrippina's sons, were as of yet too young to vie for power of their own, and too close to Rome—and to the emperor—for Livia to easily eliminate. Given time, I had no doubt that they, too, would come under threat, obstacles in Livia's path to power by virtue of their very existence.

I at last understood my sister's letter to me, its veiled warning telling of mothers willing to do anything for the advancement of their sons. Agrippina had already suspected Livia meant me and my unborn child harm, but her words could do nothing for me now. Tiberius was and would remain, if Livia had her way, the sole successor to my grandfather's empire. Augustus's hopes for a blood heir would be eradicated.

Agrippa had put on his very best clothing and now stood at the port, his eyes blinking rapidly as they fought the sun's strength, which was magnified tenfold by the water. He muttered something and slapped his own face in an effort to wake himself from the haze he wandered through in his mind, and his guards exchanged glances. His fits were becoming worse, and his periods of true lucidity ever rarer.

One of the guards stepped closer to the youth and whispered aggressively in his ear, a hand on his arm both supporting and threatening him. "Pull yourself together. My master has finally convinced the emperor to pay you a visit. This could be your chance to return to Rome, to set all our plans into action at last."

Agrippa swayed on his feet. He could barely remember the soldier's real name. He always called them Rufus, after the first red-haired guard who had promised him that his chance for power was not yet lost. Since then, over five years had passed, and still he remained on the cursed island of Planasia. Perhaps Rufus had been wrong.

He was no longer certain why power mattered, why Rome mattered. Nor had he ever figured out who it was that sent guard after guard, claiming to work on his behalf in an effort to bring him to power. Agrippa half thought he had imagined it all.

One of the guards, perhaps the second or third incarnation of Rufus, had told him that if he ceased to cooperate, if he tried to alert the other guards, then they would kill his sister, Julia. He didn't know if he believed them anymore, or if he cared. For all he knew, she was already dead. Sometimes he wished he were, too.

A flurry of movement on the ship attracted Agrippa's attention. Soldiers, garbed in their finest gear as if for a triumph, shining shields in hand, were assembling. Something was happening.

An old man emerged onto the ship's deck, surprisingly small and wan in appearance, especially when surrounded by the polished leather and gleaming metal of a dozen well-built, helmeted soldiers. Agrippa squinted, swaying again. It was Augustus. His grandfather.

Augustus slowly disembarked, careful not to get caught up in his own toga, and approached Agrippa. His gray eyes, although sunken in age, were still coldly calculating. *That* Agrippa remembered well, however scattered his mind might be. But this man was tinged with sickness, not the steely strength he always remembered his grandfather possessing. Augustus, seemingly immortal before now, was fading.

The old man and the youth stood opposite one another, each of them appraising and assessing without dialogue. The assembled guards stood by silently, observing the aged emperor and his errant grandson.

At last, Agrippa opened his mouth to speak. "Grandfather." He managed a solemn greeting and a respectful bow of his head.

The trace of a hopeful smile touched the emperor's lips, but his eyes remained calculating. "Are you well, grandson? I received a report that suggested you had… improved." His choice of wording was careful, measured. He had never liked to speak aloud of his grandson's madness.

To say such words was to confirm it, an admission of weakness, of failure.

Agrippa smiled in return. "I am *quite* well, Grandfather. Come, and let me show you the fishpond where I like to swim." He reached out to grasp the emperor's hand, as he had when he was just a small boy, but Augustus pulled back, all hint of a smile now gone.

"Grandfather?" Agrippa asked. He swayed again, trying to find his balance. "Let me show you."

The emperor's expression became resigned, sad. He smiled again, but it did not reach his eyes. He knew for certain then that there was no chance of restoration for his wayward, mad grandson. Agrippa would see his twenty-fifth summer that year. He should have been in the prime of his life, but he was too far gone for his future to be salvaged.

Augustus gestured for the young man to lead the way. Agrippa showed his grandfather the fishpond and invited him to swim even as he jumped in, still fully dressed in his finest clothing. Naturally, the emperor declined. He did not stay for dinner, but instead ordered the ship to prepare for immediate departure.

Agrippa followed Augustus's retinue to the port, watching the preparations. When all was ready for the ship to get underway, Augustus turned to his grandson with a sigh. His eyes held a sad determination. "Farewell, Agrippa."

The youth smiled and nodded, and then the emperor was gone without a single backwards glance, disappearing below deck.

Later that evening, the same guard who had steadied Agrippa at the port and whispered into his ear beat him severely.

"You fucking mad fool!" he hissed, slapping Agrippa across the face for the umpteenth time. "All you had to do was be sane for a few hours, and you couldn't even manage that! You have ruined everything!"

Agrippa cried out his apologies, but they fell on deaf ears. A rough blow to his stomach silenced him entirely. The guard—another iteration of Rufus—was in a rage, dispensing the fury his own nameless master would no doubt visit upon him when his time on Planasia as a guard expired and he returned to Rome.

The next day, Agrippa thought it had all been a dream, a vision of Augustus that visited him in his sleep. Only his aching body suggested otherwise, and it was then that Agrippa knew his madness had won the better of him at last.

The summer afternoon was wretchedly hot, even for late August. Julia and Scribonia were sprawled on couches, slaves dutifully fanning them even as sweat drenched their own, overworked bodies. A platter of fresh fruits was laid out before the women but remained untouched. Even the thought of reaching out a hand to select an apple or a fig was unbearable in such weather.

None of Julia's plots over the past six years had come to fruition, and she found herself more and more resigned to her fate, at long last. She had curated a comfortable existence for herself, with access to whatever foods and wines she desired and occasional trips to the market in Rhegium, a chance to stretch her legs amongst some degree of civilization. Her efforts were now focused on maintaining what life she had managed to develop over her long years in exile.

She had been too long removed from Rome, and too many of her connections had died or themselves been exiled from the city's limits, strewn uselessly across the empire. Her father's power was secure, and Julia had finally accepted that she would not succeed in ousting him. Perhaps it was her age catching up to her, but she found herself less and less worried about it all.

A knock at the door reached her drowsy ears, but she ignored it, her eyes closed in rest. A slave would see who it was, no doubt a confused delivery boy who did not know where the kitchen door was located. He would be set straight soon enough.

Julia heard the doors open then, and the initial quiet voices were suddenly raised. She frowned, opening her eyes as she fought away the last traces of sleepiness that fogged her mind. Perhaps it was not a lost delivery boy after all.

Three guards, bedecked in all their official military gear, were approaching her, hands resting on their swords in silent warning. One of the household's slaves stood by the still open door, her eyes horrified as more guards entered the villa. The slaves stopped their fanning and backed away, eyes lowered as they pressed themselves to the atrium's walls, hoping to escape notice.

Julia jumped up from her couch, seething at the unexpected and uninvited intrusion. "What is the meaning of this?" she snapped at them, but they paid her no mind. Two guards approached either side of her, each firmly grabbing an arm, while the third watched, his face set.

Julia yelped and tried to wrench her arms free from their grasp, but to no avail. Scribonia herself was being seized by a fourth guard even as she struggled to rise from her couch.

"Leave her alone!" Julia yelled as her mother wailed.

Still the guards did not speak, but instead began to drag her down the hallway. Scribonia, restrained, did not follow, and her wails faded as Julia moved further away and out of sight.

They passed by the bedrooms, and Julia's fear began to rise in earnest. "What is the meaning of this?" she asked, her voice quivering. Her mind, and heart, were racing. "What is happening? I demand that you tell me at once! Such treatment is unacceptable! I am the daughter of your emperor, and I order you to unhand me immediately."

The guards dragging her did not slow, but the third one spoke at last even as they continued to move. "Augustus is dead. Tiberius is emperor." His words were formal, emotionless. A mere statement of fact.

Julia felt as if she fainted for a moment, the blood rushing from her head as she briefly lost not only her vision, but her senses. She shook herself, trying to catch her breath, to think, even as she understood that the world as she knew it was crumbling all around her. There was no time, no time to think, to plan.

The guards reached a small door at the end of the hallway. Julia had never bothered to look at it too closely, since it had been used only for storage. It was this door that they opened, revealing a small, windowless room.

The third guard, who had followed them, passed inside first, and he began to throw out what odds and ends were in the room: a box or two, a broken broomstick, an empty bucket. A fourth guard appeared with a jug of water and a small sack of bread, which he set carelessly on the floor of the room before disappearing.

Julia was shaking. Only the grip of the soldiers on either side kept her on her feet. "Where is my mother?" she asked quietly. Her voice trembled.

The guard who had informed her of her father's death was again the one to answer her. "She will live."

Julia's legs collapsed at his words, because she understood then that she would die. This little room was to be her death; she would be walled up and left to die like the Vestal Virgins of old, if they had failed to keep Rome's hearth alight. This, then, was to be her final punishment.

The guards dragged her into the room and deposited her without another word, slamming the door behind them. She heard it latch and, not long after, the sound of hammering. That door would never open again while she still lived.

They would not even give her the honor of an outright execution. Tiberius was too cowardly to stir up public outcry by shedding her blood directly—the blood of Augustus himself. Instead, she would starve, a slow death that would spare Tiberius's image, from being known as a murderer of women. No one would know the truth of it.

It was dark and stuffy inside the little room. Julia considered rationing the water and bread, extending her life until someone might help her. Perhaps Scribonia could escape her own captors and free her, and they would flee, leaving Rome and her cursed family far behind. Perhaps she had allies still, somewhere in the vast expanse of her father's empire.

But Julia knew, deep down, that such thoughts were wishful thinking. She sought out the jug of water with shaking fingers and gulped half of it before curling into a ball on the hard floor. At last the hammering on the door ceased, and she was entirely alone in the darkness.

CHAPTER XLIV

AGRIPPA POSTUMUS

There was commotion at the villa as Agrippa's guards sighted an incoming ship. It was the end of August, very nearly September, but still too early for the autumn supply ship to be expected. No one knew what was happening, but they were preparing for the worst.

Agrippa didn't particularly care. He wandered unnoticed out to the fishpond he enjoyed so much, watching the creatures swim about, all of them resigned to their life within the stone confines they found themselves in—much like himself. It was a stark contrast to his panicked guards, running about with confused expressions as they tried to plan for whatever was about to happen.

He was unaware of the passage of time as he watched the fish, and eventually he decided to join them. There was little else to do; no one had come to retrieve him or to tell him what was going on. Agrippa pulled off his clothing and left it in a pile on the ground before plunging in, dispersing the alarmed fish with his sudden entrance.

He floated on his back, watching the sun above as it progressed on its journey across the sky. Eventually, some of the fish, intrigued by their visitor now that he remained so still, swam up to Agrippa's pale body, nosing at his fingers and toes as they determined if he was something edible. A twitch of the youth's fingers sent them scattering, and Agrippa smiled, closing his eyes as he floated. The warmth of the afternoon soothed his burns, which, although healed years ago, still seemed to ache periodically, for reasons he couldn't understand.

Shadows dimmed the sun's light that warmed his eyelids, and Agrippa frowned. He didn't like clouds, but they would soon pass, as they always did.

The shadows strengthened rather than dissipating, and Agrippa at last opened his eyes. Where he expected to find clouds, he saw a bevy of soldiers, armored and helmeted. They all watched him, their expressions unreadable, and their hands were resting on sheathed swords.

A guard he faintly recognized gestured to him and spoke, but Agrippa couldn't hear him. His ears were submerged. The man gestured again, and his lips continued to move. At last, Agrippa shifted his position, treading water in the middle of the fishpond. The guard spoke again, and his words were quiet, with a hint of something that Agrippa thought he had long ago forgotten: kindness.

"Come on out, lad. We'll get you dried and fed." He waved at the youth, encouraging him to swim to the rocky edge of the pool.

Agrippa did as he was bade, rolling onto his stomach and paddling over to the guard without hesitation. He had little desire to fight them, not anymore. The man stooped over, offering an arm to help pull him from the fishpond, which Agrippa accepted.

Shortly, he stood at the pond's edge, naked and dripping water as the sun beat down on his body, already beginning to dry it. The guard who had helped him from the water bent to retrieve Agrippa's clothes and headed back towards the villa. Agrippa followed obediently, unashamed of his nakedness.

The first stab did not hurt. Agrippa looked down at his stomach to see the tip of a sword poking out, a bright red liquid dripping from it onto the rocks below. With surprise, he realized the liquid was his own blood. The second attack came just after the first sword was withdrawn, and Agrippa fell to his knees. After the third, he lost count, falling backwards and staring up at the sky once more as his blood spilled from his body and into the fishpond.

The fish, alarmed, retreated, their clean water muddied by the unknown coppery substance. A bird flew low overhead, crying out as it watched the scene of carnage below. Agrippa's pale, scarred body was still at last, his blank eyes open to a sky he no longer saw.

"Well, that's that, then," the guard who had been leading the youth back to the villa said. "May Tiberius live long." The others were silent, observing the results of their work.

One of the soldiers who had been stationed at the villa watched from afar, rubbing his temples to fight the headache he felt coming on. Although his master had already begun to make other plans since Agrippa's failure to be recalled to Rome in the spring, he still would not be pleased to find out about the youth's execution. The political landscape was changing, and rapidly.

CHAPTER XLV

OVID

Graecus wheezed when he entered Ovid's presence, and it must have taken no less than five minutes for the old slave to catch his breath in order to speak. Frankly, Ovid was surprised that he was still alive, and he fully expected him to drop dead at any moment. The only inconvenience would be locating a new, affordable slave that had any idea how to run a proper household.

"Messenger… for you…. *dominus*," Graecus gasped out, steadying himself by placing a hand against the wall. His other hand clutched at his chest.

Ovid remained calm, finishing the sentence he was in the middle of writing without any rush. He had long ago stopped experiencing a surge of hope whenever a messenger was announced. In the end, it always proved to be nothing of any real use to him, just one disappointment after another.

He had now spent six years in Tomis. His letters and poems were regularly and reliably sent off to his wife in Rome, but they had failed to produce any results, despite Fabia's best efforts; he did not blame his dear wife in the least. Augustus, rigid and unforgiving man that he was, had not been moved by his pleas, nor by his praises, however well worded they were. Ovid was slipping into obscurity, and he worried the people of Rome would forget him entirely. Fabia remained his only certainty, but even she, Ovid worried, might begin to neglect him, if things did not soon change for the better.

The poet finally finished writing his sentence and set the pen down carefully. "Send him to me."

Graecus nodded and prepared himself to traverse his way back to the waiting messenger. Ovid waited.

A messenger in plain clothing finally appeared, looking somewhat worse for wear; the man had clearly traveled in a rush. He delivered a sealed scroll to the poet before nodding and stepping back, waiting for Ovid to read its contents.

The letter was from Fabia. Her few words were written hastily, the ink smudged; she had not taken the proper amount of time to let the papyrus dry before she had rolled and sealed it. None of that mattered, though, not once Ovid had read the letter's contents, his eyes skimming back across the words a second and then a third time as he digested the news. Augustus had died, and Tiberius had come to power. Rome and its empire were in new hands. His wife awaited further instruction.

"Will you be sending a response?" the messenger asked, seeing that Ovid had finished reading the letter, though he still clutched the scroll with intensity.

The poet did not answer, instead re-reading Fabia's words yet again. He could not decide if Augustus's death was good news or bad. On the one hand, his years of work had been wasted, since the intended recipient was no longer able to read or appreciate his letters and poems; what if he had been making at least some dent in the emperor's austerity after all these years? On the other hand, Tiberius might prove to be a new, sympathetic ear to his cause, one Ovid had previously overlooked. He hoped his mistake would not prove too costly now that the empire's balance of power had shifted.

The messenger still waited for Ovid's answer. "Yes, I will. Go get something to eat. I will send a letter with you this evening, and you will depart at once for Rome. Do not linger on the way; I will give you money aplenty to book passage on the fastest ship from here to Byzantium, and then onwards to Rome. You will place my message directly into my wife's hands, and she, too, will make sure that your efforts are well rewarded."

The messenger nodded and disappeared in search of the kitchen. Ovid pushed aside his newest poem and carefully laid out a fresh piece of papyrus, picking up his pen once more and beginning to write, the fresh ink shiny in the lamplight.

WE MUST CHANGE TACTICS, FABIA. TIBERIUS MAY YET RECALL ME TO ROME, BUT HE WOULD NOT DO SO ALONE. LIVIA NOW, MORE THAN EVER, IS IMPORTANT TO OUR FUTURE. TAKE CARE TO FIND OUT WHAT YOU CAN, AND TO ALWAYS PRESENT YOURSELF, AND ME, MOST WELL TO HER. THERE IS HOPE YET, IF WE PLAN ACCORDINGLY.

Ovid set the letter aside to dry before he rolled and sealed it. With any luck, it would reach Rome in a month.

The poet selected yet another fresh slip of papyrus, and he began to draft a new piece, a consolation to Livia that recognized the esteemed lady's hardships and implored her to rely upon her trusted son, Tiberius, following the death of her much beloved husband. He sang the praises of Livia and her son—the new emperor—without reservation.

As long as Ovid lived, he would not cease working towards his recall to Rome. His plans to threaten Aulus all those years ago were now long forgotten, discarded not long after the disappearance of the slave family. There was no point in lingering on failed plots; time was, as always, of the essence. The city of Rome was everything to him, and he vowed to set his eyes upon its landscape a final time before Pluto claimed him for his realm.

Perhaps the only thing Ovid valued more, if pressed to tell, was his dear Fabia. He closed his eyes and remembered her, how her blonde curls fell down her back, how the faint, fresh scent of roses always seemed to accompany her as she moved from room to room; he could almost hear her girlish laugh, so sweet as it tickled his ears.

Ovid cast a small prayer upwards to the gods that he might at least see her again, somehow, even if Rome remained beyond his grasp. He could not bear to press on otherwise.

Seven years had now passed since I arrived on Trimerus; six years had passed since Titus left the island in search of my lost child. In that time, I had received only one letter from him, via Lucius. There were a few words scribbled on a ratty scroll, only letting me know that he had found my son.

That letter had come five years ago, and since then there were no other updates, no other news of my child's wellbeing, nor that of Titus. It was for the best, even though it wrenched my heart with each passing day. My son would see his seventh summer that year, and yet I could only imagine him as the helpless infant he had been, torn screaming from my arms so soon after his birth.

I could not even keep Titus's letter, lest it be discovered by one of Livia's spies or any other undesirable figure that had crept in amongst the endless cycle of guards and slaves. They were all nameless and faceless to me now, and any one of them could be my enemy. I treated each with cold suspicion, isolating myself from them all.

Lucius had passed away two years ago. He had never fully recovered from what had started out as a small illness, his cough worsening and wracking his body. He had wasted away slowly, the last vestiges of his true strength seeming to have faded ever since he had delivered Titus's letter safely into my hands. It was as if he felt that he had fulfilled his promise to me.

I remembered visiting him on his deathbed. The commander of my guards at the time had been less than kind, but I used all manner of threats and bribes to convince him to allow me a final visit to my old friend. At last, I had succeeded.

"Lucius," I had said softly, holding his cold hand, uncertain if he could even hear me. Already his skin was pale, his breathing shallow and intermittent. "Thank you, for everything." I knew he would understand all that those words encompassed. I could never fully express my gratitude for his role in saving my son's life.

At my statement, his eyelids had fluttered but did not open. He had to try several times before his raspy voice would work. Even then, I had to lean in close to hear his words. "My dear, I am so very happy that I could be of service." A series of coughs wracked his body for an indeterminable amount of time before he could speak again. "I ask a final favor. Set my birds free for me. I can't care for them properly now, and I would hate for them to suffer."

I had squeezed his hand in silent affirmation and followed his orders, opening cage after cage in the atrium of his villa. Many of the birds flew away at once through the space's open roof, chirping their excitement as they began a new adventure, while others remained for a while, hopping about on the floor and pecking in hungry confusion at the dark pieces of marble that were dotted throughout the mosaic, perhaps thinking they were seeds. I smiled sadly as I watched them, recalling the little sparrow Lucius had gifted to me so long ago. She had lived a long life, for her kind, but death had claimed even her.

Lucius passed away the following day. I was not permitted to attend his cremation.

His villa remained vacant now, and it had begun to fall into disrepair. It seemed that no one in his family wanted to visit or maintain his much-loved residence, but perhaps that was for the best. I could imagine no one else living there.

Lucius's slaves had all disappeared once it became obvious that no heirs were likely to lay claim to the villa—or to come to account for them. My guards had looked the other way; they were not paid to keep track of slaves, and so did not have any reason to waste their time or energy hunting them down. The slaves had purchased passage on supply ships when they could, no doubt carrying with them what small treasures their elderly master had accumulated over his lifetime, intending to sponsor their futures. I bore them no ill will, hoping that they might find some measure of happiness in their illicit freedom. It was more than I could expect for myself.

My companion Claudia had been sent back to Rome a year past, after producing a stillborn infant. None of the guards in service at that time had been willing to claim responsibility for it, and I had not been surprised. It made me remember Silanus and his own weakness, a trait I had come to learn was common to many men. Although I bore pity for Claudia, it was outside my power to help her. Such was the way of the world.

Monimos remained at the villa and was fatter than ever. I expected his heart to stop at any moment, but he continued on, overseeing the other slaves and guzzling the best of the wine until there often was far less in the storeroom than had been delivered on the supply ship. There was no friendship between us, despite the fact that we became Trimerus's longest serving residents. We never spoke of all that had transpired during the first year of my *exilium*.

Artemis, her skills as a cook constantly growing and improving, had been snatched away to Rome as a specialized slave. The guards must have carried back tales of her meals when their tour of duty on Trimerus expired, their words reaching important ears. I did not know who she was to serve next, but I hoped she would find success, and possibly even freedom, in her future.

The graves of Aurelia and Publius were side by side at the island's highest point, now grassy and overgrown, each marked only by a large, misshapen rock. Although I held them both vividly in my memory, I did not visit their resting place often: it was too painful.

My sister Agrippina wrote me an annual letter, and her most recent had reported that my daughter Aemilia had finally been married to a certain Marcus Junius Silanus Torquatus, an aspiring politician who, in a cruel coincidence, was a relative of my own lover years ago, the cowardly father of my bastard child. I did not know the extent of their familial relation, but I hoped that they were nothing alike: my daughter deserved better. Regardless, Aemilia had produced a son in very short order and, according to Agrippina, appeared to be happy and healthy. I was now a grandmother, at the age of thirty-three.

Aemilia never wrote to me herself. Although my sister tried to blame this on my daughter's new, busy life as a wife and mother, I suspected that someone had poisoned Aemilia against me. Then again, even if my daughter *had* written to me, there was no guarantee her letters would be allowed to reach the island. It was probably better for her future if she had nothing to do with me at all, and I bore her no ill will for it.

As for my little sister, the only unblemished grandchild of Augustus, she had produced a third son whom everyone affectionately called Caligula, or 'little boot,' after the footwear of his father's soldiers. Agrippina and her children had gone on a campaign of retribution with her husband in Germania, quashing the barbarians who had dared rise against the emperor only a few years ago.

"Mistress?" a guard asked me, his young face hesitant as he interrupted my thoughts. I did not recall his name, and I did not ask it now. He, like the others, would be gone next spring, Trimerus a distant memory for him.

I raised my eyebrows in silent response, suggesting that he continue.

"The supply ship has been sighted. It's late, considering it should have arrived a few weeks ago at the latest, but it's here now, on the horizon, and will arrive tomorrow, most likely. The commander thought you would like to know."

I nodded an acknowledgment, and the soldier left me in peace.

The ship, in addition to the usual supplies, also bore an official messenger. He spoke with the commander privately, and they were ensconced alone together for quite some time. The guards were too busy unloading boxes to notice, but my interest had been piqued. I lurked in the atrium, watching the hallway for signs of movement. I did not recall the last time a proper messenger had visited Trimerus, and I did not know whether the news would be good or bad.

When the pair at last emerged from the commander's room, both were solemn. The messenger departed towards the kitchen for refreshment, nodding an acknowledgment to me as he passed by. The commander appraised me silently for a moment before speaking.

"Mistress, if you would please join me." He held back the door hanging to his bedroom, a gesture suggesting that I was to enter. I did so quietly, without question. I chose my moments of quiet rebellion carefully these days, and complaining about the propriety of my reception in his bedroom was not worth the effort.

When the door hanging was back in place, the commander turned to face me. He sighed. "I will inform the other guards in short order, but thought it best if you knew first, given your station. The emperor has died. Tiberius now reigns."

My legs felt weak, but I stiffened them. I would not collapse, not now. Not after all I had survived. "When?" I couldn't manage more than the one word.

"Last summer. We didn't receive word because the autumn supply ship last year had already departed for us, and they did not yet know." The commander gave a small shrug. No ships came to the island during winter, and so the messenger had simply been sent with the next dispatch of supplies.

I nodded, my thoughts racing as I sought to process the information. My grandfather had been elderly, but death always seemed to come as a shock, no matter when it arrived and who it claimed.

"What else?" I could tell from the way he was shifting his weight that there was something more he would tell me, although he seemed hesitant to do so.

"Your mother and brother have also... died." I detected the slightest of pauses before his final word.

"Died?" I prompted. I knew there was more to it than that.

The commander shifted his weight again, searching for his next words.

"How?" I asked, impatient, although I already suspected the answer. It could be no coincidence that so much of my remaining family had been decimated all at once.

"Your brother was executed last summer. There were no details provided about your mother, but her death, too, is certain." He watched me apprehensively, perhaps waiting for a mental break, for tears and unleashed fury.

I stared out the small bedroom window, the water of the Adriatic a shockingly vivid hue of blue that early summer day. I had no doubts that Livia had whispered in Tiberius's ear, urging him to eliminate Agrippa Postumus, who remained a threat to his power so long as he lived, even with his debilitating madness. That was the fate of a male in our cursed family. We were no better than the vicious hyenas of Africa, turning on one another in an endless effort to establish dominance.

My mother's death, despite all her conniving and plotting, surprised me more than that of my poor little brother. Women were often spared the death sentences enacted upon their husbands, brothers, and sons, whatever their own crimes and faults. Livia and Tiberius were taking no chances, it seemed, but clearly they had wanted to avoid an outright execution. I did not dwell on how they might have killed her instead.

"And me?" I asked at last. I kept my gaze on the rolling waters of the sea, endless and eternal. I expected to feel the cold metal of the commander's sword against my neck at any moment. "Am I, too, to die?"

I thought back to Marcus, to Gaius, to the countless others I had never identified who had all been Livia's pawns. One after another, they had been watching me, waiting for their orders to change. Perhaps that time had finally come. I closed my eyes, inhaling the salty ocean breeze that had become the inescapable breath of my everyday existence.

The commander answered. "No, mistress. I received instructions that we are to continue on as we always have. You are to remain on

Trimerus, in *exilium*. As usual, there will be a change of guards each year, and you will stay here."

I opened my eyes again to the sea. I didn't feel relieved at his words. Instead, I felt nothing, a blankness that stretched from my mind to my heart and seeped into every bone of my body. I was to remain here, a prisoner.

Perhaps Livia and Tiberius would one day change their minds. Perhaps one day I might be recalled to Rome to serve some purpose, to fulfill some role that they had thought up for me. Perhaps one day they might decide to kill me after all, deciding that I was too much of a threat to their power to be allowed to live. Or perhaps I would remain on Trimerus, an island of oblivion, lost to the world I once knew so well. As always, only time would tell what fate had in store for me.

CHAPTER
XLVII

TITUS

Titus sighed, removing his furred cloak and tossing it to the ground. He had finally warmed up, and the wolf skins covering his body had begun to prove stifling. Although it was summer in Dacia, it remained cool this high up in the mountains, sheltered as they were by the immense trees of the ancient forest. It was a wild, dangerous region, and Rome wanted to bring it to heel.

"Hold it like this," he said, extending his arm that held the curved Dacian sword.

Two young boys, about seven years old, looked up at the soldier's hand, squinting as they intensely studied his grip. One of them was darker in coloring, smaller, while the other was taller and lighter in skin. Nevertheless, they were brothers in all the ways that truly mattered.

Both boys extended their own small hands, clutching wooden swords that were miniatures of Titus's own. The man took the time to adjust their fingers and move their small legs into more appropriate stances.

"Scorilo," Titus said, shifting the darker boy's fingers once more, "keep them light, like this. It allows for easier movement." The boy nodded solemnly, focused on keeping his fingers exactly as Titus had instructed.

"Duras," Titus said next, shifting his attention to the other boy and similarly changing his grip. "Very good."

Titus set them to lightly sparring, a routine exercise they had practiced before, and stepped back to observe. They improved with every session. Within a handful of years, they would wield proper blades rather than the wooden toys they now practiced with.

Duras did not know the truth of his heritage. He was too young to understand yet, and so Titus did not tell him. He did not tell him that he was the great-grandson of the recently deceased emperor of Rome. He did not tell him that his birth mother, whom he resembled more and more each day, remained a prisoner on a remote island in the Adriatic.

Titus did not tell him all these things and more, not just because he was too young to comprehend, but because Titus did not understand it all himself. He did not know if or when he would return to Rome, or how to tell Julia's son all that had happened, and all that he was. He did not know what would become of the boy, what path he would take.

Duras accidentally hit his adopted brother with the wooden sword, and Scorilo cried out in anger and pain. Titus, sighing, went to separate the boys before they got into a scuffle. The children were fiercely loyal to one another, but they could fight like wolves when their blood was up. Both would be strong warriors one day, whether they fought for Rome or against it.

Titus was uncertain of the future, but he had made a promise, once, to a woman he loved very much. He had said that he would protect her son, and he intended to keep his word, whatever the cost.

The story continues in…

DAUGHTER OF EXILE

AVAILABLE SEPTEMBER 2024

Aemilia Lepida was closer to becoming empress than anyone knew when she was betrothed to Claudius—but her parents' disgrace leads to the dissolution of her engagement, and her life changes forever.

Aemilia comes of age in Rome at a dangerous time, one in which her heritage makes her a desirable pawn in the schemes of others. Her own efforts to restore her family's honor place her on a treacherous path of vengeance and intrigue that will consume her life even as it ultimately reveals a strength she never knew she possessed.

Meanwhile, Titus begins a journey harder and longer than he could have imagined, spanning from Rome to Dacia and back again. He will sacrifice more than he bargained for as he struggles to accept his new identity: a deserter in hiding, shielding a secret that could disrupt the empire, not knowing if he will ever again see the woman for whom he has upended his life.

Aemilia and Titus, and those around them, must decide whether their differences will keep them apart, or if Julia and her exile—their sole unifying connection—will be enough to bind them together, perhaps saving all their lives.

AUTHOR'S NOTE

This novel largely stems from the research I conducted on the phenomenon of Julio-Claudian island exile while I was an undergraduate at Princeton University. My finished work (*Julio-Claudian exilium ad insulam*) won the 2014 Department of Classics John J. Keaney Prize for Best Senior Thesis.

Many of the characters in this book are real historical figures, and I have tried to stay as true as possible to known events, dates, names, and relationships. Where a date is uncertain, I have used a combination of (1) what best fits the story and (2) what can be academically surmised.

For example, the execution of Julia the Younger's husband, Paullus, is known to have occurred sometime between 1 and 14 CE. I chose the year 7 CE because this roughly aligns with when Agrippa Postumus was exiled for his own treason, and it is entirely possible—probable, even—that these events are related. Furthermore, Paullus must have been dead before 8 CE when the pregnant Julia the Younger was exiled. Had she been carrying a legitimate child of her husband (even if he himself was a traitor), it is unlikely that Augustus would have cast her and the infant out; her exile thus suggests that it was known with certainty that Paullus was not the father, which indicates that he must have been dead long enough for Julia's indiscretion to be obvious.

However, the survival of Julia the Younger's child in this book is wholly imagined. Historically, it is most likely that the infant either died on its own or was killed shortly after birth.

The planned rescue of Julia the Younger and Agrippa Postumus is attested to in history, although the details are murky, and I took some liberties to fit my plot. For example, there is uncertainty *which* Julia was the subject of the rescue (the younger or the elder) and which of them was the mastermind—and there is no evidence that any would-be rescuers reached the islands and their inhabitants. Similarly, the involvement of Sempronius Gracchus (a known lover of the elder Julia) in this plot is my own invention.

There *was* a second rescue attempt on behalf of Agrippa Postumus, in which the island was actually reached—but this occurred shortly after his execution. They instead absconded with his ashes and a pretender impersonated him for approximately two years before being killed. This is not included in *The Longest Exile*.

Notably, the fact that Julia the Younger survived 14 CE (when her mother and brother were killed, amongst other historical figures) suggests that she was likely innocent of any true political plotting and was not considered a potent threat to Tiberius.

Augustus did visit Agrippa Postumus a final time in the spring of 14 CE, before his own death, but ultimately did not recall his grandson to Rome. Augustus was fixated on a blood heir; had there been any chance that the emperor thought the wayward Agrippa Postumus could rule, he no doubt would have pursued this avenue—yet he did not. Historically, it is generally accepted that there was something quite 'wrong' with Agrippa Postumus; he was said to possess a violent temper and a degree of insanity. A modern viewpoint to be considered is that the youth developed a severe mental illness of some sort, which presented in his mid-to-late teenage years.

Following the death of Augustus, Agrippa Postumus was killed, likely in an outright execution as depicted in this novel, while the elder Julia truly was walled up in a room and left to starve—a grisly, drawn-out death that was not an unheard-of execution method for Roman women. Scribonia, who accompanied her daughter into exile of her own volition, both to Pandateria and then to Rhegium, lived another two years, presumably dying of natural causes in her mid eighties.

The exact cause of Ovid's exile has never been determined with absolute certainty, although it is generally thought that he may have held some knowledge of the plots that Paullus and Agrippa Postumus were involved in, as well as having produced works (such as his *Ars Amatoria*) which offended Augustus and the emperor's moral legislation. Ovid never returned to Rome, but his writing lives on; of particular note with respect to this book are his *Tristia* and *Epistulae ex Ponto*, written during his exile, which are available fairly widely in translation.

The food in this book is all inspired by actual recipes from ancient Rome. I particularly drew from the compilation put together by Andrew Dalby and Sally Grainger in *The Classical Cookbook* (revised edition, 2012).

The old man Lucius, the guards (including Rufus and Titus), and the slaves in *The Longest Exile* are invented characters. For the lattermost—the slaves—I have tried to present an accurate view of what their lives might have been like, which, in many instances, was not pleasant. Slaves in the Roman empire came from all over—often they were conquered peoples—and were considered the property of their owners. They had no personal rights, could not legally marry or own property, and were subjected to the whims of their masters. While we see that Julia the Younger views Aurelia, in some ways, almost as a mother, at the end of the day, she was still a slave—a treasured possession. Similarly, we see the abhorrent treatment of the slave girl Aphrodite: rape, being forced into performing actions against her will at the threat of death, and more. This was, sadly, not uncommon.

Finally, I would like to note that much of written history focuses on those by whom it is written—which, throughout time, has often been men in positions of power. The lives of common people, women, and the enslaved are known about through what the history-writers chose to include—often flavored by their own preconceived or biased notions—and (perhaps less subjective, but sometimes more of a puzzle to be pieced together) what the archaeological record tells us. With this novel, I hope to shed light on a fascinating Roman woman about whom little academic scholarship exists, and to tell her story—or at least my version of it. I hope I have done her justice, and I hope you will read on in *Daughter of Exile* to learn more about Julia, her daughter Aemilia, and what fate has in store for them against the backdrop of an increasingly turbulent empire.

ACKNOWLEDGEMENTS

To my husband, Gabriel—thank you for convincing me to sit down and actually write this book (instead of just talking about it), and for supporting me over the years as my relentless cheerleader and partner in all things.

Professor Harriet Flower, my research supervisor at Princeton when I first delved into the topic of Julio-Claudian island exile, was the first person to casually suggest to me that some of my work might be interesting to develop into historical fiction. That single comment stuck in the back of my mind for years, and this book (and its sequel) are the result. Thank you for helping guide my research, encouraging my creative streak, and reading an early draft of this novel. I am so very grateful to have had you as a mentor over the years.

I would also like to specifically thank the Class of 1955 Senior Thesis Fund at Princeton, which made a large part of my research possible by funding my visit to the islands of Pandateria (modern Ventotene) and Pontia (modern Ponza). Although neither of these islands play a significant role in this book (Pandateria is mentioned in passing as the location to which the elder Julia was exiled before being moved to Rhegium), both have archaeological sites which were integral to my academic research. Furthermore, spending time on these islands—where

ACKNOWLEDGEMENTS

Julio-Claudians lived and died in exile—helped me to grasp, even if only slightly, what being trapped there might have been like.

Jacques de Spoelberch, thank you for believing in this project over the course of several years. It's so much better for your advice and critique.

To my parents, thank you for always encouraging my love of reading and writing.

Kiki, I miss you every day. Thank you for walking across my keyboard, sitting in my lap, and trying to knock over my wine glass as I wrote.

Bubbles, you are gone but not forgotten. We love and miss you. Is it weird to say I've never felt so supported (or judged) by a horse, before or since you?

Lastly, to you, the reader—thank you for joining me on this journey. I hope you enjoyed it, and I hope you'll read more of my work.

ABOUT THE AUTHOR

Tana Rebellis is a pen name of Kasey Morris, who also writes romantic comedies. She studied Classics at Princeton University and then Classical Archaeology at Oxford. When not reading, writing, or working, she's spending time with her animals and her husband on their farm in Virginia.

www.TanaRebellis.com
Instagram: @TanaRebellis
Twitter (X): @ExploreClassics

Printed in Dunstable, United Kingdom